DON DELILLO'S
THE NAMES

"Almost every page of *The Names* gives evidence of its author's brilliance and originality."
—Gene Lyons, *Newsweek*

"It would be my guess that those readers who enjoyed Lawrence Durrell's *Justine* and John Fowles' *The Magus* would want to read *The Names*. These books share the same sort of exotic atmospheres and settings. *The Names* not only accurately reflects a portion of our contemporary world but, more importantly, creates an original world of its own."
—Mark Smith, *Chicago Sun-Times*

"Exceptional—a startling and potent work of fiction."
—Arthur J. Sabatini, *Philadelphia Inquirer*

"[DeLillo's] breakthrough...rewards reading and rereading with hard-eyed insights....DeLillo sifts experience through simultaneous grids of science and poetry, analysis and clear sight, to make a high-wire prose that is voluptuously stark."
—Al J. Sperone, *Village Voice Literary Supplement*

"DeLillo verbally examines every state of consciousness from eroticism to tourism, from the idea of America as conceived by the rest of the world to the idea of the rest of the world as conceived by America, from mysticism to fanaticism."
—Christopher Lehmann-Haupt, *The New York Times*

"DeLillo is a master of style, creating in his novels intricate and meaningful stories. *The Names* is his best and most ambitious work to date; easy to read...almost impossible to decipher fully."
—Rob Swigart, *San Francisco Chronicle*

"Extraordinary...that rarity of current fiction: a mysterious, suspenseful story that is also an ambitious novel of ideas...Like Stone's *A Flag for Sunrise*, it is an exciting novel of politics that reverberates on many nonpolitical levels as well...Don DeLillo has written his finest book. *The Names*—a haunting, powerful work of art—will be among the most discussed books of the year."
—Dan Cryer, *Newsday*

Also by Don DeLillo

Americana

End Zone

Great Jones Street

Running Dog

Ratner's Star

White Noise

Libra

Mao II

Underworld

The Body Artist

Pafko at the Wall

Cosmopolis

THE NAMES

DON DELILLO

THE NAMES

Vintage Contemporaries

Vintage Books

A Division of Random House, Inc. | *New York*

Vintage Books Edition, July 1989

Copyright © 1982 by Don DeLillo

All rights reserved under International and Pan-American
Copyright Conventions. Published in the United States by
Random House, Inc., New York, and simultaneously in Canada
by Random House of Canada Limited, Toronto. Originally
published by Alfred A. Knopf, Inc., in 1982.

Library of Congress Cataloging in Publication Data
DeLillo, Don.
The names.
I. Title.
PS3554.E4425N3 1983   813'.54   83-5763
ISBN 0-679-72295-5 (pbk.)

Manufactured in the United States of America

The author gratefully acknowledges the support of the John Simon Guggenheim Memorial Foundation. A printed shout from the housetops goes as well to Atticus Lish, in fond appreciation.

The Island

1

FOR A LONG TIME I stayed away from the Acropolis. It daunted me, that somber rock. I preferred to wander in the modern city, imperfect, blaring. The weight and moment of those worked stones promised to make the business of seeing them a complicated one. So much converges there. It's what we've rescued from the madness. Beauty, dignity, order, proportion. There are obligations attached to such a visit.

Then there was the question of its renown. I saw myself climbing the rough streets of the Plaka, past the discos, the handbag shops, the rows of bamboo chairs. Slowly, out of every bending lane, in waves of color and sound, came tourists in striped sneakers, fanning themselves with postcards, the philhellenes, laboring uphill, vastly unhappy, mingling in one unbroken line up to the monumental gateway.

What ambiguity there is in exalted things. We despise them a little.

I kept putting off a visit. The ruins stood above the hissing traffic like some monument to doomed expectations. I'd turn a corner, adjusting my stride among jostling shoppers, there it was, the tanned marble riding its mass of limestone and schist. I'd dodge a packed bus, there it was, at the edge of my field of vision.

One night (as we enter narrative time) I was driving with friends back to Athens after a loud dinner in Piraeus and we were lost in some featureless zone when I made a sharp turn into a one-way street, the wrong way, and there it was again, directly ahead, the Parthenon, floodlit for an event, some holiday or just the summer sound-and-light, floating in the dark, a white fire of such clarity and precision I was startled into braking too fast, sending people into the dashboard, the backs of seats.

We sat there a moment, considering this vision. It was a street in decline, closed shops and demolition, but the buildings at the far end framed the temple perfectly. Someone in the back seat said something, then a car came toward us, horn blowing. The driver stuck an arm out the window to gesture. Then his head appeared, he started shouting. The structure hung above us like a star lamp. I gazed a moment longer and backed out of the street.

I asked Ann Maitland, who sat alongside, what the man had called me.

"Masturbator. It's standard. A Greek will never say anything he hasn't already said a thousand times."

Her husband Charles reprimanded me for not knowing the word. To Charles it was a mark of one's respect for other cultures to know the local terms of abuse and the words for sex acts and natural wastes.

We three were in the front seat. Behind were David Keller and his new young wife Lindsay and a man named Stock, a Swiss or Austrian located in Beirut, here to do business with David.

There was always someone at dinner who was in town to do business with one of the regulars. They tended to be heavyset men, these guests, northern, raw. Eager faces, strong accents. They drank too much and left in the morning.

With Ann's help I worked out our location and headed toward the Caravel, where Stock was staying.

"Isn't it awful?" Lindsay said. "I haven't been to the Acropolis. Two and a half months, is it, David?"

"Shut up. They'll think you're an idiot."

"I'm waiting for my curtains."

I told her she wasn't the only one who hadn't been there and tried to explain why I'd been slow to make the pilgrimage.

Charles Maitland said, "The thing is there, isn't it? Climb the hill. Unless it's some sort of perverse celebrity you're angling for. The man who turns his back to the peerless summit."

"Is that a trace of envy I hear? Grudging admiration?"

"Climb the hill, James. The thing is right there. It looms. It's close enough to knock you sideways."

He had a way of feigning gruff impatience. It was a role he found himself comfortable in, being the eldest among us.

"That's just it," I said. "That's the point."

"What do you mean?" Ann said.

"It looms. It's so powerfully there. It almost forces us to ignore it. Or at least to resist it. We have our self-importance. We also have our inadequacy. The former is a desperate invention of the latter."

"I didn't know you were so deep," she said.

"I'm not normally."

"You've clearly studied the matter."

"The bloody thing has been there for millennia," Charles said. "Climb the hill, have your look and then descend at an even pace, step by step, placing one foot ahead of the other."

"Is it really that easy?"

I was beginning to enjoy myself.

"I think you ought to grow a beard or shave your head," Ann said. "We need a physical demonstration of your commitment to these deep ideas. I'm not sure you're altogether serious. Give us something to believe in. A shaved head would do wonders for this group."

I drove past a sidewalk full of parked cars.

"We need a Japanese monk," she said to Charles, as if this were an answer they'd been seeking.

"Shave your head," Charles told me wearily.

"This is why your car is too small for six," Ann said. "It's Japanese. Why didn't we take two cars? Or three?"

David Keller, a husky blond Nebraskan of forty or so, said to me earnestly, "Jim, I think what our friends are trying to point out to you, boy, is that you're a fool, running a fool's errand, in a fool's world."

"You drive, David. You're too drunk to talk. Lindsay knows what I mean."

"You don't want to climb it because it's there," she said.

"Lindsay cuts to the heart of things."

"If it weren't there, you'd climb it."

"This woman has a gift," I said.

"We met on a plane," David said. "Somewhere over the ocean. Middle of the night. Local time." He was drawing everything out. "She looked so great. In her Pan Am flight socks. You just wanted to hug her, you know? Like an elf. Her hair kind of delectably frazzled. You wanted to give her a brownie and a glass of milk."

When I pulled up at the Caravel we realized Stock was asleep. We got him out easily enough. Then I dropped the others and went home.

I was living in a residential area that curls around the lower slopes of Lycabettus Hill. Most of the people I knew were here or nearby. The deep terraces spill over with lantana and jasmine, the views are panoramic, the cafés full of talk and smoke into the early hours. Americans used to come to places like this to write and paint and study, to find deeper textures. Now we do business.

I poured myself some soda water and sat outside awhile. From the terrace the city stretched to the gulf in smoky vales and rises, a seamless concrete village. Rare nights, for whatever atmospheric reasons, you could hear planes taking off down by the water. The sound was mysterious, full of anxious gatherings, a charged rumble that seemed a long time in defining itself as something besides a derangement of nature, some onrushing nameless event.

The phone rang twice, then stopped.

I flew a lot, of course. We all did. We were a subculture, business people in transit, growing old in planes and airports. We were versed in percentages, safety records, in the humor of flaming death. We knew which airline's food would double you up, which routes connected well. We knew the various aircraft and their configurations and measured this against the distances we were flying. We could distinguish between bad-weather categories and relate them to the guidance system of the plane we were on. We knew which airports were efficient, which were experiments in timelessness or mob rule; which had radar, which didn't; which might be filled with pilgrims making the *hadj*. Open seating never caught us by surprise and we were quick to identify our luggage on the runway where that was the practice and we didn't exchange wild looks when the oxygen masks dropped during touchdown. We advised each other on which remote cities were well maintained, which were notable for wild dogs running in packs at night, snipers in the business district at high noon. We told each other where you had to sign a legal document to get a drink, where you couldn't eat meat on Wednesdays and Thursdays, where you had to sidestep a man with a cobra when you left your hotel. We knew where martial law was in force, where body searches were made, where they engaged in systematic torture, or fired assault rifles into the air at weddings, or abducted and ransomed executives. This was the humor of personal humiliation.

"It is like the Empire," said Charles Maitland more than once. "Opportunity, adventure, sunsets, dusty death."

Along some northern coast at sundown a beaten gold light is waterborne, sweeping across lakes and tracing zigzag rivers to the sea, and we know we're in transit again, half numb to the secluded beauty down there, the slate land we're leaving behind, the peneplain, to cross these rainbands in deep night. This is time totally lost to us. We don't remember it. We take no sense impressions with us, no voices, none of the windy blast of aircraft on the tarmac, or the white noise of flight, or the hours waiting. Nothing sticks to us but smoke in our hair and clothes. It is dead time. It never happened until it happens again. Then it never happened.

I took a boat in two stages to Kouros, an obscure island in the Cycladic group. My wife and son lived there in a small white house with geraniums in olive oil cans on the roof edge and no hot water. It was perfect. Kathryn was writing reports on the excavation at the south end of the island. Our boy, who was nine, was working on a novel. Everyone is writing away. Everyone is scribbling.

When I got there the house was empty. Nothing moved in the streets. It was a hundred degrees, four o'clock, relentless light. I crouched on the roof, hands clasped above my eyes. The village was a model of irregular geometry, the huddled uphill arrangement of whitelime boxes, the street mazes and archways, small churches with blue talc domes. Laundry hung in the walled gardens, always this sense of realized space, common objects, domestic life going on in that sculpted hush. Stairways bent around houses, disappearing.

It was a sea chamber raised to the day, to the detailing light, a textured pigment on the hills. There was something artless and trusting in the place despite the street meanders, the narrow turns and ravels. Striped flagpoles and aired-out rugs, houses joined by closed wooden balconies, plants in battered cans, a willingness to share the oddments of some gathering-up. Passageways captured the eye with one touch, a sea green door, a handrail varnished to a nautical gloss. A heart barely beating in the summer heat, and always the climb, the small birds in cages, the framed approaches to nowhere. Doorways were paved with pebble mosaics, the terrace stones were outlined in white.

The door was open. I went inside to wait. She'd added a rush mat. Tap's writing table was covered with lined sheets. It was my second visit to the house and I realized I was scrutinizing the place, something I'd done the first time as well. Was it possible to find in the simple furniture, in the spaces between the faded walls, something about my wife and son that had been hidden from me during our life together in California, Vermont and Ontario?

We make you wonder if you are the outsider in this group.

The meltemi started blowing, the nagging summer wind. I stood by the window, waiting for them to appear. White water flashed outside the bay. Cats slipped out of hidden places in the rough walls and moved stretching into alleyways. The first of the air booms came rolling across the afternoon, waves from some distant violence, making the floor tremble slightly, window frames creak, causing plaster dust to trickle between abutting walls with an anxious whispering sound. Men were using dynamite to fish.

Shadows of empty chairs in the main square. A motorcycle droning in the hills. The light was surgical, it was binding. It fixed the scene before me as a moment in a dream. All is foreground, wordless and bright.

They arrived from the site on a motor scooter. Kathryn had a bandanna around her head and wore a tank top over baggy fatigue pants. It was in its way a kind of gritty high fashion. Tap saw me at the window and ran back to tell his mother, who didn't quite catch herself from looking up. She left the scooter at the edge of a stepped street and they came up toward the house single file.

"I stole some yogurt," I said.

"So. Look who's here."

"I'll pay you back a little at a time. What are you up to, Tap? Helping your mom revise the entire history of the ancient world?"

I grabbed him under the arms and lifted him to eye level, making a noise that exaggerated the strain involved. I was always making lionlike noises, rough-housing with my kid. He gave me one of his tricky half smiles and then put his hands squarely on my shoulders and said in his small monotone, "We had a bet when you would come. Five drachmas."

"I tried to call the hotel, tried to call the restaurant, couldn't get through."

"I lost," he said.

I gave him a sideways toss and put him down. Kathryn went inside to heat pots of water that she would add to their baths.

"I liked the pages you sent. But your concentration fell off once or twice. Your hero went out in a blizzard wearing his rubbery Ingersoll."

"What's wrong with that? It was the heaviest thing he had. That was the point."

"I think you meant Mackintosh. He went out in a blizzard wearing his rubbery Mackintosh."

"I thought a Mackintosh was a boot. He wouldn't go out with one Mackintosh. He'd wear Mackintoshes."

"He'd wear Wellingtons. A Wellington is a boot."

"Then what's a Mackintosh?"

"A raincoat."

"A raincoat. Then what's an Ingersoll?"

"A watch."

"A watch," he said, and I could see him store these names and the objects they belonged to, for safekeeping.

"Your characters are good. I'm learning things I didn't know."

"Can I tell you what Owen says about character?"

"Of course you can tell me. You don't have to ask permission, Tap."

"We're not sure you like him."

"Don't be cute."

He bobbed his head like a senile man in the street having a silent argument with himself. In his miscellany of gestures and expressions, this one meant he was feeling a little sheepish.

"Come on," I said. "Tell me."

"Owen says 'character' comes from a Greek word. It means 'to brand or to sharpen.' Or 'pointed stake' if it's a noun."

"An engraving instrument or branding instrument."

"That's right," he said.

"This is probably because 'character' in English not only means someone in a story but a mark or symbol."

"Like a letter of the alphabet."

"Owen pointed that out, did he? Thanks a lot, Owen."

Tap laughed at my tone of pre-empted father.

"You know something?" I said. "You're beginning to look a little Greek."

"No, I'm not."

"Do you smoke yet?"

He decided he liked this idea and made smoking gestures and talking gestures. He spoke a few sentences in Ob, a coded jargon he'd learned from Kathryn. She and her sisters spoke Ob as children and now Tap used it as a kind of substitute Greek or counter-Greek.

Kathryn came out with two handfuls of pistachio nuts for us. Tap cupped his hands and she let one set slowly run out, raising her fist to lengthen the spill. We watched him smile as the nuts clicked into his hands.

Tap and I sat cross-legged on the roof. Narrow streets ran down to the square, where men sat against the walls of buildings, under the Turkish balconies, looking wine-stained in the setting sun.

We ate our nuts, putting the shell remnants in my breast pocket. Above the far curve of the village was a ruined windmill. The terrain was rocky, dropping steeply to the sea. A woman stepped laughing from a rowboat, turning to watch it rock. The broad motion made her laugh again. There was a boy eating bread at the oars.

We watched a deliveryman, powdered white, carry flour sacks on his head into the bakery. He had an empty sack folded over the top of his head to keep flour out of his hair and eyes and he looked like a hunter of white tigers, wearing the skins. The wind was still blowing.

I sat inside with Kathryn while the boy took his bath. She kept the room dark, drinking a beer, still in her tank top, the bandanna loose around her neck now.

"So. How's the job coming? Where have you been spending time?"

"Turkey," I said. "Pakistan now and then."

"I'd like to meet Rowser sometime. No, I wouldn't."

"You'd hate him but in a healthy way. He'd add years to your life. He has a new thing. It's a briefcase. Looks and feels like a briefcase. Except it has a recording device, a device that detects other recording devices, a burglar alarm, a Mace-spraying device and a hidden tracing transmitter, whatever that is."

"Do you hate him in a healthy way?"

"I don't hate him at all. Why should I hate him? He gave me the job. The job pays well. And I get to see my family. How would I get to see my little expatriate family if it weren't for Rowser and his job and his risk assessments?"

"Is he adding years to your life?"

"I enjoy it. It's an interesting part of the world. I feel I'm involved in events. Sure, sometimes I see it from a different perspective. Yours, of course. It's just insurance. It's the world's biggest, richest companies protecting their investments."

"Is that my perspective?"

"Don't I know what you hate by this time?"

"There ought to be something higher than the corporation. That's all."

"There's the orgasm."

"You've had a long tiring trip." She drank from the bottle. "I think I distrust the idea of investing, somehow, more than corporations themselves. I keep saying 'somehow.' Tap catches me at it. There's something secret and guilty about investing. Is that a foolish thing to believe? It's the wrong use of the future."

"That's why they use small print to list stock prices."

"Secret and guilty. How's your Greek?"

"Terrible. I leave the country for three days and forget everything. I know the numbers."

"Numbers are good," she said. "They're the best place to start."

"At dinner the other night I asked for chicken shit instead of grilled chicken. I got the accent wrong so the waiter didn't know what I was saying anyway."

"How did you know you said chicken shit?"

"The Maitlands were there. Charles pounced. Are we having dinner?"

"We'll go to the quay. Did you get a room?"

"There's always a room for me. They fire the cannon when they see my boat rounding the point."

She passed the bottle across to me. She looked tired from her work at the excavation, physically beat, her hands full of marks and cuts, but she was also charged by it, bright with it, giving off static. There must be a type of weariness that seems a blessing of the earth. In Kathryn's case it was literally the earth she was combing so scrupulously for fire marks and artifacts. I saw nothing in it myself.

Her hair was trimmed to the nape and she was brown and a little leathery, wind-seared around the eyes. A lean woman, small-hipped, agile and light in her movements. There was a practicality about her body. She was built to a purpose, one of those padders through rooms, barefoot, in swishing corduroys. She liked to sprawl over furniture, arms dangling, legs stretched across a coffee table. She had a slightly elongated face, sinewy legs, quick deft hands. Old photographs of Kathryn with her father and her sisters showed a directness that caught the camera, engaged it fully. You felt this was a girl who took the world seriously. She expected it to be honest and was determined to be equal to its difficulties and testing times. She gave an unbalancing force and candor to the pictures, especially since her father and sisters customarily wore expressions that were studies in Canadian reserve, except when the old man was soused.

Greece, I believed, would be her shaping environment, a place where she might carry on the singleminded struggle she'd always thought life was supposed to be. I mean the word "struggle" as an undertaking, a strenuous personal engagement.

"I'd like to take Tap to the Peloponnese with me," I said. "He'll love the place. It's haunted. All those fortified heights, the mist, the wind."

"He's been to Mycenae."

"He hasn't been to Mistra, has he? Or down to the Mani. Or to Nestor's palace. Honest-hearted Nestor."

"No."

"He hasn't been to sandy Pylos, has he?"

"Relax, James, would you."

"Come September, what happens? I think we ought to know where he's going to school. We ought to be making arrangements right now. When do you stop digging? Where do you plan to spend the winter?"

"I don't have plans. We'll see."

"What have you found here anyway?"

"Some walls. A cistern."

"Were the Minoans as bright and gay as we're led to believe? What have you found besides walls?"

"It was a small settlement. Some of it's under water. The sea's risen since then."

"The sea's risen. No frescoes?"

"Not a one."

"What pickups? Coins, daggers?"

"Storage jars."

"Intact?"

"Fragments."

"Big jars? Big as the ones at Knossos?"

"Not nearly," she said.

"No frescoes, no silver-inlaid daggers, tiny broken pots. Are the pots unpainted?"

"Painted."

"Dumb luck," I said.

She grabbed the bottle and drank, partly to conceal traces of amusement. Tap came in, a little shiny after his bath.

"We have a brand new kid," she said. "I'd better hurry and take my bath so we can feed him."

"If we don't feed him, he'll blow away in this wind."

"That's right. He needs ballast. Do you think he knows what ballast is?"

"He's writing a prairie epic, not a sea epic, but I think he knows anyway. Five drachmas says he knows."

He turned on a light. I'd arrived expecting him to be changed in appearance. He'd always seemed vaguely delicate to me, small-boned. I thought the open life would transform him physically. There might be something of the wild boy about him. The sun and wind would crack his skin a little, mark up the tidy surface. This unpremeditated life of theirs would break him out of his containment, I thought. But he looked about the same. A little darker, that was all.

The essential Thomas Axton now stood before me. Arms crossed on his chest, left foot forward, he spoke in his uninflected manner about ballast in ships. He seemed to be speaking through a hollow stalk. It was the perfect voice for Ob.

When Kathryn was ready we walked down to the harborfront. This wasn't an island abandoned to tourism. It was hard to get to, had one shabby hotel and a few rocky beaches, the best of them inaccessible except by boat. Even in midsummer there were only a couple of orange backpacks propped against the fountain, no wandering shoppers or places to shop. We would eat in one of the two identical restaurants. The waiter would spread the paper covering and drop utensils and bread onto the table. He would bring out grilled meat or fish and a country salad and some wine and a soft drink. Cats would appear under the chairs. The wind would shake the canopy and we would tuck the paper covering under the elastic band beneath the table top. A plastic ashtray, toothpicks in a glass.

She preferred satisfactions that were basic. This was Greece to her, the burning wind, and she was loyal to the place and the idea. At the site she worked with trowels, root clippers, dental picks, tweezers, whatever else they used to move dirt and extract objects. Inches a day. Days the same. Stooped in her five-foot trench. At night she wrote reports, made charts, mapped out the soil changes and heated water for her bath and Tap's.

She'd started out washing clothes for the dig director and fieldworkers. She also prepared lunch from time to time and helped clean the house where most of the staff lived. After budget cuts and defections, the director, Owen Brademas, gave her a trench. That's the kind of operation it was. The director wore bathing trunks and played the recorder.

This was her first dig. She had no experience and no degree and was paid nothing. After we split up she'd read the details of this excavation in something called a fieldwork opportunities bulletin. Volunteers accepted. Travel and lodging paid by individual. Field gear provided.

It was interesting to see, back then, how progressively certain she became that this was the future. Other jobs she'd had, good ones, jobs she liked, never took hold so powerfully, the way this mere prospect took hold. The event gathered force. I began to understand it wasn't just a reaction to our separating and I didn't know how to take this. It's almost comic, the number of ways in which people can find themselves diminished.

Against my lassitude she operated at peak levels. Sold things, gave things away, stored things in people's garages. It had struck her with the pure light of a major saint's vision. She would sift dirt on an island in the Aegean.

She started learning Greek. She ordered tapes, bought dictionaries, found a teacher. She went through a couple of dozen books on archaeology. Her study and planning were carried on in a fusion of anticipation and controlled rage. The latter had its source in my own living person. Every day made her more certain of my various failings. I compiled a mental list, which I often recited aloud to her, asking how accurate it was in reflecting her grievances. This was my chief weapon of the period. She hated the feeling that someone knew her mind.

1. *Self-satisfied.*

2. *Uncommitted.*

3. *Willing to settle.*

4. *Willing to sit and stare, conserving yourself for some end-of-life event, like God's face or the squaring of the circle.*

5. *You like to advertise yourself as refreshingly sane and healthy in a world of driven neurotics. You make a major production of being undriven.*

6. *You pretend.*

7. *You pretend not to understand other people's motives.*

8. *You pretend to be even-tempered. You feel it gives you a moral and intellectual advantage. You are always looking for an advantage.*

9. *You don't see anything beyond your own modest contentment. We all live on the ocean swell of your well-being. Everything else is trivial and distracting, or monumental and distracting, and only an unsporting wife or child would lodge a protest against your teensy-weensy happiness.*

10. *You think being a husband and father is a form of Hitlerism and you shrink from it. Authority makes you uneasy, doesn't it? You draw back from anything that resembles an official capacity.*

11. *You don't allow yourself the full pleasure of things.*

12. *You keep studying your son for clues to your own nature.*

13. *You admire your wife too much and talk about it too much. Admiration is your public stance, a form of self-protection if I read it correctly.*

14. Gratified by your own feelings of jealousy.

15. Politically neuter.

16. Eager to believe the worst.

17. You will defer to others, you will be acutely sensitive to the feelings of strangers, but you will contrive to misunderstand your family. We make you wonder if you are the outsider in this group.

18. You have trouble sleeping, an attempt to gain my sympathy.

19. You sneeze in books.

20. You have an eye for your friends' wives. Your wife's friends. Somewhat speculative, somewhat detached.

21. You go to extremes to keep your small mean feelings hidden. Only in arguments do they appear. Completing your revenge. Hiding it even from yourself at times. Not willing to be seen taking your small mean everyday revenge on me, which, granted, I have sometimes abundantly earned. Pretending your revenge is a misinterpretation on my part, a misunderstanding, some kind of accident.

22. You contain your love. You feel it but don't like to show it. When you do show it, it's the result of some long drawn-out decision-making process, isn't it, you bastard.

23. Nurser of small hurts.

24. Whiskey sipper.

25. Underachiever.

26. Reluctant adulterer.

27. American.

We came to refer to these as the 27 Depravities, like some reckoning of hollow-cheeked church theologians. Since then I've sometimes had to remind myself it was my list, not hers. I think it was a fair analysis of her complaints and I took a self-destructive pleasure in calling out the accusations as if from her own unforgiving heart. Such was my mood those days. I was trying to involve her in my failings, make her see how she exaggerated routine lapses, make her appear shrewish to herself, the bitch of legend.

Every day I'd recite a few entries, go into deep meditation, working up new ones, polishing old, and then come back at her with the results. For aggravating effect I'd sometimes use a female voice. It was a week-long operation. Most of the items brought silence. Some made her laugh sarcastically. I had to learn that people who try to be perceptive about themselves are taken for self-hectoring fools, although it's more accurate to say I was trying to be perceptive about her. The oral delivery was a devotional exercise, an attempt to understand through repetition. I wanted to get inside her, see myself through her, learn the things she knew. Thus Kathryn's cutting laughter. "Is this what I'm supposed to think of you? Is this the picture I have in my mind? A masterpiece of evasion. This is what you've compiled."

What a funhouse mirror is love.

By the end of the week I was using a vibrant liturgical voice, sending it toward the distant ceiling of our renovated Victorian house in Toronto's east end. I sat on the striped sofa in the living room, watching her separate her books from mine (bound for different garages), and I stopped reciting long enough to ask casually, by the way, "What would happen if I followed?"

Now, six thousand miles from that cobblestone street, the family sits down to dinner. Ten octopus carcasses hang over a clothesline near our table. Kathryn goes into the kitchen to exchange greetings with the owner and his wife and to look at the heated trays, the meat and vegetables lurking beneath oil slicks.

A man standing near the edge of the quay lifts his cane to waggle a warning at some children playing nearby. Tap would use this detail in his novel.

2

OWEN BRADEMAS used to say that even random things take ideal shapes and come to us in painterly forms. It's a matter of seeing what is there. He saw patterns there, moments in the flow.

His pain was radiant, almost otherworldly. He seemed to be in touch with grief, as if it were a layer of being he'd learned how to tap. He expressed things out of it and through it. Even his laughter had a desolate edge. If it was all sometimes too impressive, I never doubted the unsparing nature of whatever it was that haunted his life. Many hours we spent in conversation, the three of us. I used to study Owen, trying to figure him out. He had an unsettling mental force. Everyone was affected by it to one degree or another. I think he made us feel we were among the fortunate ordinary objects of the world. Maybe we thought his ruinous inner life was a form of devastating honesty, something unique and brave, a condition we were lucky to have avoided.

Owen was a naturally friendly man, lank, with a long-striding walk. My son enjoyed spending time with him and I was a little surprised at how quickly Kathryn developed a fondness, a warm regard, whatever a woman in her mid-thirties feels toward a sixty-year-old man with a western voice and a long stride.

Her eagerness to work amazed and confounded him. She went

at it like someone half her age. This was inconsistent with the style of a fading operation. It was a dig that would never be published. From forty people, the first time I visited, they were down to nine. Still, she worked and learned and helped keep things going. I think Owen enjoyed being shamed. He'd emerge from one of his midday swims to find her at the bottom of an abandoned hole, swinging a railroad pick. The high sun funneled in on her, the wind passed over. Everyone else was in the olive grove, eating lunch in the shade. Her attitude was a precious dissonance, something as intimate, pure and unexpected as a moment from his own past, flaring in the mind. I picture him standing at the edge of the pit with a bath towel fastened at the waist, in torn tennis sneakers, breaking out in abandoned laughter, a sound that always struck me as a cue to some deep and complicated passion. Owen yielded himself completely to things.

Sometimes we talked half the night. I felt these were useful hours beyond whatever rambling things we found to say. They gave Kathryn and me a chance to speak to each other, see each other, from either side of Owen's intervening position, in Owen's refracting light. They were his conversations really. It was mainly Owen who set the tone and traced the subject matter. This was important. What she and I needed was a way to be together without feeling there were issues we had to confront, the bloody leftovers of eleven years. We weren't the kind of people who have haggard dialogues on marriage. What dulling work, all ego, she would say. We needed a third voice, subjects remote from us. This is why I came to put a high practical value on those conversations. They allowed us to connect through the agency of this wan soul, Owen Brademas.

But I don't want to surrender my text to analysis and reflection. "Show us their faces, tell us what they said." That's Owen too, Owen's voice coursing warmly through a half-dark room. Memory, solitude, obsession, death. Subjects remote, I thought.

An old man came with breakfast. I took my coffee out to the small balcony and listened awhile to French voices on the other side of the partition. A white ship crossed in the distance.

I saw Tap walking across the square to get me. Sometimes we walked to the site, going the first part of the way along a walled mule path humming with flies. The cab route was roundabout, a dirt road that skirted the higher parts of the island and never lost the sea. It was possible, if you looked to your left about halfway along the route, to get a distant glimpse of a white monastery that seemed to hang from the top of a rock column in the middle of the island.

We decided to take the taxi. It was outside the hotel, where it always was, a grayish Mercedes that sagged badly. The roof light was busted and one of the fenders was orange. In ten minutes the driver turned up, sucking his gums. He opened the door. A man was lying across the back seat, asleep. We were all surprised. The driver shouted at the man to wake him up. Then he went through it again to get the man off the seat and out of the cab. He kept talking and shouting as the man wandered off.

The taxi smelled of ouzo. We rolled down the windows and settled back. The driver headed along the harborfront, then turned up the last of the streets and went south. It wasn't until we'd been on the dirt road for five minutes that he said something about the sleeping man. The more he talked, the less irritated he became. As he unraveled the event and analyzed it, he began showing amusement. Whenever he paused to think back on it, he couldn't help laughing. The event was a funny one after all. He grew more animated and seemed to be relating another incident involving the same man. Tap and I looked at each other. By the time we got to the excavation we were all laughing. Tap was laughing so hard he opened the door and almost tumbled out of the car.

There were eighteen trenches extending nearly to the water's edge. There was an old mining car on a track. Pottery fragments in labeled boxes were kept in a shack with a thatched roof. The watchman was gone but his tent remained.

It was a dazed landscape. The sense of spent effort was almost total. What the scientists were leaving behind seemed older to me than what they'd found or hoped to find. The true city was these holes they'd dug, the empty tent. Nothing that was lodged in the scarps could seem more lost or forgotten than the rusted mining car that had once run dirt to the sea.

The trench area overlapped an olive grove. Four trenches were in the grove, a head in a straw hat visible in one of them. From our elevated level we could see Kathryn closer to the water and in the sun, stooped over with a trowel. No one else was around. Tap walked on past her, giving a little wave, and went to the shack to wash pottery shards. The other thing he did was collect tools at the end of the day.

Kathryn ducked out of sight and for a moment nothing moved in the dancing glare. Only light, sea dazzle, on the calm surface. I realized a mule was standing just inside the olive grove. All over the island donkeys and mules stood motionless, trick figures hidden in the trees. The air was still. I used to long for thunderstorms and bare-legged women. I was twenty-five before I realized stockings were sexy.

The same white ship came into view.

That night Owen played the recorder for ten or fifteen minutes, a small musing sound that floated over the dark streets. We sat outside the house on a small terrace that faced the wrong way. The sea was behind us, blocked by the house. Tap appeared in the window to tell us he might be going to bed soon. His mother wanted to know if this was a request for silence.

"No, I like the recorder."

"I'm relieved and grateful," Owen said. "Sleep well. Pleasant dreams."

"Gobood nobight."

"Can you say it in Greek?" I said.

"Greek-Ob or Greek-Greek?"

"That might be interesting," Kathryn said. "Greek-Ob. I never thought of that."

Owen said to Tap, "If your mother ever takes you to Crete, I know a place you might be interested in seeing. It's in the south-central part of the island, not far from Phaistos. There's a group of ruins scattered in the groves near a seventh-century basilica. The Italians excavated. They found Minoan figurines, which you already know about. And there are Greek and Roman ruins scattered all over. But the thing you might like best is the code of law. It's in a Dorian dialect and it's inscribed on a stone wall. I don't know if anyone's counted the words but they've counted the letters. Seventeen thousand. The law deals with criminal offenses, land rights and other things. But what's interesting is that the whole thing is written in a style called *boustrophedon.* One line is inscribed left to right, the next line right to left. As the ox turns. As the ox plows. This is what *boustrophedon* means. The entire code is done this way. It's easier to read than the system we use. You go across a line and then your eye just drops to the next line instead of darting way across the page. Might take some getting used to, of course. Fifth century B.C."

He talked slowly in a rich voice, lightly graveled, a regional chant of drawn-out vowel sounds and other ornaments. His voice carried drama in it, tuneful history. It was easy to understand how a nine-year-old might feel snug in such narrative rhythms.

The village was quiet. When Tap turned out his bedside lamp the only visible light was the candle stub burning among our wine glasses and crusts of bread. I felt the day's glassy heat under my skin.

"What are your plans?" I said to Owen.

They both laughed.

"I withdraw the question."

"I'm maneuvering long-distance," he said. "We may be able to finish the field season. After that, your guess is as good as mine."

"No plans to teach?"

"I don't think I want to go back. Teach what? To whom?" He paused. "I've come to think of Europe as a hardcover book, America as the paperback version." Laughing, clasping his hands. "I've given myself over to the stones, James. All I want to do is read the stones."

"Greek stones, I assume you mean."

"I've been sneaking up on the Mideast. And I'm teaching myself Sanskrit. There's a place in India I want to see. A kind of Sanskrit pavilion. Extensive inscriptions."

"What kind of book is India?"

"Not a book at all, I suspect. That's what scares me."

"Everything scares you," Kathryn said.

"Masses of people scare me. Religion. People driven by the same powerful emotion. All that reverence, awe and dread. I'm a boy from the prairie."

"I'd like to go to Tinos sometime soon."

"Lord you're crazy," he said. "The Virgin's feast?"

"Pilgrims by the thousands," she said. "Mostly women, I understand."

"Crawling on hands and knees."

"I didn't know that."

"Hands and knees," he said. "Also in stretchers, in wheelchairs, carrying canes, blind, bandaged, crippled, diseased, muttering."

She laughed, saying, "I'd like to see it."

"I'd be inclined to give it a miss myself," I said.

"I'd really like to go. Things like that have great force, somehow. I imagine it must be beautiful."

"Don't expect to get anywhere near the place," he told her. "Every square foot is given over to crawling and supplication. Hotel space is nonexistent and the boats will be jam-packed."

"I know what disturbs you two. They're white people, they're Christians. It's not all that remote from your own experience."

"I have no experience," I said.

"You went to church."

"As a child."

"Doesn't that count? I'm only saying that's not the Ganges they're swarming into. On some level it touches you in disturbing ways."

"I can't agree," Owen said. "My own experience as a bystander, an occasional observer, is totally, totally different. Campus-brand Catholicism, for instance. Well-lighted space, bare altar, open faces, communal handshaking. None of these smoking lamps, these dark sinuous images. This is gilded theater, what we see here. We're almost off the map."

"You're not a Catholic," I said.

"No."

"What are you, what were you?"

The question seemed to confuse him.

"I had an odd upbringing. My people were devout in not very

conventional ways, although I guess I'm obliged to think that convention depends on cultural surroundings."

Kathryn changed the subject for him.

"Something I meant to tell you, Owen. About two weeks ago, a Saturday, remember we broke up early. Tap and I came back here, he took a nap, I lugged a chair up to the roof, sat drying my hair, going over notes. Nothing stirred down there. About ten minutes into my reading a man came out of the shadows somewhere in the lower village. He walked over to a motorcycle on the wharf. Crouched over it, inspecting this or that surface. Out of nowhere a second man showed up. Didn't even nod at the first man, didn't see him as far as I could tell. There was another motorcycle at the other end of the wharf. The second man stood straddling his bike. The first man moved into similar position. I could see both men, they couldn't see each other. They kick-started their bikes at the same instant, Owen, precisely, and went roaring off in opposite directions, up into the hills, two streams of dust. I'm convinced neither of them even heard the other."

"How lovely," he said.

"Then silence again. Two lines of dust vanishing in the air."

"You could see the event shaping itself."

"Yes, there was a tension. I saw the elements begin to fit. The way the second man walked to the other end of the wharf. The clear shadows."

"And then it disintegrated, literally, in dust."

Owen lapsed into thought, as he often did, stretching his legs, pushing the chair back against the wall. He had a tapered face with large shocked eyes. His hair was sparse. Pale brows, a bald spot. Sometimes his shoulders seemed cramped in the long narrow frame.

"But we're still in Europe, aren't we?" he said, and I took this to be a reference to some earlier point. He came out of these thoughtful pauses saying things that weren't always easy to fit into the proper frame. "No matter how remote you are, how far into the mountains or islands, how deep-ended you are, how much you want to disappear, there is still the element of shared culture, the feeling that we know these people, come from these people. Something beyond this is familiar as well, some mystery. Often I feel I'm on the edge of knowing what it is. It's just beyond reach, something that touches me deeply. I can't quite get it and hold it. Does anyone know what I mean?"

No one knew.

"But on the subject of balance, Kathryn, we see it here every day, although not quite as you've described. This is one of those Greek places that pits the sensuous against the elemental. The sun, the colors, the sea light, the great black bees, what physical delight, what fertile slow-working delight. Then the goatherd on the barren hill, the terrible wind. People must devise means to collect rainwater, buttress their houses against earthquakes, cultivate on steep rocky terrain. Subsistence. A deep silence. There's nothing here to soothe or refresh the landscape, no forests or rivers or lakes. But there's light and sea and sea birds, there's heat that rots ambition and stuns the intellect and will."

The extravagance of the remark surprised him. He laughed abruptly, in a way that welcomed us to share a joke at his expense. When he finished his wine he sat upright, legs drawn in.

"Correctness of detail. This is what the light provides. Look to small things for your truth, your joy. This is the Greek specific."

Kathryn put down her glass.

"Tell James about the people in the hills," she said, and in she went, yawning.

I wanted to follow her to the bedroom, lift her out of the sailcloth skirt. So much stale time to sweep aside. Jasmine budding in a toothbrush glass, all the senses rush to love. We nudge our shoes away and touch lightly, in shivers, feeling each other with an anxious reverence, alert to every nuance of contact, fingertips, floating bodies. Dip and lift again, arms around her buttocks, my face in the swale of her breasts. I groan with the burden, she laughs in the night wind. A parody of ancient abduction. Tasting the salt moisture between her breasts. Thinking as I lumber toward the bed how rhythmic and correct this beauty is, this simple thing of curves, human surfaces, the shape those island Greeks pursued in their Parian marble. Noble thought. The bed is small and set low, a swayback mattress hard at the edges. In time our breathing finds the same waver, the little cadence we will work to demolish. Some clothes slip off the chair, belt buckle ringing. That gaze of hers. Wondering who I am and what I want. The look in the dark I've never been able to answer. The look of the girl in the family album who asserts her right to calculate the precise value of what is out there. We take care to be silent. The boy in his own bed on the other side of the wall. This stricture is seamed so evenly into our nights we've come to believe there would be less pleasure without it. From the beginning, when he was taking shape in her, we tried to guide ourselves away from forceful emotions. It seemed a duty and a preparation. We would make ready a well-tempered world, mur-murous, drawn in airy pastels. Noble thought number two. My mouth at the rim of her ear, all love's words unvoiced. This silence is a witness to broader loyalties.

"It started simply enough," Owen said. "I wanted to visit the monastery. There's a trail that meanders in that general direction, barely wide enough for a motor scooter. It cuts through a vine-yard, then climbs into the dusty hills. As the terrain rises and drops, you get intermittent views of those rock masses farther inland. The monastery is occupied, it's a working monastery according to local people, and visitors are welcome. The trouble with the path is that it disappears in thick shrubbery and rockfall about two miles from the destination. No choice but walk. I left the machine and started off. From the end of the path it's not possible to see the monastery or even the huge rock column it's attached to, so I found myself trying to reconstruct the terrain from those hurried glimpses I'd had a quarter of an hour earlier, on the scooter."

I could see her in the dark, moving along the bedroom wall, taking off her blouse as she went. The window was small and she passed quickly from view. A dim flash, the bathroom light. She closed the door. The sound of running water came from the other side of the house, where the toilet window was, like the sputter of something frying. Dark again. Owen tipped his chair against the wall.

"There are caves along the way. Some of them looked to me like tomb caves, similar to the ones at Matala on the Libyan Sea. There are caves everywhere in Greece, of course. A definitive history is waiting to be written of cave habitation in this part of the world. It amounts to a parallel culture, I would imagine, right up to the nudists and hippies on Crete in recent years. I wasn't surprised, then, to see two figures, male, standing at the entrance to one of these caves, about forty-five feet above me. The hills have a greenish cast here, most of them are rounded at the top. I hadn't yet reached the pinnacle rocks, where the monastery is. I pointed ahead and asked these men in Greek if this was the way to the monastery. The odd thing is that I knew they weren't Greek. I felt instinctively it would be to my advantage to play dumb. Very strange, how the mind makes these calculations. Something about them. A haggard look, intense, fugitive. I didn't think I was in danger, exactly, but I felt I needed a tactic. *I am harmless, a lost traveler.* There I was, after all, in walking shoes and a sun hat, a little canvas bag on my back. Thermos bottle, sandwiches, chocolate. There were crude steps cut into the rock. Not at all recent. The men wore old shabby loose-fitting clothes. Faded colors mostly, Turkish sort of pants, or Indian, what younger travelers sometimes wear. You see them in Athens around cheap hotels in the Plaka and in places like the covered market in Istanbul and anywhere along the overland route to India, people in ashram clothes, drawstring clothes. One of the men had a scraggly beard and he was the one who called down to me, in Greek more halting than my own, *'How many languages do you speak?'* Strangest damn thing to ask. A formal question. Some medieval tale, a question asked of travelers at the city gates. Did my entry depend on the answer? The fact that we'd spoken to each other in a language not our own deepened the sense of formal procedure, of manner and ceremony. I called up, *'Five,'* again in Greek. I was intrigued but still wary and when he beckoned me up I took the steps slowly, wondering what people, for how many centuries, had lived in this place."

I had to concentrate to see her. Back in the bedroom, by the wall, in darkness. I tried to induce her to look this way by an act of will. She'd put on a chamois cloth shirt, one of my discards, good for sleeping alone, she'd told me smiling. An overlong garment, tailored in the old-fashioned way, it reached almost to her knees. I waited for her to see me staring in. I knew she'd look.

This knowing was contained in the structure of my own seeing. We both knew. It was an understanding between us that bypassed the usual centers. I might even have predicted within a fraction of a second when her head would turn. And she did look up, briefly, one knee already lowered to the edge of the bed, and what she saw was Owen's elbow jutting across the window frame from his position in the tipped-back chair, Owen talking, and beyond this the spare calm educated face of her husband, violent in candlelight. I wanted a sign, something to interpret as favorable. But what could she give me in a crowded moment in the dark even if she knew my mind and wanted to ease it? That was the shirt she was wearing when she took a swipe at me with a potato peeler in one of the first of the dark days, our bird bath covered with snow.

Reluctant adulterer.

"There were two others near the cave entrance. One a woman, strong-featured, heavy, with cropped hair. The man was sitting just inside the entrance writing in a notebook. There was a stone fireplace nearby. Inside the cave I saw sleeping bags, knapsacks, straw mats, other things that didn't register clearly. The people were filthy, of course. Hair stringy with dirt. That particular clinging dirt of people who no longer notice. Dirt was their medium by now. It was their air, their nightly warmth. We sat outside the cave mouth on ledges, carved steps, rolled-up sleeping bags. One of the men pointed out the monastery, which was clearly visible from here. I decided to accept this as a friendly and reassuring gesture and tried not to notice the way they were studying me, inspecting minutely. We spoke Greek throughout, their version of it a mixture of older forms and *demotikí*, or what people actually speak."

He told them he was involved in epigraphy, his first and current love, the study of inscriptions. He went off on private expeditions, leaving the Minoan dig to his assistant. He'd recently come back from Qasr Hallabat, a ruined desert castle in Jordan, where he'd seen the fragmented Greek inscriptions known as the Edict of Anastasius. Before that he'd been to Tell Mardikh to study the Ebla tablets; to Mount Nebo to see the pavement mosaics; to Jerash, Palmyra, Ephesus. He told them he'd gone to Ras

Shamrah in Syria to inspect a single clay tablet, about the size of a man's middle finger, that contained the entire thirty-letter alphabet of the Canaanite people who lived there well over three thousand years ago.

They seemed excited by this, although no one referred to it until Owen was getting set to leave. He thought in fact they were trying to conceal their excitement. As he talked further about Ras Shamrah they were very still, they were careful not to look at each other. But he sensed an interaction, a curious force in the air, as though each of them sat in a charged field and these fields had begun to overlap. It turned out in the end they were interested in the alphabet. They explained this to him almost shyly in their defective Greek.

Not Ras Shamrah. Not history, gods, tumbled walls, the scale poles and pumps of the excavators.

The alphabet itself. They were interested in letters, written symbols, fixed in sequence.

Tap washed pottery shards in pans of water, scrubbing them with a toothbrush. The more delicate pieces he cleaned with a small paintbrush, fine-bristled.

Kathryn and a male student worked a device called a rocking screen. The young man troweled dirt from a tall pile into a plastic bleach bottle with the upper section cut off. He spread this dirt onto a horizontal screen equipped with handles and held in position at elbow height by a bracketed wooden framework. Kathryn gripped the handles and rocked the dirt through the fine mesh, one hour, two hours, three hours.

I sat in the shade, watching.

At twilight she and I walked down through the village to one of the fishing boats tied up at the pier. A small crucifix was nailed to the door of the wheelhouse. We sat on deck and watched people eating dinner in the two restaurants. She knew the owner of the boat and his sons. One of the sons had worked at the excavation, helping to clear the site and then digging trenches. The other son was limited in the work he could do, having lost a hand to dynamite.

This second man stood about thirty yards away, beating an octopus against a rock. The small beach where he stood was littered with broken things and thick plastic sheeting. He held the octopus by the head and smashed its tentacles against the rock, over and over.

"I had an erotic fantasy last night while Owen was talking about those people."

"Who was in it?" she said.

"You and I."

"A man who has fantasies about his wife?"

"I've always been backward in these matters."

"It must be the sun. The heat and sun are famous for generating this kind of thing."

"It was nighttime," I said.

We talked awhile about her nephews and nieces, other family matters, commonplaces, a cousin taking trumpet lessons, a death in Winnipeg. It seemed we could stray from Owen's evening seminars. We could talk to each other behind his back, as it were, as long as we didn't get too close to the basic state of things between us. The subject of family makes conversation almost tactile. I think of hands, food, hoisted children. There's a close-up contact warmth in the names and images. Everydayness. She had one sister in England, two in western Canada, people in six provinces altogether, Sinclairs and Pattisons and their extensions in insulated houses with aluminum siding at the back and half a cord of wood stacked against the sides. This is life below the white line, the permafrost. People sitting in renovated kitchens, decent, sad, a little bitter in an undirected way. I felt I knew them. Bass fishermen. Presbyterians.

When children race out of rooms the noise of their leaving remains behind. When old people die, she'd once been told, they leave a smell on things.

"My father hated that hospital. He'd always feared doctors and hospitals. He never wanted to know what was wrong. All those tests, that whole year of tests, I began to think he would die of tests. He preferred not knowing. But once they put him in the hospital, he knew."

"He needed a drink. He kept telling me. It became a complicated joke between us."

"Many drinks."

"I wish he could have gone to this subterranean place in Athens I sometimes go to with David Keller. When someone asks whether they have bourbon, the bartender says smugly, 'Yes, of course, James Beam, very good.' "

"James Beam. That is very good. He liked his bourbon."

"He liked American things."

"A common failing."

"Despite the propaganda he kept hearing from one of his children."

"Four years now, isn't it?"

"Four years. And that incredible thing he said near the end. 'I commute all sentences. Pass the word. The criminals are forgiven.' Which I will never forget."

"He could barely speak."

"Deadpan. Absolutely deadpan to the end."

This talk we were having about familiar things was itself ordinary and familiar. It seemed to yield up the mystery that is part of such things, the nameless way in which we sometimes feel our connections to the physical world. *Being here.* Everything is where it should be. Our senses are collecting at the primal edge. The woman's arm trailing down a shroud, my wife, whatever her name. I felt I was in an early stage of teenage drunkenness, lightheaded, brilliantly happy and stupid, knowing the real meaning of every word. The deck gave off a dozen smells.

"Why is Tap writing about rural life during the Depression?"

"He talks to Owen. I think it's interesting that he writes about real people instead of heroes and adventurers. Not that he doesn't go overboard in other ways. Flamboyant prose, lurid emotions. He absolutely collides with the language. The spelling is atrocious."

"He talks to Owen."

"I gather these are episodes from Owen's boyhood. People he knew and so on. I don't think Owen even knows this stuff is being put on paper. It's an interesting story, at least as it emerges from our son's feverish imagination."

"A nonfiction novel."

A man finishing a peach tossed the pit into the sidecar of a motorcycle as it turned the corner where he happened to be standing. The timing was perfect, the toss deceptively casual. What rounded out the simple beauty of the thing was the fact that he did not look around to see who noticed.

"I hope we don't become one of those couples who start getting along after they split up."

"That may be better," she said, "than not getting along at all."

"I hope we don't become one of those couples who can't live together but can't live apart."

"You're getting funny in your old age. People have commented."

"Who?"

"No one."

"We got along, didn't we, in the important ways? Our attachment is deep."

"No more marriage, ever, for this lady, to anyone."

"It's strange. I can talk about these things with other people. But not with you."

"I'm the killer bitch, remember?"

Another man had joined the first, the boat owner's son. They stood on the narrow gravel beach, in the light of the second restaurant, each beating an octopus against the rock, taking turns, working to a rhythm.

"What's next?"

"Istanbul, Ankara, Beirut, Karachi."

"What do you do on these trips?"

"Policy updates, we call them. In effect I review the political and economic situation of the country in question. We have a complex grading system. Prison statistics weighed against the number of foreign workers. How many young males unemployed. Have the generals' salaries been doubled recently. What happens to dissidents. This year's cotton crop or winter wheat yield. Payments made to the clergy. We have people we call control points. The control is always a national of the country in question. Together we analyze the figures in the light of recent events. What seems likely? Collapse, overthrow, nationalization? Maybe a balance of payments problem, maybe bodies hurled into ditches. Whatever endangers an investment."

"Then you pay."

"It's interesting because it involves people, waves of people, people running in the streets."

A donkey stood motionless in the back of a three-wheel pickup that was parked near the bakery. A man sat smoking at the wheel.

Twin boys, teenagers, walked with their father along the harborfront. The man wore a suit and tie, his sons wore knitted V-neck sweaters. He walked between them and each boy held him by an arm. They walked in a measured stately way, beautiful to watch. The boys were closer to eighteen than thirteen. They were dark and somber and looked straight ahead.

Tap was at his desk, writing.

In the room I put things in my overnight bag, planning to be on the early boat to Naxos, on to Piraeus from there. I heard someone whistling outside. A single birdlike note, repeated. I went out to the balcony. Two men played backgammon at a folding table set against the hotel wall. Owen Brademas stood under a tree across the street, looking up at me, arms crossed on his chest.

"I went up to the house."

"They're asleep," I said.

"I thought you'd all be up there."

"She's up at five tomorrow. We both are."

"It isn't necessary for her to be at the site so damn early."

"She has to heat water and make breakfast and do fourteen other things. She writes letters, she reads. Come on up."

There were five or six other villages on the island. Owen lived just outside the southernmost of these in a concrete dwelling called he dig house. It was located about a mile from the excavation. His assistant and the remaining fieldworkers also lived there. People in the houses scattered along the route from this village to that one must have wondered at the night-riding man sitting tall and awkward on his motor scooter, passing between the barley fields, the bamboo windbreaks.

I used a towel to clean off the chair on the balcony and then I carried out a spindle chair with an upholstered seat. Intermittent wind came biting up off the water.

"Is this an imposition, James? Just say so."

"It'll be another hour or two before I'm ready to sleep. Sit down."

"Do you sleep?"

"Not as well as I used to."

"I don't sleep," he said.

"Kathryn sleeps. I used to sleep. Tap sleeps, of course."

"It's pleasant here. Our house isn't well sited. It seems to catch and retain heat."

"What is it you find on those stones, Owen, that's so intriguing?"

He stretched his body, easing into an answer.

"At first, years ago, I think it was mainly a question of history and philology. The stones spoke. It was a form of conversation with ancient people. It was also riddle-solving to a certain degree. To decipher, to uncover secrets, to trace the geography of language in a sense. In my current infatuation I think I've abandoned scholarship and much of the interest I once had in earlier cultures. What the stones say, after all, is often routine stuff. Inventories, land sale contracts, grain payments, records of commodities, so many cows, so many sheep. I'm not an expert on the origin of writing but it seems to be the case that the first writing was motivated by a desire to keep accounts. Palace accounts, temple accounts. Bookkeeping."

"And now?"

"Now I've begun to see a mysterious importance in the letters as such, the blocks of characters. The tablet at Ras Shamrah said nothing. It was inscribed with the alphabet itself. I find this is all

I want to know about the people who lived there. The shapes of their letters and the material they used. Fire-hardened clay, dense black basalt, marble with a ferrous content. These things I lay my hands against, feel where the words have been cut. And the eye takes in those beautiful shapes. So strange and reawakening. It goes deeper than conversations, riddles."

"Why do you call this an infatuation?"

"Well it just is, James. It's an unreasoning passion. It's extravagant, foolish, probably short-lived."

All this with sweeping gestures, in open vocal rhythms. Then he laughed, although it may be more accurate to say he "laughed out," as one cries out or calls out. So much that he said and did had a tone of trustful surrender to it. It was my guess that he lived with the consequences of self-discovery and I suspected this was a more exacting hardship than anything the world might have worked out for him.

"And these people in the hills. You'll go back?"

"I don't know. They talked about moving on."

"There's a practical element. What they eat, where they get it."

"They steal," he said. "Everything from olives to goats."

"Did they tell you this?"

"I surmised."

"Would you call them a cult?"

"They share an esoteric interest."

"Or a sect?"

"You may have a point. I got the impression they're part of a larger group but I don't know if their ideas or customs are refinements of some wider body of thought."

"What else?" I said.

Nothing. The moon was nearly full, lighting the edges of wind-driven clouds. The backgammon players rolled their ivory dice. The board was still there in the morning, set at the edge of the table, as I hurried toward the gray boat, low-riding in the calm, looking sad, half sunken. I prepared to work through the Greek lettering on the bow in my laborious preschool way but it was an easy name this time, after the island. *Kouros.* It was Tap who'd told me the name of the island derived from a colossal statue found toppled near an ancient gravesite about a hundred years ago. It was a traditional *kouros*, a sturdy young man with braided hair who stood with his arms close to his nude body, his left foot forward, an archaic smile on his face. Seventh century B.C. He'd learned this from Owen, of course.

3

AWAKE. The pulsing cry of doves. I have to concentrate to form a sense of whereabouts. Up, into the world, crank the shutters open. The beekeeper in the garden of the British School marches in his hooded bonnet to the box hives. I take the coffee mug from the drain basket, set the water boiling. Mount Hymettus is a white shadow, summer mornings, a vaporous reach to the gulf. Today's a market day, a man is chasing peaches down the steep street below the terrace restaurants. A pickup has hit his, knocking a bushel off the end, and the peaches come down the asphalt surface in wobbling rows. The man is trying to head them off, running low to the ground and making sweeping motions with his arm. A boy stands under the mulberry trees, hosing down the floor of the restaurants. Where the pickups have met, a vast gesturing goes on between the driver of one vehicle and a friend of the stooped and running man. An envelope of Nescafé, a leftover donut. The phone is ringing, the first of the day's wrong numbers. Doves lighting on the still tips of cypresses. The men from the café around the corner come into view, watching the peaches roll. They lean into the street with care, evaluating gravely, prepared to extend only so much in effort and gesture. Honeybees rise clustered in the dusty light.

I walk to the office, where I make myself another cup of coffee and wait for the telex to address me.

Marriage is something we make from available materials. In this sense it's improvised, it's almost offhand. Maybe this is why we know so little about it. It's too inspired and quicksilver a thing to be clearly understood. Two people make a blur.

Charles Maitland and I discussed this, sitting on a bench in the National Gardens, where it was fifteen degrees cooler than in the bright city around us. Kids walked by, eating rings of sesame bread.

"You're talking about modern marriage. Americans."

"Kathryn is Canadian."

"New World then."

"I think you're out of touch."

"Of course I'm out of touch. And a good thing too. Spare me from being in touch. The point is that the thing you describe has nothing to do with *wedlock.*"

He produced the word like a gold coin between his teeth. Handsome battered face. Burst capillaries, streaked blue eyes. He was fifty-eight, a half shambles, broad, ruddy, silver-browed, racked by fits of coughing. Sundays he drove alone to a field outside the city and flew his radio-controlled model plane. It weighed nine pounds and cost two thousand dollars.

"True," I said. "Wedlock was the last thing Kathryn and I thought we'd entered. We hadn't entered a state at all. If anything, we'd broken out of states and nations and firm designs. She used to say this marriage is a movie. She didn't mean it wasn't real. The whole thing flickered. It was a series of small flickering moments. But at the same time calm and safe. A day-to-day life. Restrained, moderate. I thought if you didn't want anything, your marriage was bound to work. I thought the trouble was that everyone wanted. They wanted in different directions. Tap, coming along, reinforced the feeling that we were making it up day by day, little by little, but sanely, contentedly, with no huge self-seeking visions."

"I'm thirsty," he said.

"A drink would kill you."

"It flickered. It was a series of flickers. You were calm and safe."

"We had incredible fights."

"When the old girl gets here, we're going for a drink."

"I'm having lunch with Rowser. Come along."

"Christ, no. Christ, not him."

"Be a sport," I said.

Shaded paths. Watercourses and stone fountains. A dense green place with towering trees that provided a fan vaulting, a cover against the enlarged-heart panics of central Athens. The landscape had a pleasing randomness. It was an enticement to wander foolishly, to get lost without feeling you were part of a formalist puzzle, a garden of hedge traps and designed escapes. A dozen men talked politics under a pine tree. Intermittently Charles listened, translating for me. He and Ann had been married twenty-nine years (she was seven or eight years younger than he was). In that time he'd held various jobs involving the security of overseas branches of British and American corporations. He now worked on a consulting basis, advising mainly on fire safety, something of a drop in status and income, considering the living to be made in terror.

They'd lived in Egypt, Nigeria, Panama, Turkey, Cyprus, East Africa, the Sudan and Lebanon. These stays were anywhere from one year to four. They'd lived elsewhere, including the States, for shorter periods, and they'd been through a number of things, from house arrest and deportation, Cairo '56, to heavy shelling and infectious hepatitis, Beirut '76. Ann talked about these episodes in a tone of remote sadness, as if they were things she'd heard about or read in the newspaper. Maybe she felt unqualified to share the emotions of the native-born. The Lebanese were the victims, Beirut was the tragedy, the world was the loser. She never mentioned what they themselves had lost in any of the places they'd lived. It was Charles, finally, who told me that everything in their small home in Cyprus had been stolen or destroyed when the Turks rolled over the countryside and he implied this was only one of several ruinous events. They'd seemed, the troops, to have a deep need to pull things out of walls, whatever was jutting—pipes, taps, valves, switches. The walls themselves they'd smeared with shit.

There was a protocol of coping, of making do, and Ann was expert. I was learning that reticence was fairly common in such matters. There was a sense in which people felt it was self-incriminating to speak out against these violations. I thought I sometimes detected in people who had lost property or fled, most frequently in Americans, some mild surprise that it hadn't happened sooner, that the men with the six-day beards hadn't come much earlier to burn them out, or uproot the plumbing, or walk off with the prayer rugs they'd bargained for in the souk and bought as investments—for the crimes of drinking whiskey, making money, jogging in shiny suits along the boulevards at dusk. Wasn't there a sense, we Americans felt, in which we had it coming?

Port Harcourt, Nigeria, Ann said, was the only real regret. There was sweet crude in the delta, a howling loneliness. Charles was doing security and safety for a refinery built by Shell and British Petroleum. She fled to Beirut and the war in the streets. The marriage lost some of its conviction but made eventual gains in the category of rueful irony when BP's assets were nationalized.

They didn't want to go back home. Too many years of elaborate skies, lithe people with plaited hair, red-robed, in bare feet. Or was that England today? They thought they might retire to California, where they had a son in graduate school, some kind of raving savant by the sound of it—a mathematician.

"The idea is to learn the language," Charles said, "but not to let them know. This is what I do. I don't let people know unless absolutely pressed."

"But then what good is it?"

"I listen. I listen all the time. I pick up things, listening. I have an advantage in this regard. I'm not only a foreigner. I don't *look* as if I speak Greek."

"This is an incredible distinction, Charles. Are you serious?"

"You want to pick up whatever you can."

"But don't you do business here occasionally?"

"One does business in English. Surely you've come to suspect this."

"If I ever learn the language, I'll speak it as often as possible. I want to talk to them, I want to hear what they're saying. These men arguing, there's something serious, almost loving about it. I want to interrupt, ask questions."

"You won't pick up anything, talking to them."

"I don't want to pick up anything."

"Using my method, you'll learn infinitely more."

"Charles, your method is crazy."

"What about a Heineken then? Is it possible in this country to get beer in green bottles?"

"Seriously, do you speak Arabic?"

"Of course."

"I envy that. I really do."

"Ann's a brilliant linguist. She's done translation, you know. She's very good."

"My kid speaks Ob. It's a kind of pig Latin. You insert *o-b* in certain parts of words."

Charles hunched forward, his cigarette burning to the filter.

"Something almost loving," he mumbled, glancing at the men around the tree.

"You know what I mean. There's a certain quality in the language."

"You want to interrupt. You want to ask questions."

I watched Ann cross to us, emerging from a ring of poplars. A gait with a pleasing sway. Even at a distance, her mouth showed the small pursed conceit of a remark in the making. We stood, flanking her, and headed down a path toward the nearest gate.

"At any given time," she said, "half the women in Athens are having their hair done by the other half."

"They've worked wonders, clearly," Charles said.

"It is such confusion. I'd still be there had it not been for no-shows and dropouts. James, I've never realized. You have khaki hair."

"It's brown."

"If jeeps had hair, it would look like yours. He has khaki hair," she told Charles.

"Leave him alone. He's having lunch with George Rowser."

"He's having lunch with us. Where are we off to?"

"We'll have dinner," I said.

"Good. Shall I call anyone?"

"Call everyone."

"What are all these people doing in the park?" she said. "Greeks hate fresh air."

I pulled down a book on mythology for Tap. I took it to the cash register. The woman there directed me to a man across the room. I gave him the book and followed him to his little desk. He took a thick pad, wrote out a sales slip and gave it to me, without the book. I took the sales slip to the woman at the cash register. She took my money, stamped the slip and gave it back to me with my change. I put the stamped document in my pocket and went to the little desk. The man had wrapped the book and was sealing the package with transparent tape. He wanted my sales slip. I took it out of my pocket and gave it to him. He gave me a carbon copy. I put it in my pocket and left with the neatly wrapped book.

My life was full of routine surprises. One day I was watching runners from Marathon dodge taxis near the Athens Hilton, the next I was turning a corner in Istanbul to see a gypsy leading a bear on a leash. I began to think of myself as a perennial tourist. There was something agreeable about this. To be a tourist is to escape accountability. Errors and failings don't cling to you the way they do back home. You're able to drift across continents and languages, suspending the operation of sound thought. Tourism is the march of stupidity. You're expected to be stupid. The entire mechanism of the host country is geared to travelers acting stupidly. You walk around dazed, squinting into fold-out maps. You don't know how to talk to people, how to get anywhere, what the money means, what time it is, what to eat or how to eat it. Being stupid is the pattern, the level and the norm. You can exist on this level for weeks and months without reprimand or dire consequence. Together with thousands, you are granted immunities and broad freedoms. You are an army of fools, wearing bright polyesters, riding camels, taking pictures of each other, haggard, dysenteric, thirsty. There is nothing to think about but the next shapeless event.

One day I went out to find the streets full of children wearing costumes. I didn't know what the occasion was, what was being commemorated. In the center of Athens there were hundreds of these children in elaborate masquerade. They walked hand in hand with their parents or ran among the pigeons in front of the war memorial. Children as cowboys, elves, moonwalkers, oil sheiks with black beards, toting briefcases. I didn't ask what it meant. I was happy not knowing. I wanted to preserve the surprise in an opaque medium. This happened many times in large and small ways. Athens was my legal home but I wasn't ready to give up tourism, even here.

In the flower market I saw a priest and a deacon come out of the church behind the stalls, leading a group of people who carried crosses and other objects. The priest had wild eyes and a flaring beard, the people may have been mourners. They walked once around the church and went back inside.

To be taken constantly by surprise was not the worst thing that could happen to a man living apart.

Rowser traveled under a false name. He had a total of three identities and owned the relevant paper. His office outside Washington was equipped with a letter-bomb detector, a voice scrambler, an elaborate system to prevent break-ins. He was a man who never quite took the final heavy step into foolishness and pathos, despite the indications. His life itself was the chief indication, full of the ornaments of paranoia and deception. Even his hoarse voice, a forced whisper, seemed a comic symptom of the clandestine environment. But Rowser's massive drive, his will to see things through, overpowered everything else.

He was a businessman. He sold insurance to other businessmen. The subjects were money, politics and force.

I met him in the bar off the lobby of the Grande Bretagne, one of the duskier haunts, plush chairs, soft voices. He was a stocky man with glasses, going bald. He was drinking mineral water and making notes when I walked in.

"Sit down. I'm back from Kuwait."

"Are they killing Americans?"

"Not so you'd notice," he said. "Not openly. What have you got for me?"

"George, can I order a drink?"

"Order a drink."

"Turkey is an education in how far people will go to make a point. Except no one agrees on what the point is."

"What else is new?"

"The weather was good."

"Did you go to the mosques?"

"Not this trip," I said.

"I can't understand how people go to Istanbul and don't do the mosques. I can spend hours in one mosque."

"I was there on business, George."

"Very good. But you can always make time for a mosque."

"Are you religious?"

"Get away from me. I like the awe, that's all."

"Impressive architecture. I concede that much."

"No pictures. I have entree to Vatican pictures no one gets in to see without stunning credentials. I want to see the stuff in Naples. The hidden rooms."

"Who do you know?"

"I have a cardinal in the States."

The waiter came, head tilted, a faintly mocking look in his eyes. I ordered a beer. Rowser's ultra-secure briefcase sat next to him in the soft chair. It was full of painstaking assessments, I was sure. Data on the stability of the countries he'd been visiting. Facts on the infrastructure. Probabilities, statistics. These were the music of Rowser's life, the only coherence he needed.

What connected us was risk.

He'd started in this line of work by gathering material for people who wrote scholarly reports on large-scale death and destruction. Rowser had a gift for numbers and a temperament that enabled him to separate mathematical techniques and actuarial science from the terrifying events he culled for his figures. In universities and research centers he attended any number of conferences at which people discussed such choice calamities as reactor meltdowns, runaway viruses and three-day spasm wars.

Somebody had to tell us what our chances were. Rowser's problem was that he didn't have the breadth and penetration to succeed as a risk analyst. He knew what he was, a night-school hustler, a man who figured the angles, brusque, enterprising, chained to late nights and caffeine. He was no game theorist or geopolitician. He had no system of assumptions and principles. What he had was a set of interlocking facts he'd drawn from tons of research material on the cost-effectiveness of terror.

There had been over five thousand terrorist incidents in the past decade.

Kidnappings were routine business.

Ransom requests of five million dollars were not unusual.

In this decade a quarter of a billion dollars in ransom money had been paid to terrorists.

Business executives were prime targets.

U.S. executives led the world, being targeted with particular frequency in the Middle East and Latin America.

Simple. He convinced a medium-sized insurance company to sell ransom policies to the multinationals. His job was to figure the risk of enrolling applicants for coverage. He read everything in the public record on terror and traveled widely to set up lines of data-gathering that helped him draw conclusions about overseas operations, the attitudes of host countries, political currents in general. Secrecy was important. If a terrorist group knew that a certain corporation insured its executives against kidnap and ransom, they'd clearly want to consider an action.

The man of narrow outlook becomes immersed. Rowser occupied himself profoundly in the customs and attitudes of the secret life. His thoroughness was compulsive and regenerative, a pathological condition. He stopped carrying company ID, he committed phone numbers and addresses to memory, he spent small fortunes on electronic devices. I don't think he became involved in these things as some men do, because they verge on something deep and unseen, a dream life or alternate self. He wasn't the kind of man who plays at danger. I think he was simply scared. Risk had become a physical thing.

"What's that?"

"A book I bought my kid."

"I'm a two-time loser," he said.

"We're only separated, George."

"Get divorced."

"Why?"

"Absolutely. I don't even remember them. If they walked down the street together, I'd go right by."

"I don't want to discuss marriage. I did that an hour ago."

"Drink your beer, we'll go."

"Where are we having lunch?"

"I don't eat lunch. My doctor told me to drop one meal. We'll walk around the block. I want an overview on Turkey."

"It's damn hot out there."

"I don't like talking where it may not be secure. Drink down your beer, we'll go."

"It's insurance. That's all it is, George. Nobody's listening."

"I'm the kind of person he doesn't like to break a habit. I started doing things this way and maybe it's not necessary anymore. Maybe it was never necessary, looking objectively. But a habit is the toughest thing to break for this type person. There is no logic in most habits. This is exactly why they take such hold. A habit is a death grip to somebody like me."

The harsh dry scrape in his voice was halfway poignant. I first met Rowser at a seminar on foreign investments. Many voices besides his own at the Hay-Adams that day. Curious, I thought, how all these regional accents converged on the same sets of words. The language of business is hard-edged and aggressive, drawing some of its technical cant from the weapons pools of the south and southwest, a rural nurturing in a way, a blooding of the gray-suited, the pale, the corporate man. It's all the same game, these cross-argots suggest.

By this time Rowser was head of development for the Northeast Group, a subsidiary of a two-billion-dollar conglomerate he referred to as "the parent." No more edgy executives. The Northeast Group specialized in political risk insurance for corporations with foreign holdings. In recent years U.S. assets had been seized in two dozen countries and businessmen were looking for financial protection. All those grave Zaireans, those Pakistanis with their sensual lips and bright smiles, voices in melodic ascent, what sweet-natured technocrats they made, running the plants we'd designed and financed, using our very jargon.

Rowser and his group were writing political risk insurance in impressive amounts. They sold portions of the original policies to syndicates in order to spread risk and generate whatever cash flow the parent did not supply. He broadened his data collection network and installed a few key people called risk analysts, the title he'd felt unworthy of in the days when he gathered facts for the end of the world. This was the job he offered me. Associate director of risk analysis, Middle East.

I was a freelance writer, something of a Renaissance hack. Booklets, pamphlets, leaflets, all kinds of institutional litter for government and industry. Newsletters for a computer firm. Scripts for industrial films. Tax-planning strategies, investment strategies. We had three meetings. At the time I was ghosting a book on global conflict for an Air Force general associated with one of Rowser's old encampments, the Institute of Risk Analysis at American University. Rowser had seen early pages of the manuscript and it was possible he'd been impressed by the way I'd reshaped the general's muddled thinking. The general was a living wilderness. Everyone in the risk community knew this.

Rowser told me that material flowed into Athens from various control points around the Mediterranean, the Gulf and the Arabian Sea. It needed structuring, it needed perusal by someone with intellectual range. He wanted a view that was broader than the underwriter's or statistician's.

A tallish fellow with an educated face and khaki hair might be just what he needed for the region.

I turned him down. Kathryn, Tap and I were living in an old gabled house in the Champlain Islands, a place her father had owned, and we liked it there, among farms and apple orchards, a lake culture lying between the Green Mountains and the Adirondacks. My grubstreet ways suited us. We had a picture of ourselves as people who needed little. Kathryn was managing a crafts school on North Hero, one island up from us, and the occasional presence in our home of laconic young potters and quilt-makers gave the place a dusting of old-fashioned virtue. We wanted Tap to grow up in North America.

A year later we were in Toronto, dividing our books, and Kathryn was speaking Greek to a tape machine. So much for North America. I got in touch with Rowser. He had a man for the region but said he was interested in talking to me. I said it had to be Athens. He'd try to work it out, he told me. It took three months.

I'd have a steady job, an office, a secretary, a schedule and clear-cut responsibilities while my wife worked in a trench and my son wrote a novel. A happy pair. They were the freelancers now but I couldn't shake the feeling that I was the one taking the major risk. There was nothing to come back to if I failed, no place in particular I belonged. They were my place, the only true boundaries I had. I went, I set out, as a man on a dangerous journey, feeling a grimness and will I'd never felt before.

Self-satisfied, willing to settle.

What are my qualities? This was a question that nagged at the whole affair. Passion, character, fortitude and wit. Cunning and dumb luck. I'd have to command something of all of these. Is this why people try to force events, to find out how complete they are and what they've managed to accumulate of drifting fortune? Some kinds of loneliness are an accusation. Do we feel this is what we are, broken down to entity, unpigmented?

The rocky brown island, the chalk village, the men spreading their yellow nets, all these forms of emitted light. The layered Minoan soil, ochre and rust and soot, and the shards of painted pottery, these are the passions that saturate the world. And it was Rowser, walking uphill past the jewelry shops along the pedestrian mall, half panting, who was the middleman of all this hazardous love. Rowser in his insurance man's gray suit.

"Lloyd's wants to declare the Gulf a war zone," he said. "That could double the tanker premium."

"How do you know?"

"I got some playback from a Kuwaiti defense meeting. They're figuring a worst-case scenario. Lloyd's is. Tanker hulks littering the strait. The robed ones are muttering in their beards. Even the parent is nervous about the prospect. It impacts on almost everything they're involved in."

"A war zone."

"It has a ring, doesn't it."

He wanted to know about Turkey. I had precise figures for nonperforming loans. I had classified telex traffic between bank branches in the region. I had foreign exchange factors, inflation rates, election possibilities, exports and imports. I had cars lined up for gasoline, daily power cuts, no water coming out of household taps, crowds of unemployed young men standing on corners, fifteen-year-old girls shot to death for politics. No coffee, no heating oil, no spare parts for combat aircraft. I had martial law, black markets, the International Monetary Fund, God is great.

I'd been given the scrambled telexes by my friend David Keller, a credit head at the Mainland Bank. Much of the other material I'd been given by our control for Turkey. The streets of Istanbul were data in their own right, the raw force, the unraveling. The rest came from our contacts at the World Bank and various research institutes.

We'd circled back and were heading downhill, single file, along a narrow sidewalk. He talked to me over his shoulder.

"Where are you from? Did I ever ask?"

"Medium-sized town. Pennsylvania."

"I'm from Jersey City."

"What do you want me to say, George? We're a long way from home?"

We crossed the street to avoid a deposit of soap suds.

"Do I want to go to the Acropolis?"

"Everybody goes," I told him.

"Is there climbing?"

"They all do it. The lame, the halt."

"What's up there exactly that I have to see it?"

"You go to Naples to look at dirty pictures."

"I have to finagle that. This is nothing," he said.

Five minutes later we were in the office, two modest rooms connected by an arched opening. My secretary, a middle-aged woman who liked to be called Mrs. Helen, was at a funeral in the north somewhere.

Rowser took off his shoes and asked to see telexes, notes, memoranda, whatever I could give him. Stamped documents, rows of figures. As he settled into his reading I felt myself beginning to perceive the silence, the eerie calm that closed in gradually every time I came in here from the street. The building was in a cul-de-sac, a preciously quiet spot in a city hardened to noise. Noise is a kind of rain to Athenians, an environment shaped by nature. Nothing can prevent it.

"When do you leave, George?"

"Tomorrow."

"TW?"

"Right."

"Expect a stop."

"It's nonstop."

"Expect a stop. Shannon or Goose Bay."

"Why?" he said.

"They take off without full tanks. They tell you it's too hot here and the fuel expands. Or the runway's too short and the fuel is heavy. It's the fuel all right. More expensive here. They like to fill up elsewhere."

"It comes back to that."

"No escape," I said.

He went back to his reading. I sat at my desk with a lemon drink, watching him. He had a dozen nervous gestures. He touched his face, his clothes, blinking almost constantly. I imagined him stranded in Goose Bay. Big empty remote innocent Labrador. Scraped-clean-by-the-wind Labrador. No politics, no risk. The place would be an offense to him, a white space he could not know through numbers. He would die there, gesturing.

Summer nights belong to people in the streets. Everyone is outdoors, massed against the stonescape. We reconceive the city as a collection of unit spaces that people occupy in a fixed order of succession. Park benches, café tables, the swinging seats on ferris wheels in the carnival lots. Pleasure is not diversion but urgent life, a social order perceived as temporary. People go to movies set up in vacant lots and eat in tavernas that are improvised according to topography. Chairs and tables appear on sidewalks, rooftops and patios, on stepped streets and in alleys, and amplified music comes gusting across the soft night. The cars are out, the motorcycles and scooters and jeeps, and there are arguments, radios playing, the sound of auto horns. Horns that chime, that beep, that squeal, that blast a fanfare, horns that play popular tunes. Young men on the summer hunt. Horns, tires, crackling exhausts. This noise is annunciatory, we feel. They are saying they are on the way, they are close, they are here.

Only the men in their local cafés keep indoors, where the light is good and they can play pinochle and backgammon and read newspapers with enormous headlines, a noise of its own. They are always there behind the floor-to-ceiling windows, skeptics before the cadences of life, and in winter they will still be there, in place, wearing hats and coats indoors on the coldest nights, tossing cards through the dense smoke.

People everywhere are absorbed in conversation. Seated under trees, under striped canopies in the squares, they bend together over food and drink, their voices darkly raveled in Oriental laments that flow from radios in basements and back kitchens. Conversation is life, language is the deepest being. We see the patterns repeat, the gestures drive the words. It is the sound and picture of humans communicating. It is talk as a definition of itself. Talk. Voices out of doorways and open windows, voices on the stuccoed-brick balconies, a driver taking both hands off the wheel to gesture as he speaks. Every conversation is a shared narrative, a thing that surges forward, too dense to allow space for the unspoken, the sterile. The talk is unconditional, the participants drawn in completely.

This is a way of speaking that takes such pure joy in its own openness and ardor that we begin to feel these people are discussing language itself. What pleasure in the simplest greeting. It's as though one friend says to another, "How good it is to say 'How are you?'" The other replying, "When I answer 'I am well and how are you,' what I really mean is that I'm delighted to have a chance to say these familiar things—they bridge the lonely distances."

The seller of lottery tickets comes dragging along, his curious stave all blazoned with flapping papers, and he calls a word or two into the dimness, then walks some more.

The motion is toward the sea, the roads lead to the sea, the cars come down as though to spawn among the warships and trawlers. In a taverna along the coast we were nine for dinner, lingering well past midnight over wine and fruit. The Kellers, David and Lindsay. The Bordens, Richard and Dorothy (Dick and Dot). Axton, James. A Greek named Eliades, black-bearded, deeply attentive. The Maitlands, Ann and Charles. A German doing business.

For most of its duration the dinner progressed like any other. The Bordens told a story in alternating voices about having car trouble on a mountain road. They walked to a village and drew a picture of a car for a man sitting under a tree. Dick traveled a lot and drew pictures wherever he went. He was friendly, cheerful, prematurely bald and told the same stories repeatedly, using identical gestures and intonations. He was an engineer who spent most of his time in the Gulf. Dot was a mother of twin girls, talkative, cheerful, weight-conscious (they both were), an energetic shopper, ready to lead expeditions to American brand names. Dick and Dot were our comic book couple. Once their stories were told, they were content to make background noises, to laugh easily and pleasantly, rewarding us for the allowances we made.

"I'm good at faces, bad at names," she said to the Greek.

I watched Lindsay talk with Charles Maitland. Other voices at my ear, an old man strumming a guitar near the wine casks. She was the youngest of us by a wide margin. Light hair worn long, light blue eyes, hands crossed on the table. A mood of calm, a sun-bather's marginal apartness. She had a broad face, conspicuously American, and of a type, the still hopeful outer suburbs, the face in the train window, unadorned, flushed by some outdoor task.

Charles said something that made her laugh.

This clear sound in the music and dense talk called up the voices of women passing below my terrace at night. How is it possible that one syllable of laughter, a spray in the dark, could tell me a woman was American? This sound is exact, minutely clear and telling, and I'd hear it rise through the cypresses across the street, Americans, walking, single file along the high wall, lost tourists, students, expatriates.

"Travel is a kind of fatalism," Charles was telling her. "At my age, I'm beginning to sense the menace ahead. I'm going to die soon, goes the refrain, so I'd better see the bloody sights. This is why I don't travel except on business."

"You've lived everywhere."

"Living is different. One doesn't gather up sights in quite the same way. There's no compiling of sights. I think it's when people get old they begin to compile. They not only visit pyramids, they try to build a pyramid out of the sights of the world."

"Travel as tomb-building," I said.

"He listens in. The worst kind of dinner companion. Chooses his moments." He made a fist around his cigarette. "Living is different, you see. We were saving the sights for our old age. But now the whole idea of travel begins to reek of death. I have nightmares about busloads of rotting corpses."

"Stop," she said.

"Guidebooks and sturdy shoes. I don't want to give in."

"But you're *not* old."

"My lungs are shot. More wine," he said.

"I wish I could see a merry twinkle in your eyes. Then I'd know you were kidding."

"My eyes are shot too."

Lindsay was in some ways the stabilizing center of our lives together, our lives as dinner companions, people forced by circumstance to get along. In a way, despite her age, it was logical. She was the one most recently removed from a fixed life. It said something about the world of corporate transients that we saw her as a force for equilibrium. No doubt she gave David the latitude he needed. She would enjoy his moments of dangerous fun and be uncritical of the corollary broodings.

Second wives. I wondered if there was a sense in which they felt they'd been preparing for this all along. Waiting to put the gift to use, the knack for solving difficult men. And I wondered if some men tore through first marriages believing this was the only way to arrive at the settled peace that a younger woman held in her flawless hands, knowing he'd appear one day, a slurry of blood and axle grease. To women, these men must have the glamour of a wrecked Ferrari. I could see how David would be one of these. I envied him this reassuring woman, at the same time not forgetting how much I valued the depth of Kathryn's resolve, her rigorous choices and fixed beliefs. This is the natural state.

The German, named Stahl, was talking to me about refrigeration systems. Below us a slack tide washed against the narrow beach. A waiter brought melon, whitish green with spotted yellow rind. These mass dinners had shifting patterns, directional changes of conversation, and I found myself involved in an intricate cross-cut talk with the German, to my right, on air cooling, and with David Keller and Dick Borden, at the other end and other side of the table, on famous movie cowboys and the names of their horses. David was going to Beirut the next day. Charles was going to Ankara. Ann was going to Nairobi to visit her sister. Stahl was going to Frankfurt. Dick was going to Muscat, Dubai and Riyadh.

Two children ran through the room, the guitarist started singing. At the far edge of auditory range, through all the cross-talk, I heard Ann Maitland, in conversation with this man Eliades, switch briefly from English to Greek. A phrase or short sentence, that was all, and she probably had no motive except to clarify or emphasize a point. But it seemed an intimacy, the way her voice softly closed around this fragment, it seemed a contact of some private kind. How strange, that a few words in a foreign language (the local language, spoken at surrounding tables) could float through to me, suggesting the nature of a confidence, making the other dialogue seem so much random noise. Ann was probably a dozen years older than he was. Attractive, bantering, sometimes unsure of things, drawn taut, with a self-mocking imperial way about her and beautiful sorry eyes. Did I begrudge her a sentence in Greek? About Eliades I knew nothing, not even which one of us he was connected to, or in what way. He'd arrived late, making the customary remark about normal time and Greek time.

"Topper," Dick Borden said. "That was Hopalong Cassidy's horse."

David said, "Hopalong Cassidy? I'm talking about *cowboys*, man. Guys who got down there in the shit and the muck. Guys with broken-down rummy sidekicks."

"Hoppy had a sidekick. He chewed tobacky."

David got up to find the toilet, taking a handful of black grapes with him. I drew Charles into the colloquy with the German, deftly, and then went around the table to David's chair, sitting across from Ann and Eliades. He had bitten into a peach and was smelling the pit-streaked flesh. I think I smiled, recognizing my own mannerism. These peaches were a baffling delight, certain ones, producing the kind of sense pleasure that's so unexpectedly deep it seems to need another context. Ordinary things aren't supposed to be this gratifying. Nothing about the exterior of the peach tells you it will be so lush, moist and aromatic, juices running along your gums, or so subtly colored inside, a pink-veined golden bloom. I tried to discuss this with the faces across the table.

"But I think pleasure is not easy to repeat," Eliades said. "To-morrow you will eat a peach from the same basket and be disappointed. Then you will wonder if you were mistaken. A peach, a cigarette. I enjoy one cigarette out of a thousand. Still I keep smoking. I think pleasure is in the moment more than in the thing. I keep smoking to find this moment. Maybe I will die trying."

Possibly it was his appearance that gave these remarks the importance of a world view. His wild beard covered most of his face. It started just below the eyes. He seemed to be bleeding this coarse black hair. His shoulders curved forward as he spoke and he rocked slightly at the front edge of the chair. He wore a tan suit and pastel tie, an outfit at odds with the large fierce head, the rough surface he carried.

I tried to pursue the notion that some pleasures overflow the conditions attending them. Maybe I was a little drunk.

Ann said, "Let's not have metaphysics this evening. I'm a plain girl from a mill town."

"There is always politics," Eliades said.

He was looking at me with a humorous expression. I thought I read a tactful challenge there. If the subject was too delicate, he seemed to be saying, I might honorably go back to cowboys.

"A Greek word, of course. Politics."

"Do you know Greek?" he said.

"I'm having a hard time learning. I've felt at a constant disadvantage since my first day in this part of the world. I've felt stupid in fact. How is it so many people know three, four, five languages?"

"That is politics too," he said, and his teeth showed yellowish in the mass of hair. "The politics of occupation, the politics of dispersal, the politics of resettlement, the politics of military bases."

Wind shook the bamboo canopy and blew paper napkins across the floor. Dick Borden, at the head of the table, to my left, talked across me to his wife, who was on my immediate right, about getting on home to relieve the sitter. Lindsay brushed past my chair. Someone joined the old guitarist in his song, a man, dark and serious, turning in his chair to face the musician.

"For a long time," Dot said to the German, "we didn't know our exact address. Postal code, district, we didn't know these things." She turned to Eliades. "And our telephone number wasn't the number on our telephone. We didn't know how to find out our real number. But I told you this, didn't I, at that thing at the Hilton?"

The peach pit sat on Eliades' plate. He leaned forward to extend a cigarette from his pack of Old Navy. When I smiled no, he offered the pack down one side of the table, up the other. Ann was talking to Charles. Was this the point in the evening at which husbands and wives find each other again, suppressing yawns, making eye contact through the smoke? Time to go, time to resume our murky shapes. The public self is weary of its gleam.

"It is very interesting," Eliades was telling me, "how Americans learn geography and world history as their interests are damaged in one country after another. This is interesting."

Would I leap to my country's defense?

"They learn comparative religion, economics of the Third World, the politics of oil, the politics of race and hunger."

"Politics again."

"Yes, always politics. There is no place to hide."

He was smiling politely.

Ann said, "Do you need a ride, Andreas? We're about to leave, I think."

"I have my car, thank you."

Charles was trying to signal the waiter.

"I think it's only in a crisis that Americans see other people. It has to be an American crisis, of course. If two countries fight that do not supply the Americans with some precious commodity, then the education of the public does not take place. But when the dictator falls, when the oil is threatened, then you turn on the television and they tell you where the country is, what the language is, how to pronounce the names of the leaders, what the religion is all about, and maybe you can cut out recipes in the newspaper of Persian dishes. I will tell you. The whole world takes an interest in this curious way Americans educate themselves. TV. Look, this is Iran, this is Iraq. Let us pronounce the word correctly. E-ron. E-ronians. This is a Sunni, this is a Shi'ite. Very good. Next year we do the Philippine Islands, okay?"

"You know American TV?"

"Three years," he said. "All countries where the U.S. has strong interests stand in line to undergo a terrible crisis so that at last the Americans will see them. This is very touching."

"Beware," Ann said. "He is leading up to something."

"I know what he's leading up to. When he says two countries fight, I understand him to mean the Greeks and the Turks. He is leading up to poor little Greece and how we've abused her. Turkey, Cyprus, the CIA, U.S. military bases. He slipped in military bases a while back. I've been wary ever since."

His smile broadened, a little wolfish now.

"This is interesting, how a U.S. bank based in Athens can lend money to Turkey. I like this very much. Okay, they are the southeast flank and there are U.S. bases there and the Americans want to spy on the Russians, okay. Lift the embargo, give them enormous foreign aid. This is Washington. Then you also lend them enormous sums privately, if it is possible to call a bank the size of yours a private institution. You approve loans from your headquarters in the middle of Athens. But the documentation is done in New York and London. Why is this, because of sensitivity to the feelings of Greeks? No, it is because the Turks will be insulted if the agreements are signed on Greek soil. How much face could a Turk bring to such a meeting? This is considerate, I think. This is very understanding." His shoulders curved forward, head hanging over the table. "You structure the loan and when they can't pay the money, what happens? I will tell you. You have a meeting in Switzerland and you restructure. Athens gives to Ankara. I like this. This is interesting to me."

"Oh dear," Ann said. "I think you have the wrong man, Andreas. This is not David Keller. You want David. He's the banker."

"I am James. The risk analyst."

Eliades sat back in his chair, arms spread wide in a request for pardon. It wasn't much of an offense, the facts being what they were, but the small error had robbed his moral force of its effectiveness. A boy was clearing the table. Charles leaned my way to collect some money.

"Need a ride?" he said.

"Came with David."

"That doesn't answer my question."

"Where *is* the cowboy?"

Eliades poured the last of the wine into my glass. His fingers were coppery with nicotine. For the first time all night he stopped his determined observing. Names, faces, strands of conversation. The old man sang alone, a cat walked the rail above the beach.

"What is a risk analyst?"

"Politics," I said. "Very definitely."

"I am glad."

Dick and Dot offered to take the German to his hotel. Charles moved next to me while he waited for the change to come. The man who made change, the most important job in the country judging by the look of such men, sat at a desk full of papers, with a hand calculator and a metal box for money in front of him, and he wore a tie and jacket and knitted V-neck sweater, and had graying hair cropped close and shadowy jowls, and was wide, thick and despotic, the only stationary presence in that part of the room, where waiters and other family members moved back and forth.

Eliades walked as far as the parking area with the departing people. I heard the Bordens laughing out there. The waiters wore tight white shirts with the edges of their short sleeves folded back. There were three of us at the table now.

"Not a bad evening," Ann said. "As these things go."

"What do you mean?"

"Not a bad evening."

"How do these things go?" Charles said.

"They simply go."

"What, they shoot out toward infinity?"

"I suppose they do in a sense. James would know."

"No French tonight to tell us how shifty the Lebanese are," he said. "No Lebanese to tell us how the Saudis pick their feet in business meetings. No one to say about Syrians from Aleppo, 'Count your fingers after you shake hands with them.' "

"No one from the Midlands selling smoke alarms."

"Yes, remember Ruddle."

"His name was Wood."

"The fellow with the bad eye. The eye that drifted."

"His name was Wood," she said.

"Why would I think Ruddle?"

"You're tired, I suppose."

"What does fatigue have to do with the name Ruddle?"

Charles coughed into the hand that was curled around his cigarette.

"What about you?" he asked her. "Tired?"

"Not very. A little."

"When are you off?"

"A seven o'clock flight actually."

"That's mad."

"Isn't it insane? I'll have to be out the door at five."

"But that's mad," he said without conviction.

"No matter. I sleep on planes."

"Yes, you do, don't you?"

"What do you mean?" she said.

"By what?"

"James heard. A note of accusation. Are people who sleep on planes less mentally alert? More in touch with our primitive nature perhaps? How easily we descend. Is this what you're saying?"

"Christ, what energy."

There was a long moment in which we seemed to be listening to ourselves breathe. Ann toyed absently with the remaining utensils, a knife and spoon. Then she stopped.

"Does anyone know why we're sitting here?" she said.

"That gangster is counting out change."

As Eliades headed back, there was a stir at a far table, people talking in loud voices, laughing, someone getting up to point. Others looked over the rail. I watched Andreas walk over there and look down to the beach. He motioned us over.

A woman came out of the sea, tawny hair clinging to her shoulders and face. It was Lindsay in her sea-jade summer dress, twisted slightly at the hips, sticking wet. Her laughter rang among our voices, clear as bell metal, precisely shaped. Using both hands she scooped hair from the sides of her face, head tilted back. Ten yards behind was David, bent over, retching in knee-deep water.

Happy babble from the taverna.

He emerged now, still in his blazer and Italian pants, his sleek black slip-ons, and Lindsay laughed again, watching him walk sopping in small circles, making those coarse noises. He moved heavily, like a plaster-cast man, arms held out from his body, legs well apart. A waiter aimed a light nearly straight down, helping Lindsay find her shoes, and she stopped laughing long enough to call *efharistó, merci, thank you,* and the sound of her voice set her laughing again. She stepped into the shoes, her body glistening a little, beginning to tremble. David was standing nearly upright now, limbs still spread wide. Only his head was lowered, as though he'd decided to study the sandy-wet shoes for an explanation. He was coughing hoarsely and Lindsay turned to point him toward a stone path. People started returning to their tables.

David called up, "The water's no good to drink."

"Oceans ordinarily aren't," Charles said.

"Well I'm just advising people."

"Did you swim or wade?" Ann said.

"We swam out to the float but there is no float."

"That's a different beach. You want the one just south of here."

"That's what Lindsay said."

We went back to the table as they started climbing the path through the trees. Charles got his change, he and Ann said goodnight. Eliades disappeared into the kitchen, coming back a moment later with four glasses of brandy clustered in his hands.

"The owner," he said. "Private stock."

I thought of Kathryn, who liked a fingerbreadth of Metaxa on raw nights, sitting up in bed to read and sip, her mouth warm with it, later, in the dark. Prophetic significance. All those northern nights lapped in snow, the world shocked white under Polaris, our hushed love smelling of Greek booze.

"Tell me, Andreas, what were you doing in the States?"

"Refrigeration systems."

"Cheers," I said.

"Cheers."

Swallowing slowly.

"You're connected with the German fellow then."

"Yes, Stahl."

"And Stahl is here to do business with Dick Borden?"

"No, with Hardeman."

"Who is Hardeman?"

"He is the banker's friend. I thought your friend."

"David's friend."

"But he didn't come. We think his flight was delayed. A sand-storm in Cairo."

Lindsay stood ten feet away, shyly, as though we might send her from the room. She'd been wringing out the hem of her dress and the fabric was full of spiral twists. Andreas extended a glass and she came forward, followed by a boy with a mop.

"This is so nice. Thank you. Cheers."

"Where's David?" I said.

"He's in the men's room, freshening up."

This set her off again, laughing. She barely got the sentence out before her face went tight with glee. I put my jacket around her shoulders. She sat there rigid with laughter, her face looking synthetic, an object under measured stress.

"Freshening up," she said again, and sat there shivering, crying with laughter.

In time she began to settle down, whispering her thanks for the brandy, drawing the jacket more closely around her, whispering her thanks for the jacket. A mood of soft withdrawal. She was too self-conscious to return the pampering smiles of people at other tables.

"I don't have to ask if you like to swim," Andreas said.

"I don't think what we did was really a swim. I don't know what to call it."

"A David Keller," I said.

"Right, it was a Keller. But I went willingly."

"Have you been to the islands?" he said.

"Only the one-day tour," she whispered. "I'm waiting for my curtains."

"That's a line she uses," I told Andreas. "No one knows what it means."

"We're still moving in really. This is all new to me. I'm only learning to count. The numbers are fun. Do you know the alphabet, James?"

"Yes, and I can tie my own shoes."

"Andreas, is it absolutely necessary to know verbs? *Must* we know verbs?"

"I think it will help," he said. "You seem to be very active."

Both men were singing again. The customer, a man with dark hair and a full mustache, was looking directly at the guitarist, who stood against the wine casks, one foot up on a chair, head slightly tilted toward his bent left hand. The song gathered force, a spirited lament. Its tone evoked inevitable things. Time was passing, love was fading, grief was deep and total. As with people in conversation, these men appeared to go beyond the soulful routine woe of the lyrics. Their subjects were memory and tragic narrative and men who put their voices to song. The dark man was intense, his eyes still fixed on the old musician, never wavering. He was charged with feeling. His eyes were bright with it. The song called up a luminous fervor and he seemed to rise slightly in the chair. The men were twenty feet apart, voices shading into each other. The guitarist looked up then, a spare figure with gray stubble, someone's second cousin, the man we see asleep at corner tables all through the islands. For the rest of the song they looked at each other, strangers, to something beyond. A blood recollection, a shared past. I didn't know.

I sat with David on his terrace above the National Gardens, across from the Olympic Stadium, looking toward the Acropolis. Pentelic marble old and new. The prime minister lived in a two-bedroom apartment in the next building.

"They pay some heavyish coin."

He was talking about his more difficult postings. He sat in his damp clothes, minus the shoes and blazer, drinking beer. He was a fairly large man, just beginning to flesh out, slow-moving in a vaguely dangerous way.

Noise in short bursts issued from motorcycles crossing the dark city. Lindsay was asleep.

"The gamier the place, or the more ticklish politically, or the more sand dunes per square mile, obviously they sweeten the pot, our New York masters. The dunes in the Empty Quarter reach eight, nine hundred feet. I flew over with a guy from Aramco. Forget it."

In Jeddah the fruit bats swooped out of the night to take water from his pool, drinking in full flight. His wife, the first, came out of the house one day to find three baboons pounding on the hood and roof of their car.

In Tehran, between wives, he invented the name Chain Day. This was the tenth day of Muharram, the period of mourning and self-flagellation. As hundreds of thousands of people marched toward the Shahyad monument, some of them wearing funeral shrouds, striking themselves with steel bars and knife blades affixed to chains, David was hosting a Chain Day party at his house in North Tehran, an area sealed off from the marchers by troops and tank barricades. The partygoers could hear the chanting mobs but whether they were chanting "Death to the shah" or "God is great," and whether it mattered, no one knew for sure.

The thing he feared in Tehran was traffic. The apocalyptic inching pack-ice growl of four miles of cars. The drivers' free-form ways. Cars kept coming at him in reverse. He was always finding himself driving down a narrow street with a car coming toward him backwards. The driver expected him to move, or ascend, or vanish. Eventually he saw what was so fearful about this, a thing so simple he hadn't been able to isolate it from the larger marvel of a city full of cars going backwards. *They did not reduce speed when driving in reverse.* To David Keller, between wives, this seemed an interesting thing. There was a cosmology here, a rich structure of some kind, a theorem in particle physics. Reverse and forward were interchangeable. And why not, what was the difference really? A moving vehicle is no different moving backwards than it is moving forwards, especially when the driver regards the whole arrangement as if he were on foot, able to touch, to bump, to brush his way past vague obstacles in the street. This was the second revelation of David's stay in Tehran. *People drove as if they were walking.* They veered idiosyncratically, these fellows with their army surplus field jackets and their interesting sense of space.

In Istanbul, earlier, he used to tell people he wanted to get Mainland New York to approve purchase of a jeep-mounted recoilless rifle, plus jeep, to get him to and from the rep office. More seriously he talked about armoring his car. "Armoring your car," he told me, "is known as a major expenditure proposal. Forty thousand dollars. Allowing your driver to carry a gun is known as a small arms shipment to the Marxist-Leninist Armed Propaganda Squad. Not that the driver would give them the piece. They'd take it after they blew you both away with anti-tank grenades and AK-47s."

This summer, the summer in which we sat on his broad terrace, was the period after the shah left Iran, before the hostages were taken, before the Grand Mosque and Afghanistan. The price of oil was an index to the Western world's anxiety. It provided a figure, $24 a barrel, say, to measure against the figure of the month before or the year before. It was a handy way to refer to our complex involvements. It told us how bad we felt at a given time.

"How's Tap doing?"

"The kid writes novels, he eats octopus."

"Good. That's great."

"How are yours? Where are they living?"

"Michigan. They're doing fine. They love it. They *swim.*"

"What's your first wife's name?"

"Grace," he said. "That's a first wife's name, isn't it?"

"Does Lindsay talk about having kids?"

"Shit, Lindsay'll do anything. She's crazy. Did she tell you she found a job? Great break, she's been getting antsy for something to do. She'll teach English at one of these language schools. It's an escape from the bank wives and their get-togethers."

"I haven't noticed you two hosting any dinner parties for Mainland people here on business. Or evacuees from disturbed areas. You're the credit head, aren't you?"

"Disturbed areas. That's what we call them all right. Like snow flurries on a weather map. Dinner parties in this division are famous for eyewitness accounts of very large groups of people marching on embassies and banks. Also famous for unrelenting politeness. All the ethnic groups and religious subgroups. Can you seat a Druze next to a Maronite? They're all more or less multinationalized but who knows what lies underneath? We have a Sikh who carries the mandatory sect knife somewhere on his person. Sometimes I'm careful what I say without knowing precisely why. Grace used to handle things when we were in Beirut and Jeddah and Istanbul. She handled things beautifully in fact. Lindsay I don't think would be all that adept. I think she'd stand there laughing."

"What about the Americans?"

"Eerie people. Genetically engineered to play squash and work weekends. That swim made me hungry."

David drank slowly but steadily whenever possible. In the course of a long Sunday lunch on the eastern shore or a night almost anywhere, his voice would begin to rumble and drone, grow friendlier, taking on paternal tones, and in his large blond face a ruined child would appear, barely discernible in the slack flesh, a watcher, distant and contrite.

"Our office in Monrovia has a guy on the payroll whose job is catching snakes. That's all he does. He goes to employees' houses on a regular basis, through the yard, the garden, the hedges, catching snakes."

"What's he called officially?"

"The snake catcher."

"That's remarkably direct," I said.

"They couldn't come up with a buzz word for snake, it seems."

This was the summer before crowds attacked the U.S. embassies in Islamabad and Tripoli, before the assassinations of American technicians in Turkey, before Liberia, the executions on the beach, the stoning of dead bodies, the evacuation of personnel from the Mainland Bank.

"Does Kathryn ever get to Athens?"

"No."

"I meet my kids in New York," he said.

"That's easier than going to the island."

"We eat banana splits in the hotel room. They cost eight dollars each."

"Did Grace ever attack you physically?"

"She's not a physical person, Grace."

"Ever hit her? I'm serious."

"No. Ever hit Kathryn?"

"We've scuffled. No clean blows. She took a run at me once with a kitchen thing."

"What for?"

"She found out I went to bed with a friend of hers. It led to words."

"The friend made sure she found out?"

"She let on, somehow. She sent signals."

"So you nearly got spiked with an ice pick."

"It was just a potato peeler. What annoyed the friend was my perceived indifference. It was one of those situations. You find yourself in a situation. Alone with Antoinette. The two of you have felt the usual secret lustings. The normal healthy subatomic lustful vibrations. These are feelings that get acted on when man and wife split up. Suddenly there's an Antoinette, destiny in her eyes. But Kathryn and I hadn't split up. We hadn't done anything. The situation just arose. The combination of circumstances."

"What situation? Paint a picture."

"Never mind a picture."

"Her apartment?"

"Her house. Diagonally across the park from ours."

"Summer, winter?"

"Winter."

"The plant-filled parlor room. The glass of wine."

"Something like that."

"The intimate talk," he said.

"Yes."

"Always the intimate talk. This woman is divorced, right?"

"Yes."

"The sadness," he said.

"There was sadness, yes. But it had nothing to do with her divorce. She'd just lost her job. The CBC. They fired her."

"The sadness."

"All right the sadness."

"The longing."

"Yes, there was longing."

"The need," he said.

"Yes."

"In the starry night, in the parlor room, sipping dry white wine."

"It was a good job. She was upset."

" 'Comfort me, comfort me.' "

"Anyway I gave the impression of wavering. I must have

drawn back. This was inexcusable, of course. I hesitated, I showed uncertainty. We did the thing finally. We couldn't end our friendship, commit our crime, without finishing what we'd started. So we did the thing. We eked out a fuck. What an idiot I was. Antoinette got her sweet revenge."

"She let on."

"She let on. And in letting on she didn't fail to communicate this half-heartedness of mine. I don't know how she did this without being direct, which I gather she wasn't. I suppose in fables and parables, in allegories. The language of women and children. This is what got Kathryn really furious, I think. Not just the sex, the friend. The way I went about it. I committed a crime against the earth. That's what made her want to carve my ribs."

"Did it clear the air? This knife fight?"

"Beginning of the end."

"We married young," he said. "We didn't know anything. You know the story. Little or no experience. Grace said I was the first, more or less the first, *really* the first, the first in any important way."

We laughed.

"I knew our marriage was shot to hell when we started watching TV in different rooms," he said. "If her sound was up loud enough, I could hear her change channels in there. When she went to the same channel I was watching, I switched channels myself. I couldn't bear watching the same stuff she was watching. I believe this is called estrangement."

"You're not going to become a stereotype, are you?"

"What do you mean?"

"It's bad enough you have a new young wife. You don't want to be thought of as one of these men with an old wife and old kids back in the States. These are the wives who weren't dynamic enough to keep up with men like you in the great surge of your multinational career. The old wives and old kids are gray and stooped, sitting in front of TV sets in the suburbs. The wives have head colds all the time. The old dogs are listless on the patios."

"At least my new young wife isn't a fantasy wife. A stewardess or model. You know Hardeman? His second wife is a former ball girl for the Atlanta Braves. She used to sit along the left-field line waiting for foul balls. I think she found one in Hardeman."

David was casual about most bank matters. He told me what the bank was doing in Turkey and gave me telexes and other paper that detailed loan proposals. These documents impressed Rowser, particularly the ones marked confidential in block letters. I guess David felt there was little or no danger in giving this particular classified material to a friend. We were serving the same broad ends.

"Sometimes I wonder what I'm doing in some of these places. I can't get the Empty Quarter out of my mind. We flew right over the dunes, man, nothing but sand, a quarter of a million square miles. A planet of sand. Sand mountains, sand plains and valleys. Sand weather, a hundred and thirty, a hundred and forty degrees, and I can't imagine what it's like when the wind's blowing. I tried to convince myself it was beautiful. The desert, you know. The vast sweep. But it scared me. This Aramco guy told me he can stand on the airstrip they have out there and he can hear the blood flowing in his body. Is it the silence or the heat that makes this possible? Or both? Hear the blood."

"What were you doing flying over this place?"

"Oil, boy. What else? Big field. We're financing some construction."

"You know what Maitland says."

"What does he say?"

"Opportunity, adventure, sunsets, dusty death."

David went in to get me a beer and another for himself. I was wide awake and feeling hungry. A faint light was visible in the sky, the Parthenon emerging, two-dimensional, a soft but structured image. I followed him to the kitchen and we started eating whatever was lying loose, mainly pastry and fruit. Lindsay came in to complain about the noise. She wore a nightgown with a ruffled hem and we smiled when we saw her.

In these early hours the sky seems very near street level. The street extends from eastern sky to western. It's always a surprise, entering the boulevard by first light when there's no traffic, being able to see things as unconnected, the embassy mansions with their period detail, objects coming out of the gloom, mulberry trees and kiosks, and to make out the contours of the street itself, a place of clear limits, we see, with its own form and meaning, appearing in the stillness and marine light to be almost a rolling field, a broad path to the mountains. Traffic must be a stream that binds things to some denser perspective.

The boulevard was empty only momentarily. A bus moved past, drowned faces pressed against the windows, and then the little cars. Four abreast they came, out of the concrete hollows to the west, the first anxious wave of the day.

The way home was uphill into narrower streets, severely graded toward the pine woods and gray rock of Lycabettus. I stood by the bed in my pajamas, feeling vaguely unstuck, my habits no longer bound to hers. The tides and easements of custom. Our book of days. The canaries on the back balconies were singing, already women were beating rugs, and water fell to the courtyard from rows of potted plants, ringing on the bright stone.

That was my day.

4

THE BODY was found at the edge of a village called Mikro Kamini, an old man, bludgeoned. This village lies about three miles inland, among terraced fields that soon give out before the empty hills and the massive groupings farther in, the pillars and castellated rock forms. The landscape begins to acquire a formal power at Mikro Kamini. There's suggestion of willful distance from the sea, willful isolation, and the fields and groves abruptly end nearby. Here the island becomes the bare Cycladic rock seen from the decks of passing ships, a place of worked-out quarries, goat-bells, insane winds. The villages nestled on the coast seem not so much a refuge for seagoing men nor a series of maze structures contrived to discourage entrance by force, make a laborious business of marauding; from here they are detailed reliefs or cameos, wishing not to attract the attention of whatever forces haunt the interior. The streets that bend back on themselves or disappear, the miniature churches and narrow lanes, these seem a form of self-effacement, a way of saying there is nothing here worth bothering about. They are a huddling, a gathering together against the stark landforms and volcanic rock. Superstition, vendetta, incest. The things that visit the spirit in the solitary hills. Bestiality and murder. The whitewashed coastal villages are talismans against these things, formulaic designs.

The fear of sea and things that come from the sea is easily spoken. The other fear is different, hard to name, the fear of things at one's back, the silent inland presence.

At the house we sat in the slanted living room in low cane chairs. Kathryn made tea.

"I talked to people at the restaurant. A hammer, they said."

"You'd think a gun. Land disputes between farmers. A shotgun or rifle."

"He wasn't a farmer," she said, "and he wasn't from that village. He lived in a house across the island. He was apparently feeble-minded. He lived with a married niece and her children."

"Tap and I went through there my first visit. I took Owen's motor scooter, remember? You gave us hell."

"Senseless killings are supposed to happen in the New York subways. I've been edgy all day."

"Where are those people from the cave?"

"I've been thinking about them too. Owen says they've gone."

"Where is Owen?"

"At the site."

"Swimming above the sunken ruins. That's my image of him. An aging dolphin."

"The conservator came back today," she said. "He'd gone off to Crete with someone."

"What does he do?"

"Preserves the finds. Puts the pieces together."

"What are the finds?" I said.

"Look, this work is important. I know what you think. I'm feeding some fanatical impulse."

"Does Owen think it's important?"

"Owen's in another world. He's left this one behind. That doesn't mean it's futile work. We find objects. They tell us something. All right, there's no more money for things. No more photographers, no geologists, no draftsmen. But we find objects, we come upon features. This dig was designed partly as a field school. Help students learn. And we are learning, those who've stayed."

"What happens next?"

"Why does something have to happen next?"

"My friends the Maitlands have entertaining arguments. I wish we could learn that skill. They don't waver from an even tone. It's taken me all this time to realize they've been arguing since I've known them. It's an undercurrent. They've made a highly developed skill of it."

"Nobody just digs," she said.

Church bells, shuttered windows. She looked at me through the partial darkness, studying something she hadn't seen, possibly, in a long time. I wanted to provoke, make her question herself. Tap came in with a friend, Rajiv, the son of the assistant field director, and there were noises of greeting. The boys wanted to show me something outside and when I turned in the doorway, going out, she was pouring a second cup, leaning toward the bench where the tea things were, and I hoped this wasn't the moment when we became ourselves again. The island's small favors and immunities could not have run out so soon. Bringing something new into being. After the bright shock fades, after the separation, there's the deeper age, the gradual language of love and acceptance, at least in theory, in folklore. The Greek rite. How fitting that she had a male child, someone to love fiercely.

The bells stopped ringing. Tap and Rajiv took me along a path near the top of the village. The cut-paper brightness of doors and flowers. The curtains lifted in the wind. They showed me a three-legged dog and waited for my reaction. A shapeless old woman in black, with a red clay face, a black head-scarf, sat outside a house below us, shelling peas. The air settled into an agitated silence. I told them every village has its three-legged dog.

Owen Brademas came up out of the dark, striding, his shoulders set forward against the steep grade. He carried a bottle of wine, holding it aloft when he saw me at the window. Kathryn and I went out and watched him take the stairs two at a time.

I had an insight. He is a man who takes stairs two at a time. What this explained I'd no idea.

They spent a moment together in the kitchen talking about the dig. I opened the wine, put a match to the candles and then we sat drinking in the wind-stirred light.

"They're gone. They're definitely gone. I was there. They left garbage, odds and ends."

"When was the old man killed?" I said.

"I don't know that, James. I've never even been to that village. I have no privileged information. Just what people say."

"He was dead twenty-four hours when they found him," Kathryn said. "That's the estimate. Someone came from Syros. Prefect of police, I think he's called, and a coroner apparently. He wasn't a farmer, he wasn't a shepherd."

"When did they leave, Owen?"

"I don't know that. I went there only to talk. Out of curiosity. I have no special information."

"Senseless killing."

"A feeble-minded old man," I said. "How did he get across the island?"

"He could have walked," she said. "It's what the people in the restaurant think. There's a way to do it on foot if you know the paths. It's barely possible. The theory is he wandered off. Got lost. Ended up there. He often wandered."

"That far?"

"I don't know."

"What do you think, Owen?"

"I saw them only that one time. I went back because they'd seemed so interested in what I told them. There didn't seem to be a danger in going and I wanted to get more out of them if I could. Obviously they were determined to speak Greek, which was a drawback but not a crucial one. The fact is they probably had no intention of telling me who they are and what they were doing there, in any language."

But there was something he wanted to tell them. An odd fact, a remnant. He thought they'd be interested in this, being zealots of the alphabet or whatever they were, and he hadn't thought of mentioning it the first time they talked.

When he went to Qasr Hallabat to see the inscriptions, he'd

taken the Zarqa–Azraq road, traveling north from Amman, veering east into the desert. The fortress was in ruins, of course, with cut basalt blocks strewn everywhere. Latin, Greek, Nabatean inscriptions. The order of the Greek stones was totally upset. Even the blocks still standing were out of place, upside down, plastered over. All this done by the Umayyads, who used the stones without regard for the writing on them. They were rebuilding the previous structure, the Byzantine, which had been built from the Roman, and so on, and they wanted building blocks, not edicts carved in Greek.

All right. A lovely place to wander around in, full of surprises, a massive crossword for someone in the Department of Antiquities. And all of this, the castle, the stones, the inscriptions, is situated midway between Zarqa and Azraq. To Owen, to someone with Owen's bent for spotting such things, these names are seen at once to be anagrams. This is what he wanted to tell the people in the hills. How strange, he wanted to say, that the place he was looking for, this evocative botched ruin, lay between perfect twin pillars—place-names with the same set of letters, rearranged. And it was precisely a rearrangement, a reordering, that was in progress at Qasr Hallabat. Archaeologists and workmen attempting to match the inscribed blocks.

The mind's little infinite, he called all this.

I went inside for fruit. With the bowl in my hand I stopped at the door to Tap's room and looked in. He lay with his head turned toward me, wetting his lips in his sleep, a sound like a fussy kiss. I glanced down at the papers on his makeshift writing table, a board jammed into an alcove, but it was too dark to read the painstaking loops and slants.

Outside we talked awhile about his writing. It turned out Owen had learned a few days ago that his own early years were the subject matter. He didn't know whether to be pleased or upset.

"There are many better topics he could find. But I'm happy to learn I've kindled an interest. I'm not sure I want to read the result, however."

"Why not?" I said.

He paused to think about this.

"Don't forget," Kathryn said, "this is fiction we're talking about, even if the nonfiction kind. Real people, made-up remarks. The boy has a fix on the modern mind. Let's show him a little more respect."

"But you said he changed my name."

"I made him."

"If I were a writer," Owen said, "how I would enjoy being told the novel is dead. How liberating, to work in the margins, outside a central perception. You are the ghoul of literature. Lovely."

"Have you ever written?" she said.

"Never. I used to think it would be grand to be a poet. I was very young, this was long ago, I'm sure I thought a poet was a delicate pale fellow with a low-grade fever."

"Were you a delicate pale fellow?"

"Awkward, maybe, but strong, or strong enough. In the tall-grass prairie what you did was work. All that space. I think we plowed and swung the pick and the brush scythe to keep from being engulfed by space. It was like living in the sky. I didn't know how awesome it was until I went away. It grows more awesome all the time, the memory."

"But you've taught in the Midwest and West."

"Different places."

"Not Kansas?"

"Not the prairie. There isn't much left. I haven't been home in thirty-five years."

"And you never wrote a poem, Owen? Tell the truth," she said, playing lightly at something.

"I was a plodder, kind of slow, I think, one of those gawky boys who stands around squinting into the glare. I worked, I did chores, a dutiful son, unhappy. But I don't think I so much as scribbled a single line of poetry, Kathryn, not one."

The flames went flat, shot down, unstable in the wind. The trembling light seemed to wish an urgency on us. I was taking wine in half-glass bursts, getting drier all the time. The others rambled calmly toward midnight.

"Solitude."

"We lived in town for a time. Then outside, a lonely place, barely a place at all."

"I was never alone," she said. "When my mother died I think my father made a point of filling the house with people. It was like one of those old stage comedies in which the main characters are about to set sail for Europe. The set is full of luggage. Friends and well-wishers keep showing up. Complications develop."

"We were in the middle. Everything was around us, somehow equidistant. Everything was space, extremes of weather."

"We kept moving. My father kept buying houses. We'd live in a house for a while and then he'd buy another. Sometimes he got around to selling the old one, sometimes he didn't. He never learned how to be wealthy. People might despise a man for that but everyone liked him. His house-buying was anything but ostentatious. There was a deep restlessness in him, an insecurity. He was like someone trying to slip away in the night. Loneliness was a disease he seemed to think had been lying in wait for him all along. Everyone liked him. I think this worried him somehow. Made sad by friendship. He must have had a low opinion of himself."

"Then I was a man. In fact I was forty. I realized I saw the age of forty from a child's viewpoint."

"I know the feeling," I said. "Forty was my father's age. All fathers were forty. I keep fighting the idea I'm fast approaching his age. As an adult I've only been two ages. Twenty-two and forty. I was twenty-two well into my thirties. Now I've begun to be forty, two years shy of the actual fact. In ten years I'll still be forty."

"At your age I began to feel my father present in me. There were unreal moments."

"You felt he was occupying you. I know. Suddenly he's there. You even feel you look like him."

"Brief moments. I felt I'd become my father. He took me over, he filled me."

"You step into an elevator, suddenly you're him. The door closes, the feeling's gone. But now you know who he was."

"Tomorrow we do mothers," Kathryn said. "Except count me out. I barely remember mine."

"Your mother's death is what did it to him," I said.

She looked at me.

"How could you know that? Did he talk to you about it?"

"No."

"Then how could you know that?"

I took a long time filling the glasses and composed my voice to sound a new theme.

"Why is it we talk so much here? I do the same in Athens. Inconceivable, all this conversation, in North America. Talking, listening to others talk. Keller threw me out at six-thirty the other morning. It must be life outdoors. Something in the air."

"You're half smashed all the time. That's one possibility."

"We talk more, drunk or sober," I said. "The air is filled with words."

He looked past us, firmly fixed, a lunar sadness. I wondered what he saw out there. His hands were clasped on his chest, large hands, nicked and scarred, a digger and rock gouger, a plowboy once. Kathryn's eyes met mine. Her compassion for the man was possibly large enough to allow some drippings for the husband in his supplication. Merciful bountiful sex. The small plain bed in the room at the end of the hotel corridor, sheets drawn tight. That too might be a grace and favor of the island, a temporary lifting of the past.

"I think they're on the mainland," Owen said.

How could you understand, he seemed to be asking. Your domestic drama, your tepid idiom of reproach and injury. These ranks of innocent couples with their marriage wounds. He kept looking past us.

"They said something about the Peloponnese. It wasn't entirely clear. One of them seemed to know a place there, somewhere they might stay."

Kathryn said, "Is this something the police ought to be told?"

"I don't know. Is it?" The movement of his hand toward the wine glass brought him back. "Lately I've been thinking of Rawlinson, the Englishman who wanted to copy the inscriptions on the Behistun rock. The languages were Old Persian, Elamite and Babylonian. Maneuvering on ladders from the first group to the second, he nearly fell to his death. This inspired him to use a Kurdish boy to copy the Babylonian set, which was the least accessible. The boy inched across a rock mass that had only the faintest indentations he might use for finger-grips. Fingers and toes. Maybe he used the letters themselves. I'd like to believe so. This is how he proceeded, clinging to the rock, passing below the great bas-relief of Darius facing a group of rebels in chains. A sheer drop. But he made it, miraculously, according to Rawlinson, and was eventually able to do a paper cast of the text, swinging from a sort of bosun's chair. What kind of story is this and why have I been thinking about it lately?"

"It's a political allegory," Kathryn said.

"Is that what it is? I think it's a story about how far men will go to satisfy a pattern, or find a pattern, or fit together the elements of a pattern. Rawlinson wanted to decipher cuneiform writing. He needed these three examples of it. When the Kurdish boy swung safely back over the rock, it was the beginning of the Englishman's attempt to discover a great secret. All the noise and babble and spit of three spoken languages had been subdued and codified, broken down to these wedge-shaped marks. With his grids and lists the decipherer searches out relationships, parallel structures. What are the sign frequencies, the phonetic values? He wants a design that will make this array of characters speak to him. After Rawlinson came Norris. It's interesting, Kathryn, that both these men were at one time employed by the East India Company. A different pattern here, again one age speaks to another. We can say of the Persians that they were enlightened conquerors, at least in this instance. They preserved the language of the subjugated people. This same Elamite language was one of those deciphered by the political agents and interpreters of the East India Company. Is this the scientific face of imperialism? The humane face?"

"Subdue and codify," Kathryn said. "How many times have we seen it?"

"If it's a story about how far men will go," he said, "why have

I been thinking about it? Maybe it bears on the murder of that old man. If your suspicions about the cult are well-founded, and if they are a cult, I can tell you it probably wasn't a senseless killing, Kathryn. It wasn't casual. They didn't do it for thrills."

"You saw them and talked to them."

"That's my judgment. I could be wrong. We could all be wrong."

I looked ahead to the walls of my hotel room. Standing by the bed in my pajamas. I always felt silly in pajamas. The name of the hotel was Kouros, like the village, the island, the ship that provided passage to and from the island. Singly knit. The journey that shares the edges of destinations. Mikro Kamini, where the old man was found, means small furnace or kiln. I always felt a surge of childlike pride, knowing such things or figuring them out, even when a dead body was the occasion for my efforts. The first fragment of Greek I ever translated was a wall slogan in the middle of Athens. *Death to Fascists.* Once it took me nearly an hour, with a dictionary and book of grammar, to translate the directions on a box of Quaker Oats. Dick and Dot had to tell me where to buy cereal with multilingual instructions on the box.

"I have a feeling about night," Owen said. "The things of the world are no longer discrete. All the day's layers and distinctions fade in the dark. Night is continuous."

"It doesn't matter whether we lie or tell the truth," Kathryn said.

"Wonderful, yes, exactly."

Standing by the bed in my pajamas. Kathryn reading. How many nights, in our languid skin, disinclined toward talk or love, the dense hours behind us, we shared this moment, not knowing it was matter to share. It appeared to be nothing, bedtime once more, her pillowed head in fifty watts, except that these particulars, man standing, pages turning, the details repeated almost nightly, began to take on mysterious force. Here I am again, standing by the bed in my pajamas, acting out a memory. It was a memory that didn't exist independently. I recalled the moment only when I was repeating it. The mystery built around this fact, I think, that act and recollection were one. A moment of autobiography, a minimal frieze. The moment referred back to itself at the same time as it pointed forward. *Here I am.* A curious reminder that I was going to die. It was the only time in my marriage that I felt old, a specimen of oldness, a landmark, standing in those slightly oversized pajamas, a little ridiculous, reliving the same moment of the night before, Kathryn reading in bed, a dram of Greek brandy on the bedside table, another reference forward. I will die alone. Old, geologically. The lower relief of landforms. Olduvai.

Who knows what this means? The force of the moment was in what I didn't know about it, standing there, the night tides returning, the mortal gleanings that filled the space between us, untellably, our bodies arranged for dreaming in loose-fitting clothes.

Living alone I never felt it. Somehow the reference depended on the woman in the bed. Or maybe it's just that my days and nights had become less routine. Travel, hotels. The surroundings changed too often.

"An early night for Owen."

"Maybe an early season," she said. "The chairman of the graduate program paid a visit. He's been in Athens, conferring with the ASCS. A re-evaluation is in progress. But it may be good news in the long run. We could get going again as early as April next year. May at the latest. That's the word."

"With Owen?"

"With or without. Probably the latter. No one knows what Owen's plans are. It's this loose structure that's caused so much trouble around here."

"Trouble for everyone but you."

"Exactly. I'm the one who's benefited. And Owen is sure I'll be able to come back. So. At least we have a rough idea how things stand. It's what you've been wanting."

How easy it was to sit there and reorganize our lives across the jet streams and the seasons. We were full of ideas, having learned to interpret the failed marriage as an occasion for enterprise and personal daring. Kathryn was specially adept at this. She loved to round on a problem and make it work for her. We discussed her proposals, seeing in them not only distance and separation but a chance to exploit these. Fathers are pioneers of the skies. I thought of David Keller flying to New York to eat banana splits with his children in a midtown hotel. Then back across the sea to consolation and light, Lindsay tanning bare-breasted on their terrace.

Kathryn and I agreed. She and Tap would go to London at summer's end. They would stay with her sister Margaret. They would find a school for Tap. Kathryn would take courses in archaeology and allied disciplines. And I would find it easy, if expensive, to visit. London was a three-hour flight from Athens, roughly seven hours closer than the island was.

"In April you return."

"I ought to be able to find a better house to rent, now that I know people here. And Tap will follow as soon as school is over. It could be worse."

"I'll get to see the Elgin marbles," I said.

We also agreed I would sleep on the sofa that night. I didn't want to leave them alone after what had happened in the other village.

"I'll have to find clean sheets. We can put a chair at one end of the sofa. It's not long enough."

"I feel like a kid sleeping over."

"What excitement," she said. "I wonder if we can handle it."

"Is that a wishful note I hear?"

"I don't know. Is it?"

"An uncertainty, a suspense?"

"It's not something we can sit around discussing, is it?"

"Over local wine. We're stuck in a kind of mined landscape. It's easier when Owen is here. I admit it."

"Why do we bother?"

"We were practical people in marriage. Now we're full of clumsy aspirations. Nothing has an outcome anymore. We've become vaguely noble, both of us. We refuse to do what's expedient."

"Maybe we're not as bad as we think. What an idea. Revolutionary."

"How would your Minoans have handled a situation like this?"

"A quickie divorce probably."

"Sophisticated people."

"Certainly the frescoes make them out to be. Grand ladies. Slim-waisted and graceful. Utterly European. And those lively colors. So different from Egypt and all that frowning sandstone and granite. Perpetual ego."

"They didn't think in massive terms."

"They decorated household things. They saw the beauty in this. Plain objects. They weren't all games and clothes and gossip."

"I think I'd feel at home with the Minoans."

"Gorgeous plumbing."

"They weren't subject to overwhelming awe. They didn't take things that seriously."

"Don't go too far," she said. "There's the Minotaur, the labyrinth. Darker things. Beneath the lilies and antelopes and blue monkeys."

"I don't see it at all."

"Where have you looked?"

"Only at the frescoes in Athens. Reproductions in books. Nature was a delight to them, not an angry or godlike force."

"A dig in north-central Crete has turned up signs of human sacrifice. No one's saying much. I think a chemical analysis of the bones is under way."

"A Minoan site?"

"All the usual signs."

"How was the victim killed?"

"A bronze knife was found. Sixteen inches long. Human sacrifice isn't new in Greece."

"But not Minoans."

"Not Minoans. They'll be arguing for years."

"Are the facts that easy to determine? What, thirty-five hundred years ago?"

"Thirty-seven," she said.

We sat facing the hill that loomed above the village. It didn't take me long to see how shallow my resistance was to this disclosure. *Eager to believe the worst.* Even as she was talking I felt the first wavelets break on the beach. Satisfaction. The cinnamon boys, boxing, the women white and proud in skirts like pleated bells. Always the self finds a place for its fulfillments, even in the Cretan wild, outside time and light. She said the knife had been found with the skeleton of the victim, a young man fetal on a raised structure. The priest who killed him was also found. He was right-handed and knew how to sever a neck artery neatly.

"How did the priest die?" I said.

"Signs of an earthquake and fire. The sacrifice was linked to this. They also found a pillar with a ditch around it to hold blood. Pillar crypts have been found elsewhere. Massive pillars with the sign of the double ax. There's your massiveness, James, after all. Hidden in the earth."

We were silent awhile.

"What does Owen say?"

"I've tried to discuss this with Owen but he's weary of Minoans, it seems. He says the whole tremendous theme of bulls and bulls' horns is based on cuckoldry. All those elegant women were sneaking into the labyrinth to screw some Libyan deckhand."

I laughed. She reached over the candles, put a hand to my cheek, leaned forward, standing, and kissed me slowly. A moment that spoke only its own regretful ardor. Sweet enough and warm. A reminiscence.

Observing the rules I stayed outside until she fixed up the sofa for me and went to bed. In the morning we would make it a point to talk of routine things.

Tap came to Athens for two days with his friend Rajiv and the boy's father, who was connected with the Department of Art History at Michigan State. I'd talked to him several times at the site, a heavyset man named Anand Dass, stern and friendly, moving impressively through the rubble in tennis shorts and a spotless cotton shirt. His son seemed always to be dancing around him, asking questions, grabbing hold of the man's arm, his hand, even the loops in his belt, and I wondered whether Rajiv's fourteen months in America and five weeks in Greece had put him at such a bewildering distance from the sum of known things that only his father's dark anchoring bulk could ease the disquiet.

He was a likable boy, he bounced when he walked, Tap's age but taller, and he wore flared trousers for his trip to Athens. I met them in Piraeus, a bleached-out day, empty and still. It was my notion to give the boys an auto tour of Athens but I kept getting lost. Beyond the central landmarks the streets looked identical. The modern apartment blocks, the bright awnings over the balconies, the walls marked with acronyms of political parties, an occasional old sepia building with a terra-cotta roof.

Anand sat next to me talking about the island. There had been no water at all for two days. A dry southerly was blowing fine sand over everything. The only fruits and vegetables in the village stalls were those grown on the island itself. It would be a month before he was back in East Lansing. Green. Trees and lawns.

"You might have picked an easier place to dig."

"This is Owen," he said. "Owen is famous for this. He thinks he is going to India next. I told him forget it, you know. You won't get funding, you won't get permission, you will die in the heat. He pays no attention to weather, this man."

"He enjoys the sense of ordeal."

"He enjoys it. This is exactly true."

We cruised down endless streets, near deserted. Two men walked along biting into peaches, heads jutting and twisted, their bodies drawn awkwardly back to escape the spill.

"You know what happened," Anand said.

He'd changed his voice in such a way that I knew immediately what he was referring to.

"I was there."

"But it wasn't the first. There was another about a year ago. Another island. Donoussa."

"I don't know the name."

"It's in the Cyclades. Small. A mail boat once a week from Naxos."

The boys were speaking Ob in the back seat.

"A hammer," he said. "It was a young girl. From very poor people. She was crippled. She had some kind of paralysis. I heard it just before I left. Someone from Donoussa was in the village near the dig."

I turned a corner into a traffic jam. A man stood outside his car with hands on hips to look ahead to the source of the trouble. A figure of transcendent disgust. There were buses, trolley buses, taxis, horns blaring, then stopping almost simultaneously, then blaring again, as if to suggest a form for this ordeal—a stately panic. Rajiv asked his father where we were and Tap said, "Lobost obin spobace."

It took half an hour to find our first destination, the apartment building where friends of Anand lived and where he and his son would spend the night. The following evening we would all go to the airport. Rajiv was flying to Bombay with these friends, a young couple. His mother would meet him there and they would go to Kashmir, where Anand's family had a summer home.

After we'd dropped them, Tap said, "Can we drive around some more?"

"I bought food. I think we ought to go home and eat it."

"I like driving around."

"I showed you the wrong stuff. We'll do better tomorrow."

"Can we just drive?"

"Don't you want to see things?"

"We'll see things while we drive. I like driving."

"You're not driving. I'm driving. Aimless driving. Will the island still be fun with Rajiv gone?"

"I'm staying."

"One of these days you'll be going back to school."

"They're still digging. When they stop I'll go to school."

"You like the hard life. You're a couple of hardy people. Soon she'll be dressing you in animal skins."

"It'll have to be donkeys or cats. There must be a million cats there."

"I can see the two of you sailing around the world in a boat made of reeds and cat hair. Who needs school?"

He looked out the window for a while.

"How come you don't have to work?"

"I'll stick my head in the door around noon tomorrow. Things are quiet now. It's Ramadan. That affects the pace of things in the countries where most of our business is."

"Wait, don't tell me."

"It's an Islamic month."

"I said wait. Couldn't you wait?"

"All right, what are people not allowed to do during Ramadan?"

"They're not allowed to eat."

"They're not allowed to eat till sundown. Then they eat."

"Think of some more."

"We're almost home. I notice you've got Rajiv speaking Ob. Does your mother think you're overdoing it a bit?"

"She hasn't said anything. I learned it from her, don't forget."

"If you become Ob-sessed, I blame her. Is that the idea?"

He turned to me abruptly, a little wild-eyed.

"Don't tell me what that's called. I'm thinking. Just wait, okay?"

When I pulled up it was nearly dark. The concierge stood outside the building, a man about my age with the forceful dark look of his profession, organized loitering. They were arrayed along the sidewalk, four or five of them, thumbing their amber beads, men of inevitability and fate, presences. They stare into the middle distance. Sometimes they gather at the barber shop, serious talk, dipping their knees in turn. They attend the entrances, they sit in the marble lobbies. A man or woman walking down the street, someone of interest for whatever reason to the concierges, is passed in effect from one to the other, a stray plane tracked to the pole. Not that they are curious. The barest scattering from a common center moves them only to suspicion. Cars come and go, people wait at the bus stop, a man paints the wall across the street. This is enough for anyone.

But Niko had never seen my son. His arms went up. He came forward to open the door on the passenger's side, smiling widely. Children were the full becoming. They stirred a mystical joy in people. They were centered, always in light, in aura, scooped up, dandled, sung to, adored. Niko spoke Greek to Tap as he'd never spoken to me, with vigor and warmth, eyes shining. I see my son in the small tumult of the moment. He knows he has to handle this alone and does it conscientiously enough, shaking the man's hand, nodding madly. He is not experienced at hearty rapport, of course, but his effort is meticulous and touching. He knows the man's pleasure is important. He has seen this everywhere on the island and he has listened to his mother. We must be more precise in the details of our responses. This is how we let people know we understand the seriousness and dignity of their feelings. Life is different here. We must be equal to the largeness of things.

At the airport the next evening I stood with Rajiv and Tap under the status board, talking about the destinations and wondering what Rajiv saw when he came across words like Benghazi and Khartoum. I wondered what Tap saw.

"Will you be glad to go back to India for good?" I said. "Your father thinks sometime next year."

"Yes, I'll be glad. It's not so cold and I like school there. We run races and I'm very fast."

"Is he very fast, Tap?"

"He's pretty fast. He's faster than a three-legged dog."

"So this is good. He has one more leg than I."

"What will you study when you get back?" I said.

He held his breath at most questions. His face grew intense, he evaluated the implications, the depths of meaning. I watched him puff up his chest as he prepared to deliver an answer.

"Mathematics. Hindi. Sanskrit. English."

Later I watched from a distance as Anand said goodbye to the boy. Being a father seemed his natural talent. There was something reassuring in him, a strong settling presence that must have made Rajiv feel his aircraft would glide toward the Arabian Sea on the soft air of his own father's commanding. The boy was preparing to enter hushed places. Out of this bedlam of departing people and the voices that gather around them, he would take an escalator down to the area restricted to passengers. The people with documents, the lounge, the softer chairs, the more purposeful waiting. At the boarding gate, the last of the static chambers, the stillness is more compact, the waiting narrowed. He will notice hands and eyes, the covers of books, a man with a turban and netted beard. The crew is Japanese, the security Japanese, all this planned by his father. He hears Tamil, Hindi, and begins curiously to feel a sense of apartness, something in the smell of the place, the amplified voice in the distance. It doesn't feel like *earth*. And then aboard, even softer seats. He will feel the systems running power through the aircraft, running light, running air. To the edge of the stratosphere, world hum, the sudden night. Even the night seems engineered, Japanese, his brief sleep calmed by the plane's massive heartbeat. The journey is a muted pause between the noise of Athens and the roiling voice of Bombay.

We went to the observation deck.

He was traveling with two people he knew. Still, it was a considerable event for a nine-year-old, a separation based on thrust, speed and altitude, fiercer, more intense for this reason than the parting of the following day, when Tap would go with Anand back to the island.

It was an hour to sunset. Tap had a secret eye on a group of men in leisure suits and Arab dress, talking softly. A dense light lay on the gulf. Faint shapes in the haze, destroyers and merchant ships. We watched the planes take off.

"I heard something else," Anand said. "They were there a long, long time. Do you know about the rock shelter?"

"Which island are we talking about?"

"Kouros. There were three men, one woman. In a rock shelter."

"Owen told me."

"They were there a long time. Through the entire winter if you can imagine it. The murder on Donoussa was a year ago. I don't know for a fact that there were any foreigners on Donoussa then. There was a murder, that's all I know. Same type of weapon."

He was looking out toward the runway.

"Several questions," I said. "Did you ever see these people? Around the dig, in the village nearby? Did you ever go up toward the monastery? Owen told you what they look like, didn't he, how they dress?"

"I never saw people like this anywhere on the island. The island is a damned uninteresting place. Who comes? That's a nice enough village where Kathryn rented the house. But what else is there? You never see anyone. Greeks come now and then. Old French or German couples. These people would stand out. Believe it."

"How do you know they spent the winter in that cave?"

"Owen told me. Who else? He's the only one who's seen them."

"Anand, they didn't drop out of the sky. Other people must have seen them. They had to step off a boat. They had to make their way to the shelter."

"Maybe they arrived at different times, one by one, and they were not so disheveled then, or filthy and hungry. No one noticed."

"He didn't tell me they were there for such a long period."

"Owen is selective," Anand said. "You mustn't be hurt."

We laughed. Tap made his way closer, pointing toward the runway. We saw a 747 lift slowly in the silver haze, the blast wave reaching us before the plane banked over the gulf. Anand watched it out of sight. Then we walked down to the car and headed back to Athens.

"They were eating," Tap said.

"Who was eating?"

"The Arabs at the airport when we were waiting for the plane to take off. They had food."

"So what?"

"It's Ramadan."

"That's right, it is," I said.

"The sun was still out."

"But maybe they're not Muslims."

"They looked like Muslims."

"What does a Muslim look like?"

"He doesn't look like you or me."

"The first year I taught in the States," Anand said, "they all wanted to come to me for lessons in meditation. A Hindu. They wanted me to teach them how to breathe."

"Did you know how to breathe?"

"I didn't know how to breathe. I still don't know. What a joke. They wanted to control their alpha waves. They thought I could tell them how to do this."

All through dinner Anand talked about religion with Tap. Undreamed sights. Vultures circling the towers of silence, where Parsees leave their dead. Jains wearing gauze over their mouths to keep from breathing insects and killing them. Serious people, Tap saw. He was enjoying himself, his fork in a melon wedge in the garden taverna. He grew watchful and still as Anand described ash-gray men wandering naked with begging bowl and staff, holy men, sadhus, walking out their lives in mud and dust.

I kept waiting for Tap to ask about his own religion, if he'd ever had one or if his parents had and what happened to it if they had. We were doubters, I might have told him. Skeptics of the slightly superior type. The Christian dispersion. It was one of many things Kathryn and I agreed on, rockbound doubt, not that we'd ever discussed it. It was just there, or not there, something we knew about each other. The quasi-stellar object, the quantum event, these were the sources of our speculation and wonder. Our bones were made of material that came swimming across the galaxy from exploded stars. This knowledge was our shared prayer, our chant. The grim inexplicable was there, the god-mass looming. If we see God as a being, I might have said to Tap, the only true response is the wandering sadhu's. Go naked in a scatter of ashes, stand in the burning sun. If there is *God*, how could we fail to submit completely? Existence would be decrease, going clean. And adding beauty to the world, Kathryn might say. To her the spectacle had merit even if the source was obscure. They would be beautiful to see, leaning on staffs, mind-scorched, empty-eyed, men in the dust of India, lips moving to the endless name of God.

The alphabet.

Later I sat alone outside, hearing the day-end noise die slowly, voices in the terrace restaurants, the two-part drone of insects in the cypress trees. True night. The Doppler bursts of motorcycles taking the hill.

Anand had said the island was safe, he was sure of it, they were gone. I asked him how many times Owen had been to the rock shelter. Many. But Owen had told me he saw them only once; when he went back a second time, they were gone. Anand said he was in a position to know about Owen's absences from the site. Owen had seen them more than once. Believe it.

Early the next morning I watched their boat move off. A full day's trip even if the connecting boat was on time. Already Kathryn would be at the site, picking away with a grapefruit knife and tweezers. "Sherding" they called it. Washing the finds. Boxing the finds. Labeling the boxes. And she'd be on the roof when the boat came into view, a flashlight rigged above her record sheets, her cross-section drawings of the scarp.

Each blazing day she grew into something slightly newer. The wind blew so hot it stripped the bougainvillea of flowers. Water was being rationed, the phones were out. But the conservator was back, gluing pots together, giving them chemical baths. There was activity. One of the students was sinking a trench in the olive grove. Things were not finished. There were always finds to make.

She would walk down to the dock and watch him come off the boat with his knapsack and half smile.

Home.

Through Istanbul the long cabs passed in the gloom, Olds 88s, Buick Roadmasters, Chrysler limousines, DeSotos with busted mufflers, the Detroit overstocks of the decades, a city of dead cars. From the air all the cities looked like brown storms collecting, traps of heat and dust. Rowser sent me to Cairo for one day to finish an update for the local associate, a man who'd suffered a stroke in the lobby of the Sheraton. Cairo the radarless airport, Cairo the flocks of red-dyed sheep crossing downtown streets, the roofless buses, people hanging over the sides. In Karachi there was barbed wire, broken glass cemented to the tops of walls, trucks carrying trees in burlap sacking. Military governments always plant trees. It shows their gentle side.

In the Istanbul Hilton I ran into a man named Lane, a lawyer who did work for the Mainland Bank. The day before he'd run into Walid Hassan, one of David Keller's credit officers, at the Inter-Con in Amman. I'd last seen Hassan in Lahore, the Hilton, where we'd run into each other at the front desk, each of us signing a document allowing us to have a drink in the bar that lay behind an unmarked door off the lobby. In the bar we ran into a man named Case, who was Lane's boss.

Case had come from Nairobi with a one-sentence story. When Kampala fell to the Tanzanian forces, people greeted them with flowers and fruit and beat their own captured troops to death in the street.

All these places were one-sentence stories to us. Someone would turn up, utter a sentence about foot-long lizards in his hotel room in Niamey, and this became the solid matter of the place, the means we used to fix it in our minds. The sentence was effective, overshadowing deeper fears, hesitancies, a rife disquiet. There was around us almost nothing we knew as familiar and safe. Only our hotels rising from the lees of perennial renovation. The sense of things was different in such a way that we could only register the edges of some elaborate secret. It seemed we'd lost our capacity to select, to ferret out particularity and trace it to some center which our minds could relocate in knowable surroundings. There was no equivalent core. The forces were different, the orders of response eluded us. Tenses and inflections. Truth was different, the spoken universe, and men with guns were everywhere.

The one-sentence stories dealt with our passing grievances or small embarrassments. This was the humor of hidden fear.

Back in Athens I went around to visit Charles Maitland in his apartment. He lived on a quiet street lined with oleanders about a block and a half away from me, just below the library of the American School of Classical Studies. It was his habit, opening the door to someone, to turn immediately and shuffle toward the living room, leaving the caller slightly unsure of his welcome. The gesture had the assurance and precision of superior breeding behind it but all it meant was that Charles grew impatient with conversation in doorways.

It was a small apartment with many objects from Africa and the Middle East. He was just back from Abu Dhabi, where he'd been discussing alarm systems for refineries.

"Are they killing Americans?" I said.

He sat by the window, shirt unbuttoned, in slippers, drinking a beer. A copy of *Jane's Fighting Ships* was on the floor near his feet. I made myself a drink and wandered along the bookshelves.

"I want them to use magnetic sensors," he said. "They're reluctant, it seems. The usual convoluted process. I've passed through a hundred partitioned offices. What are you drinking? Did I make that?"

"You don't know how."

"Don't look at my books. It makes me nervous when people do that. I feel I ought to follow along, pointing out which ones were gifts from fools and misfits."

"They're Ann's books, most of them."

"When will you finally cast aside this way of seeing? It's defeating, you know."

"You're two distinct people, aren't you? They're hers, most of them. You read manuals, specification sheets."

"Tell me about Cairo," he said. "There's a city for you."

"Forty degrees Celsius."

"Nine million people. You need at least nine million people before you've earned the right to call yourself a city. The heat is impressive, isn't it?"

"The sand is impressive. There was an old man with a broom sweeping sand off one of the airport roads."

"Damn it, I miss the sand. He was sweeping it back, was he, into the desert? Good man."

"I was only there a day."

"That's all it takes. Great cities take a day. This is the test of a great city. The traffic, the sewage, the heat, the telephones. Marvelous. Get David to tell you about the traffic in Tehran. Now there's traffic for you. There's a city."

"I've heard him."

Hacking laughter.

"They're all coming out, you know."

They'd been coming out in Pan Am 747s, in VC10s, in Hercules C-130s, in C-141 StarLifters. They flew to Rome, Frankfurt, Cyprus, Athens.

Tennant heard gunfire as he left Tehran for the airport. It was the tenth straight day of gunfire for Tennant. People in Mashhad counted six straight days. Iran Oil Services chartered planes for the oilfield personnel and their families. Five hundred people arrived in Athens one day. Three hundred the next.

Athens took on the soft glow of an executive refuge, an old storytelling kingdom where men from many lands gathered to weave their tales of gunfire and chanting mobs. We who lived there began to feel we hadn't fully appreciated the place. Stability was rare, it seemed, in the cities of the eastern Med, the Gulf, well beyond. Here was our own model of democratic calm.

They would come on scheduled flights out of Beirut, Tripoli, Baghdad, out of Islamabad and Karachi, out of Bahrain, Muscat, Kuwait and Dubai, the wives and children of businessmen and diplomats, causing room shortages in Athens hotels, adding stories, new stories all the time. This would happen in the first month of the new Islamic year. The men staying behind were encouraged by their embassies to take vacations, at the very least to stay indoors whenever possible. The first month was the holy month.

From the window I watched a priest come down a sidestreet toward the building. They moved like ships, these men in their black cassocks and cylindrical hats, wide and rocking. Sunday.

"Why aren't you flying your plane?"

"Should I be?"

"Ever since I've been here you've gone out on Sundays."

"Ann thinks I'm trying to develop a sense of ruined dignity.

It would be impaired, this sense, if I were to stand in a dusty field with a model plane buzzing about my head. There's nothing ruined in such a scene. It's merely pathetic. When older men do certain things alone, it means you must pity them. Things boys are thought to do. There's something suspect in this whirling ship of mine. That's the theory."

"Not Ann's theory."

"It's a theory. I haven't finished shaving, my shirt is open. All ways to enlarge my ruined dignity, according to her."

"Is she right?"

"They're her books," he said evenly.

"Business problems. Are you having trouble coming up with assignments?"

He waved a hand.

"Because I can always talk to Rowser."

"Spare me."

"He's not so bad. Once you understand the way his mind works."

"How does his mind work?"

"On-off, zero-one."

"Binary. How do minds in general work? Anyone's. Christ, we're out of beer. Are there stores open seven days a week after death?"

The tribal mask was wood and horsehair, grimacing. Heavy-lidded eyes, geometric nose. I almost told Charles about the murders in the Cyclades. But going over it mentally I found the subject so closely tied to Owen Brademas there was little to say without bringing him into it. A character study of Owen would be necessary. The material was his, the suggestion of a sense behind the killings. I didn't think I was up to providing a background, on a sleepy late-summer day, and Charles appeared in no mood to take one in.

"I don't mind working for Rowser at all," I said. "I told Kathryn. This is where I want to be. History. It's in the air. Events are linking all these countries. What do we talk about over dinner, all of us? Politics basically. That's what it comes down to. Money and politics. And that's my job. Yours too."

"I'm in the world, granted. I've always been in the world. But I don't know that I like it anymore."

"All of us. We're important suddenly. Isn't it something you feel? We're right in the middle. We're the handlers of huge sums of delicate money. Recyclers of petrodollars. Builders of refineries. Analysts of risk. You say you're in the world. That's profound, Charles. I wouldn't have reacted to that a year ago. I would have nodded absent-mindedly. It means something to me now. I came here to be close to my family and I'm finding something more. Seeing them. But also just being here. The world is here. Don't you feel that? In some of these places, things have enormous power. They have impact, they're mysterious. Events have weight. It's all gathering. I told Kathryn. Men running in the streets. People. I don't mean I want to see it blow up. It's a heightening, that's all. When the Mainland Bank makes a proposal to one of these countries, when David flies to Zurich to meet with the Turkish finance minister, he gets a feeling, he turns a little pinker than he already is, his breath comes faster. Action, risk. It's not a loan to some developer in Arizona. It's much broader, it has a serious frame. Everything here is serious. And we're in the middle."

"How do minds work?" he said.

"What?"

"What does the latest research show?"

"I don't know what you're talking about."

"It's in the air. It's history. It's turning pinker all the time."

His voice had the abruptness of someone who talks to strangers in the subway. It was naked. There was an element of injured self in it. Whatever the tone indicated, I didn't think there was any point in responding.

I went out to the terrace. It was one of those sandblasted days. The city was achromatic, very dense and still. A woman came out of a building and walked slowly down the street. She was the only person in sight, the one thing moving. In the emptiness and glare there was a mystery about her. Tall, a dark dress, a shoulder bag. Locusts droning. The brightness, the slow afternoon. I stood watching. She stepped off the curbstone without looking back this way. No cars, no sound of cars. Was it the empty street that made her such an erotic figure, the heat and time of day? She drew things toward her. Her shadow gave a depth to things. She was walking in the street and even this was powerful and alluring, an act that had erotic force. The body presumes on the machine. An arrogance that's sensual. That nothing else moved into view, that she walked with a lazy sway, that her dress was the kind of fabric that clings, that her buttocks were hard and tight, that the moment of her passage in the sun went by so slowly, all these things made sexual drama. They weighed on me. They put me in a near trance of longing. That's what she was, hypnotic, walking down the middle of the street. Long slow empty quiet Sundays. When I was a boy these were the days I hated. Now I looked forward to them. Prolonged moments, dead calm. I needed this one day, I'd found, of simply being.

Ann was in the living room when I went back inside. Her face seemed bleached, eyes large and pale. She held a drink.

"Don't look at me."

"I thought you were out," I said. "On the phone Charles said you were at the flower market."

"It closes at two. I got here just before you did actually."

"Been hiding from me."

"I suppose I have."

"Where is Charles?"

"Napping."

"What an interesting couple. They take turns disappearing."

"Sorry, James, really."

"I ought to be going anyway."

"Don't be so glum. What are you drinking?"

"You're having problems then."

"That's the nature of the beast, isn't it? Our son is planning a visit. Peter. We'll repair it by then. Our duty is clear. Did you notice, he didn't finish shaving? He always seems on the verge of doing some great sort of comic turn. He lapses into comedy all the time. I wonder if he knows. The man's actually a gifted comic. I mean half shaven. He won't let me go with him to fly his plane. He doesn't want to be *seen*."

There was a ready-made quality about the way she spoke. Tired nonstop fluency. It came raining out. Tension and fatigue made her overbright, almost frantically eager to string sentences together, any sentences. She used pitch as an element of meaning. What she said was beside the point. It was the cadences that mattered, the rise and fall of the ironic voice, the modulations, the stresses. What we lacked was a subject.

"Have we spoken since Nairobi? I came back with some wonderful dirty words. My sister collects them for Charles. The life they lead, let me tell you. A house servant, a gardener, a man for the horses, a night guard, a day guard. But there's no butter, there's no milk."

Her eyes wouldn't meet mine.

"The Tennants are here, you know. We'll all go to dinner this week. They don't much like it here. They want to go back to Tehran. They're determined, regardless of danger."

She'd met the Tennants in Beirut. Earlier they'd lived in New York. In four years there, the Tennants said, no one ever bothered them. No one was rude or abusive. They were never threatened or mugged. They walked everywhere, they said in a tone that pretended to wonder why such a thing should be considered remarkable. This is what people said when they wanted to pay formal tribute to New York.

We walked everywhere.

"I feel sad for them," she said. "They were only just getting the feel. It takes more time in some places than others. I mean when people aren't shooting, of course. When they're shooting, you just go about your business, head down. You don't have to worry about getting the feel or learning the rhythm. It's all rather dramatically done for you. Where you can go, when you can go there."

In Beirut she used to go all the way to the airport to mail a letter. Some days they'd put it in a box, some days they'd give it back to her. In the end this is what brought them out. It wasn't the local hepatitis, the cholera to the north, even the steady gunfire. It was the arbitrary nature of things. Moods and whims. Nothing the same two days running. Stray events. Life shaped by men whose actions had the wanton force of some sudden turn in nature. Often the men themselves didn't know how they would act from one moment to the next and this put her on constant edge. She couldn't follow the thoughts behind the eyes. Checkpoints, men's eyes. The women kept washing floors. It seemed to be what they did in difficult times. During the worst of the fighting they kept on washing floors. They washed floors long after the floors were clean. The uniform motions, the even streaks. Unvarying things, she saw, must have deeper value than we know.

"Don't look at me," she said again.

"You're not so hard to look at, you know."

"Stop. I'll be a grandmother one of these days."

"Is Peter married?"

"Hardly. He tends to be dithery in his relations with people. I wish I could learn that kind of indecisiveness myself. Forever plunging. That's your Ann Maitland, dearie."

"Should we talk, you and I?"

"I thought men talked to other men. You know, buy each other foaming mugs of stout, do a little back-slapping. Things look better in the morning sort of thing."

"Charles isn't talking."

"No, he isn't, is he? He'd much rather sleep."

"Charlie's baffled."

"It's just an affair," she said. "I've had others."

"I wonder what I say to that."

"Nothing. We'll repair it. We have in the past. It requires sequences that have to be completed, one after the other. Distinct stages of development. The funny thing is I haven't learned the drill as well as he has. I do badly at it. I make things difficult for all concerned. Poor James. I'm sorry."

The voice was her own now, reflective and balanced, connected to something. She leaned forward to touch my hand. The world is here, I thought.

At first I thought the concierge was ten or fifteen years older than I was. The small girl clinging to his leg I took to be a granddaughter. It was a while before I saw I would have to adjust the relative levels, bring his age down, mine up. Most Greek men at forty seem totally fixed, part of the settled earth, assigned by time and custom to a particular set of duties, a certain face, a walk, a way of saying and doing. I was still waiting to be surprised by life. I was always coming or going, he was *there*, out on the sidewalk or behind his desk in the dark lobby, doing his records, drinking coffee.

He didn't know a word of English. My Greek was so tentative and insecure I began to wish I could avoid the man. But it wasn't possible to get by him without a sentence or two passing between us. He might ask about Tap, remark on the weather. Understanding him, answering correctly, was like making my way through a dream. I used to squint into his face, trying to pick a word out of the surge and glut, something that might give me a clue to what the subject was.

Hot.

Hot.

Very hot.

If I came into the lobby with groceries in a clear plastic bag he'd look over from his slot behind the desk and name the items one by one. At times I found myself repeating what he said or even saying the words before he did, when I knew them. I would lift the bag slightly as I walked by, making it easier for him to see. Bread, milk, potatoes, butter. The concierge had this power over me. He had the advantage, the language, and what I felt most often, passing in or out of his presence, was a childlike fear and guilt.

Aside from a limited vocabulary I had severe shortcomings when it came to pronunciation. Place-names were a special problem. Whenever I got off the elevator with a suitcase, Niko would ask where I was going. Sometimes he did this with a small hand-twisting gesture. A simple thing, destination, but often I had difficulty telling him. Either I'd forget the Greek word or I'd have trouble pronouncing it. I'd put the accent in the wrong place, mess up the x sound, the r that follows the t. The word would come out flat and pale, a Minnesota city, and I'd head off to the airport feeling I'd been unable to satisfy some obscure requirement.

In time I began to lie. I would tell him I was going to a place that had a name I could easily pronounce. What a simple, even elegant device this seemed. Let the nature of the place-name determine the place. I felt childish, of course. This was part of his power over me. But the lies began to worry me after a while in a way that had nothing to do with childishness. There was something metaphysically disturbing about them. A grave misplacement. They were not simple but complex. What was I tampering with, the human faith in naming, the lifelong system of images in Niko's brain? I was leaving behind in the person of the concierge an enormous discrepancy between my uttered journey and the actual movements I made in the external world, a four-thousand-mile fiction, a deep lie. The lie was deeper in Greek than it would have been in English. I knew this without knowing why. Could reality be phonetic, a matter of gutturals and dentals? The smoky crowded places where we did business were not always as different to us as the names assigned to them. We needed the names to tell them apart, in a sense, and I was playing fast and loose with this curious truth. And when I returned, how foolish I felt as he asked me how things had gone in England, Italy or Japan. Retribution. I might have been wishing an air crash on myself or an earthquake on an innocent city, the city whose name I had uttered.

I also lied when I went to Turkey. I could handle the word for Turkey, it was one of my better words, but I didn't want Niko to know I went there. He looked political.

That night I thought of Ann, the cities she'd lived in, what kind of bargains she'd struck with her husband and lovers. I thought of her affairs, sentimentally, as preparations for the loss she knew was coming. It was her husband's job that took her to a place, then took her away. Places, always places. Her memory was part of the consciousness of lost places, a darkness that ran deep in Athens. There were Cypriots here, Lebanese, Armenians, Alexandrians, the island Greeks, the northern Greeks, the old men and women of the epic separation, their children, grandchildren, the Greeks of Smyrna and Constantinople. Their true home was to the spacious east, the dream, the great idea. Everywhere the pressure of remembrance. The black memory of civil war, children starving. Through the mountains we see it in the lean faces of men in flyspeck villages, stubble on their jaws. They sit beneath the meter on the café wall. There's a bleakness in their gazing, an unrest. How many dead in your village? Sisters, brothers. The women walk past with donkeys carrying bricks. There were times when I thought Athens was a denial of Greece, literally a paving over of this blood memory, the faces gazing out of stony landscapes. As the city grew it would consume the bitter history around it until nothing was left but gray streets, the six-story buildings with laundry flying from the rooftops. Then I realized the city itself was an invention of people from lost places, people forcibly resettled, fleeing war and massacre and each other, hungry, needing jobs. They were exiled home, to Athens, which spread toward the sea and over the lesser hills out into the Attic plain, direction-seeking. A compass rose of memory.

5

PEOPLE WERE always giving her shirts. Their own in most cases. She looked good in everything; everything fit. If a shirt was too loose, too big, the context would widen with the material and this became the point, this was the fit. The shirt would sag fetchingly, showing the girl, the sunny tomboy buried in hand-me-down gear. She used to snatch things off hangers in Yonge Street basements, the kind of shapeless stuff men wore north. These were stores with hunting knives in faded scabbards in the window, huge khaki anoraks with fur-lined hoods, and she'd grab a pair of twelve-dollar corduroys that became immediately hers, setting off her litheness, the close-skinned physical sense she expressed even sprawled across an armchair, reading. Her body had efficient lines that took odd clothing best, the weathered, the shrunken, the dull. People were pleased to see her in their workshirts, old sweaters. She was not a friend who asked many favors or required of others a steadfastly sympathetic nature. They were flattered, really, when she took a shirt.

I stood watching from the deck. In the west the sun was banded, fading down a hazy slate horizon. We moved along the rocky coast and came booming in heavy gusts around the point. The village danced in light. As we approached there was a momentary lull, landward. Things seemed to pause to let the flesh tone seep in. Contours were defined, white walls massed around the bell-tower. Everything was clear and deep.

The ship passed into a silence. Protected now. Old men came out to catch the hawsers.

I saw her walk with Tap into the square. The shirt she wore was identifiable from a distance. Long, straight, tan, with brass studs and red-rimmed epaulets. She wore it outside her jeans. A *carabiniere* shirt. Long sleeves, sturdy fabric. The nights were getting cool.

I hadn't seen the shirt in years but easily recalled who had given it to her.

She asked about Cairo. I left my bag at the hotel desk. Up the cobbled streets, jasmine and donkey shit, the conversational shriek of older women. Tap walked on ahead, knowing she had something to tell me.

"We had a strange visit. A figure from the past. Out of absolutely nowhere."

"Everyone is from the past."

"Not everyone is a figure," she said. "This person qualifies as a figure."

We were taking unnaturally long strides on the broad steps. Some girls sang a song that began with the words *one two three.*

"Volterra," I said.

She glanced.

"You're wearing his shirt. Practically an announcement. Not only that. The moment you started talking I knew you were going to say something about him. I realized the shirt meant more than the season is starting to change."

"That's amazing. Because the funny thing is I didn't even know I had the bloody shirt. Frank left three days ago. I found the shirt this morning. I'd totally forgotten the thing existed."

"A mock heirloom as I recall. Those were the days when he wasn't sure what he wanted to look and sound like to others. The young man obsessed by film. What was he doing here? Slow down, I hate this climb."

"He was passing through. What else? He drops in, he passes through. That's the way Volterra operates."

"True enough."

"He'd been in Turkey. He thought he'd drop in. Brought along his current lady. She kept saying, 'People with cancer always want to kiss me on the mouth.' Where does he find them?"

"Too bad. I'd like to have seen him. He was coming here, I was going there."

"You're claiming foreknowledge. You knew I was going to say something about him."

"The old psychic motor is still running. When I saw you in the shirt I thought of him right away. Then Tap walked on ahead in his half-downcast all-knowing manner. You started to say something and it hit me: she's heard from Frank. How did he know you were here?"

"I wrote once or twice."

"So he knew we'd separated."

"He knew."

"Do you think that's why he dropped in?"

"Ass."

"How is he? Does he still sit with his back to the wall in restaurants?"

A man and his small sons were mending a net. Kathryn stopped to exchange greetings in the set manner, the simple questions that brought such satisfying replies, the ceremony of well-being. I stepped between the gathers of yellow mesh and with an effort caught up to Tap.

Volterra came out of an old textile town in New England, a place with a dime store, one or two handsome public buildings in decline. A man in trail boots jerked the lever on a cigarette machine in the entranceway of a diner. Women drove station wagons, sometimes just sitting at the wheel, parked, trying to remember something. It was the last generation of station wagons. His father did odd jobs, the movie theater closed. But there were falls, the sound of rushing water. It was a northern sound, it smelled of the north. There was something pure in it.

His mother had mental problems. Frank was the youngest of four. She was thirty-seven when he was born and she seemed now to be longing for senility. She wanted to sit in a warm corner and let the past fall slowly over her. Confused recollection was a state she felt was earned. It was a gratifying punishment, a sinking away from the life struggle. Her situation was exemplary. Let the children see how God does these things to people.

The dark brick mill ran skeleton shifts, was always on the verge of shutting down. Men wore trail boots, wilderness boots, insulated hunting shoes.

In New York he went to a school for private detectives, working in the stock rooms at Macy's during the day. The school, called an academy, was located off the lobby of a hotel full of West Indians. It was a crazy and money-wasting idea, he said, but it marked his freedom, it meant New York. You were a stranger and could do these things. Two months later he enrolled in film school at NYU.

He cut news footage for a network affiliate in Providence. After writing a number of unfinished scripts he headed west to do technical films for companies with names like Signetics and Intersil. California was full of technocratic amaze. That's where the visionaries were, developing an argot, playing galactic war games on the display screens in computer research centers. Kathryn and I lived in Palo Alto then, happily on the fringe of things, sanding our secondhand chairs. She worked for Stanford University, the Center for Information Processing, where she helped students and faculty use computers in their research and course work. I was turning out the usual run of low-paying freelance work, most of it for high technology firms in the area.

I wrote a script for a film that Volterra directed. He was fast and inventive with an offhand manner toward the work and many ideas about film, the state of film, the meaning of film, the language of film. He spent a lot of time with us. We went to the movies and marched against the war. The two things were connected. The flag-tailored kids were connected, the streets were connected, the music, the marijuana. I stopped smoking grass when the war ran down.

He was full of comic sorrows, self-dramatizing impulses,

wasted-looking in a way that marked a style more than a set of depressing circumstances, and he seemed most content with himself cursing the chill mist that blew across the hills. He had a narrow face and the feral eyes of a boy absorbed in the task of surviving. The style, the psychological intrigues were elements he played off this deeper thing. When he filled out, later, and grew the second or third of a number of experimental beards, I thought I was still able to detect that early fearfulness of his, the schemer's flexible logic, whatever it takes to get the edge.

He started a filmmaking collective in San Francisco. The group shared all tasks, did two documentaries. The first concerned war protests and the police. The second was a story of the love affair, outside marriage, of a middle-aged woman well known in Hillsborough society. The movie became notorious locally for this reason and well-known on a wider basis for a forty-minute segment detailing an afternoon of sex and conversation. For legal reasons the movie had only fitful distribution and eventually none at all, but people talked about it and wrote about it and there were private screenings for months on both coasts. The running time was two hours, the woman's lover was Volterra.

Film. This is what there was, to shoot film, cut film, screen it, talk about it.

The collective fell apart when a conglomerate bought rights to the second documentary, changed the title, changed the names, hired stars and re-shot the whole thing as a feature, using a veteran director and four writers. It was one of those strange transferences in which people conspire to lose sight of a central reality. But what was the reality in this case? There were a dozen questions about ethics, manipulation, the woman's motives. The documentary was edged in politics and hate. Frank was a name in the business.

He would go on to features himself, of course, dropping from sight for long periods, insisting on closed sets when he worked. Long before that he was a force in our lives. He made us think about our modest expectations. His drive to make movies was so powerful we couldn't help feeling anxious hopes on his behalf. We were involved with Volterra. We wanted to defend him, explain him, make allowances for his obsessions, believe in his ideas for uncompromising films. He provided an occasion for reckless loyalties.

When we told him Kathryn was pregnant he showed an emotion deep enough to confirm our own awe, the remarkableness of what we'd commonly made, this almond curve, detailed and living. We didn't know we were ready for a child until Frank's reaction showed us how beside the point readiness can seem to be.

Parenthood eventually deepened our sense of moderation, our not-wanting. It was Frank who left us wondering at this way of life but ultimately confirmed in it. This is one of the balances of a stimulating friendship.

There's no denying his effect on Kathryn. He stood outside her measures of a person's worth. He made her laugh, she sparked to him. The sweet mean narrow face, the uncombed hair. He was a genuine talent, a commitment, the one person whose excesses and personas she needed to indulge. It was bracing to have one's principles challenged. It clarified her vision of things, to be able to defend him to herself, this man who would sit with her in a restaurant on a redwood deck and recount in earnest deadpan detail the methods and bents, the *hand-grips*, of some woman he'd lately spent a night with. The exception was valid if it was large enough. He had the charm of a vast and innocent ego.

This was before the film about the woman from Hillsborough. Kathryn would refuse to see it.

He liked to turn up unexpectedly and made it hard for people to reach him when they wanted to. He lived in borrowed apartments much of the time. Already he was building tunnels in and out. Our feelings for him were sometimes deflected because of this. Long periods went by. We'd hear he was out of the country, underground, back east. Then he'd show up, hunched against the night, moving through the door in a half prowl, nodding, touched to see us looking much the same.

A glancing love.

. . .

"There's more," Kathryn said. "He talked with Owen."

Star fields, ruined time. Nearby a man with a flashlight and donkey hauling garbage in black bags. The hill was empty depth against the streaming night, the medieval sky in Arabic and Greek. We drank dark wine from Paros, too full of night and sky to use the candles.

"I only listened to bits and pieces. It was mostly about the cult. Owen is less vague about them now. They're a cult pure and simple. They qualify. I don't like listening to that."

"I know."

"He makes an exercise of it. All that speculation. He knows I'm tired of it but in this case I can't really blame him for going on at such length. Frank was absolutely fascinated. He prompted, he questioned Owen endlessly. They spent seven or eight solid hours talking about the cult. One night here, one at the dig house."

"Why was Frank in Turkey? Is he doing a movie?"

"He's hiding from a movie. He left the set, the location, whichever it was. He didn't say where they were shooting but I know it's the fourth straight project he's abandoned. The second one to reach the shooting stage."

"Where is he now?"

"I don't know. He took the Rhodes steamer. It stops at two or three islands along the way."

"Did you see his last film?"

"It was wonderful. Just a great piece of work. All Frank's. No one else could have done it. It had his tension in it. Do you know? His way of cutting short extravagant things. Oh I loved it."

"That was about the time we were getting set to wind it up."

"I went to that revival house on Roncesvalles. I walked. How many miles?"

"Past Bathurst."

"Past Dufferin."

"Going to the movies. What was I doing?"

"It felt so good to go to a movie alone. Do you know?"

"I think I must have been watching television. What a crucial difference."

"You were working on your list," she said.

"*Your* list."

"I've never organized your so-called depravities in my mind. That was your game."

"True, all true. How broken I must have been, to be watching television. There you were, striding past Dufferin in your boots and padded clothes like some dyke in a modern children's story."

"Thank you."

"To the movies."

"It felt so good to walk."

"Not just any movie either."

"Remember the argument over the car?"

"The squirrel in the basement. That one tree that flamed in the autumn."

"How strange to be nostalgic about the end of a marriage."

I saw him before I heard him, Owen Brademas (his shape) advancing softly up the stairs, knees high as he climbed, heedful, long-limbed, trailing the glow from his flashlight.

"But you're sitting in the dark."

I said, "Why were you pointing your light down behind you?"

We spoke almost simultaneously.

"Was I? Didn't realize. I know the way so well."

"Darkness makes us sentimental."

Kathryn brought a glass, I poured some wine. He switched off the light and settled into a chair, stretching.

The storytelling voice.

"I realize finally what the secret is. All these months I've wondered what it was I couldn't quite identify in my feelings about this place. The deep-reaching quality of things. Rock shapes, wind. Things seen against the sky. The clear light before sundown that just about breaks my heart." Laughing. "Then I realized. These are all things I seem to *remember*. But where do I remember them from? I've been to Greece before, yes, but never here, never to a place so isolated, never these particular sights and colors and silences. Ever since I got to the island I've been remembering. The experience is familiar, although that's not the right way to put it. There are times you do the simplest thing and it reaches you in a way you didn't think possible, in a way you'd once known but have long since forgotten. You eat a fig and there is something *higher* about this fig. The first fig. The prototype. The dawn of figs." Laughing out. "I feel I've known the particular clarity of this air and water, I've climbed these stony paths into the hills. It's eerie, this sense. Metempsychosis. It's what I've been feeling all along. But I didn't know it until now."

"There's a generic quality, an absoluteness," I said. "The bare hills, a figure in the distance."

"Yes, and it seems to be a remembered experience. If you play with the word 'metempsychosis' long enough I think you find not only *transfer-of-soul* but you reach the Indo-European root *to breathe.* That seems correct to me. We are breathing it again. There's some quality in the experience that goes deeper than the sensory apparatus will allow. Spirit, soul. The experience is tied up with self-perception somehow. I think you feel it only in certain places. This is my place perhaps, this island. Greece contains this mysterious absolute, yes. But maybe you have to wander to find yourself in it."

"An Indian concept," Kathryn said. "Or is it? Metempsychosis."

"A Greek word," he said. "Look straight up, the universe is pure possibility. James says the air is full of words. Maybe it's full of perceptions too, feelings, memories. Is it someone else's memories we sometimes have? The laws of physics don't distinguish between past and future. We are always in contact. There is random interaction. The patterns repeat. Worlds, star clusters, even memories perhaps."

"Turn on the lights," I said.

Again he laughed.

"Am I growing soft-headed? Could be. I've reached an age."

"We all have. But I wish you'd stayed with figs. I understood that."

He rarely supported his arguments or views. The first sound of contention sent him into deep retreat. Kathryn knew this, of course, and moved protectively to other subjects, always ready to attend to his well-being.

Terror. This is the subject she chose. In Europe they attack their own institutions, their police, journalists, industrialists, judges, academics, legislators. In the Middle East they attack Americans. What does it mean? She wanted to know if the risk analyst had an opinion.

"Bank loans, arms credits, goods, technology. Technicians are the infiltrators of ancient societies. They speak a secret language. They bring new kinds of death with them. New uses for death. New ways to think about death. All the banking and technology and oil money create an uneasy flow through the region, a complex set of dependencies and fears. Everyone is there, of course. Not just Americans. They're all there. But the others lack a certain mythical quality that terrorists find attractive."

"Good, keep going."

"America is the world's living myth. There's no sense of wrong when you kill an American or blame America for some local disaster. This is our function, to be character types, to embody recurring themes that people can use to comfort themselves, justify themselves and so on. We're here to accommodate. Whatever people need, we provide. A myth is a useful thing. People expect us to absorb the impact of their grievances. Interesting, when I talk to a Mideastern businessman who expresses affection and respect for the U.S., I automatically assume he's either a fool or a liar. The sense of grievance affects all of us, one way or another."

"What percentage of these grievances is justified?"

I pretended to calculate.

"Of course we're a military presence in some of these places," I said. "Another reason to be targeted."

"You're a presence almost everywhere. You have influence everywhere. But you're only being shot at in selected locales."

"I think I hear a wistful note. Canada. Is that what you mean? Where we operate with impunity."

"Certainly you're there," she said. "Two-thirds of the largest corporations."

"They're a developed country. They have no moral edge. The people who have technology and bring technology are the death-dealers. Everyone else is innocent. These Mideast societies are at a particular pitch right now. There's no doubt or ambiguity. They burn with a clear vision. There must be times when a society feels the purest virtue lies in killing."

Talking with my wife on a starry night in the Greek archipelago.

"Canadians are stricken by inevitability," she said. "Not that I defend the capitulation. That's what it is. Pathetic surrender."

"We do the wrong kind of killing in America. It's a form of consumerism. It's the logical extension of consumer fantasy. People shooting from overpasses, barricaded houses. Pure image."

"Now you're the one who sounds wistful."

"No connection to the earth."

"Some truth in that, I guess. A little."

"I like a little truth. A little truth is all I ever hope for. Do you know what I mean, Owen? Where are you? Make a noise. I like to stumble upon things."

I knocked over a glass, enjoying the sound it made rolling on coarse wood. Kathryn snatched it at the edge of the table.

"Talk about stumble," she said.

"The worst thing about this wine is that you can get to like it."

A light high on the hill. We waited through a silence.

"Why is the language of destruction so beautiful?" Owen said.

I didn't know what he meant. Did he mean ordinary hardware —stun grenades, parabellum ammo? Or what a terrorist might carry, some soft-eyed boy from Adana, slung over his shoulder, Kalashnikov, sweet whisper in the dark, with a flash suppressor and folding stock. He sat quietly, Owen did, working out an answer. The way was open to interpretation, broader landscapes. *Wehrmacht, Panzer, Blitzkrieg.* He would have a patient theory to submit on the adductive force of such sounds, how they stir the chemistry of the early brain. Or did he mean the language of the mathematics of war, nuclear game theory, that bone country of tech data and little clicking words.

"Perhaps they fear disorder," he said. "I've been trying to understand them, imagine how their minds work. The old man, Michaeli, may have been a victim of some ordering instinct. They may have felt they were moving toward a static perfection of some kind. Cults tend to be closed-in, of course. Inwardness is very much the point. One mind, one madness. To be part of some unified vision. Clustered, dense. Safe from chaos and life."

Kathryn said, "I have one point to make, only one. I thought of it after James and I talked about the finds in central Crete, human sacrifice, the Minoan site. Is it possible these people are carrying out some latter-day version? You remember the Pylos tablet, Owen. Linear B. A plea for divine intercession. A list of sacrifices that included ten humans. Could this murder be a latter-day plea to the gods? Maybe they're a doomsday cult."

"Interesting. But something keeps me from thinking they would accept a higher being. I saw them and talked to them. They weren't god-haunted people, somehow I know this, and if they believed some final catastrophe was imminent they were waiting for it, not trying to prevent it, not trying to calm the gods or petition them. Definitely waiting. I came away with a sense that they were enormously patient. And where's the ritual in their sacrifice? Old man hammered to death. No sign of ritual. What god could they invent who might accept such a sacrifice, the death of a mental defective? A street mugging in effect."

"Maybe their god is a mental defective."

"I talked to them, Kathryn. They wanted to hear about ancient alphabets. We discussed the evolution of letters. The praying-man shape of the Sinai. The ox pictograph. Aleph, alpha. From nature, you see. The ox, the house, the camel, the palm of hand, the water, the fish. From the external world. What men saw, the simplest things. Everyday objects, animals, parts of the body. It's interesting to me, how these marks, these signs that appear so pure and abstract to us, began as objects in the world, living things in many cases." A long pause. "Your husband thinks all this is bookish drool."

Our voices in the dark. Kathryn reassures, James issues mild denials. But he wasn't far wrong. I had trouble enough getting Greek characters straight; picturesque desert alphabets were a little too remote to keep me interested. I didn't want to become an adversary, however. He'd probably withheld some things, misled us slightly, but I didn't think these were pieces of strategy so much as instances of personal confusion. And in his present silence I thought I sensed a dreaminess, a drift into memory. Owen's silences were problems to be worked out. Night is continuous, he'd said. The lulls, the measured respites were part of conversation.

"It's possible they've killed another person," he said after a while. "Not here, Kathryn. Not anywhere in Greece."

His turn to reassure. This was considerate, his quickness to ease her fears for Tap's safety. I could imagine from that point on she would no longer feel so protective and affectionate. He was the friend who brought the bad news.

"I received a letter from a colleague in Jordan. He's with the Department of Antiquities there. He knows about the cult, I'd written him. He tells me there was a murder two or three months ago which resembles this one in several respects. The victim was an old woman, near death, lingering for some time. She lived in a village at the edge of the Wadi Rum, the great sandstone desert in the southern part of the country."

Kathryn stood against the white wall. She wanted a cigarette. Twice a year since she'd given them up she wanted a cigarette. I always knew. Moments of helpless tension, an imbalance in the world. They broke the rules, so will I. She used to go through the house groping in dark closets for a lone Salem left faded in some coat pocket.

"They found her outside the mud-brick house where she lived with relatives. She'd been killed with a hammer. I don't know whether it was a standard claw hammer like the one used here."

I said, "Is this what you and Frank Volterra talked about for two nights?"

"Partly. Yes, he wanted to talk. To talk and listen."

"Is that where he's gone?"

"I don't know. He seemed to be considering it. Something about the place excited him. I made the trip myself once, some years ago; there are inscriptions, simple graffiti mostly, camel drivers scratching their names on rocks. I described it to him. We talked about it at some length, the idea of these people, this mad scene being played out in a vast beautiful silent place. The man almost frightened me with his attentiveness. To be listened to so closely can be disconcerting. It implies an obligation on the speaker's part."

"Frank's not your everyday tourist. Did you tell him about Donoussa?"

"I don't know anything about it. Only that a young girl was killed. My assistant heard it from someone."

"Also a hammer," I said.

"Yes. A year ago."

A claw hammer. Is this what he'd meant when he talked about the language of destruction? Simple hand tool of iron and wood. He liked the sound of the words apparently, or the look of them, the way they were bonded perhaps, their compact joinder, like the tool itself, the iron and wood.

If you think the name of the weapon is beautiful, are you implicated in the crime?

I poured more wine, suddenly tired, feeling drumheaded and dumb. It didn't seem logical, the hangover preceding the drunk, or concurrent with it. Owen said something about madness or sadness. I tried to listen, realizing Kathryn was gone, inside some-where, sitting in the dark or in bed already, wanting us to take these murders somewhere else. I would go down the hill with him in the small beam of his flashlight, watch him ride off on the undersized machine, legs crowding the handlebars. Then to my hotel, one flight up, the room at the end of the hall.

Owen was talking again.

"In this century the writer has carried on a conversation with madness. We might almost say of the twentieth-century writer that he aspires to madness. Some have made it, of course, and they hold special places in our regard. To a writer, madness is a final distillation of self, a final editing down. It's the drowning out of false voices."

The custom in warm weather is to hang curtains in doorways. The solid finish of the village yields to human needs. Surface shapes are engagingly disturbed. The wind blows, houses open to the passerby. There's no clear feeling of mysterious invitation. Only of stillness moved inside, stillness darkened, the grain of the inner day.

The rooms are plain and square, immediate, without entranceways or intervening spaces, set at street level, so close to us as we walk in the narrow passage that we feel uneasy about intruding. The Greek in conversation crowds his listener and here we find the same unboundaried exercise of life. Families. People clustered, children everywhere, old women in black sitting motionless, rough hands folded in sleep. The bright and vast and deep are everywhere, sun-cut clarity, the open sea. These modest rooms mark out a refuge from eternal things. This is the impression we have, Tap and I, a sense of modesty, of nondescriptness, only glimpsing as we pass, careful not to appear too curious.

Above the stepped streets there were occasional open spaces, stronger wind. I followed Tap past a large well with a conical iron cap. A woman with an open umbrella sat on a mule, waiting. Cats moved along the walls, watched from roof ledges, cankerous, lame, mangy, some of them minute, the size of a woolen glove.

Climbing. The sea appeared, the ruined windmill to the east. We paused to catch our breath, looking down on a church with an openwork belfry of some patchy rose-pink hue, a rude and pretty touch in all the layered white. A single small church might press together half a dozen surfaces in unexpected ways, sea-waved, domed, straight-edged, barrel-vaulted, a sensuous economy of shapes and arrangements and cross-influences. We heard the hoarse roar of a donkey, an outsized violent sound. The heat felt good.

I showed Tap a postcard my father had sent. It had a picture on it of the Ranchman's Café in Ponder, Texas. My father had never been to Texas as far as I knew. He lived in a small house in Ohio with a woman named Murph.

Tap had received the same kind of postcard. In fact almost all my father's communications for two or three years had been in the form of postcards showing the Ranchman's Café.

The message on his card, Tap said, was the same as the message on mine. He didn't seem surprised by this.

A distant lazy drone. Cicadas. We'd seen them come whirring out of olive trees to sail into walls, dropping in a dry stunned rustle. The wind began to gather force.

Tap led me to an unpaved area of houses with courtyards, the upper limit of the village. There were tall gateways here, some of them located a fair distance in front of the houses to which they belonged. Seen from certain angles these gateways framed a barren hilltop or the empty sky. They were artless arrangements, free of the texts they put before us, material cleanly broken from the world.

We climbed a rock path that worked around a shoulder of land and curled out of sight of the village. A whitewashed chapel across a defile, abrupt in brown earth. We were high up now, in the sweep of the wind and sea, stopping frequently to find fresh perspectives. I sat at the edge of a narrow stand of pine, wishing we'd brought water. Tap wandered into a rocky field just below. The wind came across the defile with a sound that changed levels as the current increased in speed and reached the trees, rushing, from a pure swift surge of air to something like a voice, an urgent emotion. Tap looked up at me.

Ten minutes later I got to my feet and walked out into the sun. The wind had died. I saw him standing fifty yards away in the steep field. He was absolutely still. I called to him, he didn't move. I walked that way, asking what was wrong, calling the words out across the immense silence around us, the drop-off into distances. He stood with his knees slightly flexed, one foot forward, head down, his hands at belt level, held slightly out from his body. Arrested motion. I saw them right away, lustrous black bees, enormous, maybe a dozen, bobbing in the air around him. At twenty yards I heard the buzzing.

I told him not to worry, they wouldn't sting. I moved in slowly, as much to reassure Tap as to keep the bees from getting riled. Burnished, black-enameled. They rose to eye level, dropped away, humming in the sun. I put my arm around him. I told him it was all right to move. I told him we would move slowly up toward the path. I felt him tense up even more. His way of saying no, of course. He was afraid even to speak. I told him it was safe, they wouldn't sting. They hadn't stung me and I'd walked right through them. All we had to do was move slowly up the slope. They were beautiful, I said. I'd never seen bees this size or color. They gleamed, I told him. They were grand, fantastic.

Raising his head now, turning. Did I expect relief, chagrin? As I held him close he gave me a look that spoke some final disappointment. As if I could convince him, stung twice before. As if I could take him out of his fear, a thing so large and deep as fear, by prattling on about the beauty of these things. As if I could tell him anything at all, fake father, liar.

We held that inept stance a moment longer. Then I took his arm and led him through the field.

Kathryn and I had dinner on the harborfront with Anand Dass. She knew what was in the kitchen and gave our orders to a boy who stood with his arms crossed on his chest, nodding as she listed the items. The food and supply boat was docked nearby, a single-masted broad-beamed vessel with mystical eyes painted on the bow. No one wanted to talk about the cult.

"It was flawless. A perfect flight. I mean it, those Japanese, they impress me. When I learned they have their own security at the Athens airport, I knew I would send him JAL."

"You go to the States soon," I said.

"The whole family, we converge, what an event," he said. "Even my sister is coming."

"Do you come back in the spring?"

"Here? No. The University of Pennsylvania takes over the whole operation. I'll be back in India by then."

Kathryn passed the bread around.

"In any case I'm not interested in underwater work," he said. "Outside my frame."

"What do you mean?" I said.

He looked at Kathryn. She said to me, "They're going to concentrate on the submerged ruins. They'll alternate. Next season, underwater work. Following year, back to the trenches."

"This is new," I said.

"Yes."

"But I don't think we'll ever alternate," Anand said. "I think we're finished for the season, the decade, the century, whatever."

He had a strong laugh. People stood along the quay, talking in last light. I leaned back in the chair and watched Kathryn eat.

The argument was long and detailed, with natural pauses, and moved from the street to the terrace, into the house, finally up onto the roof. It was full of pettiness and spite, the domestic forms of assault, the agreed-upon reductions. This seemed the point, to reduce each other and everything else. What marriage is for, according to her. Our rage was immense but all we could show for it, all we could utter, were these gibes and rejoinders. And that we did poorly. We weren't able to take advantage of the clear openings. It didn't seem to matter who got the better of it. The argument had an inner life, a force distinct from the issues. There were surges, hesitations, loud voices, laughter, mimicry, moments in which we tried to remember what we wanted to say next, a pace, a range. After a while this became our only motive, to extend the argument to its natural end.

It began on the way up to the house.

"Bitch. You knew."

"I've been trying to find an alternative."

"This means no England."

"We could still go to England."

"I know you."

"What do you know?"

"You want to dig."

"I didn't want to tell you the plan had broken down until I had some kind of alternative."

"When will you tell me about the alternative? When the alternative breaks down?"

"Shut up, ass."

"I know what this means."

"I don't know what it means. How could you?"

"I know how you think."

"What does it mean? I don't know what it means."

"You won't go to England."

"Good. We won't go to England."

"That whole thing was based on your coming back here."

"We could go anyway. We could work out a plan for the summer while we're there."

"But you won't."

"Why won't we?"

"Because you won't. It's too obvious and simple. It lacks intrepidness. It was intrepid when you came up with it originally. It is now obvious and simple and dull."

"You want to see the Elgin marbles."

"It's a fallback. You hate that."

"You're a fallback."

"What are you?"

"You want to see the Elgin marbles but you won't go to the Acropolis. You want to see the rip-off, the imperialist swag in its proper surroundings."

"Hopeless. How the hell did I ever imagine I could come here?"

"Swag. I got that from Tap."

"I hate this climb."

"You keep saying."

"I'm not the man—never mind."

"You never were. You're not the man you never were."

The argument had resonance. It had levels, memories. It referred to other arguments, to cities, houses, rooms, those wasted lessons, our history in words. In a way, our special way, we were discussing matters close to the center of what it meant to be a couple, to share that risk and distance. The pain of separation, the fore-memory of death. Moments of remembering her, Kathryn dead, odd meditations, pity the sad survivor. Everything we said denied this. We were intent on being petty. But it was there, a desperate love, the conscious hovering sum of things. It was part of the argument. It was the argument.

We walked the rest of the way in silence and she went in to check on Tap, who was sleeping. Then we sat on the terrace and began immediately to whisper at each other.

"Where will he go to school?"

"Back on that, are we?"

"Back on that, back on that."

"He's way ahead of them. He can start a little later if necessary. But it won't be necessary. We'll work it out."

"He's not so way ahead. I don't think he's way ahead."

"You distrust his writing. Something in you recoils from that. You think he ought to be diagramming sentences."

"You're crazy, you know that? I'm beginning to see."

"Admit it."

"Why did it take me so long to see what you are."

"What am I?"

"What are you."

"You enjoy telling me that you know how I think. How do I think? What am I?"

"What are you."

"I feel things. I have self-respect. I love my son."

"Where does that come from? Who asked? You feel things. You feel things when they're in your interest. You feel things when they further your drive, your will to do something."

"Ass of the universe."

"Pure will. Where's the heart?"

"Where's the liver?" she said.

"I don't know why I came here. It was crazy, thinking something might come of it. Did I forget who you are, how you consider the simplest things people say and do an affront to your destiny? You have that, you know. A sense of personal destiny, like some German in the movies."

"What's that mean?"

"I don't know."

"What movie, ass?"

"Come to my room. Come on, let's go to the hotel, right now."

"Whisper," she said.

"Don't make me hate myself, Kathryn."

"You'll wake him up. Whisper."

"I'm fucking pissed off. How can I whisper?"

"We've had that argument." Bored.

"You make me hate us both."

"That's an old tired argument." Bored. The worst remarks were bored ones. The best weapons. Bored sarcasm, bored wit, bored tones.

"But what about Frank? We haven't had that argument in a while, have we? How is it he just happened to drop by? Did he want to talk over old times?"

She was laughing. What was she laughing at?

"What a pair, you two. The ragged self-regarding artist, the secretly well-to-do young woman. How many intimate little lunches did you and Frank have while I was doing my booklets and pamphlets? All those diminutive things I was so good at. That minor status you hated so much and still hate in me. What sexy currents passed in the air? Buddy-buddy. Did he ask you up to one of those dreary flats he was always holed up in? He spent half his life looking for bottle openers in other people's kitchens. Did that make it sleazier, sexier? Did you talk about your father's money? No, that would have made him hate you. That would have made him want to fuck you in all the wrong ways, so to speak. And what about Owen, the way you look out for his interests, his curious interests, that half-flirtish thing that comes over you." I went into my female voice routine, a tactic I hadn't used since the recitation of the 27 Depravities. "Are you sure, Owen honey, you never wrote a single line of poetry when you were a lonely farmboy under that big prairie sky?"

"Fobuck yobou."

"That's right."

"You stupid."

"That's right. Bilingual."

"You're just shit."

"Whisper, whisper."

She went inside. I decided to follow, feeling my way in the dark. Soft noise, a light around the corner. She was in the bathroom, pants down, seated, when I moved into the doorway. She tried to kick at the door, one arm flailing, but her legs were caught in the jeans and the arm wasn't long enough. Water music. Too urgent to be contained.

"What were you laughing at before?"

"Out."

"I want to know."

"If you don't get out."

"Say it in Ob."

"You bastard."

"Would you like a magazine?"

"If you don't go. If you don't get out."

The argument worked in such a way that we kept losing the sequence. It moved backwards at times, then advanced abruptly, passing over subjects. There were frequent changes in mood. Moods lasted only seconds. Bored, self-righteous, injured. These injured moments were so sadly gratifying that we tried to prolong them. The argument was full of satisfactions, the major one being that we did not have to examine what we said.

"It lacks intrepidness."

"Get out."

"You'll build a reed boat."

"James, son of a bitch, I want you out of here."

"You'll live in a gas balloon that circles the earth. A seven-story balloon with ferns in the lobby."

"I'm serious now. If you don't get out. I really mean this."

"You'll take him to the Museum of Holes. So he'll have a better understanding of your life work. Dirt holes, mud holes, tall holes, short holes."

"You bastard, I'll get you for this."

"Pee pee pee pee pee pee pee."

"You stupid."

"Don't you realize that as long as you have to sit down to pee, you'll never be a dominant force in the world? You'll never be a convincing technocrat or middle manager. Because people will know. She's in there *sitting down.*"

I stayed on the terrace for a while. Then I climbed the short stairway to the roof. Flashing lights in the harbor. He was awake, I could hear them talking and laughing. What were they laughing at? She came up, tossed me a sweater and sat on the ledge.

"Your son's afraid you might frobeeze."

"What?"

"Frobeeze tobo dobeobath." Amused.

"I wish you'd stop doing that. Both of you."

"Issue a formal order."

"Why did you come up here?"

Amused. "He sent me."

"I want to see him. Wherever you two end up. You'll send him."

"Issue a command. We'll route it through the system."

"Bitch. You knew."

"How do you think I feel? I wanted to come back here."

"To dig."

"You make me insane sometimes."

"Good."

"Shut up."

"You shut up."

"You're afraid of your own son. It disturbs you, that there'll always be a connection."

"What connection?"

"We find things. We learn."

"What do you learn?"

"I never minded what you did. I know you've always arranged your life around things you couldn't possibly fear losing. The snag in this plan is your family. What do you do about us? But I never minded what you wrote. It's your present occupation I despise. I would hate your life. I would hate doing what you do. That awful man."

A high-pitched voice. "That awful man."

"The travel alone would drive me crazy. I don't know how you stand it. And the job."

"We've heard all this." Bored.

"What am I, who am I, what do I want, who do I love. A Harlequin romance."

"Make sense."

"Make sense. If only you knew. But you're so small and whining."

"I'm the ass of the universe. That implies a certain scope, a dimension."

"You'll be an alcoholic. That's what you'll be. I give you a year. Especially if you don't go back to North America. You'll drift into it here. You'll find yourself packing a flask to take to Saudi Arabia. If you're better off without it, you're an alcoholic. Remember that."

"That's your father's line."

"That's right. But he wasn't better off without it. He was a dead soul either way. You're different."

"I like what I'm doing. Why can't I make you understand that? You don't listen. Your view is the only view. If you don't like something, how could anyone like it? If you're better off without it, he'd say, pouring another bourbon. And I *like* his writing. I think it's fantastic. I've told him that. I've encouraged him. You're not the only one who encourages him. You're not the sole support. And I'll tell you how you think. I'll tell you exactly. You need things to be committed to. You need belief. Tap is the world you've created and you can believe in that. It's yours, no one can take it from you. Your archaeology is yours. You're a wonderful amateur. I mean it, the best. You make the professionals seem like so many half-ass triflers. They just dabble, they putter. It's your world now. Pure, fine, radiant. He'd pour another bourbon. If you're better off without it. He liked his bourbon all right. What was the name of that boat, where we talked? The fisherman pounding the octopus. Boats are either saints or women, except when they're places."

I put the sweater on.

"You know how it is with Canadians," she said. "We love to be disappointed. Everything we do ends up disappointingly. We know this, we expect this, so we've made disappointment part of the inner requirement of our lives. Disappointment is our native emotion. It's our guiding spirit. We arrange things to make disappointment inevitable. This is how we feed ourselves in winter."

She seemed to be accusing me of something.

The terrace was L-shaped. From the longer of the segments, the east, where I sat doing a pronoun exercise in my book on modern Greek, I saw a familiar figure in red shorts and t-shirt go running across the street and along the restaurant wall, where he passed quickly from sight, the first of two familiar figures I would see that day.

It was David Keller, toning up. I put down the book, delighted to have an excuse to do so. Then I went outside and headed up through a small dusty park toward the pine woods that form a band around Lycabettus Hill. As I walked through the opening in the fence I heard my name called. Lindsay was behind me, also tracking the runner.

We walked into the woods and found a path that looked as though it might suit someone running, being set at less of a lateral slant than the others. The pine floor was dry and pale. There were no shrubs or bushes and it was possible to see a fair distance up into the woods.

"Why does he come all the way up here to run?"

"He likes the woods. Someone told him it's better to run on rough terrain."

"A milder heart attack."

"He was serious about sports. He needs to hear himself breathe, he says. He was football, basketball crazy."

"The dogs will get him in here."

"Dogs like him," she said.

She walked lazily, swaying, hands clasped behind her. From an opening in the trees we saw part of the sprawl toward Hymettus, white buildings, a white city in this September sun. She seemed often to be thinking some amusing thought, perhaps something so nearly inseparable from a private perception she could not share it easily. She was shy with people but eager to receive, never wary or distrustful. Her eyes were full of humor, fond remembering. Her favorite stories concerned men making fools of themselves heroically.

"I like it here. It's so still."

"He has a kind of shagginess. As far as dogs."

"They really do. They follow him."

We saw him coming back this way, pounding crookedly on the narrow path, dancing over tree roots and stones. We stepped out of the way. He went past grunting, breath blasting, his face twisted and stretched, looking unfinished. We found a crude bench in the sun.

"How long will you stay?" she said.

"Awhile. Until I begin to feel I know it here. Until I begin to feel responsible. New places are a kind of artificial life."

"I'm not sure I know what you mean. But I think that's a Charles Maitland type remark. A little weary. I also think people save up remarks like that, waiting for me to come into range."

"It's your own doing."

"Sure. I'm so innocent."

"How are your storefront English lessons going?"

"It's not exactly a storefront and I think I'm learning more Greek than they're learning English but aside from that it's going well."

"It's not that we think we see innocence. We see generosity and calm. Someone who'll sympathize with us over our mistakes and bad luck. That's where all these observations come from. Mistakes in life. We try to make pointed remarks out of the messes we've created. A second chance. A well-turned life after all."

Below us two dobermans ranged along a draw. The woods were marked with shallow draws and deeper man-made channels to carry off winter rains. We heard David approach again. The dogs went taut, looking up this way. He passed just above us, blowing, and Lindsay turned to flip a pebble at him. A girl in a school smock said something to the dogs.

"When will we get to meet Tap?"

"They're still on the island. They're laying plans."

"You make it sound sinister."

"They're sitting in the sunlit kitchen, avoiding mention of my name."

"We haven't had dinner in a while," she said.

"Let's have dinner."

"I'll call the Bordens."

"I'll call the Maitlands."

"Who else is in town?"

"Walk around the Hilton pool," I told her.

The three of us went slowly down toward the street. David talked in short bursts.

"Happen to have a canteen? What kind of friend?"

"What are you in training for?"

"Night drop into Iran. The bank's determined to be the first ones back in. I'll be leading a small elite group. Credit officers with blackened faces."

"I'm glad we're here instead of there," Lindsay said. "I don't think I'd want to be there even after the trouble ends."

"It ain't ending real soon. That's why I'm doing this commando stuff."

An old man with a setter walked along an intersecting path. Lindsay stooped over the dog, murmuring to it, a little English, a little Greek. David and I kept walking, turning into a path that ran parallel to the street, twenty feet above it. A woman walked below us, headed in the opposite direction, carrying pastry in a white box. David's breathing leveled off.

"Dresses with thin shoulder straps," he said. "A puckered bodice, you know. The kind of dress where the strap keeps slipping off and she doesn't notice for two or three strides and then she puts it back up there casually like brushing a curl off her forehead. That's all. The strap slips off. She keeps walking. We have a momentary naked shoulder."

"A puckered bodice."

"I want you to get to know Lindsay. She's terrific."

"I see that."

"But you don't know her. She likes you, Jim."

"I like her."

"But you don't know her."

"We talk now and then."

"Listen, you have to come with us to the islands."

"Great."

"We want to do the islands. I want you to get to know her."

"David, I know her."

"You don't know her."

"And I like her. Honest."

"She likes you."

"We all like each other."

"Bastard. I want us to do the islands."

"Summer's ending."

"There's winter," he said.

His probing looks disarmed me. It was a practice of his to search people's faces, determined to find a response to his vehement feelings. Then he'd show his big tired western smile, his character actor's smile. It was interesting, the esteem in which he held Lindsay, the half reverence. He wanted everyone to know her. It would help us understand how she'd changed his life.

She caught up to us now.

"Everyone's so nice," she said. "If you speak a few words of the language, they want to take you home to dinner. That's one of the things about living abroad. It takes a while to find out who the madmen are."

Near the spear leaves of a blue-green agave she turned to speak to David, her left ear translucent in the sun.

Later that afternoon, near a kiosk where I often bought the newspaper, I saw Andreas Eliades in a car with another man and a woman. The car had stopped for a light and I'd glanced that way. He was alone in the rear seat. It was one of those low-skirted broad-visored Citroëns, medieval, with slash headlights and heavy trim, a battering contraption for sieges. Above the full black beard his dark eyes were set on me. We nodded to each other, smiled politely. The car moved off.

Sherding. Crouched in the pungent earth, soft forms all about her, pink-ridged, curled, writhing, here in B zone, below the black decay. She is scraping down the square. Right-angled corners, straight sides. Her sweat is a rank reminder, the only one, that she exists, that she is separate from the things that surround her. Troweling around a stone. She remembers someone telling her that stones gradually sink through humus and loam. Clip the roots, leave the stones in place. Part of a hearth, perhaps, or wall. An incised design. A glimpse of political life. Rodents, earthworms turn the soil. She senses the completeness of the trench. It is her size, it fits. She rarely looks over the rim. The trench is enough. A five-foot block of time abstracted from the system. Sequence, order, information. All she needs of herself. Nothing more, nothing less. In its limits the trench enables her to see what's really there. It's a test device for the senses. New sight, new touch. She loves the feel of workable earth, the musky raw aroma. The trench is her medium by now. It is more than the island as the island is more than the world.

I was helpless, overwhelmed. The bare fact of it disheartened me. I couldn't see what the work signified or represented to her. Was it the struggle that counted, a sense of test or mission? What was the metaphor, exactly?

I was compelled in the end to take her literally. She was digging to find things, to learn. Objects themselves. Tools, weapons, coins. Maybe objects are consoling. Old ones in particular, earth-textured, made by other-minded men. Objects are what we aren't, what we can't extend ourselves to be. Do people make things to define the boundaries of the self? Objects are the limits we desperately need. They show us where we end. They dispel our sadness, temporarily.

She called that night to say she'd taken a job with the British Columbia Provincial Museum. She spoke haltingly, her voice full of concern. I could almost believe someone close to me had died. The British Columbia Provincial Museum. I told her that was fine, fine. I said it sounded like a wonderful museum. We were polite, accommodating. We spoke softly, moved to a gentleness we clearly felt we owed each other. Owen had helped arrange the job, through contacts. The museum was in Victoria and specialized in the culture of the Northwest Coast Indians. The museum sponsored occasional field schools. Fine, fine. We were warm to each other, considerate. I wanted her to be certain the job was good enough, what she wanted, although she wasn't sure at this point exactly what she'd be doing. She apologized for having to take Tap so far away and promised we would work out visits despite the distance. Work out meetings, trips together, long talks, father and son. Her voice was dense, chambered, the telephone a sign and instrument of familiar distance, this condition of being apart. All the tender feelings passed between us that I'd sought in recent months to revive by some jumbled luck of character, will and indirection, carried now in the static of our voices, undersea. There were many silences. We said goodnight, dark, sorry, making plans to meet in Piraeus for the trip to the airport. After that we would talk again, talk often, keep each other informed, stay in the closest possible touch.

Ashes.

In the painted evening they walk past the windmill. He points out to sea, about a hundred yards, to the place where dolphins breached, a week ago, in a softfall of violet light. It is one of those imprinted moments, part of him now, contained in island time. A fishing boat approaches in the calm that settles in at this hour. It is blood red, the *Katerina*, a life ring fixed to the mast. She smiles as he makes out the name. The motor leaves a cadenced noise.

The small Cretan rugs. The plank floors. The old lamp with its sepia shade. The donkey bag on the wall. The flowers in rusty cans on the roof, the steps, the window ledges. Tap's handprint on a mirror. The cane chair in a rectangle of light.

In the morning they leave. From the top deck of the boat they see the white village rocking in the mist. How brave and affecting it is, houses clustered on a windy rock, news and reassurance. They eat the food she has packed, sitting low in their slatted bench, out of the wind. He asks her the names of things, ship parts, equipment, and later they walk across the lower deck to trace the system of ropes and anchor chains.

The sun is obscured in dense ascending cloud. Soon the island is a silhouette, a conjecture or mood of light, scant and pale on the iron sea.

The Mountain

6

THE AIRCRAFT veered into position, halting. We waited for clearance. I looked out the window, trying to find something that might distract me from the meditative panic I always experience, the dream-rush before takeoff, all the week's measures of self-awareness in one charged moment. The pale sand stretched level in the distance. A figure was out there, a man in a flax robe. I watched him walk into nothing. Erased in chemical flame. The plane moved down the runway and I sat back, rigid, looking straight ahead.

Words sounded incomplete to me. The starts and stops in people's voices came unexpectedly. I couldn't figure out the rhythm. But the writing flowed, of course. It seemed to have a movement top to bottom as well as right to left. If Greek or Latin characters are paving stones, Arabic is rain. I saw writing everywhere, the cursive beaded slant in tile, tapestry, brass and wood, in faience mosaics and on the white veils of women crowded in a horse-drawn cart. I looked up to see words turning corners, arranged geometrically on mud-brick walls, knotted and mazed, stuccoed, painted, inlaid, climbing gateways and minarets.

I sat across the aisle from a dead man on a Yemen Airways flight from San'a to Dhahran. He died about fifteen minutes into the flight and the people traveling with him started wailing. They carried cloth-covered bundles and wailed. A man behind me remarked to his companion, "But credit extension isn't the issue here." I gripped the arm rests and looked straight ahead. We were over the Empty Quarter.

I found myself studying doors, shutters, mosque lamps, carpets. Surfaces were dense and abstract. Where figural things were present they were rendered as nuances of line or curve, taken out of nature to the level of perfect repetition. Even writing was design, not meant to be read, as though part of some unbearable revelation. I didn't know the names of things.

Forty men and women in immaculate white robes with close-fitting head-scarves filled the rear section of the plane, a Tunis Air flight, Cairo-Damascus. The women's hands were covered with small red marks, designs of some kind. At first I thought they were letters of the alphabet. Not that I knew which alphabet. Possibly the obscure language of some religious sect. Finally I decided the figures were crosses, although some might have been chevrons and others might have been variations of either of these. I couldn't tell whether the marks were ingrained or simply applied to the surface of the skin with cosmetic dye. The people had been on the plane when I boarded, all quietly in place, waiting. After we landed I looked back that way as I moved up the aisle toward the nose exit. They were still in their seats.

Women's eyes glanced away, windows were false, shadows crossed the wall in dappled patterns, architectural planes receded, prayer niches were aligned with Mecca. This last fact supplied an axis to the vapor of fleeting shapes. So much that happened seemed to happen simultaneously. Animals everywhere. The cramped passages of the souk were the least secret places. Loud voices, hanging meat. The crowd was soft, however, floating in robes, sandaled, billowing, touched by the light that fell through broken places in the roof.

I stood waiting at the baggage conveyor in the airport in Amman. The king would be arriving later that afternoon after seventeen days abroad. When the king returns to Jordan after a trip abroad, two camels and a bull are slaughtered at the airport. The drive to the palace follows.

I was staying at the Inter-Con, which was near the palace and across the street from the U.S. embassy, a not uncommon Mideast cluster. I took the oversized map I'd bought in the lobby and spread it across the bed. There they were, as Owen had said, the anagrammatic place-names. Zarqa and Azraq. Between them, west of the midway point, the hilltop fortress of inscribed stones. Qasr Hallabat.

It didn't mean anything. I'd only thought of checking the map for these places on my way up in the elevator. They were a curiosity, that was all. But I was interested to find that he hadn't invented them.

Volterra wore a battered field jacket. Paramilitary drab had always been his color, I realized. He had about two weeks' growth on his face and looked crafty and drawn. We embraced silently. He looked at me, nodding, his biblical gesture of friendship and memory and elapsed time. Then we went into the restaurant.

It was an Indian place, empty except for us and two boys, the waiters, who took our orders and then stood motionless at the end of the long dark narrow room. We sat in tall chairs and talked about Kathryn. It was she who'd given him my number in Athens. When I told him I expected to be in Amman in three weeks' time he said he would try to meet me there. He was calling from Aqaba.

"I thought you had a traveling companion, Frank."

"She's in the room watching TV."

"Where are you staying?"

"Small place near the fourth circle. You've been to Amman?"

"First time."

"Transit cranes," he said. "Beeping taxi horns."

"You've spent all this time in Aqaba?"

"On and off. It's our base. We make three-day trips into the Wadi Rum with a guide and a Land-Rover. We camp out, in our fashion. Then we go back to Aqaba to water-ski."

"I don't see you on water-skis."

"That's an abbreviation. 'Water-ski.' It's shorthand. It means everything in the world that doesn't involve looking for a bunch of crazy people in a barren waste with a guide whose true purpose is to lead us in circles."

"Why are you looking for them?"

Frank laughed. "Is this an interview?"

The boys pushed a large and elaborate serving table along the carpeted floor. On it were two cans of beer.

"Owen seemed to think the cult struck a romantic chord somewhere deep in your breast."

"When you put it that way, Jim, I don't think I'm obliged to discuss the matter further, friends or not."

"I take it back."

He poured the beer into his glass, watching me.

"I'm looking for something outside the range of expectations, you know? It's just a probe. The Wadi Rum's been filmed before, wide screen, soaring music. The place intrigues me in a totally different way. It has to be linked to this homicidal calculation. These small figures in the landscape. Brademas says these people are stalkers. They pick a victim and they watch. They wait for something. There's a particular logic."

"You've walked away from three or four projects, Kathryn told me."

"They were *safe*," he said.

Something came into his eyes, a cold light I recognized as the contempt he often summoned to respond to challenges.

"They weren't worth sticking with. They were exercises. I found myself getting interested in things because they presented a familiar theme or subject I thought I could handle differently, I thought I could give a sweet twist to. Genre crap. I was trying to force these ideas to deliver up riches they didn't contain."

His mood softened, one word to the next.

"I've been feeling the pressure. I admit it. People alighting in helicopters. Clapped-out producers. Lawyer-agents in Nazi sunglasses. They come down out of the sky. Nobody likes the way I work. I don't talk to anybody. I ban people from the set. Do you know what a dumb little napoleonic thing that is? But I do it. I like to do things in secret. I don't say a word to people who want to write about me. Two good films, made money. It happens I like doing deals. Today we do deals. You don't have to pretend money is dirty. Or a deal memo is too complicated for your sensibility. It's a Jewish science, movie-dealing, like psychoanalysis. Only what's the connection?"

"I don't know."

"Intimacy. They involve intimate exchanges. The point is I was starting to hear things. I was reading things about myself, hearing footsteps. I was the man who walks off his own set, the man who closes down productions. I started getting the feeling that my downfall was being plotted in the major capitals of the world. Volterra's time had come, you know? They weren't even going to extend me the courtesy of a finished disaster. I was wasting away above the line. Let's cordon off the area and watch him die in relative privacy."

"What have you come across out there?"

"Not a whole hell of a lot. First the desert patrol knows what I'm *about.* They don't like me sticking my head in every black tent in the area, asking questions. Second my guide is no help at all. Salim. He sees himself as a Swiss banker. Terrifically discreet and guarded. 'One does not speak of these things.' 'I cannot ask these people such a question.' Then there's Del, the traveling companion. She calls the Arabs rag-heads. Another big help. But there's something going on. These Bedouins talk to Salim, I see something passing between them that doesn't get translated. There's a rest station at a place called Ras en-Naqab. We went in there once on our way back to Aqaba. The place is on a hill and the wind comes out of the desert like a jet exhaust. Del wasn't with us that trip and Salim made right for the toilet, so I go in alone. There's only one person in the place, a white man. At first I figured he was Circassian. He's huddled over his food, eating with his fingers, right hand only, dressed in layers of loose shirts and tunics, bareheaded. I sit down, take a closer look at the guy, say to myself this guy is European. So I address him. I ask some harmless question. He says something to me in Arabic. I keep talking to him, he keeps eating. I went to get Salim that useless bastard to translate. When we got back the man was gone."

"A sighting."

"I think I made a sighting."

"Do Circassians speak Arabic?"

"I asked Salim. Yes. But I still think I made a sighting."

"Are you sure it was Arabic you heard?"

"First you interview me. Then you make an interrogation out of it."

"What do you do now?"

"Brademas gave me a name at the Department of Antiquities. When we first got to Amman I went there. This is a very soft-spoken, very cultured man. Dr. Malik. He's working with a Dutch team that's surveying sites right outside the city. He tried to discourage me. All I could get from him was the general area where the murder took place."

I said, "It stands to reason they'd move on after killing some-one."

"Brademas told me they stayed. They're somewhere in the Rum."

"He didn't tell me that."

"They changed locations but they're still there, he said. Dr. Malik told him they'd been spotted. But he wouldn't tell *me* that. I went to see him again this morning, soon as we arrived. He told me if I really want to learn something about the cult I have to go to Jerusalem. 'You must ask for Vosdanik,' he said."

Volterra liked to show skepticism by tilting his head to cast sidelong glances at the figure opposite him. Now he described his talk at the Department of Antiquities, repeating the aggrieved and disbelieving looks he'd communicated to Dr. Malik.

He was told to go to the old city, the Armenian quarter. He must ask for Vosdanik. This man has three names, four names. Vosdanik is apparently the first name of one of these three or four full names. He is a guide in the old city. This was the absolute limit of Dr. Malik's knowledge.

Frank liked doing accents.

He asked Dr. Malik to give him some names here in Jordan. He didn't want to go to Jerusalem. He didn't want to get involved with another guide. He was told Vosdanik knew about the cult.

He would be easy to find. He was Armenian. He lived in the Armenian quarter. Frank asked for more information on the Wadi Rum. There'd been a murder, after all. More than one in fact. Dr. Malik said, *"It is best we do not speak of these things."*

Volterra let his gesturing hand drop out of the air. The boys brought our food, then stood in the dimness at the end of the room. No one else came in.

"I can't surrender myself to places," Frank said. "I'm always separate. I'm always working at myself. I never understood the lure of fabulous places. Or the idea of losing yourself in a place. The desert down there is stunning at times. Shapes and tones. But I could never be affected by it in a deeply personal way, I could never see it as an aspect of myself or vice versa. I need it for something, I want it as a frame and a background. I can't see myself letting it overwhelm me. I would never give myself up to the place or to any other place. I'm the place. I guess that's the reason. I'm the only place I need."

He wanted to know about my travels. I told him I was a traveler only in the sense that I covered distances. I traveled between places, never in them.

Rowser had sent me out to these jurisdictions to perform various good works, to fill in here, do a review there, restructure some offices, see to sagging morale. It was a season of small promise. Our Iranian control was dead, shot by two men in the street. Our associate for Syria-Iraq was sending cryptic telexes from Cyprus. Kabul was tense. Ankara lacked home heating, families were moving to hotels. Throughout Turkey people could not vote unless they had their fingers dyed. This was to keep them from voting more than once. Our associate for the Emirates woke up to find a corpse in his garden. The Emirates were overbanked. Egypt had religious tensions. Foreign executives in Libya were coming home from the office to find their houses occupied by workers. It was the winter the hostages were taken in Tehran and Rowser put the entire region on duplicate. This meant all records had to be copied and sent to Athens. One of our vice-presidents, visiting Beirut, came out of his hotel to find his car being disassembled by militiamen. I opened an office in North Yemen.

Frank ordered two more beers. We talked about Kathryn. When we finished dinner we wandered around for an hour. Taxis followed us, beeping. We were in a residential area, empty, no one else on foot. A man in uniform came out of the darkness and said something we didn't understand. Another figure appeared twenty yards along the sidewalk, holding an automatic rifle. The first man pointed across the street. We were to continue our walk over there.

"Something tells me we've come upon the palace," Frank said. "The king is at home."

It took two days to get permits for the trip to Jerusalem. When we reached the Jordanian security area, Volterra and our driver took all the documents inside. I leaned against a post under the corrugated roof, watching Del Nearing blow on the lenses of her sunglasses and wipe them in circular motions with a soft cloth.

"There's an Arabic letter called *jim*," she said.

"What does it look like?"

"Don't recall. I gave the language about an hour's study."

"It could be important," I said. "It could tell me everything I need to know."

She looked up, smiling, a slight figure with a finely drawn face, her dark hair short and slicked back. She'd spent the fifty-minute drive ministering to herself, catching up on the precautions travelers take against the environment. The coating of hands. The moistening of face and neck. The delicate release of eye drops from a squat bottle. She went about these tasks apart from them, deep in thought. She gave the impression she was always behind schedule, accustomed to doing things in layers. These moments of sealed-in physical busyness were meant mainly to be spent in reflection.

"I have a disembodied feeling about this whole trip," she said. "I've been floating, like. I didn't know we were going to Jerusalem until we got into the taxi and went to pick you up. I thought we were going to the airport. He claims he told me last night. I don't use drugs anymore. Frank helped me with that. But I am disembodied, regardless. I miss my apartment, my cat. I never thought I'd miss my apartment. That must be where my body is."

Volterra came out.

"Look at her. Those oversized glasses. With her thin face and that short hair. All wrong. She looks like a science-fiction insect."

"Suck a rock, Jojo."

We got on a bus with a group of Baptists from Louisiana and rode across the river to the Israeli compound. Elaborate procedures. Del came out of the booth where women were searched and joined us at passport control, scanning the area.

"Look how they lean on those M-16s. I thought they'd be different from the Arabs and Turks. They're sloppy-looking, aren't they? And they wave those guns around, they don't care who's standing in front of them. I don't know what I expected. Neater people."

"It's going to rain," Frank said. "I want it to rain."

"Why?"

"So you'll take those glasses off."

"I don't know what I expected," she said.

"So we'll get drenched walking in the old city. So you'll catch another cold to match Istanbul. So I'll know the disaster is complete."

We shared an eight-seat taxi with Russian Orthodox nuns. The sun broke through heavy cloud as we neared Jerusalem, half gold on the tawny hills, on the limestone buildings and Ottoman ramparts. Our hotel was north of the old city. Volterra lingered at the desk to make inquiries.

We entered through the Damascus Gate and were caught at once in the polyglot surge. I felt crowded by languages, surprised and jostled as much as by donkeys loaded with produce, by running boys. Soldiers wore yarmulkas, a man lugged an eight-foot cross. Volterra spoke Italian to some people who asked directions. Merchants loaded bolts of scarlet cloth, sacks of potatoes onto wooden carts which boys would use to batter through the crowds. Coptic priests in blue, Ethiopian monks in gray, the White Father in his spotless soutane. Was religion the point or language? Or was it costume? Nuns in white, in black, full habits, somber hoods, flamboyant winglike bonnets. Beggars folded in cloaks, sitting motionless. Radios played, walkie-talkies barked and hissed. The call to prayer was an amplified chant that I could separate from the other sounds only briefly. Then it was part of the tumult and pulse, the single living voice, as though fallen from the sky.

Del was the first to wander off, disappearing down a twisted alley being torn up by workmen. Then Volterra muttered something about the Armenian quarter. We made vague plans to meet at the Western Wall.

I found a café and sat outside to sip Turkish coffee and watch shopkeepers in idle talk. Their windows were full of religious souvenirs, rows of mass-produced objects. I found this presence a bolstering force. All the crippled pilgrims in the Via Dolorosa, the black-hatted Hasidim, the Greek priests, Armenian monks, the men at prayer on patterned carpets in the mosques—these streams of belief made me uneasy. It was all a reproach to my ardent skepticism. It crowded me, it pressured and shoved. So I tended to look with a small ironic measure of appreciation at the trashy objects in the shop windows. The olivewood, glass and plastic. They counteracted to some extent the impact of those larger figures who milled in the streets, coming from worship.

I saw Del talking to an old man leaning on a cane outside a spice stall. He was white-bearded, wearing a knitted cap and sweater, a robe with a black sash, and there was an aura of stillness about him that was a form of beauty. His eyes were soft, a half-dreaming gaze, and in his face, which looked like a desert face, was an age of memory and light. It occurred to me that she was telling him something very much like this. I barely knew her, of course, but it was a thing she would do, I thought. Approach an old man in the street and tell him that she liked his face.

She saw me and came over, making her way past a group whose leader carried a banner with the letter *sigma* on it. Del had propped the sunglasses on her forehead and was peeling a green orange. There was an element of street flash about her, a winsome toughness. She moved like a shambling kid in a school corridor, raggy and sullen. I hadn't seen till now how good-looking she was. The face was proportioned and cool, eyes disregarding, a moody curve to the mouth. She gave me a slice of orange and sat down.

"I don't think he understood me."

"What were you telling him?"

"How nice he looked, standing there. What beautiful eyes. That's what I'll remember. The faces. Even those macho faggots in Turkey. You see incredible faces. How long are we staying here?"

"I leave in the morning. I have an afternoon flight out of Amman. I don't know about you two. You'll have to check the permits."

"Why are we here?"

"I'm sightseeing. You're looking for an Armenian."

"I like that jacket. That jacket's loaded with character."

"It used to be tweed."

"I love old stuff."

"It's been worn down by erosion. You can have it."

"Too big but thanks. Frank says you're lonely."

"Frank and I don't always understand each other. Our friendship depended largely on Kathryn. When he and I were alone together, even then, the subject was Kathryn, the missing link was Kathryn."

"Can't you get laid in Athens?"

"I've developed a preoccupied air. Women think I want to take them to museums."

"I don't like museums. Men always follow me in museums. What is it about places like that? Every time I turn there's a figure watching me."

"I love Frank. It's not that I don't love him. But we don't really live in the same world anymore. I love the times we had. We were in our twenties, learning important things. But it was Kathryn, really, who made the whole thing work."

I was expecting Del to ask if he'd slept with Kathryn. She had a way of looking through one's remarks, waiting for them to end so she could get to what she thought was the point. Her voice didn't quite match the blankish face. It had a sultry little disturbance in it, an early morning scratch. We looked at each other. She asked about lunch instead.

Later we waited for Volterra in a light rain. Men washing at the fountain outside el-Aqsa, arrayed barefoot at the taps. Men swaying at the Wall, beneath the long courses of masonry, moon-scarred limestone with finely chiseled margins, with rock-dwelling plants cascading out of the cracks. We stood near a fence adorned with stylized branch candlesticks. When he showed up finally, jacket collar raised against the chill, he took Del off to one side, where they had a brief unhappy exchange. He seemed to want her to go to the Wall, the section reserved for women. She looked away, her hands deep in the pockets of a nylon parka.

On the way back to the hotel he told me he'd found Vosdanik.

We walked in the dark to a restaurant near the Jaffa Gate. He didn't say why Del wasn't coming with us. It was misty and cold, we were a long time finding the place.

Vosdanik walked in, a small dark man wearing an undersized fedora. He removed the hat and coat, offered us cigarettes, remarked that stuffed pigeon was the specialty here. There was a note of serious business in his manner, a modulated note, softest when he greeted people passing near our table. We drank arak and asked him questions.

He spoke seven languages. His father had walked across the Syrian desert as a boy, a forced march, the Turks, 1916. His brother's business was rubble in Beirut. He told us his life story as a matter of course. He seemed to think we expected it.

Before he was a guide he'd worked as interpreter for a team of archaeologists at a site near the Sea of Galilee. Crews had been excavating for decades. Twenty levels were eventually uncovered, almost four thousand years of settlement. A vast cataloguing of fragments.

"They made temples that will face the east. In Egypt at that time they call the east God's land. *Ta-netjer*. The west is death, the setting sun. You will bury the dead on the west bank. The west is the city of the dead. The east is cockcrow, the rising sun.

This is where you will live, on the east bank. Put the house in the east, put the tomb in the west. Between there will be the river."

He went at the pigeon seriously, rice spilling off his fork. His remarks were well spaced, pauses for effect, for mouthfuls of food, gestures of greeting and good will as people entered.

He was the guide as storyteller. Even incidents from his own life he recounted with a degree of awe, as if he were pointing out the workmanship in a polychrome tile. There was a bump on the bridge of his nose. All his clothes looked shrunken.

At the excavation he first heard of a group, a cult, apparently nameless. An archaeologist spoke of it, a Frenchman named Texier. In the beginning Vosdanik thought the references were to an ancient cult whose members had lived in this region. It was a land of cults and sects and desert monks and stylites. Every settled group produced a scatter of rival cells. From these a man or men broke off, working toward a purer vision.

"Wherever you will find empty land, there are men who try to get closer to God. They will be poor, they will take little food, they will go away from women. They will be Christian monks, they will be Sufis who dress with wool shirts, who repeat the holy words from the Koran, who dance and spin. Visions are real. God is involved with living men. When Mohammed was, there still were men who went away from him. Closer to God, always in their mind to remember God. *Dhikr allah.* There were Sufis in Palestine, Greek monks in the Sinai. Always some men go away."

This man Texier, himself half starved and a little distant, offered clarification, sitting in the evenings under a swaying bulb beneath the excavation roof. A note pad and briar pipe. He was working backward through curves of time, arc after arc of fragments set on the ground around his chair. At intervals he spoke softly in the general direction of Vosdanik, shadowed on a wall ten yards away, beyond the shards, a man unaccustomed to listening.

The cult was not ancient as far as Texier knew. The cult was living. The members had last been seen, a handful of men, in a cliffside village some miles north of Damascus—a Christian settlement where the people at times still spoke Aramaic (or Western Aramaic or Syriac), which happened to be the language of Jesus.

Wait, wait, go slow, we said.

He ate twice as fast as we did, spoke a thousand words to every one of ours. It was his job, telling stories, supplying names and dates, sorting through the layered calamities of his city, the alleys and crypts where profound things had taken place.

It was not one of Vosdanik's seven languages, Aramaic, but he had heard it in the Christmas liturgy. The cult lived in two caves above the village. They were elusive men, rarely seen, except for one of them who occasionally came down into the streets and talked to the children. The language of the streets and schools was Arabic. But this man made efforts to speak Aramaic, amusing the children. Good reason why the others stayed above the town. They were keeping a watch, waiting for someone or something.

"They follow you like a crooked shadow," he said.

After they'd left, the body of a man was found in one of the caves, a villager, his chest full of slashes and puncture wounds, blood everywhere. The cultists were thought at first to be Druze, blondish, some of them blue-eyed—a Muslim sect living in the mountains in the southern part of the country. A murder based on religious differences, it seemed. But arising out of nothing. There'd been no trouble, no provocation. And why were the initials of the victim cut into the blade of the crude iron tool used to kill him?

Vosdanik paused, his sad face hanging in the smoke.

"You will want to hurt your enemy, it is in history to destroy his name. The Egyptians made pottery that the names of their enemies were engraved with sharp reeds. They will smash the bowls, great harm to the enemies. The same harm that if you cut his throat."

None of this was easy for us to follow. Vosdanik was involved in the textures of place, in histories, rituals, dialects, eye and skin color, bearing and stance, endless sets of identifying traits. We leaned forward, straining to hear, to understand.

He ordered more arak. I poured a scant measure of water, watching the arak cloud, a sedimentary stir. His narrative worked back to the dig, the overshadowing background, whispers of Islam, occult rabbinical doctrine, the vast embroidered mist of precepts and dreams. Shining icons, strands of hair from the Prophet's beard. He believed it all.

Slow, we told him. Go slow, give us a chance to get it straight.

He was taken back by the intensity of Volterra's questioning. It was clear he had few answers. He hadn't thought about these things and there was no reason he should have. The cult was just another mystery in the landscape. They were unremarkable to him, these men, considering where he lived, what he knew about the dark places, assassins in cloaks, the dead who walked. He told us of two other cult murders, one we knew about, the Wadi Rum, although the version he'd heard was different in some ways.

He went after the last traces of food with a thoroughness almost cleansed of pleasure and zest. To an Arab at the next table he said something that sounded like "German shepherd." A boy came with arak.

"With sweet words you make them naked," Vosdanik said to us.

"Who?"

"The Arabs. You will be soft with them you get what you want."

He offered us cigarettes. A man with half his face covered by a scarf came out of the toilet, wearing black and carrying a stick. Smoke collected near the ceiling.

"Where are they now?" Frank said.

"I hear nothing."

"Do you think there is one group, two?"

"I hear three murders, I see one pair of blue eyes."

"Were the initials on the knife in Aramaic?"

"This I don't know."

"Is there an Aramaic alphabet, or what?"

Shrugging. "No one can write it anymore. It is only sounds. It traveled in history with the Jews. It was used by itself, it was mixed with other languages. Dog-Aramaic. It was carried by religion and now it fades because of religion, because of Islam,

Arabic. It is religion that carries a language. The river of language is God."

And this.

"The alphabet is male and female. If you will know the correct order of letters, you make a world, you make creation. This is why they will hide the order. If you will know the combinations, you make all life and death."

He lit another cigarette, leaving one in the pack.

"Food for tomorrow," he said. A shy smile.

Tomorrow he would show us an Aramaic inscription on the wall of the Syrian church if we were interested. He would take us to Bethlehem, to Jericho. The columns in el-Aqsa are Crusader columns, he said. Mohammed flew to heaven from the Dome of the Rock.

After he left we stayed behind, drinking and talking, and when we hit the street we had a little trouble finding the way to our hotel.

"Let me get this straight," I said. "There was someone Texier."

"He's not important."

"Slow down. We should have left when Vosdanik left. Always leave with the guide. These alleys are full of religious fanatics."

"The archaeologist. Forget him."

"All right. We're with the cult. Where were they?"

"Somewhere in Syria," Frank said.

"What is a Druze?"

"What were the other words for the language?" he said. "Shit, did I ask about hammers?"

"I thought he spoke Hebrew."

"Who?"

"Jesus."

"He's not important. Forget him, forget what he spoke. I'm trying to concentrate on essentials. Did I ask about the victim's health?"

"He was dead, Frank."

"Before they killed him. Did they choose an imbecile, a cancer victim?"

"His health was not good. This is one of the qualities we associate with death. In all seriousness, where are we? We should have gone out the gate and found a cab."

"I thought the walk would clear our heads."

He started laughing.

"I don't think I'm drunk," I said. "It's the effect of the smoke, that's all, and then coming outside. That was a smoky place."

He thought this was very funny. He stopped walking in order to laugh, doubling up.

"What did he say?"

"Who?" I said.

"I don't know what he said. Vosdanik. Maybe it was the smoke. It was a smoky place."

He was talking and laughing at the same time. He had to lean against a wall to laugh.

"Did you pay him?"

"Damn right I paid him. We haggled. The little bastard."

"How much did you pay him?"

"Never mind. Just tell me what he said."

He crossed his arms on his midsection, bent against the wall laughing. It was a staccato laugh, building on itself, broadening in the end to a breathless gasp, the laughter that marks a pause in the progress of the world, the laughter we hear once in twenty years. I went into an alley to vomit.

Through the night I kept waking up. Scenes from the restaurant, patches of Vosdanik's monologues. His face came back to me as a composed image, movie-lit, bronzed and shaded. The prominent nose, the indentations on either side of the forehead, the crooked fingers lifting a cigarette from the pack of Montanas, the little smile at the end. He seemed a wise and sympathetic figure in this dawn projection, super-lifelike. The third or fourth time I woke up I thought of the dead man's initials cut into the weapon. Old westerns. If one of those bullets has your name on it, Cody, there's not a goldarned thing you can do about it. Spitting in the dust. Montana daybreak. Is this what I wanted to isolate from everything else he'd said, is this what I was driving up out of sleep to tell myself to remember? Initials. It was the only thing he'd said that seemed to mean something. I knew something. There was something at the edge of all this. If I could stay awake and concentrate, if I could think clearly, if I could be sure whether I was awake or asleep, if I could either snap awake completely or fall into deep and peaceful sleep, then I might begin to understand.

I sat with Del Nearing in the back of the long Mercedes, waiting for Volterra. A camel stood near the hotel entrance and the Baptists from Louisiana took turns mounting and dismounting, photographing each other.

"Frank has crazed eyes this morning. It's a look he gets now and then. The blood drains out of his eyes. Deadly."

"Where were you last night?"

"Watching TV."

"You missed the guide, the linguist."

"Not interested."

"We drank too much."

"It's not that," she said. "It's the old disease. The one that science hasn't noticed yet. He's obsessed."

The camel driver posed with a woman named Brenda.

"Why was he annoyed at you yesterday?"

"He has this sentimental idea. I'm part Jewish somewhere back on my mother's side and he expects me to think I'm coming home. I'm an idiot because I don't explore my background, I don't pay more attention to the Jewish ruins. I come mostly from the Midwest. We moved a lot. We lived in a trailer court when I was little. I got into trouble a lot, I ran away two or three times, I went sort of crazy in the Haight. I was way too young to know what was going on. Frank says if it wasn't for the Jewish underpinning I'd be a total Oklahoma drifter. He's stupid about that. I'd be a motorcycle moll, a dancer in a lounge. Everything between the coasts is Oklahoma to him. Big, dusty, lonesome."

"He makes movies there."

"He makes movies. I love his movies. See, on one level he's

fascinated by the pure American thing. The aimlessness, the drifting. That's fascinating to him, it lends itself somehow. Motels, mobile homes, whatever. But he'd dump me in a minute if I'd never mentioned being part Jewish. Now *that's* worthwhile. That's something to respect yourself for. A Jew."

Frank had nothing to say until we were across the river, sitting under the corrugated roof in the Jordanian area, past the gun emplacements, waiting for our original driver to show up.

"Do we have to go to Amman?"

The question was addressed to himself, if anyone. He wore dark glasses and kept biting skin from the edge of his thumb. The driver appeared, in jeans and elevated heels, extending his pack of cigarettes.

Amman is set on seven hills. In Arabic the word for hill or mountain is *jebel*. When we were fifteen minutes outside the city I told the driver to take us to Jebel Amman, where the Inter-Continental is located. I would pick up the suitcase I'd left there and then go with Frank and Del to the airport, where I'd catch my plane to Athens, they'd catch theirs to Aqaba, a thirty-minute flight.

"Do we have to go to Aqaba?" Del said.

Most of their clothes were there, two cameras were there, a tape recorder and other equipment in two suitcases and a canvas bag.

Five minutes later Volterra spoke for the second time.

"I have it all figured out. Once this collapses. Once the entire career goes down the tubes. I know exactly what I'll do for the rest of my life. I've been planning it since the very beginning. Because I've always known. I've known since the beginning, I've been planning since the beginning. Once the dust clears from the last failure. Once they've stopped talking about me in the tones they reserve for the once promising beginners who overextended, who burned out, who miscalculated, who didn't deliver, who ran out of luck. The tone of tepid regret, you know? The knowing tone that says those early successes were obviously accidents anyway. I know where I'll go when this happens, what I'll do." He dropped his hand from the side of his mouth. "I'll open a same-day dry-cleaning service. With the money I haven't pissed away on exploring the world for subjects, I'll go to a quiet place somewhere, one of those well-planned communities with crescent streets and picturesque lampposts, a series of town-house developments although there's no town, they've forgotten the town. A modest place. Elderly couples. Divorced women with anxious kids. Unassuming. My same-day dry-cleaning store will be in the shopping mall along with the boutique, the supermarket, the radio and TV repair, the three-in-one movie theater, the fast-food places, the travel agent, all of it. It's a community where no one knows the names of film directors. People just go to the movies, you know? That's where I'll hide out for the rest of my life. Frank's Same Day Dry Cleaning. The fucking clothes'll come whipping along on these huge fucking conveyors, a thousand pairs of tartan slacks, a thousand tennis dresses, all wrapped in shimmering plastic. You want your tartan slacks, all I do is press a button behind the counter and these serpentine conveyors go into motion, shooting the garment toward the desk in twisty looping figures. Pink sales slips flutter from the moving garments. The plastic rustles, it clings. It clings to everything—clothes, car seats, metal, human flesh. I'm behind the counter, happy to be there. People call me Frank, I call them Mr. Mitchell, Mrs. Green. 'Hi, Mr. Mitchell, think we got that piña colada stain off your tartan slacks.' I live in the back of the shop. I have a hotplate, a little Sony TV, my pornographic magazines, my wheat germ and honey shampoo, the one luxury in my life, because I fear baldness more than death. But there is one person who knows my identity, who has managed to find out. An ex–New Yorker, what else? A film society pervert who recognizes me from old photos in his collection of film journals. Word gets around. People start saying, 'He was famous for ten minutes in the seventies.' 'Who was he?' 'An actor, a gangster, I forget.' They forget. In the end they forget even the erroneous things they've been told about me. How beautiful. It's why I'm there, after all."

At the Inter-Con I found out my flight had been delayed for five or six hours. I went out to the car and stuck my head in the window. He sat with one arm around her, still in his dark glasses, his army surplus jacket, unshaven. Del seemed to be asleep.

"Come to Athens," I said.

"I don't know."

"What other possibilities?"

"I have to think about it. California maybe. Do nothing for a while."

"They know you in California. Come to Athens. I have a spare bedroom."

"I don't know, Jim."

"What about the cult?"

"I have to think about it."

"You're crazy," I said. "Forget it."

He looked straight ahead, his hand curled over her shoulder, and he spoke quietly in a tone that found fault with me for dealing in self-evident things.

"Don't tell me I'm crazy. I fucking know I'm crazy. Tell me I'm a little brave, a little determined. I want to hear someone say I follow things to the end."

When they were gone I went back to the desk, got the map out of my overnight bag and headed out into the city. From the spaces and heights of Jebel Amman it was a long walk down to the crowds around the taxi ranks near the Roman theater. The sun was warm. Men folded their robes under them, climbing into the shared cabs. I went past the columns and walked slowly up to the top of the theater. On the far side two men sat several rows apart, reading newspapers. No one else was here. The stone ran sandy white, curves lengthening in the climb. I sat one row down from the top. Traffic was a remote noise, another city. I felt solitude begin to return, a sense of elements gathering, first things. A long time passed. This theater, open to the city, was at the same time detached from it, a mental space, a park made of nothing but steps. Perfect. My mind was clear. I felt empty, alert. I took out the map and unfolded it. One of the men on the second tier unfolded his newspaper to turn a page. On the reverse side of the map of Jordan was a detailed map of Amman. I looked for a way back to the hotel that would not involve retracing my route. But I found something else. Something came to me. I didn't have to concentrate or direct my thoughts. As if I'd known all along. As if my interrupted sleep of the night before had been a mechanism of clarifying thought. Initials, names, places. In the emptiness of these moments, in the reason and ease of these sweeping curves, I realized I'd been approaching this point all morning long. I folded the map and put it back in my jacket pocket. One of the men, the higher of the two, got to his feet and walked slowly down the steps. Soft noise from the distant city.

Jebel Amman / James Axton.

7

I MET HER in a café in Kolonaki Square, a place where all
Athenians who feel they are worth seeing eventually show up to
be seen, where the women have pouty ultraviolet mouths, the
uniform is leather, the chains are gold, the futuristic object parked
at the corner is a De Tomaso Pantera, the command car of idle
fantasy, and the slender bearded men shift in their chairs, behind
dark glasses, wearing sweaters draped over their shoulders.

Ann, approaching, tilted her head to catch my eye. The warm
smile held an edge of reproof.

"Where have you been? Said she accusingly."

"Making the rounds. The Gulf and points north. Many wonders."

"You might have mentioned it, you beast."

"It was chaos, honest. I had barely enough time to arrange
visas."

"You wanted us to worry," she said.

"Ridiculous."

"You wanted us to think you'd simply run off, run away, given
it all up, given us up."

"Did you call my secretary?"

"Charlie did."

"Then you knew."

"Eventually," she said, using the word to indicate I was taking this more seriously than I was supposed to.

The main cafés and their auxiliaries were crowded into a noisy slanted space that included a small park, traffic melees, three or four kiosks layered and seamed in bright magazines. The first mild day after a grim spell. The canopies were furled to let in light, the tables extended across the sidewalks. Celebration and release. An old woman turned the crank of a barrel organ while her husband moved among the tables collecting coins. People had the happy air of survivors eager to talk of their common ordeal. Waiters moved sideways. The lottery man stood at the edge of things, bearing his notched stave.

"How nice to be back," I said. "I want to do nothing, go nowhere. A sunny winter. That's what I want. Orange trees on every street. Women in self-important boots."

"Wait until the wind starts blowing. You're high enough on Lycabettus to get the full effect."

"I want to pass time. Sit in places like this, talk about nothing."

"I have to confess I find it hard to pass time in the heart of the city. I need a seascape or vista."

"I could easily fall into this," I said. "Laze my way through life. Coffee here, wine there. You can channel significant things into the commonplace. Or you can avoid them completely."

"I wouldn't have thought you were a café wastrel."

"We all are. It's just a matter of realizing it. I'm preparing myself for the bleak years ahead. A lonely sad expatriate. Wifeless. Stumbling through seedy cafés. A friend of mine imagined a similar fate only yesterday. It involved dry cleaning. What does it all mean?"

"I don't know. Self-depreciation is a language I don't think I understand. It's so often a form of ego, isn't it, a form of aggression, a wanting to be noticed even for one's flaws. I don't know these modern languages. In fact I may be the person in your fantasy. The sad expatriate. The real one."

Men stood before the kiosks reading displays of the day's papers. The waiter opened a half bottle of wine. I smiled at Ann, turning my head, making it a look of measurement, evaluation. A look of the left eye.

"Is it possible, love affairs as functions of geography?"

She looked back, showing amused interest.

"Possibly you want to deepen the experience of a place. A place you know you will have to leave some day, most likely not by choice."

"That hadn't occurred to me," she said. "Adulterous sex as a function of geography. Do I have such obscure motives?"

"The loss of Kenya, the loss of Cyprus. You want to keep something for yourself that isn't a tribal mask or figurine. A private Cyprus, a meditation. How does a woman make these places hers as well as her husband's when after all it's his job that determines where they go, and when they go, and when they leave."

"A function of memory. I might buy that. Some women have a way of planning their memories."

"Isn't there a connection? Geography and memory?"

"You're drifting away from me."

"You're a plain girl from a mill town. I know."

"Of course there is sheer sense pleasure. Are we allowed to take that into account? Excitement."

"That's another subject. I don't find that subject agreeable."

"You want to maintain a certain decorum."

"A certain level. I don't want to succumb to jealousy. A man has jealous thoughts about a woman he's never loved, a woman who's simply a friend. He doesn't want to hear about sense pleasures. He's interested in her affairs as themes, motifs in her life."

"Just the conversation," she said, "for Kolonaki Square."

"You don't have to hate a man to enjoy his bad luck. True? And you don't have to love a woman to feel possessive toward her or resentful of her affairs."

"I don't know how serious you are. Are you serious?"

"Of course I'm serious."

"Well how nice. I think."

"I hadn't thought of it as nice or not nice."

"Or do I make a mistake in regarding myself as specially favored?"

"Probably you make a mistake. I have a history of pathological envy."

She laughed.

"You have too much time to think, James. You're alone too much, aren't you?"

"And you?"

"Wherever we've been I've managed to find things to do. Not much but enough. English lessons in the beginning. Of course I was a full-time mother and housekeeper for quite a few years. I do occasional work for the British Council here. Translation mainly. It does make a difference. I need to feel that I'm building little blocks of time. That's why the café life will never claim me."

"Have you ever thought being alone might be in some way a fullness, a completion?"

"No, absolutely."

"I believe deeply in the idea of two. Two people. It's the only sanity. The only richness."

"Of course."

"Yesterday I was in Amman, sitting in the Roman theater, and I had an odd sensation. I don't know if I can describe it but I think I perceived solitude as a collection of things rather than an absence of things. Being alone has components. I felt I was being put together out of these nameless things. This was new to me. Of course I'd been traveling, running around. This was the first quiet moment I'd had. Maybe that's all it was. But I felt I was being put together. I was alone and absolutely myself."

"Terrifying. Not that I know what you're talking about," she said.

A young man fell into the chair next to Ann's, crossed his legs, folded his arms and eased into the slouch of a ten-hour wait, the slouch of cancelled flights, half-sleep in vast rooms.

This was Peter, her son, a pointed face, curly reddish hair, wire-frame specs. He wore a checked sport coat that was a couple of sizes too large, a country gentleman's outfit with pockets for shotgun shells or corn cobs to toss to the pigs. He wanted to see a menu.

"In modern travel there are no artists—only critics," he told me.

"You're tired," Ann said.

"On the one hand there's nothing new to *make* of all this. On the other there's so much to dismiss as overrated or plain rotten. My critical sense has been given a confident charge these past weeks. It does something for a person's self-esteem when he is able to judge entire land masses as second-rate."

The Far East, from which direction Peter had come, put him in a particular mood of censure. There was a great deal of energy in his observations and it seemed to hang above the fallen body like a posthumous glow.

"Incidentally the phone rang as I was walking out the door. Athens is evidently a place where you pick up a ringing phone and it keeps ringing."

I asked him what kind of mathematics he did. He couldn't decide whether or not to tell me. He did mention that at Berkeley he was in a favorable position to study two of the esoteric wonders of our time, subjects only an adept might begin to penetrate. Pure mathematics and the state of California. There were no analogies from the real world that might help him explain either of these. He began to disappear beneath the table.

"Who was it?" she said.

"What."

"Who was on the telephone?"

"Well when I realized it wouldn't stop ringing I put it down. But he rang back. Greek fellow. Wrong number."

She tilted the wine bottle to read the label.

"It's a way of life, wrong numbers," I said. "Telephones constantly change hands. People buy them, inherit them. I learn more Greek talking to people who've dialed the wrong number—"

Finally Charles showed up, returning us briefly to our careless pace. He talked about recent arrivals and departures, local politics, Swahili curses and obscenities, growling these last into the hand that clutched his cigarette. The single oddness he conveyed, a man staying strong as he wears away, an appearance of robust corrosion, was always more apparent when I hadn't seen him for a time.

"Your son won't tell me what sort of mathematics he does. If you explain that I used to do technical writing now and then, he may consider speaking to me."

"Technical writing. He deals in truth and beauty. That's the wrong thing to say, James. Technical writing."

"I only mean I'm familiar with some of the nomenclature. I may be able to distinguish one discipline from another."

"He's not impressed," Charles said. "Look at him."

"Unimpressed. What can I do to prove myself? Give me a test."

Ann was in conversation with someone at the next table. We were all passing time.

"There is no test," Charles said. "The only test is mathematics. You've got to know the secrets. Look at him. He speaks to no one. He says he's not able to talk about it. There are certain things he can't discuss with his *professors*. It's too bloody rarefied. It makes no sense if you don't know the secrets, the codes. It means nothing, says nothing, refers to nothing, is in fact absolutely useless."

Peter Maitland ate his lunch.

"It doesn't bear on human experience, human progress, ordinary human language," Charles said. "It must be a form of zoology. It's a branch of zoology. The great ape branch. That's why men are teaching apes to communicate. So we can discuss mathematics with them." They'd been through this before. "It's interesting in itself, you see. It refers to itself and only itself. It's the pure exercise of the mind. It's Rosicrucianism, druids in hoods. The formal balances, that's what counts. The patterns, the structures. It's the inner consistencies we have to search for. The symmetries, the harmonies, the mysteries, the whisperies. Good Christ, Axton, you can't expect the man to talk about these things."

Peter said to his mother across a forkful of spinach pie, "Is he doing one of his comic bits, do you think? Will he juggle oranges next?"

She wasn't listening.

"How happy he is to be wrong," Peter said. "It's his special provenance. He loves to return to it. Of course he knows how deeply he misconstrues. This is part of the joy of the thing. The whole point is to pretend not to know. As some people protect their inexperience or fear, this man protects his knowledge of the true situation. It's a way of spreading guilt. His innocence, other people's guilt. There's a proportional relation. This is the theme of his life, pretending not to know. Keeps him going, absolutely."

He was addressing himself to me. Charles gazed past the traffic as though none of this had anything to do with him or was at worst an extension of the discourse on mathematics.

"I look forward to their retirement. They want to live in California, you know. We'll see each other on American holidays. Charlie will drink Miller Lite and watch the Super Bowl. We'll have cranberry sauce on Thanksgiving. My dear mother will finally get her tour of movie stars' homes. All the stars she's ever heard of are long dead, of course, whether she knows it or not. While she was in the jungles, the marshes and the hill stations, all the neon lights went out, one by one."

They were feeling happy again. Peter took a sip of his mother's wine, then directed another look my way, a different one, quizzical, mock angry.

"Who are you anyway," he said, "that I should tell you our secrets?"

While we laughed I wondered if I would ever see these two people in quite the same way. Peter had altered them not only by what he'd said but by a simple physical extension of the local figure they made. He was the apex, the revelation of full effect. He knew his mother's affairs, his father's weaknesses, and I felt in a sense he'd stolen these things from me. I wanted to forget him, the jut of his face, its curious outdatedness, the voice with its self-referring note of complaint. I was afraid my romance with Ann Maitland would end, my word-romance, the pleasant distant speculative longing.

Ann and Peter decided to go for a walk. We watched them cross to the small park, where they waited for a break in traffic.

"There they go," Charles said. "The twenty-four hours of my life. A.M. and P.M."

"Has he ever told you what he's doing?"

"In mathematics? Something awesome, I gather. He expects to be burnt out by the time he's twenty-five. We'll see how he adapts to that."

There was an antique air of celibacy about Peter. It had the stubborn force of some vow a boy might make when he is fourteen, high-minded, his life suddenly come to a powerful hesitancy —a pledge which the man in his scrupulous carved space might well decide to honor. I had one of my sentimental thoughts. He would meet a woman one day soon and be immediately transformed. The apparatus of complaint would fall away. His cleverness would be shamed by the power of love.

My secretary, Mrs. Helen, had glazed yellow hair and the overpolite manner of someone who wishes the atmosphere was a little less casual. A delicate scent of dusting powder hung about her comings and goings. She liked to fuss over tea and Greek verbs, which she was helping me with, and had a fondness for anything British, near British or aspiring to British.

She thought Owen Brademas was one of these. He'd been in the office earlier looking for me and although she'd invited him to wait he said he had some things to do and would return.

I read the telexes and made check marks in the appropriate boxes on several option memos. Mrs. Helen described her infant grandson's tiny hands. She called me Mr. Oxtone.

She was versed in the total range of social codes and usages. She advised me on the correct replies in Greek to everyday greetings or to inquiries about my health and she suggested phrases I might utter to someone celebrating his name day, someone else who was ill. On food and drink she was firm, insisting there was a proper order in which I might consume the coffee, the water and the crystal of rich preserves I was likely to be offered in someone's home. There was even a correct place to set the spoon once I'd finished using it.

She practiced a demon neatness around the office. She was twice divorced, once widowed, and referred to these separate events with roughly equal good humor.

When Owen showed up I saw why she thought he might be British or might at least aspire to that station. He wore a wide-brimmed velour hat, a wool scarf looped twice around the neck and trailed over one shoulder, a belted corduroy jacket, worn shiny, with elbow patches and leather buttons. He resembled, if not a Briton per se, then a British actor working down to the level of his character, a jaded expatriate in a nameless country.

"Just the man I want to see."

"Couldn't pass through town without saying hello, James."

"I need to have a theory confirmed."

We went to an *ouzerí* nearby, an old crowded smoky room with a high ceiling and posters on the columns and walls advertising English tea biscuits and Scotch whiskey. We drank and talked for three hours.

"Where have you been?"

"I stayed on the island for a time. Then I traveled in the Peloponnese. Took buses, walked, caught colds."

"Where exactly?"

"The southern Peloponnese. The middle tit."

"The Mani."

"Do you know it?"

"Only by reputation," I said. "What are you doing in Athens?"

"I want to take another look at the epigraphic collection in the National Museum. A place that interests me. It's a library of stones in effect. A huge room with shelves down both long walls, shelves down the middle, four levels high."

"Shelves full of stones."

"Many hundreds of stones, numbered. Parts of columns, walls, tablets, memorial reliefs. All inscribed, of course. A few letters in some cases are all that remain. Others with words, longer fragments. The Greeks made an art of the alphabet. They gave their letters a symmetry and a sense that something final had been made out of the stick figures of various early forms. Modern. The stones come in many sizes and shapes. No one is ever there. The caretaker follows me at a tactful distance. There is a table and a lamp. You take a stone from the shelf, put it on the table, then sit down and read what is inscribed, study the shapes."

He smiled, tipping his chair back against a column. I felt this was the picture he wanted to leave with me. A man in a room full of stones, reading.

"I went to Jerusalem with Volterra," I said.

"Jerusalem."

"Did you know that?"

"No, I didn't."

"I came back with some questions for you."

"Fine," he said. "Do my best."

"They don't concern the trip. They concern what I think I learned there, what I heard."

"This is the theory you want me to confirm."

"That's right."

"Fine," he said.

"First the old man on the island."

"The murder."

"The mentally deficient old man. His body wasn't found in the village where he lived. It was found in another village on another part of the island."

"This is correct."

"Do you happen to know the old man's name? I don't."

"He was called Michaeli. I kept hearing the name all that week."

"What was his last name?"

We were looking at each other. His face showed a melancholy easement, a deliverance almost. The noise of conversation grew around us.

"His full name was Michaelis Kalliambetsos."

"We both know the name of the village," I said. "Mikro Kamini."

"This is correct."

"What does all this mean?"

"I wouldn't look for meaning, James."

"They found a man whose initials matched the first letter of each word in a particular place-name. They either led him to this place or waited for him to wander there on his own. Then they killed him."

"Yes. This seems to be what happened."

"Why?"

"The letters matched."

"That's no answer."

"I wouldn't look for answers," he said.

"What would you look for, Owen? You said once you were trying to understand how their minds work. Pattern, order, some sort of unifying light. Is this what we're supposed to come away with?"

He stared up at the unused loft, still tipped in his chair, holding the whiskey glass against his chest.

"What about the other island?" I said. "And there was the woman in the Wadi Rum."

"I don't know the details of these crimes. Hammers. This is all I know."

"There was a murder in a Christian village in Syria. Some men lived in caves nearby. One of them tried to speak Aramaic. The initials of the victim were cut into the knife they used to slash him to death. Do you know anything about this?"

"I don't know the victim's name but I think I can tell you that his first and last names began with the same letter, and it was an *M*."

"How do you know this?"

"The village is called Malula. It lies below vast protrusions of bedrock. I was there thirty years ago. There are inscriptions in the caves."

"You've been keeping up to date. Been talking to them, haven't you? What else do you know?"

"James, why attack me? Don't you know helplessness when you see it? Look at the man who's long since given up on himself. The man who hands himself over to the nearest mob. For what, I'm not certain."

"Someone has to show an anger."

"Consider that you've done the job. What else do I know about the cult? Basically what you know."

"Do we assume these initials on the knife were in Aramaic?

The cult seems to be intent on using the local language. I gather no one writes Aramaic these days."

"I'm sure they used whatever older script they knew about or were able to find. The Aramaic *M* of eight hundred B.C. was a jagged letter, a forked lightning bolt, say. By the fourth century it had resolved itself into a graceful curve, bringing to mind the Arabic form, although this was still a long way off. Whatever version they engraved on the weapon, it was an *M* or double *M*."

"Why did they use a knife, not a hammer?"

"A different unit or group. Possibly the weapon is irrelevant. They use what they can find. I don't know."

"No one has ever mentioned victims' initials on the hammers that were found."

"A different group, different practices."

A silence. I kept waiting for him to say something about my discovery. I'd been elated, after all, when the notion came to me in that Roman theater of some alphabetic link between the victim's name and the place where he or she was killed. A terrible elation. A knowledge bounded by emptiness and fear. What did I expect, congratulations?

I told Owen about Vosdanik, his references to holy men, myth and history; to the ancient custom of scratching an enemy's name on a piece of pottery, then smashing it; to the excavation where he'd first heard of the cult; to religious visions and the language Jesus spoke.

"Nothing applies," Owen said.

He knew about the vast excavation near the Sea of Galilee. It was at Megiddo, he said, which is thought to have been the biblical Armageddon. Allusive, suggestive. (*I am alpha and omega.*) Almost everything Vosdanik had said, almost any referential clue you might follow to the cult's origin or purpose would seem to signify something, to have a sense, a content. Owen dismissed it all. They weren't repeating ancient customs, they weren't influenced by the symbolism of holy books or barren places, they weren't making a plea to Egyptian or Minoan gods, or a sacrifice, or a gesture to prevent catastrophe.

But they weren't the products of their own reveries either, the mass murderers we've come to know so well, the mass communicators, working outward from some private screen, conscious of an audience they might agreeably excite.

"We thought we knew this setting. The mass killer in his furnished room, in his century, feeding Gaines-burgers to a German shepherd. The news is full of settings, isn't it, James? You said it yourself one night. Men firing from highway overpasses, attic rooms. Unconnected to the earth. By which I think you meant nonpolitical in the broad sense. Murders that drift away from us. What waste."

We know those gaunt families whose night scoutings remind us so much of our childhood games. We know the stocking strangler, the gunman with sleepy eyes, the killer of women, the killer of vagrant old men, the killer of blacks, the sniper, the slasher in tight leather, the rooftop sodomist who hurls children into the narrow alley below. These things are in the literature, along with the screams of victims in some cases, which their murderers have thought instructive to put on tape.

Here, he said, we have a set of crimes that take us beyond all this. There is a different signature here, a deeper and austere calculation. The murders are so striking in design that we tend to overlook the physical act itself, the repeated pounding and gouging of a claw hammer, the blood mess washing out. We barely consider the victims except as elements in the pattern.

There is nothing in the literature, there is nothing in the folklore. And what a remarkable use for their humane impulses these cultists have found. Dispatching the feeble-minded outcast, the soon-to-die-anyway. Or is their choice of victims meant to be a statement that these acts are committed outside the accepted social structure, outside the easeful routines we ourselves inhabit, and should be paid scant mind. What has been lost? Think of it as an experiment in what the solitary mind does with its honed devices.

But this isn't human nature as we might study it in some prowling boy found living alone in the jungle. The cult is made up of people who were educated at some point in their lives. They read, they converse with each other. They're not totally cut off, are they?

So we talked, so we argued, taking roles, discarding them, the social theorist, the interrogator, the criminologist.

He reset his chair squarely on the floor as though to demonstrate something (I'm imagining this), demonstrate what it was we were trying to do in all this talk, set a premise for the act, put it at some fixed level with regard to the earth. But the next thing he said came out of nowhere or out of the waveforms of another occasion. Past moments had a way of surfacing in his face, in delayed recognitions, and he simply entered the spoken thought.

"I've always believed I could see things other people couldn't. Elements falling into place. A design. A shape in the chaos of things. I suppose I find these moments precious and reassuring because they take place outside me, outside the silent grid, because they suggest an outer state that works somewhat the way my mind does but without the relentlessness, the predeterminative quality. I feel I'm safe from myself as long as there's an accidental pattern to observe in the physical world."

I asked him whether he had been feeling this need for a very long time, the need to be safe from himself. The question surprised him. He seemed to believe everyone felt it, all the time. When he was a boy, he said, the safe place was church, by a river, among cottonwoods, in the shade of the long afternoons. The choir loft extended across the back wall, the pews were narrow and hard. The minister gestured, sang and orated in the open promotional manner of a civic leader, sweat-stained and pink, a large man with white hair, booming by the river. Light fell across the pews with the mysterious softness of some remembered blessing, some serious happy glimpse of another world. It was a *memory* of light, a memory you could see in the present moment, feel in the warmth on your hands, it was light too dense to be an immediate account of things, it carried history in it, it was light filtered through dusty time. Christ Jesus was the double-edged name, half militant, half loving, that made people feel so good. The minister's wife talked to him often, a narrow woman with freckled hands.

When things went bad and they moved to the tallgrass prairie, his parents joined a pentecostal church. There was nothing safe about this church. It was old, plain, set in the middle of nowhere, it leaked in wet weather, let in everything but light. A congregation of poor people and most of them spoke in tongues. This was an awesome thing to see and hear. His father fell away to some distant place, his mother clapped and wept. People's voices variously hummed and racketed, a hobbling chant, a search for melody and breath, bodies rising, attempts to heal a brokenness. Closed eyes, nodding heads. Standers and kneelers. The inside-outness of this sound, the tumbling out of found words, the arms raised, the tremble. What a strangeness to the boy in his lonely wanting, his need for safety and twice-seen light.

"Did you speak also?" I said.

His eyes in their familiar startledness, their soft awe, grew attentive now, as though he'd stopped to analyze what he was feeling and what it meant. No, he hadn't spoken. He'd never spoken. He didn't know the experience. Not that it was an experience confined to some narrow category, the rural poor, the dispossessed. Many kinds of people knew the experience. Dallas executives spoke in tongues in gospel meetings in the shimmering tinfoil Hyatt. Catholics knew the experience, and middle-class blacks of the charismatic renewal, and fellowships of Christian dentists. Imagine their surprise, these tax-paying people, he said, these veterans of patio barbecues, when they learned they were carriers of ecstasy.

But there was no reason it had to be carried out in a religious context. It was a neutral experience. You learn it, he said, or fail to learn it. It is learned behavior, fabricated speech, meaningless speech. It is a life focus for depressed people, according to the clinical psychologists.

He measured what he was saying like a man determined to be objective, someone utterly convinced of the soundness of a proposition but wondering in a distant way (or trying to remember) whether anything has been left out.

"What is left, Owen?"

"Ah. I ask myself."

"Where are you staying?"

"Colleagues have given me a room at the American School. Do you know it?"

"I live up the street."

"Then we'll see each other again. Good. I'll be here a week. Then I leave for Bombay, by freighter."

"So India is next."

"India."

"You told us once."

"India."

"Sanskrit."

"Sanskrit, Pali, Tamil, Oriya, Bengali, Telugu. It's crazy, James. Rock edicts in ancient languages. I'll see what I can before the money runs out or the rains come. When do the rains come?"

"Another thing you told us, on one of those island nights. They're on the mainland. They're in the Peloponnese."

"A supposition."

"On some level you want other people involved in this, don't you? I'm not sure you're even conscious of it but you don't want to be alone in this. With Kathryn there was no chance—she was firm about keeping a distance. In my case there was only a token interest, conversation for its own sake. But with Volterra you found a willing listener, a willing participant in a sense. He showed no reluctance, no scruples about what they did. This is a man whose interest in things can be almost deadly. He wanted to know more, he wanted to *find them*. So you pointed him in a certain direction. I'm not sure it was the best or simplest direction. I suspect you wanted to keep the local group to yourself. You didn't exactly mislead Frank. You told him the truth, the partial truth. You sent him after a second or third group, whatever the correct number. What is the correct number?"

"Most likely three. No more than four."

"One is in Greece."

"You're supposing," he said.

"One is in Jordan. One was in Syria—I don't know how long ago. Vosdanik mentioned Syria, he mentioned Jordan, he also told us about a cult murder in northern Iran. But it wasn't clear how many groups he was talking about."

"Forget it," Owen said.

"That's what I told Frank. Forget it."

They are engaged in a painstaking denial. We can see them as people intent on ritualizing a denial of our elemental nature. To eat, to expel waste, to sense things, to survive. To do what is necessary, to satisfy what is animal in us, to be organic, meat-eating, all blood-sense and digestion.

Why would a denial of these things have to end in murder?

We know we will die. This is our saving grace in a sense. No animal knows this but us. It is one of the things that sets us apart. It is our special sadness, this knowledge, and therefore a richness, a sanctification. The final denial of our base reality, in this schematic, is to produce a death. Here is the stark drama of our separateness. A needless death. A death by system, by machine-intellect.

So we talked, so we argued, the anthropologist, the storyteller, the mad logician. Strange that when we saw each other again it would not be that week, in Athens, with only half a city block between us. Maybe all the talking had brought us closer to an understanding, a complicity, than we wanted to be.

In the light of a lowering sky the city is immediate and sculptured. None of summer's white palls, its failures of distance and perspective. There are shadow-angles, highlighted surfaces, areas of grayish arcs and washes. Laundry blows on rooftops and balconies. Against an urgent sky, with dull thunder pounding over the gulf, this washwork streaming in the wind can be an emblematic and touching thing. Always the laundry, always the lone old woman in black who keeps to a corner of the elevator, the bent woman in endless mourning. She disturbs the composure of the modern building with its intercom and carpeted lobby, its marble veneer.

Some nights the wind never stops, beginning in a clean shrill pitch that broadens and deepens to a careless and suspenseful force, rattling shutters, knocking things off the balconies, creating a pause in one's mind, a waiting-for-the-full-force-to-hit. Inside

the apartment, closet doors swing open, creak shut. The next day
it's there again, a clatter in the alleys.

A single cloud, low-lying, serpentine, clings to the long ridge
of Hymettus. The mountain seems to collect weather, to give it
a structure, an aspect beyond the physical, weather's menace, say,
or the inner light of things. The sun and moon rise behind the
mountain and in the last moments of certain days a lovely dying
appears in the heights, a delivering into violet, burnt rose. The
cloud is there now, a shaped thing, dense and white, concealing
the radar that faces east.

Girls wear toggle coats. In heavy rain there is flooding, people
die. A certain kind of old man is seen in a black beret, hands
folded behind him as he walks.

Charles Maitland paid a visit, making a number of sound effects
as he got out of his rubberized slicker. He walked to an armchair
and sat down.

"Time for my midnight cup of cocoa."

It was seven o'clock and he wanted a beer.

"Where are your rugs?" he said.

"I don't have any."

"Everyone in the area has rugs. We all have rugs. It's what we
do, James. Buy rugs."

"I'm not interested in rugs. I'm not a rug person, as the Bordens would say."

"I was over there yesterday. They have some Turkomans and
Baluchis, fresh from customs. Very nice indeed."

"Means nothing to me."

"Weaving districts are becoming inaccessible. Whole countries
in fact. It's almost too late to go to the source. It is too late in many
cases. They seem to go together, carpet-weaving and political
instability."

We thought about this.

"Or martial law and pregnant women," I said.

"Yes," he said slowly, looking at me. "Or gooey desserts and
queues for petrol."

"Plastic sandals and public beheadings."

"Pious concern for the future of the Bedouins. What does that
go with?"

He sat forward now, turning the pages of a magazine on the coffee table. A sound of rain on the terrace rail.

"Who is it, do you think?" I said. "Is it the Greek? Eliades?"

He looked at me sharply.

"Just a guess," I said. "I noticed them at dinner that night."

"You noticed nothing. She would never give anyone cause to notice. Whatever she's doing, I promise you it's not being noticed."

"I know I shouldn't be bringing it up. I've no right. But it's been hanging in the air. Even your son makes reference. I don't want us to have to adopt a cryptic language or a way of avoiding each other's eyes."

"What Greek?" he said.

"Eliades. The night David and Lindsay took their famous swim. Intense man, black beard."

"Who was he with?"

"The German. There was a German. He was there to meet someone who never showed up. Someone David knows. Refrigeration systems."

"You saw nothing. I could never believe she gave anyone cause to notice."

"It's not what I saw. It's what I heard. She spoke to him in Greek."

I waited for him to tell me how stupid it was to believe this meant something. I felt stupid, saying it. But the sound of her voice, the way it fell, the way it became a sharing, a trust, drawing them away from the rest of us, the way it shaded toward a murmur—the moment haunted me, I think.

Charles didn't tell me I was stupid. He sat quietly turning the pages, possibly thinking back to that night, trying to recollect. There were so many dinners, friends, transients, so many names and accents. I could see him try to construct a summer night around that single image, Lindsay standing on the beach, in half light, laughing. He couldn't connect it. One more sadness at the middle of things.

"I went clean off the rails in Port Harcourt. She left me, you know."

"I know."

"There was no one else. Just left."

"She was lonely. What do you expect?"

"The Greek," he said, like a name mislaid. "Was it in Tunis I met him? Did we see each other later at the airport, come back to Athens together? I took him home for a drink. We all sat around and talked. An acceptable scenario, wouldn't you say? I didn't see him again until the night you describe."

We went to a movie together, went to dinner, saw a man so fat he had to move sideways down a flight of steps. The wind kept me up that night until two or three, a steady noise, a rustling in the walls.

When I walked into the lobby the next evening Niko was at the desk with his coffee cup and newspaper. His small daughter was in his lap and he had to keep shifting her to read the paper.

Cold.

Cold, I said.

Rain.

Small rain.

I talked to the girl briefly, waiting for the elevator to descend. I said she had two shoes. One, two. I said her eyes were brown, her hair was brown. She knocked the empty coffee cup into the saucer. The concierge's wife came out, a broad woman in house slippers.

Cold.

Cold.

Very cold.

Later my father called.

"What time is it there?" he said.

We talked about the time, the weather. He'd received a letter from Tap and a card from Kathryn. Printed at the bottom of the card, he said, was the following sentence: *No trees were destroyed to make this card.* This annoyed him. Typical Kathryn, he said. Most of his anger came from TV. All that violence, crime, political cowardice, government deception, all that appeasement, that official faintheartedness. It rankled, it curled him into a furious ball, a fetus of pure rage. The six o'clock news, the seven o'clock news, the eleven o'clock news. He sat there collecting it, doubled up with his tapioca pudding. The TV set was a rage-making machine, working at him all the time, giving him direction and scope, enlarging him in a sense, filling him with a world rage, a great stalking soreness and rancor.

"Do they have exact-change lanes?" he shouted out to me. "What about goat cheese, Murph wants to know. In case we might visit, which I seriously doubt."

When the violet light seeps into Hymettus, when the sky suddenly fills with birds, tall wavering spiral columns, I sometimes want to turn away. These birdforms mingle, flash, soar, change color light to dark, revolve and shimmer, silk scarves turning in the wind. Bands of light pour out of cloud massifs. The mountain is a glowing coal. How is it the city keeps on functioning, buses plowing through the dusk, while these forces converge in the air, natural radiances and laws, this coded flight of birds, a winter's day? (Kathryn would know what kind of birds they are.) Sometimes I think I'm the only one who sees it. Sometimes, too, I go back to whatever I was doing, to my magazine, my English-Greek vocabulary. I come in off the terrace and sit with my back to the sliding door.

You don't allow yourself the full pleasure of things.

A white-armed traffic cop stands in the dark, gesturing, beckoning to the gathered shapes. I hear the cadenced wail of an ambulance stuck in traffic. How hard it is to find the lyrical mode we've devised to accompany our cities to their nostalgic doom. An evolution of seeing. The sensibility that enables us to see a ruined beauty in these places can't easily be adapted to Athens, where the surface of things is mostly new, where the ruin is differently managed, the demise indistinguishable from the literal building-up and building-out. What happens when a city can't fade longingly toward its end, can't be abandoned piece by piece to its damaged truth, its layered ages of brick and iron? When it contains only the tension and paralysis of the superficial new? Paralysis. This is what the city teaches us to fear.

The ambulance stands fast, wailing in the night. The kiosks are lighted now.

8

WE STOOD by the side of the road, pissing in the wind. A hunter in a camouflage jacket came up out of the woods, called a greeting. Steam drifted up from the riverbed.

"Where do we go next?"

"We cross this range, we eat lunch, then we drive south."

"Good," he said.

"You like that idea."

"As long as we drive. I want to keep driving. I like the driving."

The mountains here contained a sense of time, geologic time. Rounded, colorless, unwooded. They lay in embryo, a process unfolding, or a shriveled dying perhaps. They had the look of naked events. But what else? It took me awhile to understand in what precise way these pale masses, southwest of Argos, seemed so strange and irreducible, in what way they worked a mental labor in me, forcing me to shift my eyes time and again, keep to the wheel, look to the road. They were mountains as semantic rudiments, barest definitions of themselves.

"Maybe it'll be warmer down there."

"How far down?"

"All the way," I said. "Where Europe ends."

"I don't mind the cold."

Tap had nothing to say about the landscape. He seemed interested in what we saw, even engrossed at times, but said nothing,
looked out the window, tramped the hills. Eventually I did the
same, talking about anything but what was out there. We let the
features gather, the low skies and mists, the hilltops edged with
miles of old walls, fallen battlements, that particular brooding
woe of the Peloponnese. It hovers almost everywhere, war memory, a heaviness and death. Frankish castles, Turkish fortresses,
ruined medieval towns, the gateways and vaulted cisterns, the
massive limestone walls, the shaft graves, the empty churches
with their faded All-Creator floating in the dome, the curved
Lord, the non-Euclidean, and the votive lamps below, the walnut
throne, the icons in the side galleries, Byzantine blood and gold.
All we did was climb, drive and climb. For three days the weather
was overcast and cold. We climbed the rubble trails, the goat and
donkey paths, the tunnel stairways, the rutted spiral tracks to
upper towns, we climbed the Gothic towers, the broad ramps of
Mycenaean palace mounds.

"When I'm swimming, Dad."

"Yes."

"And I put my head under the water."

"Yes."

"How come the water doesn't rush into my ears and nose and
fill my whole body, sending me to the bottom, where I'm crushed
by the pressure?"

South. The plains and orchards. Bare poplars in the distance,
a combed silk shimmer. This wasn't a bad road. Others unsur-
faced, some half washed off the edge of mountains, or rock-
scattered, or ending in a pile of gravel, machines scaled with gray
mud.

"That's it," he said. "That's the question. I'm finished."

Now, ahead, high above us, the hammered sheet, the broad
snowy summit of Taygetus. This is the range that thrusts down
through the Mani, the middle peninsula of the southern Peloponnese, the middle tit, Owen had called it, all mountain and wild
coast.

That whole afternoon we saw half a dozen cars, as many men with dogs and guns. A man riding a horse, a woman who walked behind him holding the horse's tail.

The towns were small, with empty streets and squares. Wind blew across the olive groves, causing a wild tremor, a kind of panic, treetops going silver. We passed rubble fields, rock walls, groups of whale-back boulders, hillsides covered with enclosures of rough stone.

We waited out a downpour in a deserted village square. An old church, a well, a cut-back mulberry tree. The rain was continuous, a single wavering surface, beating on the roof and hood. It was Christmas Day.

A mountain cloud kept rolling toward a white village, then merged with warmer air and vanished. Again it fell, like a rush or slide of timeless snow, disappearing in the air above the village.

In our mood of reticent observation, of speaking of other things, the journey through the Mani became something like a pure rite of seeing. This was appropriate, I thought. If Athens is a place where people breathe the spoken word, if much of Greece is this, then the Mani forms an argument for silence, for finding a way to acknowledge the bleakness that carries something human in it. Tap peered through the windshield, he looked at things with an odd thoughtfulness. We would see what was here, see clearly through the rain shrouds that hung in the gorges, through the bluish smoke high-piled on the coast.

We came to a town that was larger than the others, built at a crossroads, a hotel on the edge of it, two-story cement, boarded shut. I drove slowly down a narrow street to what I thought might be the main square, small as it was, halfhearted, oddly shaped, an historical pause. In the narrowness of this place the stone houses loomed. We got out in a light rain, flexing our legs, and walked toward a cobbled street that seemed to lead down to the water. Doors opened in abandoned houses, wind-swayed. We heard goat-bells nearby and passed a church, seeing three goats come over a broken wall. There were more houses with swinging doors, a butcher shop with an empty meat case, a man standing in the dark near the counter.

When we started down the stone path a wind came cutting up to meet us and we looked at each other and turned around. At the end of a street, bulking high over the road we'd just been on, was a massive anvil rock, maybe five hundred feet tall, a dark presence, a power like a voice in the sky. I spotted a café, tall windows, someone moving about. I told Tap to wait in the car and I went inside.

It was a shabby place, two tables occupied. A man stood in a doorway at the back. It wasn't clear whether he was in charge or just hanging around. It was that kind of place, run by someone who drops in when he thinks of it. I asked the man, in Greek, about hotels nearby. He made a barely perceptible sign, a head movement, the smallest action of eyes and lips. Total disdain. Utter and aloof and final dismissal of all subject matter pertaining to this question, now and forever. A soul shrug. A gesture that placed the question outside the human environment, the things men will rouse themselves to discuss.

He was a grave man with wavy black hair, a thick mustache. I crowded him, as I tended to do when speaking Greek, in order to avoid being overheard by others, and said in an earnest halting way that I had three maps of the area south of here, the area where the main road makes its deepest penetration, then turns to go up the opposite coast. And the maps were all different. And I wondered if he could look at the maps and tell me which one was accurate, if any. The people at the nearest table, not Greeks, stopped talking when I was halfway through my recitation. This made me nervous, of course. Not that it mattered to the black-haired man. He said something I didn't understand, three, maybe four words, looking past me to the front window.

The voices resumed. I bought some chocolate bars for Tap. Then I asked if there was a toilet. The man looked to his left and I asked if this meant outside and he looked again and I saw that it did.

I walked through an alley, across a muddy yard to the toilet. It was the terminal shithouse of the Peloponnese. The walls were splattered with shit, the bowl was clogged, there was shit on the floor, on the toilet seat, on the fixtures and pipes. An inch of exhausted piss lay collected around the base of the toilet, a minor swamp in the general wreckage and mess. In the chill wind, the soft sweet rain, this doleful shed was another plane of experience. It had a history, a reek of squatting armies, centuries of war, plunder, siege, blood feuds. I stood five feet from the bowl to urinate, tip-toed. How strange that people used this place, still. It was like an offering to Death, to stand there directing my stream toward that porcelain hole.

Driving slowly, nosing the car out of town, I passed the café, aware we were being watched, although I wasn't sure by whom. We headed south again, in misty light, sharing some chocolate. Soon we began seeing tower houses, tall narrow structures, flat-roofed except where broken near the top. They stood in the bare landscape, solitary pieces, chess pieces, unfigured, raised straight in the dead afternoon. They looked less like houses, former houses, than some mysterious use of the local stone.

"Was I born during the Vietnam war?"

"Don't sound so depressed. You're not scarred for life, I don't think."

"But was I?"

"Yes. It was our favorite war, your mother's and mine. We were both against it but she insisted on being more against it than I was. It got to be a contest, a running battle. We used to have terrific arguments."

"Not smart."

This is what he said on those occasions when another kid might say "dumb" or "pretty stupid." Not smart. A whole world existed in this distinction.

He was belted in, wearing a watch cap, suspended in one of his inward states. He possessed an eerie calm at such times and was capable of the most unsettling questions about himself, his degree of sanity, his chances of living past the age of twenty, figured against world conflicts, new diseases, in a studious monotone. It was almost a talent, a knack he had, these elaborate balances, the way he dwelt in his own mind as a statistician, a neutral weigher of destinies.

"What do Sherpas do?" I said.

"Climb mountains."

"What's in Arecibo?"

"The radio telescope. The big dish."

"Let me think of some more."

"Think of some more."

"Let me think," I said.

On a plateau in the distance, separated by open sky, were two clusters of tower houses, long gray forms rising out of the rocks and scrub. The houses were set at varying heights so that in aggregate they resembled a modern skyline seen from a certain distance, a certain elevation, in the rain and haze, in ruins. I felt we were coming upon something no one had approached in a thousand years. A lost history. A pair of towered cities set at the end of the continent.

They were only villages, of course, and there was nothing very lost about them. It only seemed that way, here, in the Mani, in a landscape of rocks. We found a dirt road and drove into the first of the towns. The road was unpaved all the way in, turned to mud in some places, deep pools in others. Some of the buildings were clearly inhabited, although we saw no one. There were several recent structures, made of the same stone, among the broken towers. Walled cactus gardens. House numbers in green paint. Utility poles.

"Who am I named after?"

"You know the answer to that."

"But he died."

"That has nothing to do with it. When you go back to London, ask your mother and your aunt to tell you about his eccentricities. He had some juicy quirks. That's a local fruit you ought to try. And when you go back to Victoria, write me a letter now and then."

"But why am I named after him?"

"Your mother and I both loved him. He was a sweet man, your grandfather. Even your nickname comes from him. Some of his business associates called him Tap. Thomas Arthur Pattison, get it? But the family didn't use the name much. We called him Tommy. He was Tommy, you were Tap. A couple of funny

guys. Even though you're Thomas Arthur Axton and not Pattison, we wanted to call you Tap, after him."

"How did he die?"

"You want to know how he died so you can decide whether
or not that's how you're going to die. Well there's no connection,
so forget it."

A dog slept on a mound of olive pulp. We went a short distance, then turned off the main road again, left this time, and
drove slowly up into the other towered hamlet. We saw a woman
and child retreat from a doorway, heard gunshots in the hills, two
soft bursts, hunters again. Stones were arranged in circular
figures, threshing floors. Some houses had slate roofs topped with
stones. Stones were crammed into window spaces.

"Here's one for you. What goes on at the Bonneville salt flats?"

"Rocket cars. High-speed tests."

"What do you think of when I say Kimberley?"

"Wait, let me think."

Who are they, the people in the café? Are they *members?* At
one table an old man, a chipped white cup. At the other table a
group, three or four, not Greeks. They listened when I asked
about the maps. How do I know they aren't Greek? Who are
they, what are they doing here, this desolate place, in winter?
What am I doing here, and have I stumbled across them, and do
I want to go back, to look again, to be sure, one way or the other,
with my son in hand?

"South Africa."

"Now if I get it, it's because you gave me a hint."

"Mining."

"Thanks for practically telling me."

"What is it then?"

Morose, slumped in his seat. "Diamond mining," he said.

Minutes later we approached the coast again. The last ridge of
Taygetus fell to the sea, a clean line of descent in the fading light.
I stopped the car to look at the maps. Tap pointed north, catching
sight of something through my side of the windshield, and after
a moment I was able to see a dark mass of towers set among the
terraced hills.

"I think we ought to find a hotel or rooming house. At least figure out where we are."

"Just this last place," he said.

"You like the tower houses."

He kept peering through the glass.

"Or is it the driving you like?"

"This one last place," he said. "Then I promise we can stop."

The road up was a dirt track, all stones and mud. Three or four runnels came splashing past the car, merged in places, and I began to think about the jagged rocks, the deep mud, the force of the racing water, the growing dark. Tap broke a section of chocolate from the bar, then subdivided, a piece for each of us. It was raining hard again.

"No signs. If we knew the name of this place, we could find it on the map. Then we'd know where we are for a change."

"Maybe there's someone up there we can ask."

"Although it's probably not on the map anyway."

"We can ask," he said.

The muddy streams jumped ruts and smaller stones. I spotted dead cypress trees above us. The road kept turning, there was cactus hanging off the edges, stunted brush.

"First you see something in front of the car and then it goes past the way it really is."

"Like a tree," I said.

"Then you look in the mirror and you see the same thing, only it looks different and it moves faster, a lot faster. Whoby obis thobat."

"Too bad your mother isn't here. You could have a long talk in your native tongue. Have they given her a hole in the ground yet?"

"She has an office."

"It's only a matter of time. There's a hole in the ground somewhere in British Columbia that she's determined to end up in. Is that a question you were asking?"

"There are no questions in Ob. You can ask a question but you don't say it like a question in English. You say it like a regular sentence."

The last loop in the road took us away from our destination, momentarily, and provided a look at another towered hamlet, set along a distant ridge, and still another, a smaller cluster, silhouetted on a headland way below us. We turned up onto a long straight approach to the village and then I saw something that sent a chill through me, a delayed chill (I had to think, to translate). I stopped the car and sat there, staring out over the textured fields.

It was a fallen rock, a ten-foot boulder standing by the roadcut to our left, a flat-faced reddish block with two white words painted across its width, the pigment running down off the letters in rough trickles, the accent mark clearly in place.

Ta Onómata.

"Why are we stopping?"

"It was stupid, coming up here. My fault. We ought to be finding a place to stay, some food."

"We're turning around, you mean, just when we get here?"

"You had your drive up. Now you'll have your drive back down."

"What's painted on that rock? Do you think that's what they use for road signs here?"

"No. It's not a road sign."

"What is it?"

"Just someone writing. We've seen writing on walls and buildings everywhere we've gone. Politics. We've even seen crowns, long live the king. If there's no wall around, I guess they use the nearest thing. A rock in this case."

"Is it politics?"

"No. It's not politics."

"What is it?"

"I don't know, Tap."

"Do you know what it means?"

"The Names," I said.

We found a room above a grocery store in a beaten seaside town with a rubble beach, cliffs dropping sheer to the sea. I was glad to be there. We sat each to a bed in the darkish room, attempting to put ourselves at a mental distance from the rocking car, the lurches and turns of the day. It took a while to believe we were off that last flooded track.

The old grocer and his wife invited us down to dinner. The simple room at the back of the store had a beamed ceiling and oil lamp and carved box for linens and these made for a certain order and warmth, a comfort of the spirit after all that stone. The old man knew some German and used it whenever he sensed I wasn't following what he said. From time to time I reported his remarks to Tap, mainly inventing as I went along. It seemed to satisfy them both.

The woman had white hair and clear blue eyes. Pictures of her children and grandchildren were set around a mirror. They were all in Athens or Patras except for one son, buried nearby.

After dinner we watched television for half an hour. A man with a pointer stood before a map, explaining the weather. Tap thought this was very funny. The scene was familiar to him, of course. The map, the graphics, the talking-gesturing man. But this man spoke a language other than English. And this was funny, it upset his expectations, to hear these queer words in a familiar setting, as if the weather itself had gone berserk. The grocer and his wife joined in the laughter. We all did. Possibly, to Tap, the strange language exposed the whole idea as gibberish, the idea of forecasts, the idea of talking before a camera about the weather. It had been gibberish in English as well. But he hadn't realized it until now.

We sat in the blue glow, laughing.

What do you know about them?

They weren't Greek.

How do you know that?

You see it right away. Faces, clothes, mannerisms. It's just there. A set of things. A history. Foreigners practically glow in certain local landscapes. You know at once.

How many were there?

A crowded table. But the tables in that place are small. I'd say four people. At least one was a woman. In the brief time I was in there, the glancing look I had, the animal *feel* of them, I think I sensed a guardedness, a suspicion. It's possible I'm supplying this impression after the fact but I don't think so. It was there. I didn't pick it up fully at the time. I was intent on other things. I didn't know it might mean something.

What language did they speak?

I don't know. I heard the voices as a tone, only, an undercurrent in the room. I was intent on asking my questions about hotels and maps.

Was it English, possibly?

No. Not English. I would have recognized English just from the tone, the particular quality of the noise.

What did they look like, a general impression?

They looked like people who came from nowhere. They'd escaped all the usual associations. They weren't Greek but what were they? In a sense they belonged to that worn-out café as much as any local idler does. They were in no hurry, I don't think, to find another place to sit, another place to live. They were people who found almost any place as good as almost any other. They didn't make distinctions.

All this in a glance, a walk across the room?

The feeling you get. I couldn't pick them out of a crowd of similar people, I don't know what they look like as individuals, but the general recognition, the awareness of some collective identity—yes, it's there at a glance.

What were they wearing?

I recall an old wasted aviator jacket on one man. Outer material peeling off. A hat, definitely. Someone wore a hat, a knitted skullcap, several dark colors, a circular pattern. I think the woman had a scarf and boots. I may have seen the boots when we drove past the café on our way out of town. Floor-to-ceiling windows.

What else?

Just an impression of old clothes, mixed things, some touches of brightness maybe, a sense of layers, whatever they could add on to keep warm.

What else?
Nothing.

In the morning, a couple of minutes out of town, I saw a dark shape come out of the scrub near the road, an instant with a speed and weight to it, something near the right front wheel, and I hit it, a dull sound trailing off behind us, and kept driving.

"What was it?"

"A dog," he said.

"I saw it too late. It ran right into us."

He said nothing.

"Do you want to go back?"

"What's the point?" he said.

"Maybe it's not dead. We can find somewhere to take it."

"Where could we take it? What's the point? Let's keep driving. I want to drive. That's all."

The rain was a torrent now and people started coming out of the fields, people I hadn't known were there, mostly the old and very young, shrouded in coats and shawls, riding donkeys, walking head down, leaving on tractors, whole families on tractors with umbrellas and blankets and plastic sheeting held over them as they crowded between the massive tires, moving slowly toward home.

I sat in the office alone, sending telexes, doing numbers on the calculator. It seemed to me that ever since the first of those island nights I'd been engaged in an argument with Owen Brademas. I wasn't sure what the subject was exactly but felt for the first time a weakening in my position, a danger.

I also felt I was ahead of myself, doing things that didn't correspond to some reasonable and familiar model. I would have to wait to understand.

Why had I gone to the Mani, knowing they might be there, and why with Tap? Was he my safeguard, my escape?

I read reports, drafted letters. Mrs. Helen arrived, chiding me for being in so early, for looking so worn-out. She went to the alcove to make tea, Zou Zou Bop Golden tea, which someone had brought back from Egypt.

I worked until ten that night, enjoying it, finding a deep and steady pleasure in the paperwork, the details, the close-to-child-like play of the telex, of tapping out messages. Even putting my desk in order was a satisfaction and odd comfort. Neat stacks for a change. Labeled folders. Mrs. Helen had devised for herself an entire theology of neatness and decorum, with texts and punishments. I could understand, faintly.

I went home and made soup. Tap had left his hat behind. I resolved to stop drinking, although I'd had only a couple of glasses of wine in the last week or so. It was a setting of limits I thought I needed. A firmness and clarity, a sense that I could define the shape of things.

Lindsay Whitman Keller, eating an olive.

Voices around us, some vague occasion of the Mainland Bank, a suite at the Hilton. People stood with their hands in the air, eating, drinking, smoking, or they clutched their own elbows or engaged with others in prolonged and significant handshakes.

"Is this an assigned duty?" I said.

"Spouses have no rights. Good thing I have my teaching job."

"Good thing David's not a hard-liner."

"This one I had to attend. Something to do with the future of Turkey. Unofficially, of course."

"Has the bank decided to let them live?"

"Banks plural."

"Even more ominous."

"What's your excuse?" she said.

"Hard liquor. I've been working day and night and not minding at all. This worried me."

Two men seemed to be barking at each other but it was only laughter, a story about a plane skidding off a runway in Khartoum. The bank wives stood mainly in groups of three or four in their corporate aura, tolerant, durable, suffused with a light of middling privilege that was almost sensual in its effect, in the way that a woman's arrangements with a man are a worldly thing, bargained over and handled and full of knowingness. The forced suburbia of these women's lives, the clubby limits of the 1950s in some dead American pasturage, here was a dislocation with certain seductive attributes and balances. The duty-free car, the furlough allowance, the housing allowance, the living allowance, the education allowance, the tax equilization, the foreign assignment premium. Often the women stood with a man in attendance, a flawlessly groomed Pakistani or a Lebanese in a well-tailored suit. Bankers from poor countries dressed like military men. They looked alert and precise and slightly in pain and they spoke a brisk and assured English with a blend of shortened forms. JDs were Jordanian dinars, DJs were dinner jackets.

David moved across the room in our direction. I asked Lindsay what it was about him that always gave me the impression he was pushing people out of the way. He fed his wife some cheese and took her drink.

"Always near a woman," he said to me, then turned to Lindsay. "Not to be trusted, these men who talk to women."

"Tried to call you yesterday," I said.

"I was in Tunis."

"Are they killing Americans?"

He wouldn't give the glass back to her.

"Per capita GNP is the fifth largest in Africa. We love them. We want to throw some money at them."

I gestured around us.

"Have you decided to let them live? The Turks? Or will you shut them down for ten or twenty years?"

"I'll tell you what this is all about. It's about two kinds of discipline, two kinds of fundamentalism. You have Western banks on the one hand trying to demand austerity from a country like Turkey, a country like Zaire. Then you have OPEC at the other end preaching to the West about fuel consumption, our piggish habits, our self-indulgence and waste. The Calvinist banks, the Islamic oil producers. We're talking across each other to the deaf and the blind."

"I didn't know you saw yourself as a righteous force, a righteous presence."

"A voice in the wilderness. Want to fly to Frankfurt and watch the bowl games on TV?"

"You're out of your mind."

"We can watch on a monitor at the Armed Forces studios. No problem. The bank will arrange."

"He's serious," Lindsay said.

"We're all serious," he said. "It's the start of a new decade. We're serious people and we want to do this thing."

"Let's have a quiet New Year's Eve," she said, "in that little French place up the street."

"We'll have a quiet New Year's Eve, then we'll all get on a plane to Frankfurt and watch the bowl games on TV. The Huskers go against Houston. I outright refuse to miss it."

Why was I so happy, standing in that mob of bodies? I would talk to the bank wives. I would talk to Vedat Nesin, one of the many Turks I met that year who had a name with interchangeable syllables. I would talk to a man from the IMF, an Irishman who complained that he kept walking into scenes of destruction and bloodshed that never got reported. In Bahrain he walked into a Shi'ite riot. In Istanbul he fled his hotel in a service elevator during a demonstration that no one knew was coming, that no one understood, that did not appear in local newspapers or anywhere else. It was as though the thing had never happened, as though the corridors hadn't filled with smoke and rampaging men. His fear was going undocumented in city after city. He was disturbed by the prospect that the riot or terrorist act which caused his death would not be covered by the media. The death itself seemed not so much to matter.

I embraced the wives and looked into their eyes, studying for signs of restlessness, buried grudges against their husbands' way of life. These are things that lead to afternoons of thoughtful love. I spoke to a Kuwaiti about the grace and form of characters in Arabic, asking him to pronounce for me the letter *jim*. I told stories, drank bourbon, ate the snacks and tidbits. I listened to the voices.

"You are lucky," Vedat Nesin said. "You are a target only outside your country. I am a target outside and inside. I am in the government. This makes me a marked man. Armenians outside, Turks inside. I go to Japan next week. This is a relatively safe place for a Turk. Very bad is Paris. Even worse is Beirut. The Secret Army is very active there. Every secret army in the world keeps a post office box in Beirut. I will eat this shrimp in garlic and butter. Later I will eat profiteroles in thick chocolate sauce. After Japan I go to Australia. This is a place that should be safe for a Turk. It is not."

I started out at first light, stopping only once, below Tripolis, for something to eat, and the same bluish clouds were massed down the coast, over the bays and processional headlands, but it wasn't raining this time when I reached the spot where the rutted track bends its way up to the boulder and the towered village beyond. Signs of night were hours off.

I drove slowly up the hill and left the car behind the large rock. Someone, using tar, had painted over the words we'd seen six days earlier, covered them completely. It was a level stretch to the village, sixty yards, and the sky was so low and close I felt I was walking into it, into sea mists and scattered light.

Bags of cement on the ground, stacked crates of empty bottles. A woman in black sitting on a bench in an open area of mud and stones. She had a bony face framed in a head-cloth. One of her shoes was broken, split across the instep. I spoke a greeting, nodded toward the alley that led into the village proper, asking leave to enter in effect. She paid no attention and I didn't know if she'd even seen me.

I followed the narrow unpaved passage. A millstone lay in the first ruined tower and there was cactus jutting out of other houses, stones packed solid in window slits and doorways. I kept walking into dead-ends, mud and rubble, weeds, prickly pear.

There was scaffolding on a number of structures, surprisingly, and house numbers in red as well as surveyors' marks.

I moved slowly, feeling a need to remember all this, and I

touched the walls, studied the inscription above a door, 1866, examined the crude steps, the small crude bell-tower, and noted the colors of the stone as if some importance might attach to my describing them precisely someday, the unmellowed tone of this particular biscuit brown, this rust, this sky gray.

Along the intricate and twisting paths, among the broken towers, I began to wonder if this might all be one structure, the whole village, a complex formation whose parts were joined by arches, walls, the lower rooms that smelled of animals and forage. There seemed no clear and single separation between the front and back ends of the village, between this oblong tower and that.

It was their place, I was sure. A place of hesitations and textures. An uncertain progress that was like the inner labor of some argument. The barred window, the black bees we'd seen on the island. A place that was a muffled question, as some places are shouts or formal lectures. All the buildings joined. One mind, one madness. Was I beginning to know who they were?

I came out above a slope of terraced earth, the empty sea. Several trees had become entangled in their growth, and the bare branches grappled and twisted and the smooth gray trunks were locked in what appeared a passionate and human fury. How strongly this element of humanness showed in that stark mingling. The wood resembled burnished stone. A mortal struggle, a nakedness, sex and death together.

I took a path back out the other side of the village. This was limestone, those were fig trees, that was a barrel-vaulted chamber. The names. I felt strangely, self-consciously alone. This place was returning to me a sense of my own motion through it, my stoopings into rooms, my pauses to judge the way.

There were two women now. The second was very old, trying to pick apart an orange section by section. I stood in front of them, asking if anyone lived in the town. Foreigners. Do foreigners live here? The old one made a gesture that either meant she didn't know what I was talking about or that they'd gone, the people I meant, they'd cleared out.

Do you live here alone?

One other, she said. The man of the other woman.

From the car I could see the hamlet on the far ridge. Tap and

I had passed through there on our way home, after coming across the road that led up the Laconian coast, and I thought I might find something to eat there, houses with people. I drove back down to the paved road, eventually heading northeast, climbing again.

I left the car next to a tower with a blue balcony, recently attached, and was directed by some children down a steep path, seeing a café with a small evergreen out front, trimmed with balloons. The dirt was redder here, the towers had an ochre glow. Volterra was standing in the doorway. He had his hands jammed in his pockets. His breath showed white.

I decided the only thing to do was smile. He gave me something of a measured look. But a grin emerged as we shook hands, a crooked smile, speculative, hinting at a certain appreciation. I followed him inside, a dark room with a wood-burning stove, and ate an omelette as he watched.

"These towers are strange," he said. "The older ones are three, almost four hundred years. These people spent all their time killing. When they weren't killing Turks, they killed each other."

"Where is Del?"

"In a hotel up the coast."

"Watching TV."

"Are you here to write something, Jim?"

"No."

"You know how I am about privacy. I'd hate to think you came here to do a story on me. A major piece, as they say. Full of insights. The man and his work."

"I don't write, Frank. I have a job. It doesn't involve writing anything but reports and memos."

"You used to write. All kinds of things."

"I don't write. My son writes."

"It's a subject I have to raise from time to time with certain people."

"Reluctantly."

"Reluctantly. Even friends don't always know how serious I am about this. The filmmaker on location. The filmmaker in seclusion. Major pieces. They're always major pieces."

"I only came because Owen more or less indicated they were here. It was just to see."

"What have you seen?"

"Nothing," I said.

"From the beginning Brademas talked about a design. That's what got me going. This last time he seemed close to telling me what it is. Their waiting, the way they select a victim. But he changed his mind or maybe I didn't handle it right. Maybe there's a set of forms, a right and wrong way to pursue the matter."

A man brought coffee for both of us. Two children stood in the doorway, watching me. When I smiled they edged away.

"Poor bastard," Frank said.

"Where did you talk to him, this last time?"

"Athens."

"Thanks for getting in touch."

"I know. You offered us lodging. But we were only there a day, only long enough for me to talk to him. This thing is building. I want this thing. I'm beginning to see what it's all about. Only Del, she's the only person I can stand to have around me for long periods without feeling everything's pressing in, everybody's one purpose in life is to throw me off, to set me back." Laughing. "The bitch."

"You thought the desert was a frame. What about the Mani?"

"The desert fits the screen. It is the screen. Low horizontal, high verticals. People talk about classic westerns. The classic thing has always been the space, the emptiness. The lines are drawn for us. All we have to do is insert the figures, men in dusty boots, certain faces. Figures in open space have always been what film is all about. American film. This is the situation. People in a wilderness, a wild and barren space. The space is the desert, the movie screen, the strip of film, however you see it. What are the people doing here? This is their existence. They're here to work out their existence. This space, this emptiness is what they have to confront. I've always loved American spaces. People at the end of a long lens. Swimming in space. But this situation isn't American. There's something traditional and closed-in. The secret goes back. I believe it goes back. And these tower houses, they're perfect, they give me my vertical. Old worn rugged stone the color of the land. Lines of flat land. Lines moving diagonally to the sea. Lines up and down the hills, those stone walls, like scar tissue. And the towers showing up everywhere, unexpectedly. Black and white. The natural colors hardly stray from that anyway. You could count fifty kinds of gray out there today."

"How do you make a movie out of it, out of the situation? Where is the movie?"

"Look. You have a strong bare place. Four or five interesting and mysterious faces. A strange plot or scheme. A victim. A stalking. A murder. Pure and simple. I want to get back to that. It'll be an essay on film, on what film is, what it means. It'll be like nothing you know. Forget relationships. I want faces, land, weather. People speaking whatever languages. Three, four different languages. I want to make the voices part of a landscape of sound. The spoken word will be an element in the landscape. I'll use the voices as synchronous sound and as off-screen narration. The voices will be *filmed* voices. The wind, the donkeys braying, the hunting dogs. And then this line that moves through the film. A scant narrative line. Everything else gathers around this line, hangs from it. Somebody's being watched, he's being followed. There's a pattern, something inevitable and mad, some closed-in horrible logic, and this cult is locked into it, insane with it, but calm, very patient, faces, eyes, and the victim is off in the distance, he's always in the distance, among the stones. All the elements are here. Some strong and distinct like the towers. Some set back a ways like the victim, a crippled goatherd maybe, a vague figure, throwing stones at his flock, living in one of those tin-roof enclosures up in the hills."

"Do you film the murder?"

"Eat your eggs."

"You haven't thought that far ahead."

"There won't be a murder. Nobody gets hurt. At the end they raise their arms, holding the weapons, the hammers or knives or stones. They raise their arms. That's all we see. We don't know what it means. Are they surrendering their weapons? Are they preparing to strike? Is it a gesture that means the illusion is over now, you can go on with your lives, we give you permission to go on with your lives, the film is over, the mass is over, *Ite, missa est*. This image has been in my head. The cult members raise their arms. Will they kill him once the camera stops turning? I want this question to linger."

"How do you know they won't kill him? This is what they do, after all."

"Obviously we make an agreement. We'll have to agree. If they're interested in doing the film at all, I think they'll agree to this condition. They'll see it's the only way I can do it. Whatever else they are, they're educated. I almost want to say they're reasonable. I have a sense of these people. I spent enough time with Brademas to understand certain things about them. My conviction is that they'll want to do it. The life they lead out here, what they do, seems so close to something on film, so natural to film, that I believe once I talk to them they'll see it's an idea they might have thought of themselves, an idea involving languages, patterns, extreme forms, extreme ways of seeing. Film is more than the twentieth-century art. It's another part of the twentieth-century mind. It's the world seen from inside. We've come to a certain point in the history of film. If a thing can be filmed, film is implied in the thing itself. This is where we are. The twentieth century is *on film*. It's the filmed century. You have to ask yourself if there's anything about us more important than the fact that we're constantly on film, constantly watching ourselves. The whole world is on film, all the time. Spy satellites, microscopic scanners, pictures of the uterus, embryos, sex, war, assassinations, everything. I can't believe these people won't instantly see they belong on film. Instantly. I want them to film some of it themselves. It's time for me to go back to a sharing of duties, anonymous, a collective effort. I want them to handle the camera, appear on camera, help me plan shots and sequences. I want them to recite alphabets. Strange things. Whatever they do, whatever they say and do. It'll be like nothing you know, Jim. They'll shoot some of it,

I'll shoot some. Maybe shoot backgrounds myself, landscapes. We all do something. That's appealing, that idea, right now."

"How do you get it all going?"

"I've found one," he said. "I've got one."

I'm not sure I would have known what he meant except for the look, the grim pleasure of the will, showing through. One *what*, I would have said.

He took me outside, where we stood between two carob trees and looked over the valley to the towered village I'd just been wandering through. It stood among swirling banks of earth, the terraced groves that seemed a lyrical attempt to ring the hill with steps, a rippling descent of dream trees and lunar tones. Mist pooled around the towers. The village from this distance and perspective was an aerial fancy. It had an element of medieval legend about it, something I hadn't found in the cactus and mud, where there was mystery, true, but not of folklore or narrative verse.

"Four days ago. Those towers. I found him sleeping in a damp cellar, stinking of goats. Andahl. He knows my work."

It was cold, we went back inside.

"He was with them on the island. He's still with them but the situation isn't the same. They had to leave that village and they're a little scattered now but still in one area, the Deep Mani. Five people. Andahl likes to deliver recitations. I let him recite. I'm not here to argue with the bastards."

"Why did they have to leave that village?"

"It's being developed. The whole place is being renovated. Workmen start coming in any day. Somebody wants to make guest houses out of the towers. Open the area to tourists."

"Real life," I said. "Where is he now?"

"There are caves on the Messinian coast. Some well known, very extensive. Others just holes in the sea rock. I drop him on the road that leads to the caves. I don't know where he goes after that. Last three days that's been the routine. In the morning I show up, same place. Eventually he appears. They're talking. He's trying to arrange a meeting."

"Have you asked him what the pattern is? Why they keep

a watch. How they decide who and where to strike."

"He puts a finger to his lips," Frank said.

Because part of the eastern coast is without roads of any kind, we had to cross the peninsula twice before reaching Githion, beyond the towers, a tiered port town that opens directly, almost bluntly on the sea. Sundown. We found Del Nearing in a waterfront café, writing a postcard to her cat.

"A man will say, if you ask him how many children he has, two, proudly. Then you learn he has a daughter he didn't bother to count. Only the sons count. That's the Mani."

"I wonder if I'll ever see my apartment again," Del said. "I've been trying to reconstruct it in my mind. There are large gaps. It's like parts of my life have melted away."

"Death and revenge," Frank said. "A lot of the killing revolved around the family. The house was also the fortress. That's the reason for these towers. Endless vendettas. The family is the safekeeper of revenge. They keep the idea warm. They nurture it, they promote the conditions. It's like those family sagas of crime in the movies. People respond to Italian gangster sagas not just for the crime and violence but for the sense of family. Italians have made the family an extremist group. The family is the instrument of revenge. Revenge is a desire that almost never becomes an act. It's a thing most of us are limited to enjoying in the contemplation alone. To see these families, these crime families, many of them blood relatives, to see them enact their revenge is an uplifting experience, it's practically a religious experience. The Manson family was America's morbid attempt to make a stronger instinctive unit, literally a blood-related unit. But they forgot something. The revenge motive. They had nothing to revenge. If there's going to be blood, it has to be a return for some injury, some death. Otherwise the violent act is ghastly and sick, which is exactly the way we see the Manson murders."

"Frank's people come from Tuscany. I tell him why do you talk like a Sicilian."

"Look at her. I love that face. That dull empty perfect face. How right for today."

"Suck a rock."

"Self-created," he said. "It's a blankness she wills out of her deepest being. Vapid. Does vapid say it? Maybe vapid says too much."

"If Manson is ghastly and sick," I said, "what do we have here, with our own cult?"

"Totally different. Different in every respect. These people are monks, they're secular monks. They want to vault into eternity."

"The same but different."

"Film is not part of the real world. This is why people will have sex on film, commit suicide on film, die of some wasting disease on film, commit murder on film. They're adding material to the public dream. There's a sense in which film is independent of the filmmaker, independent of the people who appear. There's a clear separation. This is what I want to explore."

It was a long dark room. A boy kept bringing pots of tea, ouzo for Frank. Del was watching an old man sitting in a corner, a cigarette hanging from the middle of his face.

"Film," she said absently. "Film, film. Like insects making a noise. Film, film, film. Over and over. Rubbing their front wings together. Film, film. A summer day in the meadow, the sky's full of heat and glare. Film, film, film, film."

It was only when she'd finished talking that she turned her attention to Frank, grabbing a handful of hair at the back of his neck and twisting his head so that he might see directly into her gray eyes. Their public affection was reserved for the times when they heckled and mocked each other. It was an automatic balance, the hands and eyes as the truth-tellers of love, the things that redeem what we say.

We went to a restaurant two doors down. There was a handful of red mullet in a basket out front. We were starting to eat when the old man hobbled in, worn down to an argument with himself, a cigarette still drooping from his mouth. This made Del happy. She decided she didn't want to talk to us anymore. She wanted to talk to him.

We watched her at his table, gesturing elaborately as she spoke, pronouncing words carefully, words in English, a few in Italian and Spanish. Frank seemed to be looking right through her to some interesting object fixed to the wall.

"She's not part of anything," he said. "She doesn't know yet whether she wants to grow up and assume responsibilities in the world. She had a miserable time most of her life. She has a tendency to give in to fate or other people. But we tell each other everything. There's an easiness between us. I've never known a woman I could be so intimate with. It's our gift as a couple. Intimacy. I sometimes feel we've known each other three lifetimes. I tell her everything."

"You told Kathryn everything."

"She never told me anything back."

"You told Kathryn more than I told her. It was a kind of challenge, wasn't it? That was the mechanism between you two. You dared her to be part of something totally unfamiliar. You wanted to shock her, mystify her. She found this interesting, I think. Something her background hadn't encompassed."

"Kathryn was equal to any challenge I could come up with. Not that I know what you mean by dares and challenges."

"Remember the shirt? She still has it. Your *carabiniere* shirt."

"She looked good in that shirt."

"She still does. It still bothers me, how good she looks in that shirt."

"Finish your wine. This is the stupidest talk I've had in ten years."

Del, the waiter and the old man were talking. The waiter was balancing an ashtray on the back of each hand.

"She's beautiful. Del is."

"Christ, yes, I do love her face. Despite what I say. It never changes. It's eerie, how it never changes, no matter how tired she is, how sick, whatever."

We sat in the hotel lobby, in almost total dark, talking. When Frank and Del went upstairs I walked through the streets above the waterfront. A strong wind came up, different from wind in an open space. It went banging through town, disturbing the surface of things, agitating, taking things with it, exposing things as temporary, subject to a sudden unreason. There were wooden balconies, chicken coops. The walls were crumbling in places and cactus grew everywhere. Figures in the light, in small rooms, wall shadows, faces.

They want to vault into eternity.

I would conceal myself in Volterra's obsession as I had in Owen's unprotected pain, his songs of helplessness.

9

I MADE MY WAY through the mud streets, the same complicated solitude. I could almost see myself, glowing in borrowed light. A voice, my own but outside me, speaking something other than words, commented somehow on the action.

I was made of denim and sheepskin. My shoes were waterproof, my gloves lined with wool.

This is the way things happen. I walk into a café in a wind-beaten town and they are right there even if I don't know it at the time. And now I duck under a stone beam on a cold smoky morning in the towered hamlet where no one (almost no one) lives and he is sitting on a blue crate, a crate for soda bottles, and there is one for me as well, upended. A fire is going, twigs mostly, and he lifts his feet off the dirt floor, putting them close to the flames, and it is nothing, a talk in a basement room with a medium-sized man who has a cold. But how else would it be? What did I expect? The only true surprise is that I am in the scene. It ought to be someone else sitting here, a man who has seen himself plain.

"What do we have?" he said. "First we have a film director and now we have a writer. This is not so strange really."

"Frank thinks I want to write about him."

"About him or about us?"

"I'm a friend of Owen Brademas. That's all. I know Owen. We've talked many times."

"A man who knows languages. A calm man, very humane, I think. He has a wide and tolerant understanding, a capacity for civilized thought. He is not hurried, he is not grasping for satisfactions. This is what it means to know languages."

He had a long face, a receding hairline, pale freckles high on his forehead. Small hands. This reassured me in some mysterious way, the size of his hands. His face was impassive. He wore a black tunic unraveling at the right shoulder. I studied, I took mental notes.

"I thought you would want to speak Greek," I said. "Or whatever the language of a particular place."

"We are no longer *in* a place. We are a little disorganized. Soon it will be all right again. Also this business with Frank Volterra is unique. What do we have? A situation we have not had before. So we are attempting to adjust."

"Are the others interested? Will they agree to be part of a film?"

"There are problems. It is a question of our larger purpose. We must consider many things. One thing is whether we are such filmic material as Frank Volterra believes. Maybe we are not. He lacks a complete understanding."

"Owen Brademas had this understanding."

"Have you?" he said.

"If we are talking about a solvable thing, a riddle or puzzle, then I have solved it, yes."

"What is your solution?"

"The letters match," I said. "Name, place-name."

He was leaning back, balanced, hands clasped on his knees, his feet still dangling over the flames. I crouched forward, wanting to feel the heat on my face. He didn't change expression, although it's possible to say that my remark, my reply, prompted him to renew his stoic mien, to inhabit it more fully. I'd made him aware of the look on his face.

"Do we seem improbable to you?"

"No," I said.

"I wonder why this is."

"I don't know."

"We ought to seem improbable. What do you think?"

"I'm not sure. I don't know."

"Something in our method finds a home in your unconscious mind. A recognition. This curious recognition is not subject to conscious scrutiny. Our program evokes something that you seem to understand and find familiar, something you cannot analyze. We are working at a preverbal level, although we use words, of course, we use them all the time. This is a mystery."

His eyes were dim, blood-flecked. He had a two-day stubble, reddish blond, darker than the hair on his head. His fingernails were yellowish and thick.

"In one sense we barely exist," he said. "It is a difficult life. There are many setbacks. The cells lose touch with each other. Differences arise of theory and of practice. For months nothing happens. We lose purpose, get sick. Some have died, some have wandered off. Who are we, what are we doing here? There is not even a threat of the police to give us a criminal identity. No one knows we exist. No one is looking for us."

He stopped briefly in order to cough.

"But in another sense we have a permanent bond. How could it be otherwise? We have in common that first experience, among others, that experience of recognition, of knowing this program reaches something in us, of knowing we all wanted at once to be part of it. When I first heard of this, before I became a member, it was in Tabriz, eight years ago. People in a hotel talked of a cult murder somewhere in the area. Much later, I cannot tell you how, I learned what the elements were. Immediately it reached me, something about the nature of the final act. It seemed right to me. Extreme, insane, whatever you wish to call it in words. Numbers behave, words do not. I knew it was right. Inevitable and perfect and right."

"But why?"

"The letters matched."

"But to kill?"

"Nothing less," he said. "It had to be that. I knew at once it was right. I cannot describe how fully and deeply it reached me. Not as an answer, not as a question. Something else totally. Some terrible and definitive thing. I knew it was right. It had to be. Shatter his skull, kill him, smash his brains."

"Because the letters matched."

"I believe you see it, how nothing else would suffice. It had to be this one thing, done with our hands, in direct contact. Nothing else, nothing less. You do see that it's correct. You see the rightness of it. You know it intuitively. The whole program leads up to this. Only a death."

He put his feet on the ground in order to cough, head down, hands covering his face. When he was finished he leaned back again, balancing, his feet in the air once more. I reached to the side for more twigs, dropped them on the fire. We sat that way in silence for a while. Andahl leaning well back, his feet raised. Axton crouched forward, looking into the fire.

"We walked through these mountains from north to south. When we came into the Mani we knew we would stay. We are set back but only for a time. What is here. This is the strength of the Mani. It does not suggest things to us. No gods, no history. The rest of the Peloponnese is full of associations. The Deep Mani, no. Only what is here. The rocks, the towers. A dead silence. A place where it is possible for men to stop making history. We are inventing a way out."

He lowered himself again, coughed into his armpit. He was wearing a strange pair of suede boots trimmed on the outside with some fleecy synthetic—women's boots, I thought. His pants were loose and brown, drawn in at the ankles.

"The large stone outside this village," I said. "Why were those words painted there?"

"Someone, leaving, painted the words."

"When you found them, you painted them over, made them illegible."

"We are not painters. It was not a good painting."

"Why did he do it?"

"There are many setbacks. We lose purpose, get sick. Some

people die, some wander off. There are differences in meaning, differences in words. But know this. Madness has a structure. We might say madness is all structure. We might say structure is inherent in madness. There is not the one without the other."

He coughed into his armpit.

"No one has to stay. There are no chains or gates. More die than leave. We are here to carry out the pattern. A small patient task. You have the word in English. Abecedarian. This is what we are."

"I don't know the word."

"Learners of the alphabet. Beginners."

"And how did you begin, how did the cult begin?"

"This can wait for another time. We will talk again if the occasion permits."

Through the rest of the conversation I found myself eliminating contractions from my speech. Not to ridicule or mimic Andahl. It was something of a surrender to the dominance these complete words seemed to possess, their stronger formulation, spoken aloud.

"Does the cult have a name?"

"Yes."

"Can you tell me what it is?"

"No, impossible. Nameforms are an important element in our program, as you know. What do we have? Names, letters, sounds, derivations, transliterations. We approach nameforms warily. Such secret power. When the name is itself secret, the power and influence are magnified. A secret name is a way of escaping the world. It is an opening into the self."

From somewhere under his tunic he took a maroon scarf and wrapped it around his head. I took this to mean we were coming to an end.

"What we have not talked about is the experience of killing," he said. "How it confirms the early sense of recognition, the perception that the program must end this way. It confirms everything. It tells us how deep we are in." He was watching me through this. "We have not talked about the sound, the hammers, a damp noise, the way she crumpled, how soft it was. We have not talked about the way she crumpled or how we kept hitting,

Emmerich sobbing, the word-building German, he could only groan and sob. Or how long it took, we have not talked about this. Or how we hit harder because we could not stand the sound, the damp sound of the hammers on her face and head. How Emmerich used the cleft end of the hammerhead. Anything to change the sound. He gouged, you know? We were hysterical. It was a frenzy but not of blood. A frenzy of knowing, of terrible confirmation. Yes, we are here, we are actually killing, we are doing it. It was beyond any horror but this was precisely what we had always seen and known. We had our proof. How right we were to tremble when we first learned the program. We have not talked about the way she crumpled or how we knelt over her, having found her weeks before, having determined her condition, having tracked her, having waited in the dust, in the silences, the burning sun, watching her drag her leg, watching her approach the place, the name, the place, all this, having matched the Greek letters, or how she crumpled, only stunned at first, a single blow, or how we knelt over her with the hammers, smashing, beating in her head, or how he gouged with the cleft end, pulling out brains, or the sight of it. We have not talked about the sight of it, how flesh gives up its bloom and vigor, how functions gradually cease, how we could seem to ourselves to be causing functions to end, one after the other, metabolism, response to stimuli, actually sensing these progressive endings in the way she sank. Or how little blood, not at all what we expected, the blood. We looked at each other, amazed at this paucity of blood. It made us feel we had missed a step along the way."

He went outside to cough. He was out there for some time, hawking and spitting. It made me think of the night I'd vomited pigeon swill in that alley in Jerusalem, an episode I now saw as a clear separation, a space between ways of existing. No wonder I'd puked. What haste my system made to reject the whole business, what an eager spew, burbling out like some chemical death. I'd leaned against the wall in a cold sweat, head bent, hearing Volterra laugh.

"Has this been of help to you?" Andahl said, coming back in, teary-eyed from his exertions.

"Of help?"

"This talk we have had. Has it given you a start? What do you think? Is there an interest, is there something here? If Frank Volterra gains a better understanding, if he learns what the method is, he may decide it is not a thing that adapts well to film. It is not a film. It is a book."

"I see. You are helping me toward the writing of a book."

"You are a writer."

"If you lose one man, you have another in reserve."

"There is no question of losing," he said. "The only question is how we will decide in the end."

"But why are you interested, either way, either form?"

"In one sense we barely exist. There are many setbacks. People die, they go out one day and disappear. Differences arise. For months nothing happens. The cells lose touch with each other. No one knows we are here. I talked to the others about a film. I myself argued for a film. Now I see there is more to discuss. We are still talking. There is bitter opposition. I must tell you that. We are talking about the value of an external object. Not a cult document but a thing outside the cult. An interface with the world. What is a book? What is the nature of a book? Why does it have the shape it has? How does the hand interact with the eyes when someone reads a book? A book throws a shadow, a film is a shadow. We are trying to define things."

"You want an external object. I am trying to understand."

"It will outlast us. This is the argument I make to them. Something to outlast us. Something to contain the pattern. We barely exist. No one will know it when we die away. What do you think, Axstone?"

I studied him for further details, a mark on the back of the hand, a way of standing, although I had no reason to collect such incidentals beyond an uncertain wish to return a truth to the landscape itself, the name-haunted place.

It was warmer now. I followed him out of the village, hurrying to keep up. A woman, the old one, appeared through an archway on the slope below us, motionless among goats browsing in the thistle-heads, a thousand feet above the sea.

Frank's car was parked behind mine. He had a black Mazda

bearing on its windshield the checkered decal that showed it was rented. Andahl got in and they drove away.

By noon I was checked out, sitting in my car outside the hotel. A merchant ship lay at anchor. Del sat next to me, cleaning the lens of a still camera with a blow-brush. Pieces of equipment were on the floor, above the dashboard, in the open glove compartment. We were talking about Frank's movies, the two features. A man's hat came sailing across the street.

"I missed the second one," I said. "I saw the first when we were living on an island in Lake Champlain. You cross the lake on a little ferry, a canal barge, that runs by a cable strung from one bank to the other."

"Don't let him know."

"What do you mean?"

"He'll get upset," she said.

"That I missed one of his movies? He wouldn't care. Why would he care?"

"He'll get upset. He's serious about things like that. He expects things from friends and he can't understand, it's beyond belief to him that a friend would not do anything, go anywhere, rob and steal, to see one of his films. He'd do it for them, he expects them to do it for him. He may be hard to get along with at times, especially when his brain is raging, like right now, he's the incredible deadly manta ray, the killer of the deep, but you know he'd do anything for you, without exception. It's all part of the same thing."

"I watched TV, Kathryn went to the movies. That was our private metaphor."

"Frank is loyal," she said. "He's serious about that. He's got a side people don't know. He more or less literally saved my life. He has that side. I wouldn't call it protective exactly. It's a little deeper. He wanted to show me I could be better than I was. It's partly because he thought the way I was living was a form of self-indulgence, which is something he hates. But he also wanted to get me out of there. I was hanging around with people on the fringes. They were people with borrowed vans. Everybody had a borrowed van or knew where to get one. I was always crossing a bridge in someone's borrowed van. I lived with a van painter for a while. We lived in his van. He painted mystical designs on vans and campers. He was after a total design environment, he used to say. Your house, your van, your garage. That was his vision. I was working in television then, a fringe job. TV is the coke medium. The pace is the same. Frank helped me with that. I always half-disgusted him. How I could think so little of myself that I would just go to waste."

She used lens tissue moistened with alcohol.

"When are you going home?"

"When he's ready," she said.

"Where do you live?"

"Oakland."

"Where does Frank live?"

"He wouldn't want me to say."

"He was always like that. Funny. We never knew where he lived. At least I didn't."

"He took me to the hospital to see my father dying. I had to be dragged if you can picture how pathetic. Do the hard things. That's a skill I don't ever want to learn."

I saw Volterra's car in the rearview mirror. He parked behind us, got out, opened the back door of my car, got in without looking at either one of us.

"What did he want?"

"He wanted to talk about books," I said.

"He wouldn't tell me why he wanted to see you."

"It's just an intuition, Frank, but I think he's doing all this on his own. I don't think they know about it. I think he may be a deserter. Or maybe they threw him out. I don't think people who believe what they believe and do what they do would even remotely consider the idea of being put on film, put in a book."

"We find out tomorrow," he said.

"Has he arranged a meeting?"

"I talk to them in the morning."

"I don't think they'll be there."

"They'll be there. And they'll listen to me. They'll see at once what I want to do and why they ought to be part of it."

"Maybe. But he was alone when you found him. He's still alone. Anything outside the cult is meaningless to them. They're locked in. They've invented their own meaning, their own perfection. The last thing they want is an account of their lives."

"What's your stake in all this?"

"I'm going home," I told him. "I saw Andahl in his pixie boots. I can go home now. If you're confused by my presence here, so am I. But I'm leaving and I'm not coming back."

"What do you do in Athens? What's your job?"

"You still think I'm here to write about you."

"What's your job?" he said.

"I'm called a risk analyst."

Del said, "A likely story." Sighting through the viewfinder.

"It's a mass of organized guesswork. Political risk insurance. Companies don't want to be caught short."

I was talking with my head turned toward Del.

"It sounds vague," she said. "It sounds vague, Frank. What do you think?"

He sat in the middle of the back seat. The play in her voice got him off course. The urgency he'd brought with him, the sense of imperative purpose, began slowly to dissolve, and with it his suspicion. He sat back, thinking. A day's wait.

"How will you do it?" she said.

She'd joined him at precisely the right moment in his meditations. He answered immediately.

"Two people from Rome. That's all I need. Kids I know. They bring the equipment on the car ferry from Brindisi. Drive down here from Patras. We go to work. I don't necessarily want to shoot twenty-two hours of film, then work it back on the editing table. We shoot whatever's here. I don't care if I end up with half an hour. Whatever the yield. It won't matter anyway. The coterie toads are all lined up. They're ready to turn. My time has come. I've sensed it the last eighteen months. People give off a musty smell. Whole projects reek. You can't believe how much pleasure it'll give them. A few seconds of pure pleasure. A platonic orgasm. Then they'll forget it completely. Once you fail, you're okay again. And this is the time. It's possible to sense these things. I sense these things across fucking oceans."

"You'll give them something to bury you for," I said.

"I'll go beyond the bounds. They can bury me or not. Some people will see it right away. They'll know exactly what I'm doing, frame by frame. The rest don't matter."

Maybe it would happen the way he believed it would. He'd meet them in a ruined tower near the sea. Strange faces in a ring. There is time and there is film time. It was a natural extension, the barest of transferals, to make the crossing, to leap into the frame. Film was implied in everything they did.

But there was Andahl. He'd introduced an element of motivation, of attitudes and needs. The cult's power, its psychic grip, was based on an absence of such things. No sense, no content, no historic bond, no ritual significance. Owen and I had spent several hours building theories, surrounding the bare act with desperate speculations, mainly to comfort ourselves. We knew in the end we'd be left with nothing. Nothing signified, nothing meant.

Andahl etched an almost human face on this hard blank surface. How could he still be one of them? He wanted something. He'd attempted to draw me in, slipping bits of information to me, withholding others temporarily. He was maneuvering toward some further contact.

He'd told me those words on the rock were put there by someone leaving. The apostate manages his own escape by revealing a secret of the organization, breaking its hold on him. He was the one who'd painted the words—the words that may have been more than a reference to what they did, that may have been their name. Someone else blotted them out. It was possible they were looking for him.

All he wanted from us was a chance to explain. These meetings were a way of turning himself toward the air of worldly reason, of conventional sense and its manipulations. He was raising a call for human pity and forgiveness.

"I've been getting to know this mountain," Frank said. "The other day I was going on foot up a narrow trail above one of the villages. There was a house up there, looked uninhabited. I peer into every structure that looks uninhabited. In my uniquely dumbfuck way I figure sooner or later I'll come across them. This was before Andahl had set up the meeting. I was scouring the hills, scouring the valleys. Now I'm on this trail when suddenly I hear behind me the sound of goat-bells. Here they come, without exaggeration, eighty-five goats, scrambling up the trail behind me, coming fast, for goats. On either side of the trail we find orchards of prickly pear. Whole fields of the stuff. I pick up the pace. I'm not running yet. I don't want to embarrass myself by running. The idea is to make it over the rise where the terrain opens up and there is plenty of room for the goats to graze without trampling me. But what happens? Fifty yards from the end of the trail I hear a pounding driving hell-bent noise. Donkeys and mules, a whole train of them, galloping down the trail at me. A guy is sitting on the lead mule. He's the muleteer, a reckless-looking bastard, a real Maniot, sitting side-saddle, reaching back to swat his mule on the rump with a long switch. And he's uttering what I took to be the muleteer's traditional cry, it sounds like the cry of a Venetian boatman poling around a sharp bend. A barbaric vowel sound. A thousand-year-old cry. I had the definite impression it was meant to urge the mules on. The goats meanwhile are jumping up my ass. They're in a frenzy of hoofs and curved horns, piling up on top of each other. Like some massive rut, the peak of the rutting cycle. And the donkeys and mules are bearing down. It's their only run of the week. All week they've plodded under heavy loads. Now they finally have a chance to run, to get loose, feel free, the wind in their manes, if they had manes, and there I was, in their path, the goats piling up behind me." He paused thoughtfully. "I didn't know whether to shit or go blind."

He would never finish the story. Del started laughing and couldn't stop. I hadn't imagined she could laugh at all but his last remark sent a light to her face, almost broke it apart in a kind of whimpering mirth. Soon Frank was laughing too. They seemed to take their good feeling beyond the story he'd been telling. She sat facing the windshield, making that helpless sound. Their laughter had points of contact, found each other like instruments in a brass quintet, communicating subtle and lovely things. Frank reached over the seat and put his hands on her breasts, awkwardly, clutching tight. His delight had to find something to grasp, to adhere to, some part of her. He narrowed his eyes, showed clenched teeth. It was his old hungry look, hungry for the limit of things. Eventually he settled back in his seat, hands clasped behind his neck. I needed Kathryn to help me see him complete, feel what we'd all felt together, years ago.

The water beyond the jetty was blowing white. They got out of the car, camera equipment slung over Del's shoulders. Frank nodded to me. They said goodbye, standing on the sidewalk, and I drove north, out of town, seeing at once the summit of Taygetus, well ahead, as I'd seen it with Tap from the other side when I first came down to the Mani, a wide reach above the hills and orchards, snow-gold in the climbing sun.

Dick and Dot, the Bordens, greeted me at the door. In the living room a few people stood holding drinks. Before the others arrived, Dick said, he wanted to show me something, and led me down a long hall to the study. The floor was layered with rugs. There were rugs hanging on the walls and rugs draped across the sofa and chairs. He showed me rugs rolled up in closets and rugs wedged under the desk. He walked me around the room, talking about the acquisition of particular rugs. Visits to dealers in Dubai, to warehouses in Lahore, to Turkish weaving areas. The color in this prayer kilim comes from the roots of certain grasses. You can tell children worked on this Bokhara because the knots aren't banged down tightly. Dot came in to ask what I wanted to drink, then joined us briefly, happy to trade voices with her husband, to recite stories about bargaining for rugs over jasmine tea, getting rugs through customs, photographing rugs for insurance purposes. Investments, she said. Supply was getting scarce, value was bound to increase, they were buying all they could. War, revolution, ethnic uprisings. Future value, future gain. And in the meantime look how lovely. When she left, Dick got down on his knees to lift the edges of rugs arranged in layers on the floor. Hexagons. Stylized flying birds. Palmette stars. He threw back the edges to show more, the mellow colors of an old kilim made by nomadic weavers, a double prayer-niche that allowed both young and old to pray. He threw back entire rugs to show the full surfaces of what lay beneath, the patterns multiplying inward. He was not thinking of investments now. There were grids and arabesques, gardens in silk and wool. He pointed out multiple backgrounds, borders with formal Kufic lettering, things drawn together in crowded surfaces, a contained and intricate rapture, the desert universe made shapely and complete. He bobbed his smallish, round and almost hairless head, speaking in a soft hypnotic singsong. Geometry, nature and God.

The living room was crowded when we got back. I was drinking raki for no good reason. David introduced me to a man named Roy Hardeman. I looked at the wall-hangings, the silk calligraphy. *They have a tendency to crowd together in doorways, leaving the cinema for instance.* A woman's voice. *One thing I will say for the English, we don't block exits.* Lindsay stood across the room, laughing. What was it about our lives that year we were together that made us so ready to laugh? We were always laughing, it seemed, as if impelled by some quality of the sky on clear nights, the mountains around us, the sea at the foot of Syngrou Street. Hardeman said something. He was a small correct American who stood with his legs together, feet slightly parted. Based in Tunis, David said. Travels widely in North Africa, Western Europe. The pinched face of a killer executive. Dot moved toward me with a bottle three-quarters full. I realized why the name seemed familiar. Refrigeration systems. He was the man who hadn't showed up the night David and Lindsay went swimming in their clothes. A sandstorm in Cairo, someone had said. But who? Dick went down the hall with three Armenians from Tehran, here to get Canadian visas. I asked David if he'd gone to Frankfurt. He paused to wonder. Charles Maitland entered, full of chummy belligerence. Ann, behind him, looked nervous, over-alert. We were all standing, a stylized fatigue, a form of waking collapse that we agreed to undergo together.

Drink and banter made us hungry and someone got together a group of seven or eight for dinner. Sometime later we were down to four, sitting in a club in the Plaka watching a belly dancer named Janet Ruffing, the wife of the operations head at the Mainland Bank. David was astonished. He leaned over to confer with Lindsay. Roy Hardeman had gone across the room to make a phone call, wincing in the noise of drums, flute, amplified guitar and bouzouki. That curious bird-footed stance.

"I heard some of them were taking lessons," Lindsay said, "but I didn't think it would get this far. This is quite far."

"Does Jack Ruffing know?"

"Of course he knows."

"I don't think he knows," David said.

Hardeman came back to the table and David explained who the dancer was. Everybody seemed to know Jack Ruffing.

"Does Jack know?" Hardeman said.

"I don't think he knows."

"Hadn't someone better tell him? Look, I asked an associate to join us for a little last-minute give-and-take. I'm leaving a day sooner than I'd planned."

"I wonder if she gets paid," Lindsay said.

Polychrome sateen. Finger cymbals and scarlet lips. We studied her wandering pelvis, watched her lean and toss and vibrate. She was all wrong, long and slender, a white-bodied bending reed, but the cheerfulness of her effort, the shy pleasure she found, made us, made me, instantly willing to overlook the flat belly and slim hips, the earnest mechanics in her movements. What innocence and pluck, a bank wife, to dance in public, her navel fluttering above a turquoise sash. I ordered another drink and tried to recall the word for well-proportioned buttocks.

When the dance ended Lindsay went looking for her in a room at the top of the stairs. The musicians took a break, the three men at the table listened to the noise in the street, the motorcycles, the music from discos and nightclubs.

"Like to dedicate this medley of tunes to the deposed shah of

Iran," David said, looking into his glass. "I run in the woods every day."

"Good country hardball," Hardeman said.

"How is Karen?"

"She likes it there. She really likes it."

"Lindsay likes it here."

"She rides," Hardeman said.

"Only keep her out of the desert."

"I have a romance with the desert. That's right, of all people. The desert winds have stirring names."

"Lindsay thinks a lot of Karen."

"I'll tell her. That's good to know. She'll be pleased."

"We may be there in March."

"Our whole division moves to London in March."

"Sudden."

"Hostile oil, both sides."

"Not that many options."

"We had to facilitate," Hardeman said.

Janet wore a skirt, blouse and cardigan but her makeup was intact, shadows, penciled outlines, arcs and bands of color, a little eerie in the muted light, on a face that was a clear work of household prose. She was happy in a certain way, as someone is happy who learns that her motives are not complicated after all.

"It was unexpected," Lindsay said. "I never thought it would get this far."

"I know, it's crazy. I saw an opening and just went for it."

"You were good."

"My bellywork isn't very advanced. I have a lot of work to do on what we call hip isolation. I'm way too conscious of what I'm doing."

"What a surprise," Lindsay said, "to walk in like that and look who's up there dancing."

"People are kind," Janet said. "It's sort of an extended tryout."

"Haven't seen Jack," David said, looking at the woman with carefully measured concern.

"Jack's in the Emirates."

"The budget problem. Right, correct."

"I do things by rote," she said to Lindsay. "That's the only way I can do things. People seem to understand."

"Well you were good. I thought you were good."

Lindsay and I listened to her analyze her body in objective terms. I tried to work up a salacious interest, I schemed at it in fact, but she was artless, open and bland, so detached from the murmurous subcurrents, the system of images, that I gave it up. In the end this would become her appeal, her arousing power, this very deadness of intent.

A waiter brought drinks, the musicians returned. I liked the noise, the need to talk loud, to lean into people's faces and enunciate. This was the true party, just beginning, a shouted dialogue lacking sense and purpose. I huddled next to Janet, asking questions about her life, easing my way into her consciousness. Slowly we evolved a mood of curious intimacy, a sympathetic exchange made of misunderstood remarks, our heads nodding in the painted smoke.

I was aware of Lindsay's amused disapproval. It spurred me on, it was sexy, the Mainland wives protecting each other from public shame. The two men played a game with Tunisian coins.

"I have to get to know you, Janet."

"I'm not even sure who you are. I don't think I have it quite straight, who belongs to what at this table."

"I like it when women call me James."

"I don't do this," she said.

"You don't do what? I love the way you move."

"You know what I mean."

"We're only talking." Moving my lips, soundlessly.

"*Only* talking?"

"It's those wavelike ripples across your belly when you dance. Say belly. I want to watch your lips."

"No, honest, I don't do this."

"I know you don't, I know you don't."

"Do you really because it's important to me. And with people here I don't want to give the wrong impression."

"Lindsay is special. She's good people."

"I like Lindsay, I really do."

"They'll leave soon. Then you and I can really talk."

"I don't want to really talk. It's the last thing I want to do."

Folk dancers linking hands across their bodies moved sideways on the small stage.

"Your lipstick is cracked in places, which only heightens the effect. I could hardly breathe while you were up there. You were imperfect, even deeply flawed, but what a heartrending American body, how acutely moving. Say thighs. I want to watch your tongue curl up in your painted mouth."

"I don't do this, James."

"When women call me James, it gives me an image of myself. It *affords* me an image. Grown-up. At last, I think, I am grown up. She is calling me James. You have gorgeous long legs, Janet. That's rare today. The way your legs emerged from that silky garment, one at a time, bent ever so slightly. *Sheer.* A sheer garment."

"I really have to leave."

"Because at heart, down deep, I'm still twenty-two years old."

"Honest, I can't stay."

"How old are you, down deep?"

"Lindsay's going to think whatever."

"One more drink. We'll talk about your body. It's supple, for starters. It has a married poignancy that single carefree bodies can't even begin to suggest. The suppleness is hard-won. I love your ass."

"This means nothing to me."

"I know."

"If I thought you were serious I'd probably laugh in your face."

"You're shielding yourself from the truth. Because you know I'm serious. And I know you know it. I have to have you, Janet. Don't you see how you affect me?"

"No. I totally do not."

"Say breasts. Say tongue."

"We were two years in Brussels, three and a half years in Rome, a year back in New York and now a year and a half so far in Greece and no one has ever talked to me this way."

"I want you. It's no longer a question of choice, a question of actual wanting. We've gone beyond that. You know it, I know it. I want what's inside that cardigan, that skirt. What kind of panties are you wearing? If you don't tell me, I'll reach right under there and pull them off your legs. Then I'll put them in my pocket. They'll be mine. That vivid and intimate thing, that object."

Lindsay, turned away from us toward the stage, was still our listener, our auditor, and in everything we said there was acknowledgment of this, although she couldn't hear a word, of course, through the flutes and bouzoukis. A dancer leaped, struck his black boot with the palm of his hand, in midair, slapped it hard.

"Here's what I want to say about your makeup."

"No, please."

"It's compelling without being sexy or lurid. That's the odd thing. It's a statement of some sort, isn't it? The body is supple, open, airy and free. The face is masked, almost bitterly masked. I'm not the kind of man who tells women who they are or what they mean, so we'll just let it lay, we'll let it rest, the face, the mask, the cracked scarlet."

"I don't do this. What am I doing listening to this? Not to mention I have to go to the ladies room."

"Let me go with you. I want to. Please."

"I'm not so indecisive I can't get up and go home. It's just a sleepiness that keeps me here."

"I know. I know exactly."

"Are you sleepy too?"

"That's it exactly. A sleepiness."

She put a hand to my face, briefly, and looked at me with a strange sympathy, an understanding of something that applied to us both. Then she went downstairs, where the toilets were.

I looked diagonally across the table to see the great Balkan head of Andreas Eliades. He sat talking to Hardeman. Remember. We'd sat with four glasses of brandy in that seaside taverna, waiting for David and Lindsay to come up from the beach. Hardeman's name, Hardeman's plane, a sandstorm in Cairo. In the passing of time, that night seemed to deepen its weave. It was like a mingled reminiscence I carried with me, the selective memories of those who were there. Moments kept coming back to me, precise textures, the brand names of cigarettes, the old guitarist's eyes, his seamed brown hand, and what the Bordens said, and who plucked a grape from the wet bunch, and where people sat, how we rearranged ourselves around the table as the evening passed through its own solid objects to become what it is now. Eliades seemed more and more the means of some connection.

We nodded to each other and I made a scattered gesture to indicate I didn't know what I was doing in a place like this. I realized Lindsay was looking at me. She sat straight across from me, an empty chair on either side of her. Andreas was at the far end, facing Hardeman, who had moved.

I said to Andreas, "We keep running into each other."

He shrugged, I shrugged.

David was between Hardeman and me. Janet's chair was to my left. Where people sat seemed important to me, although I didn't know why.

"Don't stare," I said to Lindsay. "It makes me feel you're making up your mind about something."

"About going home," she said. "Whose idea was this anyway?"

"Somebody wanted to see Greek dancing."

Andreas asked her whether she was learning verbs. Another memory, a fragment of that summer night. They tried to chat politely through the amplified sound. David leaned my way to fix me with a sad-eyed look.

"We haven't talked," he said.

"I know."

"I wanted to talk. We never get to talk."

"We'll talk soon. We'll talk tomorrow. We'll have lunch."

When he and Lindsay were gone I didn't move closer to the two men and when Janet Ruffing came back to the table she sat in Lindsay's chair. It was like a board game. Two sets of people facing each other, two sets of empty chairs. Hardeman ordered another round.

"They're talking business," I said to her. "Shipments, tonnage."

"Who is the bearded man?"

"Business. A businessman."

"He looks like one of those priests."

"He's having an affair with Ann Maitland, probably. Do you know her?"

"Why would you tell me something like that?"

"I'd tell you anything tonight. There are no strategies. I mean it. I'd tell you anything, I'd do anything for you."

"But why?"

"The way you danced."

"But you said I wasn't very good."

"The way you moved, your legs, your breasts, what you are. Never mind technique. What you are, how pleased you were with yourself."

"But I don't think that's true."

"How pleased you were. I insist on that."

"I almost think in a roundabout way you're trying to bring out my vanity."

"You're not vain, you're hopeful. Vanity is a defensive quality. It contains an element of fear. It's a look into the future, into wasting away and death." Another dancer leaped. "I'm at that certain stage in a night of drinking and talking when I see things clearly through a small opening, a window in space. I know things. I know what we're going to say before we say it."

"What did Lindsay say?"

"She only looked at me."

"Are these bank people?"

"Refrigerators."

"They're going to wonder what we're saying."

"I'd like to walk out of here with your panties in my back pocket. You'd have to follow me, wouldn't you? I'd like to slip my hand under your blouse and detach your bra. I want to sit here and talk to you knowing I've got your bra and panties in my pocket. That's all I ask. The knowledge of a bareness under your clothes. Knowing that, sitting here talking to you and knowing you were naked under your clothes, this would enable me to live another ten years, this knowledge alone, independent of food and drink. Are you wearing a bra in fact? I'm not one of those men who can tell at a glance. I've never had the self-assured powers of observation that would allow me to say that this or that woman was or was not wearing a bra. As a kid I never stood on street corners and estimated cup measurements. There goes a C cup, like that, with total self-assurance."

"Please. I think I ought to go."

"Only to put my hands under your clothes. No more than that. What we did as kids, adolescent sex, how happy that would make me. A back room in your family's summer bungalow. A mildewed room, a darkening, a sudden rain. Move against me, push me off, pull me onto you again. Worried about someone coming back, back from the lake, the yard sale. Worried about everything we're doing. The rain loosens every fresh smell in the countryside. It comes in on us from outdoors, rain-fresh, rain-washed, lovely, sweet-smelling, a chill in the summer air. It's nature, it's sex. And you pull me onto you and worry and tell me not to, not to. See how sentimental I am. How cheap and indecent. They're coming back from the lakeside bar, the one on stilts called Mickey's Landing, where you wait on tables when you're feeling bored."

"But the dancing isn't sexy to me. It's not that at all."

"I know that, I know, it's part of the point, part of the reason I want you so badly, your long, white and well-meaning body."

"Oh thanks."

"Your body has won out over marriage. It's better for the experience. It's wildly beautiful. How old are you, thirty-five?"

"Thirty-four."

"Wearing a cardigan. Is a cardigan what women wear when they don't want to talk about themselves?"

"How can I talk? This isn't real to me."

"You danced. That was real."

"I don't do this."

"You danced. This talk we're having means nothing to you and everything to me. You danced, I didn't. I'm trying to return to you some idea of how deeply you affected me, dancing, barefoot, in arm-length gloves, in filmy things, and of how you affect me right now, sitting here, so hard to find under the eyeshadow, the mascara, the lip gloss, the lipstick. The way you sit here unmoved by our talking excites hell out of me."

"I'm not unmoved."

"I want to reach you in the most direct of ways. I want you to say to yourself, 'He is going to do something and I don't know what it is but I want him to do it.' Janet."

We were all drinking Scotch. Andreas still in his raincoat.

"Your voice, when you were telling us about your body, about the lessons, the practices, the hips do this, the belly does that, your voice was four inches outside your body, it began at a point about four inches beyond your lips."

"I don't know what you mean."

"There's a lack of connection between your words and the physical action they describe, the parts of the body they describe. This is what draws me to you so intensely. I want to put your voice back inside your body, where it belongs."

"How do you do that?" A half smile, skeptical and tired.

"By making you see yourself in a different way, I guess. By making you see me, making you feel the heat of my wanting. Do you feel it? Tell me if you do. I want to hear you say it. Say heat. Say wet between my legs. Say legs. Seriously, I want you to. *Stockings*. Whisper it. The word is meant to be whispered."

"I can sit and listen to you and I can tell myself this is real and I can tell myself he means it. But it's just so foreign to me. I don't know the responses."

"James. Call me James."

"Oh shit please."

"Use *names*," I said.

"No more drinks. I don't do this."

"Neither one of us wants to go home. We want to put off going home. We want to stay here awhile longer. I'd forgotten what it was like, not wanting to go home. Of course I don't have to go home. That worrisome small force isn't pulling at me, as it pulls at you. What is waiting there that you don't want to face?" We sat awhile, thinking about this. "I'm trying to express what you're feeling, what we're both feeling. If I can do that, you may begin to trust me in the deepest way. The way that complicates, that envelops. So that when you want to stop what we're doing, the shove and force and direction of the whole night, you won't be able to."

"I wonder if you would recognize me on the street, tomorrow, without this makeup I'm wearing. Even stranger, I wonder if I would recognize you."

"The glare would be immense, the broad sunlight. We'd want to run from each other."

Greeks from the audience were on stage now, dancing, and soon tourists began approaching the edges of the platform, carrying purses with them and shoulder bags and wearing sea captain's hats, looking back at friends—looks that begged encouragement for some stupidity they thought they were about to invent.

"They'll be closing soon," she said. "I think it's really time."

She went upstairs to get her coat. I stood listening to Hardeman talk about maintenance feasibility. Andreas, attending to these remarks, took a card out of some inner pocket and extended it to me without looking up. A simple business card. I offered Hardeman some money, which he waved off, and then Janet and I went into the street.

There wasn't space to hold the sound. It crowded the night, dense waves of it, heavy with electrified force. It came out of the walls and pavement and wooden doors, the pulse of some undefined event, and we walked up the stepped street, into it, her arm linked with mine.

A man with cowhide bagpipes stood playing in the window of a small taverna. This music was a condition of the air, the weather of these old streets at half past one in the morning, and I edged her into a wall and kissed her. She looked away, her mouth smeared, saying we had to go down the other way, to the bottom of the steps, where the taxis were, if there were any. I pulled her up higher past the cabarets, the last of the Cretan dancers, the last of the singers in open shirts, and held her against the second of the old walls of falling buildings. She looked at me in a near grimace of wondering, a speculation that had the shock of waking about it, of trying to recall a somber dream. Who was he, what were we doing there? I pressed her against the wall, trying to open her coat. She said we had to get a taxi, she had to get home. I put my hand between her legs, over the skirt, and she seemed to sink a little, her head turned against the wall. I tried to get her to hold the edges of my coat to keep us covered, keep us out of the cold, while I worked at my pants. She broke away, running down some steps past a scaffold set against an old building. She ran holding her handbag by the strap and well away from her body as if it held something she thought might spill on her. She turned a corner and went uphill now, into an empty street. When I reached her and put my arms around her from behind she stood motionless. I moved my hands down her belly over the skirt and placed my knees behind hers, making her bend slightly, dip into me. She said something, then shook away and walked out of the dim light toward the wall. I pressed her against the wall. The music was far away and fading by degrees as places closed. I kissed her, lifted her skirt. Voices below us, a laughing man.

She said to me, she whispered with uncanny clarity, "People just want to be held. It's enough to be held, isn't it?"

I paused, then used my knees to move her legs apart. I worked in stages, trying to reason it, to maneuver things correctly. We took short breaths, our mouths together, as we urged each other into a rhythm and a need. I worked at her clothes, my mind racing blankly. I felt the warmth in her buttocks and thighs and I moved her toward me. She seemed to be thinking past this moment, finished with it, watching herself in a taxi heading home.

"Janet Ruffing."

"I don't do this. I don't."

We stood under an iron balcony, in the upper sector of the old town, beneath the rock mass of the north slope of the Acropolis.

10

THE GERMANS are sitting in the sun. The Swedes drift by, heads tilted sunward, an eagerness in their faces that resembles pain. The two women from Holland stand against the wall of the harborfront church, eyes closed, feeling the warmth on their faces and necks. The man we keep seeing, the one in the white linen cap, stands in a patch of sun in the Turkish cemetery, among the pines and eucalyptus, peeling an orange. The Swedes move out of sight, heading toward the aquarium. The English appear, carrying their coats into the empty square, where shadows begin to extend from the Venetian arcade, in the strange silence, the late morning light.

Three days in Rhodes. David decides it is warm enough to swim. We watch him enter, moving slowly forward, shoulders swinging, arms raised to chest level when the water reaches his midsection, the blond body, as he surfaces after the plunge, seeming to leap toward the Turkish hills, seven miles off. We sit on a low wall above the beach. The beach is empty except for boys with a spotted soccer ball. The pages of a paperback book turn in the wind. The man in the white cap comes by, asking us where he can find the museum of fish.

David's swim leaves a space which we are meant to fill with

serious talk. But Lindsay seems content to look out to sea. It is that kind of holiday. The long sightlines, the emptiness, the building wind.

After the second of his long punishing swims he comes up the beach looking four inches shorter, walking deep in sand. When he raises his head we see how happy he is to be breathing heavily and sea-beaten and freezing, his wife and his friend waiting with a hotel towel.

The next day it rains, and the day after, which reduces the mood to a purer state. I begin to see that these days are connected mysteriously to Kathryn. They are Kathryn's days.

On the afternoon of the third day a storm approaches. It comes from the east and we stand on the breakwater near the old tower to watch the waves hit gleaming on the rocks. An immense graveness fills the air. The seaward stir of clouds and glassy dusk brings on a charged luminescence, a stormlight that does not fall upon objects so much as it emanates from them. The buildings begin to glow, the governor's palace, the bell-tower, the new market. As the sky goes black the white boats shine, the bronze deer shine, the gold stone of the law courts and bank emits a painted light. Water comes surging over the high wall. There is no light except in objects.

Coming home, flying low over islands crouched in the haze, we began suddenly to talk.

"Why do I miss my countries?" David said. "My countries are either terrorist playpens or they're viciously anti-American or they're huge tracts of economic and social and political wreckage."

"Sometimes all of those," Lindsay said.

"Why can't I wait to get back into it? Why am I so eager? A hundred percent inflation, twenty percent unemployment. I love deficit countries. I love going in there, being intimately involved."

"Too intimately, some might say."

"You can't be too intimate with a Syrian, a Lebanese," he told me.

"When they allow you to monitor their economic policies in

return for a loan. When you reschedule a debt and it amounts to an aid program."

"These things help, they genuinely help stabilize the region. We do things for our countries. Our countries are interesting. I can't get interested in Spain, for instance."

"I can't get interested in Italy."

"Spain *should* be interesting. The violence is not sickening like the violence in India. But I can't get interested."

"Indian violence is random. Is that what you mean?"

"I don't know what I mean."

"I can't get interested in the Horn of Africa," I said.

"The Horn of Africa is happening. Rhodesia is happening. But we can't get interested."

"What about Afghanistan? Is that one of your countries?"

"It's a non-presence country. No office but we do business, a little. Iran is different. Collapsed presence, collapsed business. A black hole in other words. But I want everyone to know I retain a measure of affection."

This was the period after the President ordered a freeze of Iranian assets held in U.S. banks. Desert One was still to come, the commando raid that ended two hundred and fifty miles from Tehran. It was the winter Rowser learned that the Shi'ite underground movement, Dawa, was stockpiling weapons in the Gulf. It was the winter before the car bombings in Nablus and Ramallah, before the military took power in Turkey, tanks in the streets, soldiers painting over wall slogans. It was before Iraqi ground troops moved into Iran at four points along the border, before the oilfields burned and the sirens sounded through Baghdad, through Rashid Street and the passageways of the souks, before the blackouts, the masking of headlights, people hurrying out of teahouses, off the double-decker buses.

All around us the human noise, the heat of a running crowd.

Food and drink were the center of almost every human contact I had in Greece and the region. Eating, talking across rickety wooden tables, marble-top tables, tables with paper covering, wrought-iron tables, tables set together on a pebbled surface by the sea. One of the mysteries of the Aegean is that things seem more significant than they do elsewhere, deeper, more complete in themselves. Those of us pressed together around the joined tables were raised in each other's estimation to a higher light perhaps, an amplitude that may or may not have been our natural due. The food itself was a serious thing, simple as it often was, eaten with dwarf cutlery from shared plates, an effort of our single will to be where we were, extravagant in our belief in each other's distinctiveness and worth. We never had to summon a sense of occasion. It was in and around us all the time.

Andreas took me to a taverna in a half-finished street in a remote district. The place specialized in heart, brains, kidneys and intestines. I decided this choice of eating place had not been made casually. The evening was to be a lesson in seriousness, in authentic things, whatever is beyond a pale understanding, whatever persuades the complacent to see what is around them. He would use these parts of the animal's body to decorate his text. This is the real thing, *kokorétsi*, the spit-roasted entrails of the beast. These are Greeks, who eat it.

On the other hand maybe it was just another dinner in a smoky room with homemade wine in tin mugs, distinguishable from a hundred other dinners not by the food so much as by the intensity of the conversation. His conversation. His furious, good-humored, incessant and maddening talk.

He was not settled until he put his cigarette and his lighter on the table in front of him. I felt almost threatened by the gesture. Serious. A serious evening.

"Why are we having dinner, Andreas?"

"I want to find out about your Greek. You said you were learning Greek. I want to find out if you are happy here."

"Not that people need a reason to eat."

"I am always interested in talking to Americans."

"Roy Hardeman."

"Professional duty. I am not so interested. He's a good manager, very smart, but we only talk about the job. He could be a Frenchman, a German, and I would hardly notice. I don't think

there's any nationality in companies such as ours. This is submerged."

"I can't imagine you submerging your nationality."

"Okay, maybe this is why we are here. To make things clear
once again. To show our status."

"You need someone to rail at. Why not a Frenchman or German?"

"Not so much fun."

"A waiter said to us on Rhodes the other day, he said, 'You
Americans are fools. You had the Germans down and you let
them up. They were down and you did not crush them. Now
look. Everywhere.' "

"But he takes their money. We all take each other's money.
This is the role of the present government. Take the Americans'
money, do what the Americans tell us to do. It is breathtaking,
how they submit, how they let American strategic interests take
precedence over the lives of Greeks."

"It's your government, not ours."

"I am not so sure. Of course we have experience in these
matters. Humiliation is the theme of Greek affairs. Foreign interference is taken for granted. It is assumed we could not
survive without it. The occupation, the blockades, the forces
landing in Piraeus, the humiliating treaties, the distribution of
influence among the powers. What would we talk about if not
about this? Where would we find the drama that is so essential to our lives?"

"You realize your irony is fixed in considerable truth. Of
course you do. Forgive me."

"For a long time our politics have been determined by the
interests of the great powers. Now it is just the Americans who
determine."

"What is this I'm eating?"

"I will tell you. Brains."

"Not bad."

"Do you like it? Good. I come here when I'm tense. When my
job is crushing my spirit. Something like this, you know. Misery,
depression. I come here and eat brains and kidneys."

"You realize the trouble with Greece. Greece is strategically located."

"We have noticed," he said.

"So it's only natural the major powers have taken a close interest. What do you expect? My boss once said to me in his nervous raspy way, 'Power works best when it doesn't distinguish friends from enemies.' The man is a living Buddha."

"I think he must be running American policy. Our future does not belong to us. It is owned by the Americans. The Sixth Fleet, the men who command the bases on our soil, the military officers who fill the U.S. embassy, the political officers who threaten to stop the economic aid, the businessmen who threaten to stop investing, the bankers who lend money to Turkey. Millions for the Turks, all decided in Athens."

"Not by me, Andreas."

"Not by you. We are repeatedly sold out, taken lightly, deceived, totally ignored. Always in favor of the Turks. The famous tilt. It happened in Cyprus, it happens every day in NATO."

"You're obsessed by the Turks. It's a spiritual need. Are they even remotely interested in you?"

"They seem to be remotely interested in our islands, our air space."

"Strategy."

"American strategy. This is interesting, how the Americans choose strategy over principle every time and yet keep believing in their own innocence. Strategy in Cyprus, strategy in the matter of the dictatorship. The Americans learned to live with the colonels very well. Investments flourished under the dictatorship. The bases stayed open. Small arms shipments continued. Crowd control, you know?"

"They were your colonels, Andreas."

"Are you sure of that? This is interesting to me, the curious connection between Greek and American intelligence agencies."

"Why curious?"

"The Greek government doesn't know what goes on between them."

"What makes you think the American government knows?

This is the nature of intelligence, isn't it? The final enemy is government. Only government threatens their existence."

"The nature of power. The nature of intelligence. You have studied these things. Where, in your apartment in Kolonaki?"

"How do you know I live there?"

"Where else would you live but there?"

"The views are nice."

"The bidet of America, we call this place. Do you want to hear the history of foreign interference in this century alone?"

"No."

"Good. I don't have time to recite it."

In the end he did recite it. He recited everything, interrupting his meal several times to light cigarettes, order more wine. I enjoyed myself even in the sweep of judgment and enormous accusation. He had made an occupation of these matters, he had taken pains, and I think he was eager to vent his scholarship. Diligence, comprehensiveness. He was a student of Greek things. It occurred to me that all Greeks were, both in and out of politics and war. Being small and exposed, being strategic. They had a sense of the frailty of their own works, the identifying energies and signs, and they instructed each other as a form of mutual reassurance.

"Does your boss tell you that power must be blind in both eyes? You don't see us. This is the final humiliation. The occupiers fail to see the people they control."

"Come on, Andreas."

"Bloody hell, nothing happens without the approval of the Americans. And they don't even know there is a grievance. They don't know we are tired of the situation, the relationship."

"You've had five or six years of calm. Is this too long for Greeks?"

"Look how deep we are involved in the comedy. To make concessions to Turks for the sake of harmony in NATO. All arranged by Americans. Americans have played the game badly in Greece."

"And your mistakes. All your mistakes are discussed in terms of acts of nature. The catastrophe in Asia Minor. The disastrous events in Cyprus. This is the language of earthquakes and floods. But Greeks caused these things to happen."

"Cyprus is problematical. I will say this only because there is no documentary evidence. But one day the facts of U.S. involvement will emerge. I am certain."

"What am I eating?"

"This is the stomach, the stomach lining."

"Interesting."

"I don't know if I would call it interesting. It's a sheep's stomach, you know. Usually I come here alone. It has a certain meaning for me. Brains, intestines. I don't know if you can understand. Did you ever see a Greek when he dances alone? This is private, a private moment. I'm a little crazy, I think. I need a moment of eating sheep's brains now and then."

The owner stood over us, totaling the bill in machine-gun Greek. We went somewhere for dessert, somewhere else for drinks. At two in the morning we walked the streets looking for a cab. Andreas told me about events leading up to this and that and the other calamity. Whenever he had a point to make he stopped walking and seized my wrist. This happened four or five times on a single windy street. Talk came out of him like the product of some irreversible technology. We'd stand briefly in the dark, then start up again, heading toward a boulevard somewhere. He was full of night vigor, a common property of Athenians. Ten paces he'd stop again. Nuclear stockpiles, secret protocols. His politics were a form of wakefulness, the alerting force in a life that might otherwise pass him by.

"What do you want me to do, Andreas?"

"I want you to argue," he said. "It may be an hour before a taxi comes."

From the small balcony off my bedroom I looked into a room across the courtyard, a little below me. A bright day, shutters open, the room being aired. Self-possessed, a woman's room, a woman's shoes on the floor. I was in shadows, the room in clear light, utterly still, a cool space of objects and tones. What a mystery her absence was, full of unformed questions. There was something final in the scene, a deep calm, as though things had been arranged to be gazed on. Shouldn't a scene like this be marked by expectation? The woman will enter? She will enter drying her hair in a towel, bringing into the room so many things at once, so much affective motion, a lifetime's shattering of composed space, that it is possible to believe you know everything about her, just in that bundling of head and arms, that careless entrance, barefoot, in a loose robe. Alluring. This is what I missed. When the light changed, later, I would look again.

My landlord, Hadjidakis, was standing in the lobby. He was a short heavy man who enjoyed speaking English. Almost everything he said in English struck him as funny, almost every sentence ended in a laugh. He seemed happily disconcerted, making these strange sounds. After we'd greeted each other he told me he'd just seen a group of riot policemen assembled near the center of town. Nothing seemed to be going on. They were simply there, about forty of them, in their white visored helmets, black uniforms, carrying riot shields, guns and clubs. As he told the story Hadjidakis kept laughing. All the facts in the story were separated by the sound of his laughter. It was an odd juxtaposition, of course, the riot police and the laughter. The story in English had an eerie dimension it wouldn't have had in Greek. And the sight of those shields and clubs had made an impact on him.

"It gave me an emotion," he said, and we both laughed.

When I came down the next day with a suitcase, the concierge stood in the dimness, his right hand twisted in the air, the gesture of destinations.

China, I told him, *Kina*, not knowing the word for Kuwait.

I rode out to the airport with Charles Maitland, who was going to Beirut to see about a job as security officer with the British embassy there.

"I was saying to Ann. They keep changing the names."

"What names?"

"The names we grew up with. The countries, the images. Persia for one. We grew up with Persia. What a vast picture that name evoked. A vast carpet of sand, a thousand turquoise mosques. A vastness, a cruel glory extending back centuries. All the names. A dozen or more and now Rhodesia of course. Rhodesia said something. For better or worse it was a name that said something. What do they offer in its place? Linguistic arrogance, I suggested to her. She called me a comedian. She has no personal memory of Persia as a name. But then she's younger, isn't she?"

We floated past the Olympic Stadium.

"There's something to it, you know. This sweeping arrogance. Overthrow, re-speak. What do they leave us with? Ethnic designations. Sets of initials. The work of bureaucrats, narrow minds. I find I take these changes quite personally. They're a rescinding of memory. Every time another people's republic emerges from the dust, I have the feeling someone has tampered with my childhood."

"You can't prefer Leopoldville to Kinshasa."

"The Ministry of Slogans. The Ministry of Obscure Dialects."

"Zimbabwe," I said. "A drumbeat."

"A drumbeat. That's just it, you see."

"That's just what?"

"A drumbeat, a drumbeat."

Our driver eased into a gray line of taxis stretching down the thoroughfare. A woman and maimed child walked along the divide from car to car, begging. The light changed. We were almost to the airport when Charles spoke again.

"I heard about the belly dancing."

"Yes."

"An interesting night, was it?"

"Do you know her?"

"I know her husband," he said, and when he looked at me his jaw was tight and strong and I wondered if we were fixed in some near symmetry of friendships and adulteries. We walked through the doors into the towering noise of the terminal.

Two phone calls.

The first came the night I got back from Kuwait. The phone rang twice, then stopped. A little later it rang again. I hadn't been able to sleep. It was two in the morning, shutters banging in the wind.

Ann's voice.

"This will seem strange, I know."

"Are you all right?"

"Well, yes, but I've been putting this off and putting it off."

"Is Charles still in Beirut?"

"He stayed on. We have friends there. He's fine. It isn't Charles, it isn't me exactly."

For a moment I thought she wanted to invite herself over. I studied the wooden surface of the table the phone was on. In the stillness before she spoke again I concentrated intently.

"It's about this man I've been seeing. It's about him actually."

I waited, then said, "Andreas. This is the man you're talking about."

She waited. "How interesting, James. Then you know." Waited. "Yes, it's about him I've been wanting to speak to you. Did I wake you? How stupid to call at this hour. But it's been absolutely pressing in on me. I couldn't sleep. I had to tell you, I finally decided. It may be pure imagination but what if it isn't, I thought." Waited. "How interesting, that you know."

The voice was rough-edged and faint. She would be sitting beneath the African mask, a drink at her right hand.

"We've talked about you," she said. "Every so often he asks. A question about your job one day. A question about your friends, your background, small things, falling more or less naturally into the conversation. At first I barely noticed. It was one subject among many. But lately I've begun to think his interest in you may be special. Something enters the conversation. A suspense, I think I'll call it. There's a curious silence in his waiting for my responses. And he watches me. I've begun to notice how he watches. He's a watchful man, isn't he?"

"I like Andreas."

"He keeps bringing up your job. I've told him I haven't the foggiest idea what you do. All right, he changes the subject. But eventually it comes up again, perhaps a bit more directly the second time, a bit clumsily even. 'Why is his main office in

Washington?' 'Andreas, I've no idea. Why don't you ask him?' Clearly he thinks you're someone who merits attention."

"He also thought I was David Keller, didn't he, at dinner that night. You were right there. He had us mixed up, remember? I was the unscrupulous banker."

"He mentions something called the Northeast Group."

"That's the firm I work for. It's part of a monster corporation. A wholly owned subsidiary, I think is the phrase."

"If I might ask, James, what exactly do you do? Not your company but you. When you travel."

"Generally I do reviews. I examine figures, make decisions."

"Well, see, that's so vague."

"The higher the post, the vaguer the job. The people with specific duties need someone to send their telexes to. I'm a presence."

"He mentions all the travel you do. He mentions the tiny staff you have in Athens. Just a secretary, is this correct? He wonders why your main office is in Washington and not New York. He does his best not to be direct. He rather worms these subjects into the conversation. The more I think about it, the more obvious it all seems. But I didn't know how to tell you."

"What else does he mention?"

"He mentions a book you wrote on military strategy."

"Ghost-wrote. All I did was organize some facts. How the hell does he know about that?"

"That's it, you see."

"I wrote a lot of things, a dozen subjects."

"I think he's read the book."

"Then he knows more than I do. I can't remember a word of it. It was grammar and syntax to me. Why didn't he mention it? I saw him a week ago."

"Something enters the conversation when we talk about you." Waiting. "Do you hear the wind?"

"He can't be gathering information for someone. Nobody's that amateurish. And there's nothing to gather. What is there to gather?"

"Maybe I'm wrong," she said. "We've talked about other people as well. Sometimes at length. I could be imagining."

"I like Andreas. There's a size to him. There's a force. He has deep feelings and deep suspicions and he should have them, why shouldn't he, when you consider events, when you consider history. I can't see what he'd be up to, doing this. He's with a multinational. They're based in Bremen or Essen or someplace."

"Bremen."

"It doesn't add up."

"Well, then, I'm imagining."

"Unless he has friends on one of the left-wing papers here. Maybe he's playing amateur spy. The Communist papers like to print the names of foreign correspondents they think are tied to U.S. intelligence."

"It doesn't seem like him."

"No, it doesn't."

"What do I want to say? He's so human?"

"Yes."

"He is, you know. He has large feelings, as you say, but they pass very easily into a gentleness, a sympathy. How I would hate to think I was being used."

"It's not that way," I said. "If he wanted information, he couldn't possibly expect to get it without my finding out."

"Unless he thought I wouldn't tell you."

"But you have."

"Isn't it awful? He thought I'd be so smitten."

"It's not that way. There's an explanation. He said he'd call. I won't even try to get in touch. I'll wait for him to call."

"He mentioned several other things in connection with your activities."

"My activities? Do I have activities? I thought it was his activities we were concerned about."

"The more I reflect, the more I think I'm imagining."

"He said he'd call. I'll give him every chance to explain before I bring it up. When will you see him again?"

"He said he'd call. But he hasn't."

"He will. What about Charles? What about the job in Beirut?"

"I don't think so," she said.

"Were you willing to go back?"

"There?" She sounded surprised that I would ask.

"Then why would he bother seeing about a job?"

"To take taxis across the Green Line. To light up in a bloody great smile when Israeli jets break the sound barrier. He loves the roar, the boom. To pretend to be unaffected when the guns start firing round the corner. That's why he went."

The worn voice began to acquire a certain disregarding impetus. Soon it would fall into monologue, an inner speech that did not need a context or listener.

"To sit there with his beer, chatting with a colleague as the mortars rain down or whatever they do. Absolutely unmoved. I think he lived for such moments. They were the high points of Lebanon, as demonstrations were the high points of Panama when we were there. During the worst of the anti-American demonstrations he'd put on his Union Jack lapel badge and go walking right into it. How I came to hate that badge. He truly felt he couldn't be harmed, wearing it. And so he sits in someone's office in Beirut when the militiamen are active. To betray no sign of emotion. To *chat*. What's the point of getting excited, he liked to say to me. Truly believing there is good sense in this. As if getting excited had something to do with deciding to get excited, making a conscious decision to get excited. They're out there hurling grenades, firing rockets. What's the point of getting excited? What's the point?"

The second call came from Del Nearing moments before I left for the office. She was in a phone booth off the main square in Argos, the Peloponnese, waiting for the Athens bus. She just thought I'd like to know.

We sat in the living room.

"Whose furniture?"

"Rented," I said.

"What do you have to eat?"

"Nothing. We'll go out."

"When?"

"Eight-thirty, nine."

"You live like me," she said. "Hard to believe I'll be home in a day or two. I actually enjoyed the bus trip here. The bus was going somewhere. I knew where it was going."

"You lost weight."

"California. I need to tone up my orgasm. What is this I'm drinking, Jim? Jeem, I should say." I took this to be her pronunciation of the Arabic letter *jim*. "Did you have a nice day at the office, Jeem? Is this marble floor real marble, Jeem?"

She wore boots, jeans and a sweatshirt with the arms cut off. Her feet rested on the coffee table. She was drinking kumquat brandy, which I'd been trying to get rid of for months.

"Where is Frank?" I said.

"Where is Frank. All right, since you're buying me dinner and letting me spend the night. Is that all right with you, Jeem? I spend the night? Separate rooms? Just so I don't have to go to another hotel?"

"Of course."

"Well, he's still there. He's crisscrossing the mountain. Andahl didn't show up where he was supposed to. There was no meeting, no sign of him or them or anyone. The first week Frank kept saying he'd give it one more day. Pathetic. I really wanted to stay. I tried very hard. One more day, one more day. He started exploring the area north of the towers. Up where the range broadens and you lose the sea. Terrible roads, no roads at all. Rusty oak trees, gunshots all the time. I began to feel there was something deeply wasteful in all this. But what can you say to Frank once he's *in*? First I went with him. Then I stayed in the hotel. The second week he didn't say much of anything and neither did I. He kept finding another dirt track, another village. Asking people, making gestures, pointing to names on the map. I felt there was something dead, there was an emptiness at the center of all this. I tried to explain but I didn't know how and he wasn't listening anyway. So I just thought to hell with it. Let the man do what he has to. And I went to see about getting myself on out of there."

"I wonder about Andahl, if they found him, if he decided to disappear."

"Nazi backpackers. That's all they are."

"I think about the movie now and then. I *see* it at times. As Frank described it. Strong images. That landscape. He'll never find them, we'll never know if he was right."

"You mean that it works as a film, the way they live?"

"Yes, that it fits the screen. I do see it at times, powerfully."

"Film. Why do I want to throw up when I hear the term 'personal film'? 'He does personal films.' 'He makes personal statements.' 'He has a personal vision.' "

"I knew they wouldn't meet him. How could people like that be interested in somebody's film, somebody's book?"

"You were right. They were true to themselves."

I noted the dry tone. I told her it was strange, how right I'd been. I'd been right all along. I figured out the pattern. I figured out Andahl was a runaway. I told Frank the cultists wouldn't appear and they hadn't appeared.

She looked at me in the dimness.

"What pattern?" she said.

"The way they work. The whole mechanism. The whole point. It's the alphabet."

"But you didn't tell Frank."

"No, I didn't."

"You kept it to yourself."

"That's right."

We sat there. I liked watching the large room turn dark as evening deepened. She didn't say anything. I thought she must be cold, being bare-armed, the heat only beginning to rise through the building. The phone rang twice.

"I'm not sure what was behind it," I said. "I guess Kathryn. Whatever there was between them."

"What was there between them?"

"I'm sure he talked about us, all three of us. You would know better than I."

"All these years you've nursed this thing? Not letting either of them know you suspected an affair, or whatever you suspected? A night? An afternoon?"

"I let her know. She knows."

"But when you had a chance to get back at him, you took it.

You knew something he didn't know, something important to him. How did it make you feel, Jeem, keeping the secret?"

"That's part of it. The secret. It meant something to me, discovering the secret. I wasn't in a hurry to pass it on. I felt this knowledge was special. It had to be earned. It was too important to be given away. He had to earn it. Owen Brademas wouldn't tell him either. He only hinted to Frank. It would have been easy to tell him. But he didn't tell him. The knowledge is special. Once you have it, you find yourself protective of it. It confers a cult-hood of its own."

We sat quietly for a while.

"All right. Do you want me to tell you what there was between them, what went on, if anything?"

"No," I said.

"You'd rather nurse it along."

"I'd rather not know. Simple as that."

After dinner we returned to sit in the same chairs. I left the hall light on. She described her apartment, how it seemed these past months to be the only settled thing in her life, the only stillness. Small, furnished sparely, in soft light, waiting. A woman's things. She might have been the woman who comes walking into that room across the courtyard, the serene space I had watched from my balcony. Maybe this is why I went to sit on the sofa, leaning toward Del to hold her face in my hands, framing the perfect features, the wide mouth and tilted eyes, the cropped hair tailing over her ears.

"You like me, Jeem? Maybe you think I give you good time. Tell me what you like. You like dirty, you like filthy? What we do, Jeem? Say to me in little words. I don't do all the words. Some words I can do, some I don't like to do so much. They are very big, these words, hard to do. But some men like. You must tell me, Jeem. We do big words or little words?"

"I thought all the words were little."

"You are funny man, Jeem. They did not tell me this in the mountains."

"He won't stay two days," I said. "The search is as good as over."

"Why this is, Jeem?"

"You're not there anymore. You go, he goes. He'll do a certain amount of serious bitching and moaning. Then he'll give in to it. He'll give in to knowing he has to have you with him. That's when he'll pack and leave."

"I think I must be real woman, if it is true what you say."

Deadpan, a humorless voice. The moment was false. It had a specious feel to it. I realized I'd approached her, touched the edges of her face, moved my thumbs across her lips (listening to the whorish voice) not for the touch itself or because I wanted something simple from her, the scant body folded in mine. Her voice went on, mocking both of us. I sat back in the sofa, my feet on the table at a right angle to hers, my hands folded behind my neck. She folded her hands behind her neck.

I'd wanted to strike at Volterra. Sex with his woman. How primally satisfying. I didn't tell her this. She would be unsurprised, prone to make a joke, invent another voice as I'd invented voices during the week of the 27 Depravities. But it pained me to be silent. I always want to confess to women.

Completing your revenge. Hiding it even from yourself at times. Not willing to be seen taking your small mean everyday revenge.

She had one last thing to say before we went to our separate beds. If there was something I hadn't told Volterra, there was also something he had kept from me.

"He had no plans to shoot in sequence except for the ending. The ending would be the last thing he'd shoot. He told me how he'd do it. He wanted a helicopter. He wanted the cult members and their victim arranged for the murder. The pattern has been followed to this point, the special knowledge you talk about. The old shepherd is in place and the murderers are in place, with sharpened stones in their hands. Frank shoots down from as close in as the helicopter can safely get. He wants the wind blast, the blast from the rotor blades. They murder the old man. They kill him with stones. Cut him, beat him. The dust is flying, the bushes and scrub are flattened out by the rotor. No sound in this scene. He wants the wind blast only as a visual element. The severe angle. The men clutched together. The turbulence, the silent rippling of the bushes and stunted trees. I can quote him almost word for word. He wants the frenzy of the rotor wash, the terrible urgency, but soundless, totally. They kill him. They remain true to themselves, Jeem. That's it. It ends. He doesn't want the helicopter gaining altitude to signal the end is here. He doesn't want the figures to fade into the landscape. This is sentimental. It just ends. It ends up-close with the men in a circle, hair and clothes blowing, after they finish the killing."

I stayed in the living room for a while after she went to bed. I thought of Volterra in the mountains, hunched in his khaki field jacket, the deep pockets full of maps, the sky massing behind him. Sentimental. I didn't believe a word she'd said. He wouldn't follow it that far. He'd followed other things, gone the limit, abused people, made enemies, but this hovering was implausible to me, his camera clamped to the door frame. The aerial master, the filmed century. He wouldn't let them kill a man, he wouldn't film it if they did. We have to draw back at times, study our own involvement. The situation teaches that. Even in his drivenness he would see this, I believed.

It was interesting how she'd made me defend him to myself (as Kathryn used to do, defend him). Not that Del had intended this. I didn't know what she'd intended. The lie had a violence of its own, a cunning force she might have meant to direct against any or all of us, ironic, ornately motivated. How rich it was, a setting for any number of interpretations. I would have to reflect a long time before I could even begin to see what she had in mind, what complex human urging caused her to invent the story.

The story, if I thought it was true, would only make me want to fix a drink, feeling obscurely pleased.

When I passed the guest room I saw the door was ajar, the lamp still on, and I paused to look inside. In jeans and sleeveless shirt, her feet bare, she knelt on the floor. Her upper body was bent well forward, chest against knees. Her legs were together, buttocks resting on her heels. The arms pointed back along the floor, palms up. A compact gathering of curves. The curve of the head and upper body folded into the curve of the upper legs. The curve of the back and shoulders extended to her hands. The arms repeated the curve of the lower legs. Her head touched the floor.

She remained that way for a considerable time. In the morning she told me the exercise was called Pose of a Child.

I joined David, running in the woods. Rains had turned the high grass solid green. We ran along paths on different levels of the hill, moving in and out of sight of each other. His bright clothes flashed through the spindly pines.

Mrs. Helen was patient with my attempts to conjugate difficult verbs. She lectured on the niceties of pronunciation and stress, the correctness of this or that form in a given situation. We sat with our cups of tea, our embossed paper napkins. It seemed to me that the language as she taught it existed mainly as a medium of politeness between people, with odd allowances made for the communication of ideas and feelings. We ate English biscuits and talked about her family. Across the room the telex clattered numbers from Amman.

I found myself scanning the English-language newspapers for stories of assault, suicide and murder. I did the same thing when I went on a ten-day trip, checking the local papers, wherever I happened to be, for items from the daily files of the police. I found myself trying to match the name of the victim with the name of the place where the crime was committed. Initials. The victim's initials, the first letter of the word or words in the place-name. I don't know why I did this. I wasn't looking for the cult, I wasn't even looking for murder victims especially. Any crime would do, any act that tended to isolate a person in a particular place, just so the letters matched.

Again I stopped drinking, this time in Istanbul. In Athens I went running every day.

The Desert

11

IN THIS VAST SPACE, which seems like nothing so much as a container for emptiness, we sit with our documents always ready, wondering if someone will appear and demand to know who we are, someone in authority, and to be unprepared is to risk serious things.

The terminal at each end is full of categories of inspection to which we must submit, impelling us toward a sense of inwardness, a sense of smallness, a self-exposure we are never prepared for no matter how often we take this journey, the buried journey through categories and definitions and foreign languages, not the other, the sunlit trip to the east which we thought we'd decided to make. The decision we'd unwittingly arrived at is the one that brings us through passport control, through the security check and customs, the one that presents to us the magnetic metal detector, the baggage x-ray machine, the currency declaration, the customs declaration, the cards for embarkation and disembarkation, the flight number, the seat number, the times of departure and arrival.

It does no good to say, as I've done a hundred times, it's just another plane trip, I've made a hundred. It's just another terminal, another country, the same floating seats, the documents of admission, the proofs and identifications.

Air travel reminds us who we are. It's the means by which we recognize ourselves as modern. The process removes us from the world and sets us apart from each other. We wander in the ambient noise, checking one more time for the flight coupon, the boarding pass, the visa. The process convinces us that at any moment we may have to submit to the force that is implied in all this, the unknown authority behind it, behind the categories, the languages we don't understand. This vast terminal has been erected to examine souls.

It is not surprising, therefore, to see men with submachine guns, to see *vultures* squatting on the baggage vehicles set at the end of the tarmac in the airport in Bombay when one arrives after a night flight from Athens.

All of this we choose to forget. We devise a counter-system of elaborate forgetfulness. We agree on this together. And out in the street we see how easy it is, once we're immersed in the thick crowded paint of things, the bright clothes and massed brown faces. But the experience is no less deep because we've agreed to forget it.

Late in the day I walked with Anand Dass in the streets near my hotel. He looked heavier, moving through the soft air in a Michigan State t-shirt and faded jeans. He kept taking my arm as we crossed streets and I wondered why this seemed so curiously apt. Could these drivers be worse than Greeks? I was woozy from lack of sleep, that was all, and it probably showed.

"Seeing to details. Mainly interviewing people. My boss has already set things in motion."

"So this is new territory," he said.

"South Asia and so on. This will be a regional headquarters, separate from Athens once we get it going."

"But you're not coming out permanently."

"Do you need a listener? Someone to talk to about the life and travels of Owen Brademas?"

"This is precisely the fact." Clutching my forearm and laughing. "The man inspires comment, you know."

"How many times did you see him?"

"He stayed with us. Three days. And three letters since. I

didn't know I cared for the man. But I read his letters again and again. My wife was fascinated by him. The worst field director in my experience. This is Owen. He digs like an amateur."

Under a movie billboard we passed a group of North Americans in saffron robes and running shoes, their heads shaved. They stood by a sound truck handing out booklets. What could I say? They looked deeply surprised in their baldness and blotched skin, amazed to be who they were, to be real and here. The loudspeaker carried flute music and chanting voices through the noise and fumes of the yellow-top taxis.

"What are you teaching?"

"I am teaching the Greeks. I am looking at Hellenistic and Roman influences on Indian sculpture. Not a large subject but interesting. Figures of Buddha. I am getting very interested in figures of Buddha. I want to go to Kabul to see the Buddha of the Great Miracle."

"You don't want to go to Kabul, Anand."

"It's a transitional Buddha."

"You know who you sound like."

"Owen is in Lahore now. I sound just like him, don't I? Do you go there at all?"

"I go everywhere twice. Once to get the wrong impression, once to strengthen it."

"Do you want to see him? I'll give you an address."

"No. It will only depress me."

"Let me give you an address. He went to Lahore to learn Kharoshthi script."

I tried to think of something funny to say. Anand laughed and grabbed my arm and we hurried across the street toward the Gateway of India, where people were gathering as night fell, street musicians, beggars, vendors of fruit drinks and sweets.

"Do you have plans then?"

"I find I'm ready to go almost anywhere and just as ready to stay where I am."

"This is a strange profession. Risk analysis. Your local man will be kept very busy. Believe it."

"I like the idea of someone saying to me, '*West Africa.*' Not that

I'd necessarily accept. But I like the immensity of it. The immensity of landscape, of possibility. It's bizarre, how opened up my life has become. *'Think about it,'* they'll say. But there's nothing to think about. That's what's odd."

We walked through one of the archways and stood above the sea steps. A small girl followed with a baby in her arms. The crowd slowly grew.

"You should spend more time in India."

"No. Four days. That's enough."

"Tomorrow you'll come to dinner. Rajiv will want to hear about Tap. He received a letter, you know. Written in Ob."

The soft air made me sad.

"And we'll talk, you and I, about Owen."

Soft and moist, a hanging heat. People still came, talking, looking out to sea. They stood around the horn player, the man with the hand drums. There were sellers of invisible commodities, names whispered in the dark. Children kept appearing from the edges, silently crossing some margin or dividing line, cradling the shriveled infants. People drifted toward the Gateway from the street along the sea wall, from the inner streets, the edges, to stand in the warm night together and wait for a breeze. The sound of bicycle bells stuck briefly to the air.

Everything clings.

She came at me with the potato peeler, wearing my L.L. Bean chamois cloth shirt, forest green, with long tuck-in tails. I stood there half embarrassed. It was in her face, absolutely, that she would kill me. A rage that will astonish me forever. I evaded the lunge, then stood thoughtfully against the cabinet, my hands tucked into my pants, thumbs showing, like a quarterback on a cold day, waiting to rehuddle.

Ann and Lindsay came down the steps of the British Council, carrying sacks of apples and books. I hailed them from a parkside table in the square. We ordered coffee and watched stooped-over people call their destinations into the windows of passing cabs.

Lindsay carried fiction, Ann biography. I lifted an apple from one of the bags and took a lusty bite. It made them smile and I wondered if they interpreted the act as I'd instinctively meant it, meant it in a totally unformed way. To be back again among familiar things and people, alive to the levels of friendship a man enjoys with married women of a certain kind, the wives he is half in love with. Somewhere in the theft and biting of an apple there are elements of innocent erotic wishfulness and other things hard to name.

"There's a new wall slogan I've been seeing," Lindsay said. "With a date attached?"

"Greece is risen," Ann said. "And the date is the date the colonels took power. Sometime in sixty-seven."

"Four twenty-one. Or twenty-one four, as they do it here."

"Then there's the other side of the argument. Was it three weeks ago? Someone killed the head of the riot police."

"I must have missed that," I said.

"They killed his driver too. Another date. Charles said the assassins left a calling card. November seventeen. Students against the dictatorship. That was seventy-three, I think."

"David's in Turkey again."

This distracted remark, a remark that seemed to drift away from us, so softly spoken and bare, a remark that Lindsay made as an automatic response to talk of violence, prompted us to change the subject. I told them about a letter I'd received from Tap. He liked the sound the water made in the shower when it hit the plastic lining of the shower curtain. That was the letter.

Lindsay said David's kids sent videotapes. She also said she had a class to teach and hurried off after the first cup of coffee.

We knew what we wanted to discuss but waited a long moment, allowing Lindsay's departure to become complete. A crouched man jogged alongside a taxi, answering the driver's hand-twisting gesture with the name of some district to the north.

"I saw him yesterday," Ann said. "He called and we had a drink."

"I knew he'd get in touch."

"He's been away. Tried to call me apparently. He was in London."

"See? Business. That's all."

"Yes. They're moving there. The whole region apparently."

"I thought it might be that."

"So I suppose that will be the end of that. A relief actually. Doubly so."

"Also a reversal."

"Yes, I'm the one who's supposed to be dragged off to yet another distant posting. Torn from the arms of love. I'm almost overwhelmed by relief. Go to London, go to Sydney. What a surprise it is, to feel this way. Why is it I have to discover these things as I go along? As events wheel about me like buzzards? Why don't I know, in advance, just once, how I'll feel about a certain thing? I hate surprises. I'm too old. I want to wear a housecoat for the rest of my life."

"It'll take more than that."

"Shut up."

"You'll need to thicken your ankles and wear slippers without backs or sides. You'll need to be *blowzy*. Thirty pounds heavier. A little bloated, a little unkempt."

"My inner nature," she said. "Wearing flip-flops. It's perfect."

"Standing around ruddy-faced, all your weight on one leg, your hip jutting out."

"Don't look at my hands. I have old fingers."

"It was all conversation. That's all. He's a decent man. His flaws are part of a moral seriousness. Even when he was being completely unreasonable, I had to admire him for it and like him for it. Maybe he had some private suspicions he wanted cleared up. That's all. Talk. His true mission in life."

"Did you tell Charles about us?"

"Yes."

"I thought you might have."

"It wasn't an easy position I was in. It never has been. I wanted to shock him a little. Make it real to him, dispel the fog he was disappearing into. I didn't like knowing something he didn't know about his own wife."

"Anyway, that's that."

"We need Lindsay to help us understand all this. She wouldn't have to comment. Only sit and gaze."

"Already I begin to see what an odd match we were."

"Happens all the time."

" 'What do they see in each other?' "

"But isn't there something rich and living in all these entanglements, the way we've mingled our lives, all of us, chaotically or not?"

"Thank God for books," she said.

Biography. It was time I was getting to the office. We said goodbye at the corner, taking each other's hands in the way people do who want to press gladness into the flesh at the end of an uncertain time. Then I crossed the street and headed west.

Silent. The rotor wash. The rippling trees. Dust spinning around them. Their hair and clothes blowing. The frenzy.

The room with its stone hearth, marble font, its ferns and fan palms and village rugs was devised by Lindsay to make her husband feel he had put behind him, at least for a time, all airports and travel. At regular intervals she apologized for the size of the place. The marble balustrade on the terrace, the glass wall producing a sunset, the ship painting from Hydra still unhung in a corner. Too large, she'd say, letting her hands swing out. Too long, too tall, too grand. Not one of life's pressing dilemmas, we reply. But we have to remember that queasiness of this kind has always been a form of middle-class grace, especially when it arises from a feeling of privilege that is binding, privilege that does not allow easy denial, and Lindsay had arrived here, the new young wife, some weeks after David found the apartment. The place made her uneasy. It made her feel, among other things, that whatever risks David ran in places like Lebanon and Turkey were connected to the size of this room.

He was playing his collection of Pacific Jazz records, a nice relic of the fifties with their original cover paintings, the odd cello and flute. Roy Hardeman showed up, here for two days of meetings and wearing new glasses, oversized and squarish. We decided we'd have one more drink and go to dinner. An early night, Lindsay said. We needed an early night.

Hardeman's attitude, as uninvited guest, was one of temporary deference, a studious waiting for the host, the hostess, the good friend to approach some topic that might give him a chance to reason and speak competitively. He didn't have to wait long.

David said, "I keep reading about tribes or hordes or peoples who came sweeping out of Central Asia. What is it about Central Asia that makes us want to say that people came sweeping out of it?"

"I don't know," I said.

"Why don't we say the Macedonians came sweeping out of Europe? They did. Alexander in particular. But we don't say that. Or the Romans or the Crusaders."

"Do you think it's a racist term?" Hardeman said.

"White people established empires. Dark people came sweeping out of Central Asia."

"What about the Aryans?" Hardeman said. "We don't say the Aryans came sweeping out of Central Asia. They filtered down, they migrated or they simply arrived."

"Exactly. This is because the Aryans were light-skinned. Light-skinned people filter down. Dark people come sweeping out. The Turks came sweeping out. The Mongols. The Bactrians. They came in waves. Wave after wave."

"All right. But your original premise is that Central Asia is a place out of which people come sweeping. Now is it only dark people who come sweeping out of Central Asia or is it simply that Central Asia is a place out of which people of any color might come sweeping, with the exception of the Aryans? Are we talking about race, language or geography?"

"I think there's something about Central Asia that makes us want to say that people came sweeping out of it but there is also the fact that these people tend to be dark-skinned. You can't separate the two things."

"We've separated the Aryans," Hardeman said. "And what about the Huns? Certainly the Huns came sweeping out of Central Asia."

"What color were the Huns?" David said.

"They weren't light, they weren't dark."

"I should have had this conversation with someone else."

"Sorry."

"I felt I'd perceived something important and interesting, all on my own, you son of a bitch."

"Well you probably did. I'm not sure of my facts really."

"Yes you are."

"Actually I am."

"Of course you are."

"But it's an interesting premise," Hardeman said.

"Fuck you."

We went to dinner in an old mansion near the U.S. embassy. Hardeman was inhaling short Scotches. The perfect part in his hair, the geometric glasses and three-piece suit seemed the achievements of a systematic self-knowledge. This was the finished thing. He was physically compact, worked neatly into well-cut clothes, and nothing attached to him that had not been the subject of meticulous inner testing.

"Karen was saying—listen to this, Lindsay—that you both have to come and stay with us in London, soon as we're settled."

"Good. In the spring."

"In the fall would be better. We have to find a nanny."

"But you don't have children," she said.

"My original kids."

"I didn't know you had original kids."

"My first marriage."

"I didn't know," she said.

"They'll spend the summer. Karen's looking forward to finding a nanny."

David sat quietly, surrounding a beer, still unhappy over the earlier conversation.

"I saw Andreas not too long ago," I said. "We had a dinner of brains and lower organs."

"A good man," Hardeman said. "Bright, analytical."

"What does he do for the firm?"

"Sales rep. A hard worker. They love him in Bremen. Speaks German well. They tried very hard to talk him into staying."

I let a silence fall over this last remark. We ordered beer all around. When the food came we examined each other's dishes. After some discussion Lindsay and I traded plates.

"Have they told you," Hardeman said, "how Karen used to spend her evenings?"

I said I wasn't sure. Karen used to spend her evenings sitting on a stool near the right-field line in Fulton County Stadium, Atlanta, Georgia, running down foul balls hit that way by National League stalwarts. She was sixteen years old, a golden girl on grassy turf, hair reaching her waist. He met her six years later in a revolving restaurant.

"I thought it was the left-field line," David said.

"Right-field."

"She told me left."

"Couldn't have been left. It was left-handed hitters she feared most. Who was active then? You're the expert. Give us some names."

David went back to his curry. When we finished the beer, Hardeman ordered another scotch. And when he asked where the men's room was, I said I was heading that way myself.

The only water was cold. We stood with our backs to each other. I held my hands under the tap, talking over my shoulder to Hardeman, who was at the urinal.

"Did I understand you to say that Andreas is leaving the firm?"

"Correct."

"I thought I understood he was moving on to London with other key people in the region."

"Not so."

"He wants to stay in Athens then."

"I don't know what he wants."

"Is he looking for a job, do you know? Has he said anything to you at all?"

"Why would he? We don't interact at that level. I'm in manufacturing."

"I'd be interested in finding out what his plans are. It would only take a phone call."

"Make it," he said.

"I wonder if you'd do it for me. Not to Andreas. Someone in the sales department or personnel."

He was finished at the urinal and slowly wheeled in my direction. I turned my head toward the blank wall in front of me.

"Why should I?" he said.

"I'd like to know why he left, who he plans to work for. If he doesn't have plans for a new job, I'd be interested in knowing why. I'd also like to know if he intends to remain in Athens." I paused, letting the water run over my hands. "It could be important."

"Who do *you* work for?" Hardeman said.

"I'm sure David's told you."

"Does he *know*?"

"Of course he knows. Look, I can't go into details. I'll only say Andreas may have a sideline. He may be connected to something besides air cooling systems in Bremen."

"Andreas was a valuable member of the firm. Why should I involve myself in an unauthorized read-out? We work for the same people. And if he's chosen to leave, he may also choose to return someday."

"What do you know about him that may not be in his personnel file? Anything at all. One thing."

"It's not *his* identity I have doubts about."

"Very funny."

"I don't mean it to be. Sure, David's mentioned political risk insurance. He's also mentioned the scrambled telexes he occasionally sends your way, unscrambled, which I told him I thought was unconscionable, regardless of content, regardless of friendship. I may not know anything about Andreas' private life or his politics but I know the firm he's worked for these last three or four years. What do I know about you?"

What could I say, we were fellow Americans? I felt foolish, staring at the wall, my hands turning in the stream of water. My attempt to learn something was less useful than the dumbest amateur's because this is what an amateur enjoys, a men's room meeting with clipped dialogue. I wasn't even good at clipped dialogue.

He was waiting to wash his hands.

The news that Andreas was not going to London would lurk vaguely in my mind in the days to come like the knowledge of some unpleasantness whose exact nature will not surface when one tries to recall it. Maybe London was his clumsy way of ending the affair with Ann, inventing a distance between them. Maybe the story revolved around her. It was all part of the same thing, that rapt entanglement I'd spoken to her about a couple of days earlier (only to be made fun of). The world is here, the world is where I want to be.

"We promised ourselves an early night," Lindsay said.

Hardeman ordered another drink. He described the house he was renting in Mayfair. He spoke slowly but very clearly and his sentences began to extend into an elaborate and self-conscious correctness, a latticework of clauses, pure grammar. Drunk.

He and I shared the back seat in David's car. We hadn't gone two blocks when he dropped off to sleep. It was like the death of a machine-tooled part. At a red light David looked at me in the rearview mirror.

"I have an idea. Are you ready for this? Because it's one of the great ideas of my career. Maybe the greatest. I started thinking about it during dinner when I saw how much he was drinking. It came to me then. And it's developing, refining itself even as we sit here waiting for the light to change. I think we can bring it off, boy, if we're cunning enough, if we really want to do it."

"We're cunning enough," Lindsay said, "but we don't want to do it."

The idea was to put Hardeman on a plane to some distant city. There was a flight at 3:50 A.M. to Tehran, for instance, on KLM. He wouldn't need a visa to get on the plane. He would only need a visa to get out of the terminal once he was there. This was beyond our purview, David said. All we wanted to do was send him somewhere. We'd need his passport, which David was certain he'd be carrying, and a ticket, which David would purchase with one of his credit cards.

We passed my building. A moment or two later we passed their building. Lindsay stared into the window on her side.

"Once we have the ticket," David said, "we come back out to the car and get him on his feet and walk him between us into the terminal. We get him a seat in the nonsmoking area, which I'm sure he'll appreciate upon reflection, and then we face our biggest problem, which is how to get him through passport control."

Lindsay began to laugh, a little warily.

"By this time he is probably semiconscious. He can walk but can't think. If we stick the boarding pass, ticket and passport in his fist, it's possible he can make it past the booth through habit alone. But what happens then? We can't follow him through passport control. It's too much to expect that he'll look at the boarding pass and walk automatically to the right gate."

I told him there was a simple solution. We were on the airport road, doing a hundred kilometers, and he looked at me in the mirror, briefly, to make sure I was serious.

"Breathtakingly simple," I said. "All we have to do is buy two tickets. One of us takes him through the entire process, right to his seat on the plane."

Lindsay thought this was very funny. It could work after all. There was a huskiness in her laugh, the slightly surprised dawning of the idea that she was mean enough to want it to work.

"Then the one who accompanies him simply turns around and goes down the ramp and gets back on the shuttle bus, feigning illness. They'll cancel the ticket. It won't cost a dime."

David whispered, "Of course, of course."

I felt all along we wouldn't do it. It was too grand, too powerful. And as many times as I'd traveled with a visa, I didn't know whether he was right about that. I thought they examined visas at the airline counter before issuing boarding passes. But David kept on driving, kept on talking, and Lindsay began to sag in her seat as if to hide from the enormity of it all. Tehran. They would think he'd come to hold a service for the hostages.

In the end we couldn't even get him out of the car. He kept hitting his head, falling away from us, limbs floppy. It was interesting to see the concentration in David's face. He viewed the formless Hardeman as a problem in surfaces, how and where to grip. He tugged at him, he wrestled. The door-opening was small and oddly shaped and David's considerable bulk was a problem in itself. He tried kneeling on the front seat and scooping Hardeman out to me. He tried a number of things. He was completely involved in the idea, the vision. He wanted to send this man to another place.

The figure appeared in a blizzard, moving toward the house from the other side of the park, a skier in bright banded colors coming in diagonal stride, the only clear shape in that dead-even light, a world without shadow, a winter's worth of snow on the streets and cars and laid over the park benches and the bird bath in the yard, the skier digging in, working across that dreamlike space, red-hooded, masked.

You can't walk down Bay Street and pick out the Americans from the Canadians. They are alien beings in our midst, waiting for a signal. This is the science-fiction theme (SF for semi-facetious). They're in the schools, teaching our children, subtly and even unintentionally promoting their own values—values they assume we share. The theme of the corruption of the innocent. Their crime families have footholds in our cities —drugs, pornography, legitimate businesses—and their pimps from Buffalo and Detroit work both sides of the border, keeping the girls in motion. The theme of expansionism, of organized criminal infiltration. They own the corporations, the processing plants, the mineral rights, a huge share of the Canadian earth. The colonialist theme, the theme of exploitation, of greatest possible utilization. They are right next to us, sending their contaminants, their pollutants, their noxious industrial waste into our rivers, lakes and air. The theme of power's ignorance and blindness and contempt. We are in the path of their television programs, their movies and music, the whole enormous rot and glut and blare of their culture. The theme of cancer and its spread.

I stood in the window as she removed the skis and carried them up the steps. The sight of her cutting through that blown snow, appearing out of the invisible city around us, the craft and mystery of it filled me with deep delight.

George Rowser stepped out of the elevator at the Hilton in Lahore, looking pale and rumpled. He put his briefcase down, setting it between his feet, then used both hands to adjust his glasses, raising the hands toward his face, fingers extended, palms turned toward each other, in a gesture that started out as a blessing of multitudes. When he saw me in a lobby chair he walked toward the coffee shop, pigeon-toed. We ordered Kipling burgers and fresh fruit juice. Gatherings of more than six people were forbidden.

"Why am I here, George?"

"Where were you?"

"Islamabad."

"So I wanted to talk. It's not as though you were on the other side of the world."

"Couldn't we talk on the phone?"

"Be smart," he said. "In addition to which, this city has architecture. Go look at the public buildings. What would you call this architecture? Gothic, Victorian—what else, Punjabi? Why do I have the impression you know things like this?"

"Maybe it's Moghul. Or Moghul-influenced. I don't know really."

"Whatever, it's a nice blend. A very happy blend. Who were the Moghuls?"

"They came sweeping out of Central Asia."

Four or five ballpoint pens stuck out of the breast pocket of his suit coat. His briefcase was under the table, upright, wedged between his calves. I waited for him to tell me what he wanted to talk about.

"I'm getting a remote ignition device put in my car. They stick a thing on the trunk. I can start the car while I'm in the kitchen boiling an egg." He looked out into the lobby. "If it blows up, the egg tastes that much better."

"Nice. What about tear gas ducts?"

"I do defensive measures only. Are you kidding? The parent would be upset if they found out I was loading a vehicle with incapacitators. Not that it matters anymore."

"What do you mean?"

"I'm seriously thinking I may resign, Jim."

The fact that he used my name seemed almost as important as the statement that preceded it. Was he saying one thing or two?

"Choice? Or are they forcing you out?"

"There are pressures," he said. "Developments no one could have foreseen. Never mind details. I think it may be time, that's all. I need a change. We all need a change now and then."

"What kind of pressures? From the parent?"

A little bored. "The parent is a collector. They acquire companies, they adjust, they seek a balance. We're one of the companies, that's all. They look at the profit curve. That's all they know from."

"What do they see when they look at this curve?"

"What they lose one year in insurance they gain in consumer products or manufacturing. They diversify to minimize risk. You and I work at risk but not in the same sense the parent knows the word. The parent knows the word in a limited sense."

"What did Iran do to us?"

"Limited coverage. Plus reinsurance. But we got hurt like everybody else. Who could predict? I don't know anyone who predicted. A haunting failure. They're still straggling onto the beach in Greece. Like the Lebanon thing earlier. We picked the right place for our headquarters. That's one thing we did."

Hamburgers for dinner. This was Rowserlike. Skip lunch, bolt dinner, go to bed, remembering to secure all systems.

"What's happening in your life, George, outside the Northeast Group?"

"I have to wear white socks. My doctor says I'm allergic to dye."

"Tension. You ought to change your wardrobe completely. You look like an assistant principal of the 1950s in a high school on the wrong side of town. Get one of those knee-length shirts the men wear here. And some loose trousers."

"They're throwing away their London suits to wear traditional things. You know what that means, don't you?"

"Our lives are in danger."

"How's your burger?" he said.

He suggested we get a car and driver and take a ride before dark. There was a mausoleum he wanted to see. I watched him go to the desk to make arrangements. He walked in a block of heavy air, a personal zone in which movement was difficult, breathing slightly labored. Every space he inhabited seemed enclosed. There was a basic containment or frustration. His compulsive secrecy, the taking of endless precautions would explain some of this, of course. Then there were his numbers, the data he collected and sorted and studied endlessly. This took up the rest of his space.

The Mall in Lahore is a broad avenue running roughly east and west, built by, named by the British. Vehicles rush into it with the cartoonish verve of objects possessing human traits, so individualistic, so seemingly intent on playing merry hell with the boulevard's stately pretensions. Cycle rickshaws, horse-drawn taxis, minicabs painted pink, fuchsia, peacock blue, trucks and cars and scooters, bicycles weaving in and out of bullock carts, vendors wheeling massive arrangements of nuts, fruits and vegetables, buses leaning under the rooftop weight of trussed-up bundles, furniture and other objects.

What we see, Owen Brademas might say, is the grand ordering imperial vision as it is overrun by the surge and pelt of daily life.

Then there was the guard at the entrance to the local office of the Mainland Bank. An elderly turbaned fellow with enormous drooping mustache, a tunic and pajama pants, a curved dagger in his sash and a pair of pointed slippers. A relative of the doorman at the Hilton. The outfit seemed intended to register in people's minds the hopeful truth that colonialism was a tourist ornament now, utterly safe to display in public. The foreign bank he guarded was a co-survivor of the picturesque past, exerting no more influence than the man himself. The man had a single task, David told me once. To lower the steel shutters at the first sign of a demonstration.

We passed some of the buildings Rowser had referred to, the high court, the museum, and headed north.

"Tanker loadings at Kharg are down to two a week."

"Maintenance."

"The fields are looking pretty grim. Only five rigs in action, I hear from Abadan."

"Parts," I said.

"Plus which the telex and telephone are down between Abadan and Tehran."

"But you still hear."

"I hear a little."

"The bankers call it a black hole. Iran."

"Have you seen the mosques? Isfahan is the place to go. I mean gorgeous. You have to spend time in the courtyards. Spend time, relax, check the tilework. I'd give anything to get up close to one of those domes. There's a dome in Isfahan"—he shaped it with his hands.

We were stopped by traffic on the road around the old city. A man came through the fortified gate and stood at the car window looking in at us, a man with a bamboo stick, wearing a rag wrapped around his head, a military jacket with copper medals, a dozen bead necklaces, a filthy white robe, oversized army boots without laces, beads around his ankles and wrists. He had hair dyed red and carried live chickens. Rowser asked the driver what he wanted. Hundreds of people congregated near the gate. I tried to look past them into the old city. The driver said he didn't know.

"I think I'm in New York," Rowser said.

"That reminds me. I want to ask you about taking three or four weeks in early summer. I want to spend time with my son in North America."

"I don't have any problem with that."

Rowser never said yes. He said, "I don't have any problem with that." Or, "I don't see how it could hurt."

"Will you still be with the firm?"

"No," he said.

"It's imminent then."

"I don't see any reason to hang around the halls. When the time comes, you have to have the grace to disappear."

We were moving again.

"Did you ever remarry?" he said.

"I never got divorced. I'm only separated, George."

"That's a crazy way to live. Separated. Divorce teaches us things. You never learn anything being separated."

"I don't want to learn anything. Leave me alone."

"I'm only saying do one thing or do the other."

"I don't want a divorce. It's boring, it's trite."

"In these matters it's best to terminate officially. That way you forget. File the papers in your steel cabinet."

We crossed a river and pulled up in front of a tall gateway, locked for the night. Rowser spoke to the driver, who went to look for the watchman, returning in ten minutes with a man chewing betel leaf. We entered a vast garden with fountains and paved watercourses. At the far end was the tomb of Jehangir, a low red sandstone structure with a minaret at each corner. The minarets were octagonal, coming to full height in white marble cupolas. Rowser said something to our driver, who spoke to the watchman. The watchman took a socket wrench out of his back pocket and inserted it in an opening in the pavement, turning full circle. The fountains began to play.

We walked slowly toward the central chamber, hearing the sunset call to prayer from somewhere beyond the walls. A breeze blew Rowser's tie over his shoulder.

"We all need a change now and then. This is basic to anyone's sense of perspective. The type person I am, which is to say a plodder, go it slow, work the angles, worry it, piss blood over it, even this type person has to start over now and then. But maybe this type less than others. I personally hired you, Jim. This makes me responsible to a degree. I'm your sole contact with the parent. You'll have a new man in the region. He'll be hired directly by the parent or sent over from one of their other interests, other arms. It could be an uncomfortable arrangement. We're identified with each other, you and I, in people's minds. That's all I'm saying. Give it some thought."

We stood on a platform at the main arched opening, which jutted from a series of eight other archways. The exterior walls were inset with designs in white marble.

"I'm told there are better examples," Rowser said, "but this is a basic Moghul tomb, except it doesn't have a dome."

He gestured with his free hand, indicating a dome. We went inside and stood a moment, waiting for the watchman to turn on a light. The sarcophagus stood under a vaulted ceiling. I circled it slowly, running my hand over the surface. Rowser set the briefcase between his feet.

"Take my advice," he said. "Resign, find a job somewhere in the States, invest in real estate, start a retirement plan, get a divorce."

The white marble surface was inlaid with semiprecious stones in seamless floral designs and in chaste calligraphy, shaped stones, jeweled stones, delicate and free-figured. The surface ran cool and smooth. Traceries of black Koranic letters covered the longer sides of the tomb with a smaller grouping on top. My hand moved slowly over the words, feeling for breaks between the inlay and marble, not to fault the craftsmen, of course, but only to find the human labor, the individual, in the wholeness and beauty of the tomb.

It wasn't until we were walking back through the garden that I asked our driver what the words represented. They were the ninety-nine names of God.

12

IN THE MORNING I went looking for Owen Brademas. The piece of paper I'd been carrying since Bombay contained a set of directions rather than an address. The address Owen used was the Old Campus, Punjab University, strictly for receiving mail, Anand said. If I wanted to find him, I would have to look for a house with a closed wooden balcony roughly halfway between the Lohari Gate and the Kashmiri Gate in the old city.

I made my way to the edge of the old city easily enough. From the street din of motorcycles and buses to the voices of the long bazaar. The thoroughfare narrowed as I passed through the Lohari Gate, a brickwork structure with a broad towerlike fortification on either side.

Once inside I began to receive impressions, which is not the same as seeing things. I realized I was walking too fast, the pace of the traffic-filled streets I'd just left behind. I received impressions of narrowness and shadow, of brownness, the wood and brick, the hard earth of the streets. The air was centuries old, dead, heavy, rank. I received impressions of rawness and crowding, people in narrow spaces, men in a dozen kinds of dress, women gliding, women in full-length embroidered white veils, a mesh aperture at the eyes, hexagonal, to give them a view of the latticed world, the six-sided cage that adjusted itself to every step they took, every shift of the eyes. Donkeys carrying bricks, children squatting over open sewers. I glanced at my directions, made an uncertain turn. Copper and brassware. A cobbler working in the shadows. This was the lineal function of old cities, to maintain an unchanged form, let time hang with the leather goods and skeins of wool. Hand-skilled labor, rank smells and disease, the four-hundred-year-old faces. There were horses, sheep, donkeys, cows and oxen. I received impressions that I was being followed.

Signs in Urdu, voices calling over my head from the wooden balconies. I wandered for half an hour, too closed in to be able to scan for landmarks, the minarets and domes of Badshahi, the great mosque at the northwest edge. Without a map I couldn't even stop someone, point to an approximate destination. I moved into a maze of alleys beyond the shops and stalls. Intensely aware. American. Giving myself advice and directions. A woman stuck cow dung in oval disks on a low wall to dry.

I turned to see who might be following. Two small boys, the older maybe ten. They held back for a moment. Then the younger said something, barefoot, a bright green cap on his head, and the other one pointed back the way I'd come and started to walk in that direction, looking to see if I would follow.

They led me to the house Owen was in. One slender white man looking for the other, that boy had reasoned. What else would I be doing in those lost streets?

The door to his room was open. He reclined on a wooden bench covered with pillows and old carpets. There were some books and papers in a copper serving tray on the floor. A water jug on a small chest of drawers. A plain chair for me. Not much else in the room. He kept it partially dark to reduce the effects of the April sun.

He was reading when I entered and looked up to regard me in a speculative manner, trying to balance my physical make-up, my shape, proportions, form, with some memory he carried of a name and a life. A moment in which I seemed to hang between two points in time, a moment of silent urging. The house smelled of several things including the trickle of sewage just outside.

Owen looked a little weary, a little more than weary, but his voice was warm and strong and he seemed ready to talk.

(It wasn't until I'd put my hand to the marble tomb, the night before, that I knew I'd try to find him, talk to him one last time. Wasn't that the image he'd wanted me to retain, a man in a room full of stones, a library of stones, tracing the shape of Greek letters with his country-rough hands?)

"I've been preparing for this all my life," he said. "Not that I knew it. I didn't know it until I walked into this room, out of the color and light, the red scarves worn as turbans, the food stalls out there, the ground chili and turmeric, the pans of indigo, the coloring for paint, those trays of brilliant powders and dyes. The mustard, bay leaf, pepper and cardamom. You see what I've done, don't you, by coming into this room? Brought only the names. Pine nuts, walnuts, almonds, cashews. All I can tell you is that I'm not surprised to find myself here. The moment I stepped inside it seemed right, it seemed inevitable, the place I've been preparing for. The correct number of objects, the correct proportions. For sixty years I've been approaching this room."

"Anand speaks of you."

"He wrote. He told me you'd been there. I knew you'd come."

"Did you?"

"But when you stood in the door I didn't recognize you at all. I was surprised, James. I wondered who you were. You looked familiar—but in the damnedest way. I didn't understand. I thought something was *happening*. Am I dying, I wondered. Is this who they send?"

"You took it calmly, if you thought I was a messenger from the other side."

"Oh I'm ready," he said laughing. "Ready as I'll ever be. Counting the cracks in the wall."

There was a pale gray booklet in the copper tray. *Kharoshthi Primer*. I picked it up and turned the pages. Lesson number one, the alphabet. Lesson number two, medial vowels. There were seven lessons, a picture on the back cover of a stone Buddha with a halo inscription in Kharoshthi.

"The ragged mob squats in the dust around the public story-teller," he said. "Someone beats a drum, a boy wraps a snake around his neck. The storyteller begins to recite. Heads nod, heads wag, a child squats down to pee. The man tells his story at a rapid clip, spinning event after event, this one traditional, that one improvised. His small son passes through the audience with a wooden bowl for donations. When the storyteller interrupts his narrative to consider things, to weigh events and characters, to summarize for the latecomers, to examine methodically, the mob grows impatient, then angry, crying out together, 'Show us their faces, tell us what they said!' "

He was a wanderer. He wandered by bus and train and walked a great deal, walked for six weeks at one point, rock-cut sanctuary to stone pillar, wherever there were inscriptions to look at, mainly ancient local languages in Brahmi script. Anand had offered to lend him a car but Owen was afraid to drive in India, afraid of the animals on the road, the people asleep at night, afraid of being stuck in traffic on some market street with crowds moving around the car, men pushing, no space, no air. The nightmarish force of people in groups, the power of religion—he connected the two. Masses of people suggested worship and delirium, oblit-eration of control, children trampled. He traveled second-class on crowded trains with wooden seats. He walked among the sleep-ing forms in railroad stations, saw people carry rented bedding onto the trains. He slept in hotels, bungalows, small cheap lodges near archaeological sites and places of pilgrimmage. Sometimes he stayed with friends of Anand, friends of other colleagues. He would reflect. A lifetime of colleagues with their worldwide sys-tem of names and addresses. Bless them.

The rusty tin villages, the brick kilns, the water buffalo silvery

with mud. His bus always seemed to sit between diesel trucks
shooting smoke. Near Poona a dozen people sat under a banyan
tree, all wearing pink-white gauze. In Surat he wandered down
along the railroad tracks, finding a shadow city that stretched
from, was part of the real city. The uncounted were here in
shacks and tents and in the street. The streetcorner barber and eye
doctor. The ear cleaner with his mustard oil and little spoon. The
shaver of armpits. Life swarmed and brooded in the pall of smoke
from a thousand cooking fires. Hindi graffiti in blue and red.
Swastikas, horses, scenes from the life of Krishna. A man in an
Ambassador picked him up on the road outside Mysore. The man
drove with his hand on the horn, moving bullocks and people but
at their own pace, in their own weary time. He was young, with
a faint mustache, a ripe underlip, and wore a green shirt and
sleeveless pink sweater.

"You are from?"

"America."

"And you are liking India?"

"Yes," Owen said, "although I would have to say it goes beyond liking, in almost every direction."

"And you are going exactly where at the present moment?"

"Just north. Eventually to Rajsamand. This is the major destination, I would say."

The man said nothing. The car was wedged for a ten-mile
stretch between a pair of diesel trucks. HORN OK PLEASE. A long
line of trucks, a hundred trucks with turquoise grills and cabs full
of trinkets and charms, stood along the road outside a gas station,
tanks empty, pumps empty, waiting for days, drivers cooking
over charcoal fires. Men in one village wore only white, women
in a field in flared red skirts. The high-pitched voices, the characters engraved in stone. All over India he searched for the rock
edicts of Ashoka. They marked the way to holy places or commemorated a local event in the life of Buddha. Near the border
with Nepal he saw the fine-grained sandstone column that was
the best preserved of the edicts, thirty-five feet tall, a lion seated
atop a bell capital. In the countryside north of Madras he found
an edict on forgiveness and nonviolence, translated for him two

weeks later by one T. V. Coomeraswamy of the Archaeological Museum in Sarnath. To the study of Dharma, to the love of Dharma, to the inculcation of Dharma.

The man took his hand off the horn.

"Rajsamand is actually the name of a lake," Owen said. "It's somewhere in the barren country north of Udaipur. Do you know the place by any chance?"

The man said nothing.

"An artificial lake, I believe. Essential for irrigation."

"Precisely!" the man said. "This is what they do, you see."

"Marble embankments, I've been told. Inscriptions cut into the stone. Sanskrit. An enormous Sanskrit poem. More than one thousand verses."

"That is precisely the place. Rajsamand."

"Seventeenth century," Owen said.

"Correct!"

The cows had painted horns. Blue horns in one part of the countryside, red or yellow or green in another. People who painted cows' horns had something to say to him, Owen felt. There were cows with tricolor horns. There was a woman in a magenta sari who carried a brass water pot on her head, the garment and the container being the precise colors of the mingled bougainvillea that covered the wall behind her, the dark reddish purple, the tainted gold. He would reflect. These moments were a "control"—a design at the edge of the human surge. The white-clad men with black umbrellas, the women at the river beating clothes in accidental rhythms, hillsides of saris drying in the sun. The epic material had to refine itself in these delicate aquarelles. Or he needed to see it as such. The mind's little infinite. India made him feel like a child. He was a child again, maneuvering for a window seat on the crowded bus. A dead camel, stiff legs jutting. Women in a road crew wearing wide cotton skirts, nose rings, hair ornaments, heavy jewelry dangling from their ears, repairing broken asphalt by hand. HORN OK PLEASE. In the upper castes they calculated horoscopes precisely. He learned a few words of Tamil and Bengali and was able to ask for food and lodging in Hindi when necessary, and to read a bit and ask directions. The word for yesterday was the same as the word for tomorrow. Professor Coomeraswamy said that if he asked someone for details of his life, the man might automatically include details from the lives of dead relatives. Owen was taken by the beauty of this, of common memories drifting across the generations. He could only stare at the round face across the desk and wonder why the concept seemed somewhat familiar. Had he discussed it himself on one of those bright-skied nights with Kathryn and James?

"White city, Udaipur. Pink city, Jaipur."

Whole cities as aspects of control. Astrology as control. The young man was delivering the car to a rental firm fifty kilometers away. This seemed to be his job, delivering cars, driving cars, and his strong hand on the horn indicated it was a job that nourished some private sense of imperium. His name was Bhajan Lal (B.L., thought Owen routinely, checking the map for names of towns in the area) and he was interested in talking about the approaching solar eclipse. It would happen in five days, being total in the south, and was very important from scientific, devotional and cosmic standpoints. His manner was remarkable for the element of reverence it contained, a stillness he hadn't seemed to possess, and Owen looked out the window, wanting not to dwell on this cosmic event, the trampled bodies it would produce, the voices massed in chant. He was happy simply looking. The humped cattle turned at the bamboo pole, threshing stalks of rice.

"We are having the moon come across the sun, which is much the larger body, but when they are in line we are seeing one is exactly the size of the other due to relative size and relative distance from the earth. People will bathe in holy places to correct their sins."

Divinities of increase. In the countryside he heard horns and drums and followed the sound to a temple of granite and marble set in a compound that included shrines and incense stalls, people squatting against the walls, beggars, touts, flower-sellers, those who watch over your shoes for a couple of weightless coins. Owen recognized a statue of the bull mount of Shiva and walked past the musicians and across a tiered porch into the temple vestibule. It was time for the sunset puja. A white-bearded pink-turbaned priest threw flowers toward the sanctum and these were immediately swept up by a man with a fly switch. There were people with marigold garlands, a man in an army greatcoat, two women chanting, figures bundled on the floor, half sleeping, with betel-stained mouths, one of them concealed behind a kettledrum. Owen tried intently to collect information, make sense of this. There were coconuts, monkeys, peacocks, burning charcoal. In the sanctum was a black marble image of Lord Shiva, four-faced, gleaming. Who were these people, more strange to him than the millennial dead? Why couldn't he place them in some stable context? Precision was one of the raptures he allowed himself, the lyncean skill for selection and detail, the Greek gift, but here it was useless, overwhelmed by the powerful rush of things, the raw proximity and lack of common measure. Someone beat on hand drums, a green bird sailed across the porch. He was twenty-five miles from Rajsamand, in the Indian haze.

Coomeraswamy said, "But what will you do after you've seen this Sanskrit ghat of yours? I think you'll want to rest awhile, won't you? Come back to Sarnath. You'll be ready for a long rest by then."

"I'm not sure what I'll do. I don't want to think about it."

"Why don't you want to think about it? Do you feel this is not an auspicious time to go to Rajsamand?"

He had graying hair, an immense kindness in his eyes, a stab of light. *As if he knew.* Smoke hung over the plain. The soaring birds, the kites, turned slowly above the white horizon. Why didn't he want to think about it? What was beyond Rajsamand, after the pure white embankment, the peaceful lake? He studied inscriptions not only in stone but in iron, gold, silver and bronze, on palm leaves and birch bark, on ivory sheets. Bhajan Lal told him that people had been gathering for weeks, living in tents or in the open, to prepare for the solar eclipse. He blew the horn at a tonga, at men on bicycles, at a small girl with a switch walking a dozen bullocks across the road. Beggars were assembling, holy men, those who will bathe in pools to seek their release. A million people were waiting at Kurukshetra, he said, to enter the tanks of water. Owen looked out the window, saw men reclined on charpoys outside spice stalls, white vultures hunched in trees. Bhajan Lal took a long-peaked cap from a pouch on his door, showed it to Owen.

"You are having a hat with you?"

"I left it somewhere."

"It was what kind of hat precisely?"

"A round hat with a loose brim. A sun hat."

"This is for eclipse!" the young man said.

A man in a dhoti walked toward him in furious contemplation, hands behind his back. Owen smiled. Among the brown hills were fields of sugarcane, the thick stems ending in wispy flower-heads. There were no cars or trucks on the road. He walked into a barren valley. Men with yellow turbans here, cows with tricolor horns. He saw the hilltop fortress that stood above Rajsamand. The kites turned in the burning sky. How quiet here, the day of eclipse, no trucks, no buses. Past the wheat fields, the clumps of pencil cactus. Bells rang lightly, a boy on an ox-drawn cart. Owen smiled again, thinking how in the midst of this wandering among Jains, Muslims, Sikhs, the Buddhist students in Sarnath, stunned time and again by the fairytale dynamics of Hindu cosmology, he had begun to think of himself once more as a Christian, simply by way of fundamental identification, by way of linking himself to the everyday medley he found around him. When people asked, this is what he said. *Christian.* How strange it sounded. And how curiously strong a word it seemed, after all these years, to be applied to himself, full of doleful comfort.

He came to the town that was set below the fortress and walked down the main street, where water buffalo lay in shallow ditches. Stalls and shops were closed, day of eclipse, and pregnant women stayed indoors, or so the driver had advised him. A disabled truck blocked the end of the street, front tires and rims gone, body pitched forward, down like a Mausered rhino. A woman sheeted in white stood by a door, a gauzy pink cloth fixed over her mouth. Owen edged past the truck and approached a gate in a yellow wall some yards from the edge of town. On the other side of the wall was the Sanskrit pavilion, as he'd come to call it, a marble-stepped embankment stretching about four city blocks along Rajsamand Lake. He judged there were fifty steps down to the water, a descent that was suspended at intervals by platforms, jutting pavilions, several decorative arches. A miraculous space in the dullish brown distemper of the countryside, cool, white and open, an offering to the royal lake. And miraculous as well for what it was not—a ghat swarming with bathers, pundits under sunshades, those who sit erect and see nothing, the mendicant, the diseased, the soon-to-be-turned-to-ashes. There were two women at the lowermost step, beating clothes, far to Owen's left, and a boy with a melodious face, approaching. That was all. Owen walked down to the nearest pavilion, entering to stand in the shade awhile, noting the elaborately sculptured columns, the dense surfaces. Set into a platform nearby was a slate panel on which he could faintly make out a block of text about forty lines long. The boy followed him along the embankment, up and down steps, across platforms, under the arches, in and out of the three pavilions. In time Owen counted twenty-five panels encased in ornamental marble, the epic poem he'd come to see and to read, one thousand and seventeen lines in classical Sanskrit, the pure, the well-formed, the refined.

The panels were accompanied, as almost everything seemed to be, almost everywhere, by carved images of elephants, horses, dancers, warriors, lovers. Everything in India was a list. Nothing was alone, itself, unattended by images from the pantheon. The boy did not speak to him until Owen by a simple shift of the head indicated he was ready to step outside his studious bearing, the contained exaltation of this first short hour on the embankment. The women pounded clothes on the bottom step, the sound fading toward mid-lake, mid-sky, renewed before a silence could obtain.

"This is a poem of the Mewar kingdom," the boy said. "It is the early history of Mewar. It is the longest Sanskrit writing in India today. This lake is circumference twelve miles. This marble is from Kankroli. The full cost is more than thirty lakhs of rupees. You are from?"

"America."

"Where is your suitcase?"

"It's just a canvas pack and I left it under a tree up there."

"It must already be stolen."

He wore short pants, sandals, high socks, a short-sleeved shirt buttoned to the top. His eyes were serious and bright, showing an interest in the wanderer that would not be satisfied without an earnest dialogue. He inspected the man openly. Sunburnt, dusty, wide-eyed, bald on top. A shirt with a dangling button.

"Is there a place I can spend the night?"

A watch with a cracked band.

"You must go back out to the road. I will show you."

"Good."

"How long will you stay?"

"Three days, I think. What do you think?"

"Do you read Sanskrit?"

"I will try to," Owen said. "I've been teaching myself for almost a year. And this is a place I've wanted to see all that time and longer. Mainly I will study the letters. It's a handsome script."

"I think three days is very long."

"But it's beautiful here, and peaceful. You're lucky, living near a place like this."

"Where will you go next?"

The women were in red and parrot green, beating in a single motion. Where would he go next? The repeated stroke reminded him of something, the Greek fisherman he'd seen a dozen times walloping an octopus on a rock to make the flesh tender. A stroke that denoted endless toil, the upthrust arm, the regulated violence of the blow. What else did it remind him of? Not something he'd seen. Something else, something he'd kept at the predawn edge. The boy was watching him, smooth face tilted in an air of inquiry, a manner that seemed laden with mature concern. *As if he knew.* The women started up the steps, the washwork in baskets on their heads. The boy's hair gleamed nearly blue. He climbed to the top of the embankment, pointed with a smile toward the tree where Owen had left his rucksack. Still there.

Owen used the pack as a cushion, sitting cross-legged before a panel set into the nearest platform. The boy stood behind him and to the right, able to see the text over Owen's shoulder.

The letters, attached to top-strokes, were solid, firmly stanced.

It was as though the sky and not the earth offered ultimate support, the only purchase that mattered. He studied the shapes. What was it about the letter-shapes that struck his soul with the force of a tribal mystery? The looped bands, scything curves, the sense of a sacred architecture. What did he almost understand? The mystery of alphabets, the contact with death and oneself, one's other self, all made stonebound with a mallet and chisel. A geography, a gesture of the prayerful hand. He saw the madness, even, the scriptural rage that was present in the lettering, the madness of priests who ruled that members of the menial caste were to have their ears filled with molten lead if they listened to a recitation of the Vedas. It was in those shapes, the secret aspect, the priestly, the aloof, the cruel.

The boy spoke several lines aloud in a beautiful musical pitch but said he wasn't sure he had it right.

The letters were not proportioned and spaced with the care the Romans put into monumental capitals, which were frameworked in squares, half squares, fitted circles, then sketched and painted and carved in graded widths. This was a thousand lines. This was the childlike history of Mewar, terrible and fierce, and the text fairly sang of sages, maidens, caliph invaders. It seemed childlike at any rate to Owen, the child again, made to learn a language, to think in lists.

He wondered at which end of the embankment the poem began, how he could tell, whether it mattered. He could not help imagining that all this marble had been quarried, cut, laid in place, the pavilions built, arches raised, the lake *made*, to provide a setting for the words.

Together they read aloud, slowly, the man deferring to the music of the boy, pitching his voice below the other's. It was in the sound, how old this was, strange, distant, other, but also almost known, almost striking through to him from some uncycled memory where the nightmares lay, the ones in which he could not speak as others did, could not understand what they were saying.

Then the boy was gone. Owen felt the light become dim, felt it, sensed it. A wind swept down the embankment. Birds veered across the lake, crying hoarsely, crows, hurrying. An arch cast multiple shadows. Midafternoon. Empty, pale and hushed. A cock began to crow.

In Kurukshetra they would be swarming toward the tanks. Bhajan Lal had said a million people. Futile to imagine. The ash-painted men, the men fixed in one position, those with sect marks, those anointed with sandalwood paste. Owen climbed toward the trees, then turned and sat on the top step. The women gathering their skirts above their knees as they enter the water. The genealogists recording the names of pilgrims, the dates of ritual baths. The holy men in rings of glowing coals. There would be mud fireplaces, the heavy smoke of burning dung. Children with begging bowls, blind men and lepers, people dying under black umbrellas. Saved by the water, released to the water. Miracles share the landscape with death.

It was one more list, wasn't it? All he could do, all he could make. His own primitive control. The sadhus sit naked, heads raised, eyes opened wide to the sun. The contortionists bend themselves into topological knots. The chanting begins, the blowing of conch shells. They go dragging through the shallow water, arms raised, multitudes, a solid body, too many to see.

Trampled, drowned. In his fear of things that took place on such a rampant scale, was there an element of desperate envy? Was it enviable? Did they possess a grace, a beauty, as his friend Kathryn believed? Was it a grace to be there, to lose oneself in the mortal crowd, surrendering, giving oneself over to mass awe, to disappearance in others?

He crossed his arms to clutch himself against the chill. In three days he would walk into the desert.

"There's some water in that jug."

"Here," I said.

"Take some."

"Is it safe?"

Owen was gravitationally bound to the cult, as an object to a neutron star, pulled toward its collapsed mass, its density. The image is both trivial and necessary. What could he say about the attraction? Nothing that did not take the form of an example from the physical world, preferably a remote and not easily observed part of it, to suggest the edge of perception.

The dead sun was not an image. It hung over the cactus and scrub, the sand hills of this desolate western reach of the Thar, the Great Indian Desert, not far from the Pakistan border. He followed camel trails and ate a thick bread made with coarse barley. The well water was brackish, the camels wore bells, people made frequent reference to snakebite. He came across two villages in four days on foot and in buses. The villagers lived in beehive huts with thatched roofs, walls of mud and dry grass.

His mother used to tell him, "Try to be more impressive."

He stood on a broken asphalt road in a white silence, waiting for a bus. The people he'd seen some miles back had worn a type of cotton robe and the women had gathered branches from small thorny trees to use in making fires. He would have to learn the names of things.

He watched a man come hobbling toward him out of the hills. He led a goat on a rope and wore a ragged turban and the cleft white beard of the old Rajput warriors. He began talking on the other side of the road and in what appeared to be the middle of a sentence, as though continuing a conversation the two men had started some years earlier, and he told Owen about the nomadic tribes in the area, about snake charmers and wandering minstrels. The English he spoke sounded like a minor dialect of Rajasthani. He said he was a teacher and guide and he called Owen sir.

"Guide to what? There's nothing here."

He said a number of things Owen could not understand. Then he showed him a filthy length of cloth embossed with some kind of symbol. This seemed to give him official government status as a guide.

"But what is there to see that requires a guide?"

"For a feesir."

"How much?"

"As you wish."

"All I want to do is get a bus going that way, to Hawa Mandir."

No buses on this road. "You will be going to Hawa Mandir, you will need to see a lorry."

"When?"

"After certain days."

"How many days are certain days?"

The man thought about this.

"I am interested in knowing what you will guide me to if I pay your guide fee."

"Pay as you wishsir."

"But what will you show me? We're somewhere between Jaisalmer and the Pakistan border."

"Jaisalmer, Jaisalmer." He made a happy chant of it.

"And the Pakistan border," Owen said.

The man looked at him. The word for yesterday was the same as the word for tomorrow. The hawks turned in the empty sky.

"If there is no bus and if I have to wait indefinitely for another vehicle, I'll walk to Hawa Mandir."

"You will be walking into the Thar but you will never walk outsir."

"You said you were a teacher. What do you teach?"

The man tried to remember. He began a monologue that seemed to be about his early days as an acrobat and juggler, wandering between the fortress cities. The two men hunkered in the dust, the Indian talking endlessly, his right hand floating in a mesmeric gesture, his left hand clutching the rope that was fastened around the goat's neck. Owen was barely aware of his departure. He remained squatting close to the ground, leaning slightly forward, body weight supported by his calves. When the sun was white and rippling he took a dried vegetable preparation out of his pack and ate it. He wanted water but allowed himself only a token amount, trying to preserve most of what was left until the next day, midmorning, when he would look for rest and shade after five hours on foot. It was suddenly dark. He reclined on his side like the gypsy in the Rousseau painting, safe in a mystical sleep.

He was barely awake, thinking of the morning's long haul, when a small caravan of brass-studded iron carts approached, bullock-drawn, heading the same way he was. Blacksmiths and their families, the women wearing bright veils and silver trinkets. They took him to Hawa Mandir.

It was a fifteenth-century town slowly being assimilated by the desert, so much the color of the desert that Owen did not see it until they were nearly at the gates. It was being received and combined, sinking into the land, crumbling, worn away in stages. Even the dogs that sulked along the outskirts were yellowish brown and passive and barely visible. He walked through the streets and alleys. The houses were sandstone, with carved façades and flat roofs, auspicious signs on many walls. There was one long building embellished with domes and kiosks and lacy stonework balconies. There was little activity, most of it involving water. A man washed down a camel, another fastened water containers to a two-wheeled wooden cart. In minutes Owen had made his way to the edge of town. Sand began to blow.

The stone houses gave way to huts of mud and brick. Many of these were ruined, lapped in sand. Children watched him drink from his canteen. Goats moved in and out of inhabited huts. He stood on a ruined wall and scanned the horizon. There were earthen bins out there, sand-colored, conical, one or two with thatched roofs. He'd seen these elsewhere, receptacles for food and grain, the taller ones seven or eight feet high, usually set on the immediate edge of a village, men with tools, livestock tethered nearby. These bins were stark, a half dozen of them, about three hundred yards from the last of the huts. He set out in that direction.

Sand was blowing across the tawny ruins. A rough path led through gorse and thorn to the cluster of small buildings. Sandstone hills rose in regulated layers in the distance. He passed a woman and child with a gaunt cow. The child followed close to the animal, gathering dung as it fell to the ground, folding it, patting it briskly. The woman screamed something at her, lashing the air with a stick. This sound carried briefly on the wind. History. The man who stands outside it.

He could barely see by the time he approached the bins. The sand stung his face and he walked with his arm crooked in front of him, opening his eyes only long enough to glimpse the way. Something startled him, a man standing at the head of the path, dark-skinned, his hair ringleted and wild, his face uncovered despite the blowing sand. Shadows around the flat eyes, a danger in his bearing. But he was also oddly calm, waiting, wrapped in garments from neck to ankles, hands hidden, head and feet bare, and he was saying something to Owen. Was it a question? They looked right at each other. When the man repeated the words, Owen realized the language was Sanskrit and he knew at once what the man had said, although he made no conscious attempt to translate.

The man had said, *"How many languages do you speak?"*

Half the room was filled with light. He sat up, a little unsteady in his movements. I don't think I'd fully realized how exhausted and ill he was. The only strength was in his voice.

"That's a question I always dread being asked," I said. "It's a question that seems to be waiting for me wherever I go in the Mideast. I don't know why it carries such force."

"It's a terrible question in a way, isn't it?"

"But why?"

"I don't know," he said.

"Why do I think it exposes some terrible weakness or failing?"

"I don't know."

"You can answer it. Five, six."

"Counting Sanskrit. Which comes pretty close to outright cheating. In my own defense I'd have to say there was never anyone I could speak it with, except that boy on the embankment. They're teaching it again in the schools."

"Did you speak it with them?"

"On and off."

"How did you know they were there? From the group in the Mani?"

"They said there was a cell in India. They'd gone there from somewhere in Iran. I was to look for a place called Hawa Mandir."

"You took your time looking."

"It was my view, my sentiment that India would cure me of the fascination. Is there more water?"

"The jug is empty."

"You have to fill it in the street. There's a tap two houses down."

When I returned he was asleep, sitting up, his arm dangling over the side of the bench. I woke him without hesitation.

The man's name was Avtar Singh. Owen suspected this was a pseudonym and was never able to convince himself that Singh was an Indian. The man was not only an impressive mimic but seemed to look different every time Owen saw him. An ascetic, streetcorner preacher, a subway bedlamite. His physiognomy changed, his features as aspect and character. Intelligent, vain, obsequious, cruel. He'd look lean and severe one day, a mystic in shabby robes; puffy the next, physically bloated, eyes heavy and drugged.

The Greek cell had broken up and two of the members were here, recent arrivals. Emmerich was one, a man with an austere head and tight beard. The other was the woman, Bern, thick-lipped, broad, utterly silent for weeks now. She spent almost all her time sealed in one of the thatched silos.

There were two other men but Owen had little contact with them. All he knew was that they'd been with Singh in Iran, that one of them was suffering frequent cycles of chills and high fever and that they were evidently Europeans. They did not speak Sanskrit as the others did, or tried to do, and it was this as much as the group's predominant mood which indicated to Owen that the cult was nearly dead.

One day he squatted in the dust with Emmerich. They talked about Sanskrit, speaking the language itself as well as several others. Emmerich had the look of an intelligent convict, someone in for life, for murder, self-taught, self-willed, an expert on the tradecraft of a confined life, contemptuous of people who want to know what it is like—contemptuous even as he agrees to enlighten them. He is well settled in his life term, this kind of man. His crime, the largeness of it, furnishes endless material for speculation and self-knowledge. Everything he reads and learns is made to serve as a personal philosophy, an explanation, an enlargement of that brilliant single moment, a moment he has reworked, re-explained to himself, made use of. The murder has by this time become part of the dream pool of his self-analysis. The victim and the act are theory now. They form the philosophical base he relies on for his sense of self. They are what he uses to live.

"The Sanskrit word for knot," Emmerich said, "eventually took on the meaning of 'book.' *Grantha*. This is because of the manuscripts. The birch-bark and palm-leaf manuscripts were bound by a cord drawn through two holes and knotted."

An austere head, Owen kept saying to himself. His father used to laugh at the oversized straw hat he wore with his bib overalls. Passing the crossroads store. The canopy and Coca-Cola sign. The wood posts sunk in cinder block. His mother used to say, "I don't know more'n a monkey what you're talking about."

Emmerich's head was smallish, with eyes that maintained a grim distance, closely cut hair and beard. The two men squatted at angles to each other, as though delivering their remarks out into the desert.

"What is a book?" Emmerich said. "It's a box that you open. You know this, I think."

"What is inside the box?"

"The Greek word *puxos*. Box-tree. This suggests wood, of course, and it's interesting that the word 'book' in English can be traced to the Middle Dutch *boek*, or beech, and to the Germanic *boko*, a beech staff on which runes were carved. What do we have? Book, box, alphabetic symbols incised in wood. The wooden ax shaft or knife handle on which was carved the owner's name in runic letters."

"Is this history?" Owen said.

"This is not history. This is precisely the opposite of history.

An alphabet of utter stillness. We track static letters when we read. This is a logical paradox."

Bern appeared, walking once around the bin, re-entering. The bin, silo or granary. Owen would have to learn the local name. This he made his first task in new places, always.

"She will try to kill herself," Emmerich said. "She will starve herself. Already she's starting. Three, four days. It came to her like a sacred revelation. This is the perfect way. Starvation. Drawn-out, silent, losing the functions one by one. What is better in a place like India than starvation?"

"Is this the end of it? Is there another group somewhere?"

"To my knowledge this is the end of it. There are no more cells outside of this one. Maybe two or three individuals left, possibly in contact with each other, possibly not."

"Will you all die here?"

"I don't think Singh will die. He will outfox it, out-talk it. Bern will die. The other two will probably die. I don't think I will die. I've learned too much about myself."

"Isn't this why people kill themselves?" Owen said.

"Because they've discovered who they are? I admit I've never thought of that. And you. Who are you?"

"No one."

"What do you mean 'no one'?"

"No one."

They squatted like Indians, close to the ground, arms draped over their knees.

"For a long time nothing happens," Emmerich said. "We begin to think we barely exist. People wander off, people die. Many differences appear among us. We lose purpose, suffer setbacks. There are differences in meaning, differences in words."

"She won't eat. Will she take water?"

"So far she has taken it. This is to draw it out, to extend the silence. You know this. She is very doctrinaire. For such people, dying is a methodology."

"In Greece she was reluctant to talk to me."

"You aren't a member. It was only your training as an epigraphist that made you more or less welcome, your digs and travels. We saw you could be trusted. This was a quiet and scholarly and deeply intense interest. But not Bern. She didn't care. Things began to irk her in Greece. Someone stole her boots."

"What happened to the others who were with you?"

"Scattered."

These bins were made of dung and earth. There were figures in the distant fields, stooped, moving. A dusty snake curved through the weeds. The one color. Formed and ordered. The high white sun.

"But there is still the program," Emmerich said. "Singh has found a man. We are waiting for him to approach Hawa Mandir. Let's face it, the most interesting thing we do is kill. Only a death can complete the program. You know this. It goes deep, this recognition. Beyond words."

These were not kites but sparrow hawks, he decided. No chaos, no waste.

"Sometimes I ask myself," Emmerich said. "What is the function of a murderer? Is he the person you go to in order to confess?"

"He was wrong," I said, surprised at my own abruptness. "You weren't there to confess anything."

"Unless it was to acknowledge my likeness to them."

"Everybody is like everybody else."

"You can't mean that."

"Not exactly. Not stated exactly so."

"We overlap. Is that what you mean?"

"I'm not sure what I mean."

His voice grew soft. He was careful not to accuse, not to hurt.

"What do you see when you look at me?" he said. "You see yourself in twenty years' time. A damn sobering sight. It's true, isn't it? Our likeness is a kind of leap, a condition you can't help but foresee. You used to oppose almost everything I said. Less so of late. As though you've begun to hedge your bets. You see yourself, James, don't you?"

Alone, weak-willed, defenseless, taking the stairs two at a time. Was this true, was he right? I would never completely understand Owen, know his reasons, know the inner shapes and themes. This only made the likeness more plausible.

Feet flat on the ground, weight on the calves, arms draped over the knees. They hunkered in one of the bins. Singh rubbed two long stones against each other, rough-shaping them as he talked. He was a talking machine. He moved from Hindi to English to Sanskrit in the space of a single long remark. Owen was afraid of him. He was too clearly on the maniacal edge. He looked mad, spoke in a jumble of tongues, fell into cruel and sweeping laughter, eyes shut, mouth wide open, full of rotting teeth. Owen listened to him talk for much of a long afternoon and through the pale desert vespers and into the night. He was mercurial and deft, sometimes intimidating, sometimes appearing to seek favor. Not a true games-player, not an observer of the rules, Owen thought, astonished at the stupidity of this reflection. Singh was electric, messianic, crazy, the coarsely grained face set in a mass of dusty ringlets. He stopped rubbing the stones only long enough to raise his fingers in the air, indicating quotation marks around a word he used ironically or with a double meaning.

"Thar. This is a contraction of *marust'hali*. Abode of death. Let me tell you what I like about the desert. The desert is a solution. Simple, inevitable. It's like a mathematical solution applied to the affairs of the planet. Oceans are the subconscious of the world. Deserts are the waking awareness, the simple and clear solution. My mind works better in the desert. My mind is a razed tablet out here. Everything counts in the desert. The simplest word has enormous power. This is fitting because it's part of the Indian tradition. The word in India has enormous power. Not what people mean but what they say. Intended meaning is beside the point. The word itself is all that matters. The Hindu woman tries to avoid speaking her husband's name. Every utterance of his name brings him closer to death. You know this. I'm not telling you something you don't know, or am I? Indian literature has been eaten by white ants. The bark and leaf manuscripts, nibbled, gnawed, consumed. You know this. India doesn't need a literature anyway. Superfluous. India is the right brain of the world. Dancing Shiva, you know? Pure motion baby. What I'd like to do when we leave this place is go to northern Iraq and study Yezidi cryptic. You have to see this alphabet to believe it. A little Hebrew-looking, a little Persian, a little Arabic, a little Martian. This thing is cryptic because the Yezidis live among Muslims and can't stand the mothers. Total mutual loathing, right? If a Yezidi hears a Muslim in prayer he either kills the poor bugger or kills himself. That's according to the book anyway. There are other alphabets to study in that area. I could go to the marshes. I'd take the woman except she's serious about starving herself. I'd like to fuck her everywhichway to Sunday or whatever the phrase. She's the kind you fuck with a vengeance, am I right? Each sound has one sign only. This is the genius of the alphabet. Simple, inevitable. No wonder it happened in the desert."

"I don't mean to interrupt."

"I'm in no hurry," Owen said. "I'd just as soon put off the rest of it indefinitely."

"I want to hear it."

"I don't want to tell it. It becomes harder and harder. The closer we come to the end, the more I want to stop. I don't know if I can face all that again."

"I interrupted to ask about Singh's idea of the desert. Is there something clear and simple there?"

Owen looked into the shadowed part of the room.

"Singh remarked to me once, his conspiratorial aspect, fixing those flat heavy eyes on me, 'Hell is the place we don't know we're in.' I wasn't sure how to take the remark. Was he saying that he and I were in hell or that everyone else was? Everyone in rooms, houses, chairs with armrests. Is hell a lack of awareness? Once you know you're there, is this your escape? Or is hell the one place in the world we don't see for what it is, the one place we can never know? Is that what he meant? Is hell what we say to each other or what we can't say, what is beyond our reach? The sentence defeated me. I was afraid of the desert but drawn to it, drawn to the contradiction. Men will come to fill this empty place. This place is empty in order that men may rush in to fill it."

The clear voice became a chant now, almost startling in its richness and stately pace. I want to call it a funeral pace.

"To penetrate the desert truly. To learn the geography and language, wear the *aba* and *keffiyeh*, go brown in the desert sun. To infiltrate Mecca. Imagine it, to enter the city with one and a half million pilgrims, cross the border within the border, make the *hadj*. What enormous fears would a man like me have to overcome, what lifelong inclinations toward solitude, toward the sanctity of a personal space in which to live and be. But think of it. To dress as a *hadji* in two pieces of seamless white cloth, every man there in two pieces of seamless white cloth, over a million of us. To make the seven circuits of the Ka'bah. The great cubical form draped in black, imagine it, with Koranic verses embroidered in gold script. For the first three circuits we are enjoined to move at a jogging pace. There are other times when great masses gather during the *hadj*, on the plain of Arafat and for three days at Mína, but it's the circuit of the Ka'bah that has haunted me ever since I first learned of it. The three running circuits, perhaps a hundred thousand people, a swirl of white-clad people running around the massive black cube, a whirlwind of human awe and submission. To be carried along, no gaps in the ranks, to move at a pace determined by the crowd itself, breathless, in and of them. This is what draws me to such things. Surrender. To burn away one's self in the sandstone hills. To become part of the chanting wave of men, the white cities, the tents that cover the plain, the vortex in the courtyard of the Grand Mosque."

"I thought it was one big bus jam, the *hadj*."

"But do you see what draws me to the running?"

"To honor God, yes, I would run."

"There is no God," he whispered.

"Then you can't run, you mustn't run. There's no point, is there? It's stupid and destructive. If you don't do it to honor God or imitate the Prophet, then it means nothing, it accomplishes nothing."

He withdrew into a silence, a deprived silence. He'd wanted to explore the matter further, the fearsome driving rapture of it, but my rejection was the type he could not contend with. He was like a child in this respect, that silence was a place to take his hurt and shame.

"What else did Singh have to tell you?"

"He talked about the world."

"Then what happened?" I said.

He talked about the world.

"The world has become self-referring. You know this. This thing has seeped into the texture of the world. The world for thousands of years was our escape, was our refuge. Men hid from themselves in the world. We hid from God or death. The world was where we lived, the self was where we went mad and died. But now the world has made a self of its own. Why, how, never mind. What happens to us now that the world has a self? How do we say the simplest thing without falling into a trap? Where do we go, how do we live, who do we believe? This is my vision, a self-referring world, a world in which there is no escape."

His flesh was pebbled along the forehead and cheeks. He had long wrists and hands. Slowly the two stones began to take on a faintly tapered shape. He rubbed the stones for hours, then days. Bern was hallucinating. They heard her moan and chant. She crawled outside to urinate, positioned on all fours. Three of the men went looking for a stray goat to kill. Owen went to Bern's silo, not knowing why. The seal was in place, an earthen hatch-cover about three feet off the ground, held fast by a wooden bar inserted through a pair of sockets. He removed the cover and bent down to look into the silo. She sat in the dark. The floor was strewn with hay and bits of corn stalk. Her face swung toward him and she stared with no apparent recognition. He spoke softly to her, offering to get water, but there was no response. He told her how the smell of animal feed made him think of his childhood,

the grain storage elevators and backyard windmills, the Here-
fords in loading pens, the bent metal sign on the little brick
building at the edge of town (he hadn't thought of this in thirty
years): FARMERS BANK. He remained outside the bin, watching her
face float in the dead air. She looked at him.

The desert town was like the land reshaped in blocks, some odd
work of the wind as it transports sand. Singh cupped his hands
to drink from an earthenware jug. One of the other men hunkered in the dust. From this distance the town was silent most of
the time. Owen drank. When it was dark and a wind fell from
the hills he watched the ashes stir and blow around the improvised spit. The night sky appeared, the scattershot of blazing
worlds.

"Who is the man you're waiting for?"

"What man?"

"Emmerich said."

"*Atcha*. A crazy. Bonkers, you know? Wandering for years in
these parts."

"Is he close to the town? How do you know he'll head that
way?"

Singh laughing. "He is bloody close, yes."

"How do you know?"

"Just seen him. You just done ate his goat."

"An old man with a beard, more or less in rags?"

"That him, mon. He keep walking. It don't do him no good
to get no older. He on his last legs for sure. He have to sit down
and wait for vulture. Vulture do the business of the desert."

"You're waiting, then, until he enters town."

"You know this. You're a member now."

"No, I'm not."

"Of course you're a member."

"No, I'm not."

"Damn fool. Of course you are."

This time it was Owen who interrupted, breaking off the narrative to reach down for the booklet I'd left propped against the

copper tray, the primer on Kharoshthi. He returned it to its place in the tray. Gradations of brown and gray. Light retreating toward the far wall. A certain number of objects, a certain placing. He sat looking into his hands.

"What does Singh mean by 'the world'?" I said.

"Everything, everybody, whatever is said or can be said. Although not these exactly. The thing that encompasses these. Maybe that's it."

"What happened next?"

"I'm tired, James."

"Try to go on."

"It's important to get it right, to tell it correctly. Being precise is all that's left. But I don't think I can manage it now."

"You were with them. Did you learn their name?"

He looked up.

"This knowledge has managed to elude me, although I tried my damnedest to pry it out of them, wheedle it out by whatever means. Even after Singh told me I was a member, he wouldn't tell me the name of the cult."

"He was taunting."

"Yes, he began to seek me out to amuse himself, fortify himself. I was their strength in an odd way and also their observer and tacit critic, the first they'd ever had, which was another indication they were near the end."

I told Owen about the time I'd spent in the Mani, my meeting with Andahl. I told him about the massive rock on which two words had been painted, then tarred over. Andahl had painted the words, I said. It was his way of breaking clear. I told Owen I thought these words were the cult's name.

"What words were they?"

"*Ta Onómata.*"

Looking at me with curious wonder. "Damn it. Damn it, James." Beginning to laugh. "You may be right. I think you could be right. It makes an eerie kind of sense, doesn't it? The Names."

"I've been consistently right about the cult. Andahl, the name, the pattern. And I found them almost as soon as I entered the

Mani, although I didn't know it at first. It scares hell out of me, Owen. My life is going by and I can't get a grip on it. It eludes me, it defeats me. My family is on the other side of the world. Nothing adds up. The cult is the only thing I seem to connect with. It's the only thing I've been right about."

"Are you a serious man?"

The question stopped me cold. I told him I didn't understand what he meant.

"I'm not a serious man," he said. "If you wanted to compose a mighty Homeric text on my life and fortunes, I might suggest a suitable first line. 'This is the story of a man who was not serious.'"

"You're the most serious man I know."

He laughed at me and made a gesture of dismissal. But I wasn't ready to let it go just yet.

"What do you mean then? Do you think I'm not serious because I've written insignificant things, miscellaneous things, because I work for a sprawling corporation?"

"You know that's not what I mean."

"It's important for me to have an ordinary job. Paperwork. A desk and daily tasks. In my curious way I try to cling to people and to work. I try to assert a basic right or need."

"Of course," he said. "I didn't mean the question as a challenge. I'm sorry. Forgive me, James."

We fell into a silence.

"Do you realize what we're doing?" I said finally. "We're submerging your narrative in commentary. We're spending more time on the interruptions than on the story."

He poured water from the jug.

"I feel like someone in that mob of yours," I told him. "The mob that grows impatient with the professional teller of tales. Let's go on with it. Where are the people in the story?"

"It gets harder as we approach the end. I want to delay. I don't want to get on with it at all."

"Show us their faces, tell us what they said."

.   .   .

Emmerich was tracking the victim. He reported that the old man's wanderings were sometimes predictable. He tended to head west for part of the day, then northeast, then west again, then southeast. Was he describing an hourglass in the sand? At other times he roamed the hills, lived for a day or two with camel herders or one of the wandering tribes, beyond all roads. In sandstorms he sat still, as Emmerich did if he was in the area, his face covered in a head-scarf as the sun paled, the sky vanished, the wind began to keen. The man was very old, his range limited. Time, weather, his faltering gait suggested he would approach Hawa Mandir in less than two days, goatless, hungry, muttering.

Bern was vomiting blood. Three or four times a day Owen removed the hatch-cover and spoke to her. She was beyond hunger, he assumed, drifting into a spiral of irreversible attrition. He spoke softly and easily. He always had something to say. Something came to mind the moment he bent to the opening. He was visiting, he was actually chatting. He wanted to soothe her, to bathe her in his human voice. He believed she understood, although there was no sign. He brought her water once a day. She could no longer hold down water but he continued to bring it, easing through the opening and trying to get her to drink from his cupped hands. Her eyes grew daily in their sockets, her face began to fold into her skull. He sat across from her, letting his mind wander. His mind had begun to wander all the time.

Singh rubbed the stones together.

"Lovely day, what? Coolish, or would you say warmish? Depends, doesn't it?"

He made quote marks in the air, raising the index and middle finger of each hand to set off the words coolish and warmish. He studied one of the stones. *Atcha*. Okay.

"What is his name?" Owen said.

"Hamir Mazmudar."

"Does it *mean* anything?"

Singh laughed wildly, pounding the stones together. When Emmerich arrived he was gray with blown sand. He looked at Singh and pointed toward the distant fields. A figure came out of the millet, moving slowly toward town. Large birds turned in the darkening sky. Owen watched the pale moon rise. The moon was his proper body, sad and dashed.

"But he's not so far gone."

"Sick man," Emmerich said.

"Not so sick. He walks for days on end."

"His memory is gone."

"It was all we could do," Singh said, "to find out the bloke's proper name."

"Once your memory goes, you're an empty body."

"There's no point anymore, is there?"

"You're a receptacle for your own waste," Emmerich said. "From the sigmoid flexure to the anal canal."

"You know the program. You know how it has to end."

"You recognize."

"You see the rightness of it," Singh said.

"It reaches you, doesn't it?"

"It's valid."

"It's true to the premise, isn't it? It follows logically upon the premise."

"It's clean, you know? Nothing clings to the act. No hovering stuff."

"It's a blunt recital of the facts," Emmerich said. "We can put it that way if you like."

"What would you like?"

"It's sound, it's binding."

"It's utterly bloody right. I mean we're bloody 'ere, ain't we? No use 'anging about, is there? Time we nipped into town, i'n it?"

Emmerich stripped, poured water from a brass pot over his face and body, then put on a coarse shirt, loose drawstring pants, an old tribal surcoat and round felt cap. Singh came out of his silo. The smoke of cooking fires hung over the town. He went with Emmerich to the bin where the other two men were enclosed. He did not look at Owen or speak to him. English was the binding tongue of the subcontinent. The ancient Arabs wrote on bones. Singh emerged in clothes that belonged to the others, a striped robe and dark sash under a military tunic. He looked princely and insane. Emmerich followed him toward the darkening town, the one color, formed and ordered. *Hakara* is the name of the Sanskrit *b*. *Makara* is the *m*.

Owen entered one of the silos and sat in the dark. It was the smallest of the structures, five feet high, and he watched the night sky rapidly deepen, stars pinching through the haze. That was the universe tonight, a rectangle two and a half feet high, three feet long. At the lower edge of the opening he could see a narrow band of earth losing its texture to the night. Council Grove and Shawnee. The old storage elevators were frame construction until they switched to silos, see the Greek, a pit for storing grain, about the mid-1920s he thought it was. Lord the machines were wonderful, the combines and tractors, those stark contraptions flailing and bumping through the bluestem grass. He was lonely for machines. The boxy little Fords and Chevrolets. The dry goods delivery truck. The cross-country buses, a hundred and twenty horsepower. HORN OK PLEASE. He was a waterboy in the fields with a straw hat, that's what they wore, and sturdy overalls. It is necessary to remember correctly. This is the earth we dream and childishly color. The spaces. The solitary church standing in weeds. The men in overalls, with wind-beaten faces, clear-eyed, gathered outside a feed store. We want to get it right.

An enclosed wooden stairway juts out from the side of the feed store. Someone peers up. Beyond a line of raked cirrus come the towering brown combers of a midsummer rain, flat-based mounds of cloud with multiple summits. There's an element of suspense in the air. The air is charged and dense. The men in overalls stand watching. There's always a period of curious fear between the first sweet-smelling breeze and the time when the rain comes cracking down.

It is Owen who is peering skyward. He moves away from the cluster of silent men. Late again. They would be waiting at home. On the porch of an old frame house the woman sits in an arrow-back chair as the first heavy drops hit the street, raising dust in gauzy mare's-tails. Poker-faced, retaining a grudging faith in the life beyond. The life beyond would not be easy or pleasurable as she saw it. These things were not part of her system of beliefs.

But it would be just, it would be consistent with moral right, it would offer a recompense for these days and years of getting by, scraping together, finding and losing homes. She limped, his mother, and he never knew why.

The man comes out to wait, just washed, clean-shirted, a rubbing of earth, nonetheless, plainly evident in the seams of his face and hands, hard earth, irremovable. He stands looking toward the noise of the storm, one shoulder higher than the other, a way of standing and walking, common enough among men who plowed and stooped and carried posts and dug post-holes. Owen thought it was related in some way to his mother's limp.

In his memory he was a character in a story, a colored light. The bin was perfect, containing that part of his existence, enclosing it whole. There was recompense in memories too. Recall the bewilderment and ache, the longing for a thing that's out of reach, and you can begin to repair your present condition. Owen believed that memory was the faculty of absolution. Men developed memories to ease their disquiet over things they did as men. The deep past is the only innocence and therefore necessary to retain. The boy in the sorghum fields, the boy learning names of animals and plants. He would recall exactingly. He would work the details of that particular day.

The church is fifteen miles out of town. The only structure visible. Seeing it from a distance he doesn't react the way he would to a farmhouse, say, with its sprung cluster of trees set against the open sky. Small groupings of objects, breaking the deep plane of the land, this house and barn, these cottonwoods and sheds and stone walls, seem to beat against the distances, the endless dusty winds, resourceful and brave. The church is different, a lone building with a decaying gray façade, pitched roof, steeple without a bell. There are no boundaries, no trees or stream. It has no telling effect. It is lost in the sky behind it.

A couple of old motorcars sit in the weeds, World War I vintage, skimpy, with treadless tires. In time the Pontiac hearse comes off the dirt road, jouncing, four-door, a once grand but now mud-spattered vehicle, gravely dented, too ramshackle and complaining to transport the dead. Rain is gunning down on the fenders and roof. (In his memory he is at the church, waiting, as well as inside the car, crammed between the door and a woman who smells of sour milk.) The doors open and people begin edging out, including the mother, father and the boy, the squinting boy of ten or so, already growing out of his clothes, growing toward the world unwillingly. He stands by the car door, waits for the lady and an old man to emerge, then shuts the door and turns toward the church, pausing in the rain before he follows the others in.

The benches are old, the altar a plain table partly stripped of varnish. A woman holds an infant, facing out, against her breasts. There is an imprint on the wall that marks the absent upright piano. The man who will preach today is young and dark-haired and has about him a hard-set radiance. He is here to determine things, to get these people right with God. Even if he were dressed in farm clothes and seated on one of the benches, it would be easy to tell him apart from the others. The marginal farmers, the migrant workers, the odd-jobs men, the invalids, the half-breeds, the widowed, the silent, the blank. Less than thirty people present today, some of them having come on foot. They seem the off-lineage of some abrupt severance or dispossession. There is something emptied-out and loose-jointed about them. Owen notices the undiscerning gazes and draws a simple moral. Hardship makes the world obscure.

These early memories were a fiction in the sense that he could separate himself from the character, maintain the distance that lent a pureness to his affection. How else could men love themselves but in memory, knowing what they know? But it was necessary to get the details right. His innocence depended on this, on the shapes and colors of this device he was building, this child's model of a rainy day in Kansas. He had to remember correctly.

The resolute young man strokes the air as he speaks, then cuts it with emphatic gestures. In this room of bare wood and dying light he is a power, a stalking force. They are here to wrestle with each other, he says. They will get right, see the light and yield, not to him but to the Spirit. When we talk about the fallen wonder of the world, we don't mean the forests and the plains and the animals. We don't mean the scenery, do we? He tells them they will talk as from the womb, as from the sweet soul before birth, before blood and corruption.

There are many silences in his discourse. All the promises are spaced. He is building a suspense, an expectancy. Gusts of rain are washing through the wheatfields of the high plains. Let me hear that beautiful babbling brook, he says. And he watches them, urging silently now. Someone mumbles something, a man in the front row. Sky is opened, the preacher says. Rain is coming down.

He moves among them, touching a shoulder here, a head there, touching roughly, reminding them of something they'd forgotten or chosen to disregard. There is a Spirit lurking here. Show me the scripture that says we have to speak English to know the joy of talking freely to God. Ridiculous, we say. There's no such document. Paul to the Corinthians said men can speak with the tongues of angels. In our time we can do the same.

Do whatever your tongue finds to do. Seal the old language and loose the new.

The boy is spellbound by the young man's intensity and vigor. It is startling, compelling. He listens to the clear voice, watches the man roll up his shirt-sleeves and shoot a hand in this and that direction, touching people, squeezing their flesh, shaking them hard. Owen's mother is saying Jesus Jesus Jesus, softly, in her seat, in awe, exalted. There is a stirring up front, an arm flying into the air. The preacher turns, walking toward the altar, talking along with the man, exhorting. He does not rush, he does not raise his voice. The noise and hurry are in Owen's mind. The preacher turns again to face the congregation, watches the man in the front row get to his feet. Owen's father gets to his feet.

Get wet, the preacher says. Let me hear that babbling brook. What am I talking about but freedom? Be yourself, that's all it is. Be free in the Spirit. Let the Spirit knock you free. You start, the Spirit takes over. Easiest thing in the world. That's all it is. Jump in, get wet. I can hear the Spirit in you, I can hear the Spirit driving. Let it move and shake you. Get ready, it's round the bend, it's turning the corner, it's running the rapids, it's coming like nobody's business. I want to hear that beautiful babbling brook.

A silence. The sense of expectation is tremendous. The boy is chilled. Time seems to pause whenever the preacher does. When he speaks, everything starts again, everything moves and jumps and lives. Only his voice can drive the meeting forward.

Time to get wet, he says. *Get wet time.*

In the bin, the inverted lunar urn, he wondered about the uses of ecstasy, see the Greek, a displacing, a coming out of stasis. That's all it was. A freedom, an escape from the condition of ideal balance. Normal understanding is surpassed, the self and its machinery obliterated. Is this what innocence is? Is it the language of innocence those people spoke, words flying out of them like spat stones? The deep past of men, the transparent word. Is this what they longed for with that terrible holy gibberish they carried through the world? To be the children of the race? Sleep. The sleep of tired children, the great white-sheeted wave. It began to fold over him. He was exhausted, he closed his eyes. A little more, a little longer. It was necessary to remember, to dream the pristine earth.

His father stands erect, eyes closed, the noise running out of him, strangely calm and measured. Owen sees the preacher come close. His eyes are bright and queer. He has powerful forearms, high-veined, dark-veined. There are voices and rejoicing, a rash of voices, movement here and there. This speech is beautiful in its way, inverted, indivisible, *absent*. It is not quite there. It passes over and through. There are occasional prompting comments by the preacher, his reflections on what he sees and hears. He speaks conversationally of these tremendous things.

Those were plain and forthright people, thought the man crouched in the dark. Those were people who deserved better. All they had to reconcile them to exhaustion and defeat was that meager place in the wind. Those were honest people, struggling to make a way, full of the heart's own goodness and love.

The clouds are neon-edged. The light is metallic, falling across the rangeland, the plainweave fields, the old towns in their scrupulous ruin.

Bless them.

"Bless them."

He sat in the small room, motionless, looking toward a wall. The eyes were still involved in that old and recollected business, the head tilted toward his right shoulder. There was a strange radiance in his face, the slightest separation of the man from his condition, the full acceptance, the crushing belief that nothing can be done. Motionless. The telling had merged with the event. I had to think a moment to remember where we were.

"You stayed in the silo through the night."

"Yes, of course. Why would I come out, to watch them kill him? These killings mock us. They mock our need to structure and classify, to build a system against the terror in our souls. They make the system equal to the terror. The means to contend with death has become death. Did I always know this? It took the desert to make it clear to me. Clear and simple, to answer the question you asked earlier. All questions are answered today."

"Is this what the cult intended all the time, this mockery?"

"Of course not. They intended nothing, they meant nothing. They only matched the letters. What beautiful names. Hawa Mandir. Hamir Mazmudar."

The twig broom. The muted colors of the pillows and rugs. The angles of arranged objects. The floorboard seams. The seam of light and shade. The muted colors of the water jug and wooden chest. The muted colors of the walls.

We sat watching the room go dark. I judged the amount of time that had to pass before he would be ready to recite the ending, before the stillness would yield. This is what I was learning from the objects in the room and the spaces between them, from the conscious solace he was devising in things. I was learning when to speak, in what manner.

"Try to finish," I said softly.

.   .   .

Two blood-covered stones were found near the body on the outskirts of the fifteenth-century town, at first light, by a woman fetching water or by boys on their way to the fields. By this time three men would be trekking west, leaving behind a comatose woman and two other men, one dead, one merely sitting still. Eventually a constable would make his way along the rough path to the storage bins, and then a subdivisional officer, to question the one conscious person. He would be sitting in the dust, blue-eyed and sparsely bearded, without documents or money, and he would probably try to speak to them in some dialect of northwest Iran.

The trekkers dispersed without a word in the wild country before the border. The one in Western clothes, carrying a small pack, had imprinted in his passport a visa which would not expire for some months. It included the stamp of the second secretary, Embassy of Pakistan, Athens, Greece, and carried above the stamp an example of this gentleman's handsomely scripted initials.

It was interesting how he'd chosen to finish, impersonally, gazing as if from a distance on these unknowable people, these figures we distinguish by their clothing. There would be no further commentary and reflection. This was fitting. I had no trouble accepting this. I didn't want to reflect further, with or without Owen. It was enough to see him sit there, owl-eyed, in the room he'd been arranging all his life.

The alleys were full of people and noise. Bare bulbs were arrayed on strings over tiers of nuts and spices. I paused every few feet to see what was here, nutmeg and scarlet mace, burlap bags of coriander seeds and chilies, rock salt in crude chunks. I lingered at the trays of dyestuffs and ground spices, heaped in pyramids, colors I'd never seen, brilliances, worlds, until finally it was time to go.

I came away from the old city feeling I'd been engaged in a contest of some singular and gratifying kind. Whatever he'd lost in life-strength, this is what I'd won.

13

SHUTTERS DOWN, laundry hanging in a dead calm on the terraces and rooftops. There's an aura of formal accord in the stillness that falls over certain cities at fixed times of the day and week. Everyone has agreed to disappear. The city is reduced to surfaces, planes of light and shade. To the lone figure, walking these streets, the silence has the well-plotted force of something commonly willed. It is a strict observance, the wishing of a spell upon things.

This is more or less what I was thinking when the argument started. A man and woman in a basement room, shouting at each other. I crossed the street and walked through a fence-gap into the pine woods, where I sat on a bench like an old man musing. The shouting grew intense, voices overlapping. It was the only sound on this weekend afternoon except for taxis down by the Hilton, cornering in early summer pain. Now the balcony doors along the street slowly opened. The woman's voice reached a bitter shriek. The neighbors began to appear on their balconies, looking down toward the sunken windows. The man was in a raucous fury, the woman spoke at runaway speed. Several people were out there, then several more, people in pajamas, in night-dresses, in robes and shorts, children grimacing in the light. All listened to the voices below, listened carefully at first, trying to catch the drift. In their dishevelment they were oddly meticulous figures, attentive, bodies held in equilibrium as they tried to comprehend, to be reasonable and fair. Then a man in striped shorts cried out a command for quiet. A bald old man in blue pajamas cried out the same plaintive word. From all the occupied balconies, voices cried out for quiet, quiet, a brief and powerful surge. In a short time the argument subsided, dropped off to a muttered exchange, and people withdrew to their rooms, fastening the louvered doors behind them.

I was happy to be back. There was dinner with Ann, there were five new pages from Tap's nonfiction novel to read. The desk in my office was full of neat stacks of paper that I looked forward to marking up and restacking, and pink and coral roses climbed the full height of a six-story building a few blocks away. But later in the day, when I thought about the walk I'd taken, it wasn't the abandoned streets I recalled, the centuries-old slumber, or the antic look of the undergarments those roused people wore. It was the two voices, that man and woman in plain rage, battling.

British Columbia. I knew two things about Victoria. It was "English" and it was "rainy." I had no idea what kind of house they lived in, what the street looked like, how they went about their daily routine. Did he walk to school or ride a bus? Was it a school bus or a city bus? What color was the bus? These things carried a haunting importance. These were the things my own father used to ask me all the time about my own small crossings of the world. His catechism of minims and incidentals. Now I saw what he was getting at. He wanted a detailed picture in which to place the small figure, the lone figure. The only safety is in details. Here we have a certainty or two, the petty facts of time and weather that connect people across a distance. He used to ask me about the lighting in the classroom, the amount of time we took for recess, which children were assigned to close the cloakroom doors, gripping the indentations to slide the panels shut. These were formal questions, addressed to me in clusters. I had to give him names, numbers, colors, whatever I could collect of particular things. These helped him see me as real.

I had no usable details of my son's comings and goings, nothing clear, nothing intact. I had trouble seeing them, seeing Kathryn taking walks across the city. In the single year we'd spent on South Hero, in the Champlain Islands, we'd walked through a deep and empty winter, walked through blowing drifts and across the lake's stunned surface (men in fishing shanties after perch and smelt). How she'd loved it, nature at the cutting edge, alert and pure. I could not have known how pure that winter would one day seem to me, bright with detail, as though set aside for future use. We had our landscape of meditation and rough love, working it out, good days and bad. I could see the place clearly, see them in it, down to the weave of their Shetland sweaters. What I needed was a sense of the present, their living days, the things around them. They'd removed themselves from my experience of real places.

Who were they when I wasn't there? What were the secrets they were keeping? I knew them in the simplest way, the accumulation, the natural gathering of hours. Is it a personal limitation or a theory of the universe that makes me want to say this is everything? This is what love comes down to, things that happen and what we say about them. Certainly this is what I wanted from Kathryn and Tap, the seeping love of small talk and family chat. I wanted them to tell me how they'd spent their day.

Ann, that evening, leaned against the balustrade on her terrace, facing in toward the door, where I stood with a drink. It was still light, too early to go to dinner, and she was telling me that Charles had just become involved in a major project in the Gulf. He would be part of a team responsible for the safety system in a gas liquefaction plant on Das Island, due to be operational by the end of the year. He had recited a stream of data over the phone. Hundreds of millions of cubic feet of gas per day, yearly tonnage of butane, propane, sulphur. He was excited, the Arabs were excited. The Japanese, who had already contracted for most of the processed gas, were also excited. The safety apparatus was an engineering marvel and Charles could hardly wait to get started.

"When does it happen?"

"He's back here day after tomorrow. A week later he flies to Abu Dhabi and pitches up on his island."

"Summer in the Gulf."

"It's a wonderful piece of luck. We're both a little stunned by it. He needs to get immersed in something like this, something brand new."

"Complex systems, endless connections."

"These bring him peace, I think. Peace and rest. He wants to talk to you incidentally. Instructed me to make sure James didn't leave town. Bind and gag him if necessary, he said."

"I look forward to seeing the old bastard. It's been a while."

"We're going to Mycenae while he's here. It's that time again. The goat-bells and wild poppies. He loves to sit on top of the palace ruins after everyone has left. The wind makes a ghostly sound, sweeping between those hills. Mycenae is his place, as Delphi is mine. Blood and steel. This is what he says about it. Massive rocks, blood cries, something old that he claims to recognize but can't seem to define for me."

I reread Tap's pages that night. They were full of small incidents, moments of discovery, things the young hero sees and wonders about. But nothing mattered so much on this second reading as a number of spirited misspellings. I found these mangled words exhilarating. He'd made them new again, made me see how they worked, what they really were. They were ancient things, secret, reshapable.

There's a grizzled old man, a sodbuster he is called in the text, who injures his leg in a drunken fall. The support he uses to get around with is one we've all seen. It includes a crosspiece to fit under the armpit and it is usually made of wood—the wood of a white-barked tree in this case. It is called a burch cruch.

This term had a superseding rightness as it appeared on the page. It found the spoken poetry in those words, the rough form lost through usage. His other misrenderings were wilder, freedom-seeking, and seemed to contain curious perceptions about the words themselves, second and deeper meanings, original meanings. It pleased me to believe he was not wholly innocent of these mistakes. I thought he sensed the errors but let them stand, out of exuberance and sly wonder and the inarticulate wish to delight me.

Charles Maitland sat alone in the dark hush of the bar at the Grande Bretagne, a midafternoon lull. He looked up when he saw me enter. A smile broke across his face, some kind of tigerish gleam in his eye.

"You wily bastard, James. Sit, sit."

"What are you drinking? I want something long and cool."

"Long and cool, is it? What a crafty piece of work."

"What are you talking about?"

The bartender wasn't at the bar. I heard him talking to a waiter in a back room somewhere.

"I always thought George Rowser was a fool. I'm the bloody fool, aren't I?"

"Why are you a fool, Charlie?"

"Come on, come on."

"I don't know what you're getting at."

"You don't know, you don't know. In a pig's eye, Axton. You bastard, I never even suspected. I never imagined. You were damned good. I don't mind telling you I'm impressed, even a bit envious, you know. It's been a year, has it, since we've been making the rounds together? And you never slipped. You never gave me reason to wonder."

The waiter came out. Charles ordered me a drink and then simply looked at me, examining as if in retrospect, wondering what he might have missed that could have given him a clue. A clue to what? I pressed him to explain.

"I appreciate your stance," he said. "It's the only professional stance. But the channel's no longer current, is it? You're relaxing with a friend."

"What channel?"

"Come on, come on."

He was glowing with admiration and delight, pink with it, shaking a match at the end of his cigarette. I decided to wait him out. I talked about his job in the Gulf, congratulated him, asked for details. When I was halfway through my drink, he approached the subject again, fearful of being deprived of it.

"Funny how I happened to see the report. I don't keep up the way I used to. I used to read every bloody word in those digests and surveys."

"What did it say exactly?"

He smiled. "Only that the Northeast Group, an American firm selling political risk insurance, has maintained a connection with the U.S. Central Intelligence Agency since its inception. Diplomatic sources et cetera."

I found it necessary to gaze across the room, to do some retrospective thinking of my own. I was aware that I'd narrowed my eyes, looking into the half light, like an illustration of someone studying an object or development. Two men entered speaking French.

"Of course you were aware in advance of this unraveling. You knew it was blown."

"Rowser knew."

"You learned it from him, did you?"

"He's very deft for someone who sweats and twitches," I said. "Where exactly did you see the report?"

Smiling, playing the game. "Has it appeared in more than one place? I doubt it. Too soon for that. *The Middle East Security Survey*. I used to read it all the time. Fallen off in recent years. But I still subscribe. Saw the current issue, as it happens, while I was in the Gulf. Just out. The minister of petroleum's personal copy."

"Is that what he's called—the minister of petroleum?"

"The minister of petroleum and mineral resources."

"Nice."

"You were damned good, James. All this time engaged in a back-channel dialogue with CIA. I never thought George Rowser was capable of this. I must tell him someday I misjudged him."

"How was it put?"

"The way they usually put things. You know as well as I. Better no doubt. 'Diplomatic sources arriving in London from Baghdad and Amman report that security officials in the Middle

East have discovered a link et cetera, et cetera.' What I'm curious to know is whether your firm is a full-fledged proprietary or simply a convenient source of information. Not that I'm asking, you understand. They've exposed only the bare outline. I know there must be much more and it must be absolutely riveting and one day I hope to hear you tell it, James."

"Drink up. We'll have another."

"I haven't told Ann. It isn't likely this kind of special information in a confidential newsletter will filter through to the public at large. Those whose business it is to know will surely know. The rest will go on as they always have. If your past is no longer a total secret, there is still your future to consider. I thought it best to tell no one, not even Ann. No doubt your plans are well advanced by now. You'll need all possible room to maneuver."

What a joke—and no one to share it with. Rowser had taken me to that Moghul tomb to tell me in a roundabout way the same thing I'd just heard from Charles. I'd failed to listen, to understand. In his own way Rowser was intent on doing me a favor. He was resigning because the news was soon to appear and he wanted me to do the same. This is the trouble with dupes. You have to save their skin in the end. Assuming they know there's something they need to be saved from.

I refrained from getting drunk. Charles gave me another of his newly respectful looks as we said goodbye outside the hotel. I went back to the office and telexed my resignation. It was not easy to feel righteous about this.

Mrs. Helen was at her desk, getting ready to leave for the day. She'd taken to wearing high-necked blouses or silk scarves to conceal the ridges at her throat. I told her what I'd learned. The bluebird scarf around her neck gave this news a faint poignancy. I said I was leaving the firm without delay and suggested it might be a good idea for her to do the same. Someone might soon turn up, an official of the government, a journalist, a man with a quantity of explosives.

She said to me, "Pĕ pĕ pĕ pĕ pĕ pĕ pĕ."

But the next day I was back in the office, drinking tea and swiveling slowly in my chair. A look at our files now and then. Maybe that's all it involved. Data for the analysts. All those finely tuned calculations of ours, the grids of virgin numbers. It seemed almost innocent, really, as I turned it in my mind. Rowser had let them see our facts and figures— figures we'd gathered openly, by and large. But I couldn't manage to extend the seeming meagerness of the crime to my own blind involvement. Those who engaged knowingly were less guilty than the people who carried out their designs. The unwitting would be left to ponder the consequences, to work out the precise distinctions involved, the edges of culpability and regret. What Rowser received in return for his benefactions I didn't know or care. Maybe he was an agency regular, maybe just an asset or higher type dupe.

If America is the world's living myth, then the CIA is America's myth. All the themes are there, in tiers of silence, whole bureaucracies of silence, in conspiracies and doublings and brilliant betrayals. The agency takes on shapes and appearances, embodying whatever we need at a given time to know ourselves or unburden ourselves. It gives a classical tone to our commonly felt emotions. Drinking tea, spinning in the quiet room. I felt a dim ache, a pain that seemed to carry toward the past, disturbing a number of surfaces along the way. This mistake of mine, or whatever it was, this failure to concentrate, to occupy a serious center—it had the effect of justifying everything Kathryn had ever said about me. Every dissatisfaction, mild complaint, bitter grievance. They were all retroactively correct. It was that kind of error, unlimited in connection and extent, shining a second light on anything and everything. In the way I sometimes had of looking at things as she might look at them, I saw myself as the object of her compassion and remnant love. Yes, she'd decided to feel sorry for me, to forgive me for the current lapse if not the others. This cheered me up considerably.

Sooner or later I would have to pick up the phone and undertake a delicate exchange with Ann Maitland. I called just before noon, a time she was likely to be home, Charles out walking. But there was no answer. They were in Mycenae, I realized, listening to the wind.

In three or four weeks Tap would be out of school. I planned to meet him at my father's house in Ohio, then drive him back to Victoria, a journey of sufficient distance to test his predilection for riding in automobiles. There I would glimpse my wife, spend more time with Tap, decide what to do next. Some kind of higher typing, a return to the freelance life. But where would I live? What place?

When the telex began to make its noise, I left the office and went walking in the National Gardens among the plantain lilies and perfect palms.

Two days later I saw Ann at the street market near my building, the Friday market. She was hefting a melon, turning it, poking with her thumb.

"You have to press right here, at the underside. This man is angry with me. He likes to do the pressing himself. Listen to him mutter. I am touching his tiny plump early-season melon."

She handed him the fruit, which he placed on one of the weighing pans of an antique balance. There was a beggar with a Panasonic, playing loud music. We walked slowly down the middle of the street, between the stalls, the men shouting out prices.

"I've been wondering something. This is awkward."

"What have you been wondering?"

"Andreas. Have you seen him?"

"I thought you understood it was over."

"There's something I would like to have explained to him."

"Can't you do it yourself?"

"This is silly. I don't know how to get in touch with him. I can't find him in the phone book."

"Do you have a phone book? Lucky fellow."

"I went down to the Hilton. There's a phone book at the Hilton."

"I don't know, James. Maybe the phone isn't in his name. I'm sure I can remember the number if you'd like to have it."

"You're annoyed."

"You want to talk to Andreas. Why shouldn't you? But isn't he in London?"

"I was hoping you could tell me where he is."

"I thought you understood."

"People are always saying things are over."

"But they're not to be believed. Is that it?"

"Where does he live? Where was he living in Athens when you were seeing him?"

"Can't you contact him through his firm? That's the obvious solution. Call London, call Bremen."

"Where was he living?"

"Not far from the airport. Terrible place. Two concrete slabs on four concrete stilts. A street that disappears into scrub below Hymettus. In summer it's bleached white. Dust hangs in the air. Two inches of dust on the furniture and floors. I tried once to ask him why he lived there. He went into a Greek male frenzy. Not for me to inquire, plainly."

"It wouldn't matter to Andreas where he lived. I don't think he notices things like that."

"No, I don't think he does. What do you know that you're not telling me?"

The peddler of lottery tickets stood at the end of the street, between the flower sellers and the vendors of clay pots, calling the same urgent word over and over. A summons to buy, to act, to live. The risk was small, the price was low. Times wouldn't always be this good.

Today, today.

I called the number many times over a two-day period. Four of those times I got an old man whose number contained six digits, or one less than I was dialing. It was the right number as far as it went but it didn't go far enough. It needed a nine on the end. The other times there was only line noise, a frozen hum.

I didn't want to be the victim of a misunderstanding.

I took a taxi to the address Ann had given me. I climbed an exterior staircase to the second floor of the building, looked through the dusty windows. Abandoned. On the first floor a woman with a small child in her arms listened to my fragmentary questions about the man who used to live upstairs. When I was finished, she gave me the classic look, the raised brows, tutting lips. Who knows, who cares?

So I sat on my terrace, watching the light change, hearing remotely the ram's horn lament of the day's fourth and final rush hour. I had no plans. I would not be leaving the country for three weeks. I wanted to get up early, run in the woods, study my Greek (now that I had the time), sleep through the empty after-noons, fade into the spaces. I would avoid people, stop drinking, write letters to old friends. These were not plans but only private forms, outlines for a human figure. I would sit and watch.

Was it clear to him that any data passed on to the CIA, to their Foreign Assessment Center, to the Iraq or Turkey or Pakistan desk, was not related in any way to affairs in Greece? Did he understand that we were simply based here and did not gather local information? Of course he understood. The questions had to take a different form. Who was he? How far would he go to make his point? What was his point?

A silence seemed to fall. I watched a glow appear behind the mountain, a shower of light, brick orange, climbing. Then the topmost arc of the moon showed over the ridge-line. It rose in degrees, fully illuminated, a calculus-driven model of pure ascent. Soon it was free of the mountain's dark mass, beginning to vault toward the west, to silver and glint, a cold object now, away from the earth-blood, the earth-burn, but beautiful, hard, bright.

The phone rang twice, then stopped.

She had the kind of fair skin that seemed to admit light, almost to provide a passage for light. Maybe it was her guileless manner that heightened the impression of such open texture—that and her stillness, the way she collected whatever was in the air, gath-ered objectively, our conversation, our world complaints. I re-member how she turned her head once, moving into a patch of sun, her left ear going incandescent, the edge and outer whorls, light penetrating finely, and how I thought this moment was the one that would come back to me when I wanted to think of

Lindsay years from now, the haze that rimmed her downy lobe.

I told her I'd be seeing Tap soon. We climbed the street named after Plutarch, slowly, bending to the effort. The sky above Lycabettus resembled an island sky today, saturated with color, blue deeps and soundings. This island sense was enhanced by the whitewashed chapel at the top of the hill, the tending presence, not so much surrounded by the sky as adhering to it, belonging to it.

"Will you be seeing Kathryn too?"

"If she's not living in a hole somewhere up the coast."

"Does she write to you?"

"Occasionally. Usually in a rush of some kind. The last lines are always scrawled. Even in Tap's letters I don't feel her presence. Shouldn't there be a feeling of her presence behind them? It occurred to me just recently that she doesn't read his letters anymore. In a way his letters told me more about things, essential things, than hers did. We exchanged some sense of ourselves through him. A mysterious sense, an intuition. But I don't feel her presence anymore. It's another connection closed down."

"You don't feel her presence but you still love her."

"I make too much of love. This is because I've never been massively seized by it. It was never an obsessive thing for me, an obsessive tracking of someone or something. You can break clear of obsessions. Or they just dissolve. But this happened slowly. It grew around me. It covered everything, it became everything. I'll tell you what the shock is. To live apart is the shock, the seizure. This is what I register daily and obsessively."

"In novels lately the only real love, the only unconditional love I ever come across is what people feel for animals. Dolphins, bears, wolves, canaries."

We both laughed. We wondered if this was a sign of some modern collapse. Love deflected, love that could not work when it was given to a man or a woman. Things had to work. Only small children and animals in the wild could provide the conditions in which a person's love might find a means to perfect itself, might not be thwarted, dismissed, defeated. Love was turning mystical, we thought.

"When are you two going to have children?"

"We're our own children."

She smiled in the private way she had, the slowly deepening way, amused perhaps to have hit upon a truth. She'd only meant to make a small joke but had found something in the sentence that made her want to think about it.

"Seriously. You ought to have children."

"We will. We want to."

"When does he get back?"

"Tomorrow afternoon."

"Where is he?"

"It's written down somewhere. Cities, hotels, airlines, flight numbers, times of arrival and departure."

We walked under the locust trees, fifty yards away from the place where the street becomes stepped, climbing in four or five levels toward the pale crags.

"This is the conversation we were supposed to have on Rhodes," I said.

"When he went swimming?"

"He left us on the beach. There was a deep pause. We were meant to talk importantly about things."

"I couldn't think of anything. Could you?"

"No."

"That was the one day it didn't rain," she said.

"When we all squeezed together on my balcony, passing David's flask."

"Oh that plummy sunset."

We decided we'd walked far enough. There was a small narrow shop, a grocery store that offered little more than yogurt, butter, pyramid cartons of processed German milk. Two chairs and a small metal table stood on the sidewalk, waiting for us.

"You ought to make the visit a permanent one," she said. "Stay there, see what happens."

"It rains."

"Not that we don't want you back."

"She purposely chose a rainy place."

"How big the world is. They keep telling us it's getting smaller all the time. But it's not, is it? Whatever we learn about it makes it bigger. Whatever we do to complicate things makes it bigger. It's all a complication. It's one big tangled thing." She began to laugh. "Modern communications don't shrink the world, they make it bigger. Faster planes make it bigger. They give us more, they connect more things. The world isn't shrinking at all. People who say it's shrinking have never flown Air Zaire in a tropical storm." I didn't know what she meant by this but it sounded funny. It sounded funny to her too. She had to talk through her laughter. "No wonder people go to school to learn stretching and bending. The world is so big and complicated we don't trust ourselves to figure out anything on our own. No wonder people read books that tell them how to run, walk and sit. We're trying to keep up with the world, the size of it, the complications."

I sat there and watched her laugh. She wore the same jade dress she'd gone swimming in, that summer night by the sea.

I was not a happy runner. I did it to stay interested in my body, to stay informed, and to set up clear lines of endeavor, a standard to meet, a limit to stay within. I was just enough of a puritan to think there must be some virtue in rigorous things, although I was careful not to overdo it.

I never wore the clothes. The shorts, tank top, high socks. Just running shoes and a lightweight shirt and jeans. I ran disguised as an ordinary person, a walker in the woods.

The ground cover was starting to pale in the dryness and heat. I listened to myself breathe, finding a narrative cadence in the sound, a commentary on my progress. I had to break stride crossing gulleys and then push and surge to make it up the inclines. These changes in rhythm were part of my unhappiness. I had to duck under the branches of smaller trees.

It was 7:00 A.M. I was on one of the higher trails, near the paved road that curves up to the outdoor theater. Two shots sounded down below. I slowed down but kept moving, my arms still crooked at my waist. I thought I would go to the end of the path, ease into a turn, jog back the other way on the same path, walk down to the street and go home for toast and coffee. A third shot sounded. I dropped my hands to my sides, walking along the path now, looking down through the well-spaced pines. Light fell with particular softness, an amber haze in the trees.

I saw dust rising at the end of a long draw down near the path that runs above the street. I was waiting for some mechanism to take control, to tell me what to do. A man came out of the scattered dust, scrambling uphill, trying to run right up the middle of the shallow draw, slipping on the rocks and debris washed down into it or dumped there, newspapers, garbage. I backed away, keeping my eyes on him, backed slowly toward a set of steps that led up to a scenic lookout just off the road. I didn't want to take my eyes off him. The moment I turned he would see me, I thought.

He had a pistol in his right hand, gripping it not at the stock but around the trigger-guard and barrel, like something he might throw. I crouched at the base of the steps. He came up over the rise, breathing hard, a medium-sized man, barely twenty, in rolled-up jeans and sandals. When he saw me I stood straight up, I shot up, and then went motionless, fists clenched. He looked at me as though he wanted to ask directions. He leaned away from me, distracted, holding the gun out from his hip, arm bent. Then he ran to the right, hurrying through the brush at the edge of the paved road. I could hear the scratching sound his pants made in contact with the spiny foliage. Then I heard him breathing, running downhill, following the road as it dips around to the north and reaches street level.

I went to the edge of the slope. There was a clear line of sight between the lowest branches and the floor of the woods. I saw someone move, a figure close to the ground. I felt a ringing pain at my elbow. I must have banged it on something.

I went down the slope, moving from tree to tree, using the trees for whatever cover they provided and to check my rate of descent. I wanted to be conscientious. I felt an unspecified sense of duty. There was a right and wrong to all this and it involved the details of actions and perceptions. The tree bark was rough and furrowed, scaly to the touch.

It was David Keller. He tried to raise himself to a sitting position. His back was covered with dust, the shirt, the neck and head. Pine needles clung to the shirt. He was breathing heavily. The sound of men breathing, the human noise, men running in the streets.

I spoke his name and moved slowly into his field of vision, edging around, careful not to startle him. He was sitting several yards from the path, among a half dozen fairly large stones, and he was using one of them as a hand grip, arranging himself less painfully. A rust fungus spotted the stones. At first I thought it was blood. The blood was spreading over his left shoulder, dripping down on his wrist and thigh.

"Two of them," he said.

"I saw one."

"Where were you?"

"Running. Up there."

"Are you all right?"

"He ran out the other way."

"Did you get a look at him?"

"He wore *sandals*," I said.

"They waited too long. They wanted me point-blank. They were trying to be disciplined, I think. They held off, they waited. But I saw him, I saw the gun and I fucking ran right at him. I went right at him. Surprised the hell out of both of us. I went as fast as I could. I just went, I was angry, I was in a rage. I just saw the gun and charged. I think he fired once. That was the one that hit me. I was just about on top of him by the time he squeezed it off. Then the other one steps out and fires. I'm all over the first one, his gun is trapped somewhere under us. The other one was up there about fifteen feet, right by those trees. He fires one more. The first one wriggles out and takes off running. He leaped the ditch and went right off that wall. Lost his gun. It's in the ditch, I think."

Telling it made him breathe harder. He kept licking his lips and then took sweat from the back of his hand, putting the hand to his mouth. Blood dripped on the shiny red trunks.

"How bad is it?"

"Stiff, stiff. Hurts like hell. Is someone coming?"

I saw several men standing against the wall of the building across the street, looking up at us. Above them, all up and down the street, there were people on the balconies, in robes and pajamas, watching quietly.

"I've been expecting this," he said. "The only question was which country, how they'd go about it. It could have been worse, boy. Better believe it."

Lindsay stood in the hospital corridor, watching me approach. She was bright with fear, shining. I was afraid to touch her.

A man came from the Ministry of Public Order. We sat in the kitchen drinking Nescafé. He was a middle-aged man, a chain-smoker whose brisk and commanding manner grew almost entirely out of the management of his cigarettes and lighter. I asked him if anyone had claimed responsibility for the action. This is how we referred to it. It was the action.

Yes, phone calls had been made to several newspapers. A group that called itself the Autonomous People's Initiative had claimed responsibility. No one knew who they were. Considering how they'd handled the action, he said, it was yet to be decided whether or not they were to be taken seriously. The weapon found at the scene was a 9mm pistol called a CZ-75, made in Czechoslovakia.

He asked me what I'd seen and heard.

The next day there was another visitor, a man from the political section of the U.S. embassy. He showed me credentials and asked if I had any scotch. He'd just had a nice visit, he said, with David Keller in the hospital. We went into the living room, where I waited for him to ask about my job, my contacts with local people. Instead he asked about the Mainland Bank. I told him what little I knew. They lent money to Turkey, impressive sums. They had only a representative office in Turkey—no foreign bank had a full-fledged branch—so they approved these loans out of the Athens office. He knew all this, although he didn't say so. He had the look of a once fat child, milk-white, smooth-surfaced, wheezing. He was incomplete without the much-loved bulk, alluding to it every time he moved, a soft-footed man, lowering himself carefully into the chair, carefully crossing his legs.

He asked a few questions about my trips to countries in the region. He approached the subject of the Northeast Group several times but never mentioned the name itself, never asked a direct question. I let the vague references go by, volunteered nothing, paused often. He sat with the drink in his hand, having wrapped the bottom of the glass in a paper napkin he'd found in the kitchen. It was a strange conversation, full of hedged remarks and obscure undercurrents, perfect in its way.

But who were they really after?

This is it, this is the thing I can't resolve. I'd gone running at the same hour for six straight days. No sign of David at that hour except on the last of these days. Were they waiting for me? Did David precipitate the action by rushing the gunmen before they had a chance to realize this was not the man they wanted? Or did they simply mistake him for me? There would be a curious symmetry to such an error, a symmetry of misidentification, especially if we believe that Andreas Eliades was behind the action or somehow involved in it. It was Andreas who mistook me for David Keller the night we first met. He thought I was the banker. Did his companions think David was the risk analyst? The possibility is haunting, that there is an exact correspondence at the center of all this confusion, this formlessness of motive and plan and execution. A harmony.

What is the counter-argument?

There was no mix-up. David and I don't look alike, we weren't wearing similar clothes, we hadn't been following similar routines. They wanted the banker. They waited outside his building, saw him come out in running clothes, drove up to the woods and placed themselves at the end of the likeliest path.

Which do you believe?

I want to believe they plotted well. I don't like thinking I was the intended victim. It puts all of us at the mercy of events. It's one more thing to vex me with its elusiveness, its drift—a fading into distances of human figures and whatever is real and absolute about the light that falls around them. When the gunman turned my way, I was at that instant not only the intended victim but had clearly done something (I tried to remember what) to merit his special attention. But he didn't aim and fire. This is the point. It turned out that he didn't know who I was, what I was supposed to have done. I want to interpret this as a sign in my favor.

Did you think you were going to die?

A pause filled my chest, a blank fear. We stood looking at each other. I waited for the second self to emerge, the cunning un-learned self, the animal we keep in reserve for such occasions. It would impel me to move in this or that direction, strategically, flooding my body with adrenalin. But there was only this heavy pause. I was fixed to the spot. Helpless, deprived of will. Why was I standing rigid on a wooded hill, fists clenched, facing a man with a gun? The situation pressed me to recall. This was the only thing to penetrate that blank moment—an awareness I could not connect to things. The words would come later. The single word, the final item on the list.

American.

How do you connect things?

Learn their names. After I told the man from the Ministry what I'd seen in the pine woods, I told him everything else I knew, gave him all the names. Eliades, Rowser, Hardeman, all the tenu-ous connections. I gave him business cards, supplied approximate dates of conversations, names of restaurants, cities, airlines. Let the investigators work up chronologies, trace routes, check the passenger manifests. Their job was public order. Let them muse on the plausibilities.

What else?

Nothing. I reconstructed events in such a way that I was able to omit a certain name without causing the sequence to appear incomplete. It was Ann Maitland I didn't want them to know about. She was not of a type or mind to disavow this kind of protection, it seemed to me.

She and I said nothing directly to each other about the shooting. It was coded matter. It was matter we could refer to only within the limits of a practiced look. Even this became too much. We began to look past each other, as if at meadows in the distance. Was Andreas the figure we saw? Our talks became ironic pastorales, slowly paced, with repeated attempts at tenderness.

Lindsay spoke only of my coming to David's aid, which put a fine sheen on her tendency to reassure us all.

The city went white with sun and dust. Charles would labor in the Gulf, installing radio links, infrared sensors. David would recover without complications, cracking jokes in the mandatory American manner, the cherished manner of people self-conscious about death. This is the humor of violent surprise.

I see them in the primitive silkscreen the brain is able to produce, maybe eight inches in front of my closed eyes, miniaturized by time and distance, riddled by visual static, each figure a dancing red ribbon. These are among the people I've tried to know twice, the second time in memory and language. Through them, myself. They are what I've become, in ways I don't understand but which I believe will accrue to a rounded truth, a second life for me as well as for them.

People sit on the steps of the Propylaea as if in a classroom, fifty of them, listening to their guide. The faces are intent, arranged in rows on the marble heights among the common encumbrances and gear, the handbags, cameras, sun hats.

Amid the scaffolding above them a workman slips the bit of a power drill into a block of dressed stone. The shank of the drill is a full meter long and produces a noise of rotating abrasions that sings among the columns and walls.

The native stone is worn smooth, worn down by treading feet, lustrous and slick. An old box camera stands on a tripod with a black cloth hanging down. It is aimed at the Parthenon.

We approach hypnotically, walking on the smooth stones, not watching where we step. The west façade rears before us. It would take a wrenching effort to avert our eyes from it. I'd seen the temple a hundred times from the street, never suspecting it was this big, this scarred, broken, rough. How different from the spotlighted bijou I'd seen from the car that night, coming back from Piraeus, a year ago.

The marble seems to drip with honey, the pale autumnal hue produced by iron oxide in the stone. And there are stones lying about, stones everywhere as I cross around to the south colonnade —blocks, slabs, capitals, column drums. The temple is cordoned by ropes but this mingled debris is all over the ground, specked surfaces, rough to the touch, wasting in acid rain.

I stop often, listening to people read to each other, listening to the guides speak German, French, Japanese, accented English. This is the peristyle, that is the architrave, those are the triglyphs.

A woman pauses to fix her sandal.

Beyond the retaining wall the great city spreads, ringed by mountains, heat struck, steeped in calamity. The smoke of small fires hangs on the hills, motionless, fixed there. The breathless rim, cinders falling from the sky. Paralysis. Nothing will disperse but powers of sound, rising from the traffic arcs, the jittery cars locked in concrete. Bombings will become commonplace, car bombings, firebombings of offices and department stores. A blind might will seem to shake things, to course headlong through that entire year. No one claims credit for the worst of the terror.

I walk to the east face of the temple, so much space and openness, lost walls, pediments, roof, a grief for what has escaped containment. And this is what I mainly learned up there, that the Parthenon was not a thing to study but to feel. It wasn't aloof, rational, timeless, pure. I couldn't locate the serenity of the place, the logic and steady sense. It wasn't a relic species of dead Greece but part of the living city below it. This was a surprise. I'd thought it was a separate thing, the sacred height, intact in its Doric order. I hadn't expected a human feeling to emerge from the stones but this is what I found, deeper than the art and mathematics embodied in the structure, the optical exactitudes. I found a cry for pity. This is what remains to the mauled stones in their blue surround, this open cry, this voice we know as our own.

Old people sit among upright fragments along the north façade, old women in white socks and heavy shoes, men with lapel badges, a guard in his gray cap, smoking, carrying with him the official aura, the glaze of vacant hours. The old box camera remains untended on its tripod, the black hood lifted in a breeze. Where is the photographer, the old man in the battered gray jacket with sagging pockets, the man with the sunken face, dirt in his fingernails? I feel I know him or can invent him. It isn't necessary for him to appear, eating pistachio nuts out of a white bag. The camera is enough.

People come through the gateway, people in streams and clusters, in mass assemblies. No one seems to be alone. This is a place to enter in crowds, seek company and talk. Everyone is talking. I move past the scaffolding and walk down the steps, hearing one language after another, rich, harsh, mysterious, strong. This is what we bring to the temple, not prayer or chant or slaughtered rams. Our offering is language.

The Prairie

14

HE WAS in the middle of a crowd, tongue tied! There was a man in a daise like a drunkerds skuffling lurch, realing in a corner. One window had glass, three others were boarded up when the glass was broken, and it wasn't conveeniently well lighted in there, like an Indian's hut of adoby and straw. "Childs play" came a voice through the gloom. It was the widow Larsen his mother's friend that smelt of spoilt milk. Or someone said "Come across, get right" and it was directed right to him. It was like one of his teeth chattering dreams when he was in the middle of the mirky depths and they called to him from all around. He felt retched, he mumbled in his mind. "Yeeld" came another voice and it was none but the old cantankerus man with the crooked face and laim leg, known as a nefariot skeemer and rummy, natural born for bone picking. "Yeeld" he followed up. Everywhere the others were speaking, but he didn't know what they were saying. The strange language burst out of them, like people out of breath and breathing words instead of air. But what words, what were they saying? Right next to him was his father bursting forth in secret language which the boy could not decifer in the least. It sounded like a man who talks to owls. The circuit rider watched him. He smiled at the boy and nodded apealingly but his face was like a patch of midnight that has never been cleared away. A secret mockery was wrapped in his friendlyness. What was this strange tongue they spoke? Was it the language of the plains Indians? No, because we know it from the gospels and the acts. This strange and age old practise was glossylalya, to speak with tongues. To some a gift but to Orville Benton a curse and calamitty! The words echoed in his head. People burst out in sudden streams. They were like long dolerus tales being dold out one by one. Who's words were they? What did they mean? There was none to tell him in that gloomy place. Something he did not like troubled him. The same haunting feeling that he felt in the darkest nights crept over him like gang green. He felt droplets of clammy sweat form on his forhead. The circuit rider's firm hand was on his shoulder and then on his youthful head. "White words" his nodding face remarked. "Pure as the drivelin snow." His eyes bored through the middle of Orville's forhead. He stiffend visibly. The rain was like horses hooves on the roof, leaking through the patches. He took his hand off the boy's head to stretch his fingers and make the bones crack. "Yeeld" his mother said to him with a wiry look that was like a rathful warning to mind his manners, there was company coming. He wanted to yeeld. This is the point! There was nothing in the world he wanted than to yeeld totaly, to go across to them, to speak as they were speaking.

"Do whatever your tongue finds to do! Seal the old language and loose the new!"

The preacherman was gripping him with hot terrible hands. He shrank back in perfect terrour. This is the same young boy who daintilly walked through the intrales and vains of rotting cattle, dead in the pastures of fatal bacillis. He tried to speak in tongues. Orville tried! But his voice had a bedragled sound to it which he did not like. It sounded dreery with weakness. "Get wet, son" the looming face remarked. "Childs play is what we're doing." This preacherman wore regular clothes with rolled up sleeves unlike the figures of the past with long clokes and little white collars. They were safer men by the look of them! His father kept nodding his head in a way that bewilderd him. People threw an arm up with figitty fingers to shake around. He scand the church such as it was. Many were speaking now, some in a quiet manner and some raising a fuss and hubub. The circuit riding man eyed the boy. He hummed a little, cracking his bones. This was not a boy who prayed much but now he shut his eyes and prayed that he would understand and speak. His mother was speaking. His mother was on her knees on the cold floor crying out and mumbling. Many a poor soul would have envied her if he could not hear in himself the same voice of the so called spirit. These are the words of the circuit riding man. "The worldwind is here. The invisible spirit's voice. Hear it in yourself and yeeld." He trusted the voices around him. He wanted to speak in the spirit's voice. He felt an enormas wish to do so. It was sheer desire. He must do it, he wished to do it. But how could he speak if he could not understand? These words were upside down and inside out! What did they mean? The preacherman knew. He listened and said. He could interprit tongues. "The spirit is the river and the wind." Even in his creeping despair, the boy marveled a little at how these people spoke. When he tried, it was poor at best. All his words were poor clattery English like a stutterrer at the front of the class. He didn't even know how to begin, where was the whurl of his ignorant tongue. A spidery despair loomed over him. It seemed as if all the worlds ills and evils had come screaming into his head. Forboding seaped from all the gouls and hags and multy eyed creatures of his dark dreams. His dreams were heavy things. He imagined another world, peaceful and trankwel. The prairie was all around him. True there is always a creature out there that will be happy to lick and saver the curious wandrer. Bull elk roamed the plains and there were coogar to be seen in the hilly places if the roomers were correct. However this story captured a lot of disbelief in some places to be sure. "Not a coogar been seen here abouts in fifty year" remarked the old timers. But the boy did not fear any animal. This was the country of his heart. He had a personal treasure he loved, which were black leather boots with canvis lining, a gift from the big hearted Lonnie Wright, who's strange fait we have seen earlier. "A smigen a' bad news, lad" grinning sheepily. And in his boots he was a little of the full man he was yet to become, roaming the prairie and learning its ways, which were the ways of the horned lark and the rodent hunting hawk, the wild flowers and the sun hovering heavenly on the wheat. He had seen the small horned lark in its nest in the grass and weeds when it was just hatched even before it had its flight feathers when it was in danger from the natural hunger of others. But these thoughts of pity toward things that are less powerful than our selvs would not over power the shadowy rememberance of terrour. Through field and forest, dale and mountain, always on the move, like an Indian, like a short legged dwarf hidden in the tall grass, he wanted to feel the morning dew on his face and neck, he wanted to see the smokey stones of camp fires in the dawn.

"A still pool" they said to him. Were they being kindly or mean? The terrible truth is that it didn't matter. A still pool was a still pool. He dumb foundedly tried to speak. He listened, he heard, and he tried again. A strange laps of ability kept ocurring. It was like the depths of a failed skeem. "Another hair brained skeem of yours, Orville!" This was his mother's voice echoing in his head. A good woman for all of that! It was the father eating a naw a' cheese he did not understand. It was the rath of a father for his only son, who's only crime was being there, doing his chors around the house and in the fields, the same ruteen day in and out. These were the careless wants of his boyhood. What things awaited? He neither knew nor cared to wonder. He only wished to free himself from this dredful woe of incomprehen-shun. They spoke all around him and he couldn't make real sense of it. He wanted freely to yeeld but he couldn't get there or go across to them. The preacherman's anger was stamped in his eyes. He could read it like a book. It was the ominus stamp of doom. Not fury or natural pain did this straw haired boy fear but the doom of the night and the specters. Psyhcology! "When you die you go away" his mother told him, but his father had a rigamaroll of dying, with specters and surprising visits. He tried to stiful his sobbs. He felt done in and then some. It was a dream but not a dream. The gift was not his, the whole language of the spirit which was greater than Latin or French was not to be seized in his pityfull mouth. His tongue was a rock, his ears were rocks.

This was his queer discription of the situation, mumbled in his mind. He wanted to strike himself silly, but his hand was stade by the rathful look of the preacher. His arms and legs had gone to the wind, he was deaf and dumb. A jolting urge said "Run!" His legs suddenly stirred up into speed not consulting his brain in the matter of where he should go. He sped out the creakey door and into the pouring rain. Streaks of lightning leaped across the sky. A terrible energy burst through him, the energy of panick and fear. He was a strong enough boy for his age and his legs took him capably over the sogging turf. All the land was gray. The sky was black. No where did he see the gentle prairie of his careless days. Lonnie Wright was long gone. He would have opened his door to any young wafe, even a bad one. There was no where to run but he ran. The farm to market road was mud itself. His shoes squished and the lumpy mud flew onto his clothes and hands. He looked in vane for familiar signs and safe places. No where did he see what he expected. Why couldn't he understand and speak? There was no answer that the living could give. Tongue tied! His fait was signed. He ran into the rainy distance, smaller and smaller. This was worse than a retched nightmare. It was the nightmare of real things, the fallen wonder of the world.